Agents of S.U.I.T.

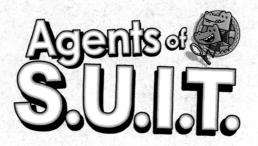

Agents of S.U.I.T.

written by **John Patrick Green**
and **Christopher Hastings**
illustrated by **Pat Lewis**
with color by **Wes Dzioba**

First Second
New York

For those who stand out, and those who blend in

:01
First Second

© 2023 by John Patrick Green

Digitally illustrated in Photoshop

Published by First Second
First Second is an imprint of Roaring Brook Press,
a division of Holtzbrinck Publishing Holdings Limited Partnership
120 Broadway, New York, NY 10271
firstsecondbooks.com
mackids.com
All rights reserved

Don't miss your next favorite book from First Second! For the latest
updates go to firstsecondnewsletter.com and sign up for our enewsletter.

Library of Congress Control Number: 2022908546

ISBN 978-1-250-85256-4 (Hardcover)
ISBN 978-1-250-88234-9 (Special Edition)
ISBN 978-1-250-88233-2 (Special Edition)

Our books may be purchased in bulk for promotional, educational,
or business use. Please contact your local bookseller or the Macmillan
Corporate and Premium Sales Department at (800) 221-7945 ext. 5442
or by email at MacmillanSpecialSales@macmillan.com.

FIRST
EDITION

First edition, 2023
Edited by Calista Brill and Steve Foxe
Cover design by John Patrick Green, Pat Lewis, and Molly Johanson
Interior book design by Molly Johanson
Color by Wes Dzioba
Printed in China by Toppan Leefung Printing Ltd., Dongguan City, Guangdong Province

10 9 8 7 6 5 4 3 2 1

BY ART
WE LIVE

Prologue

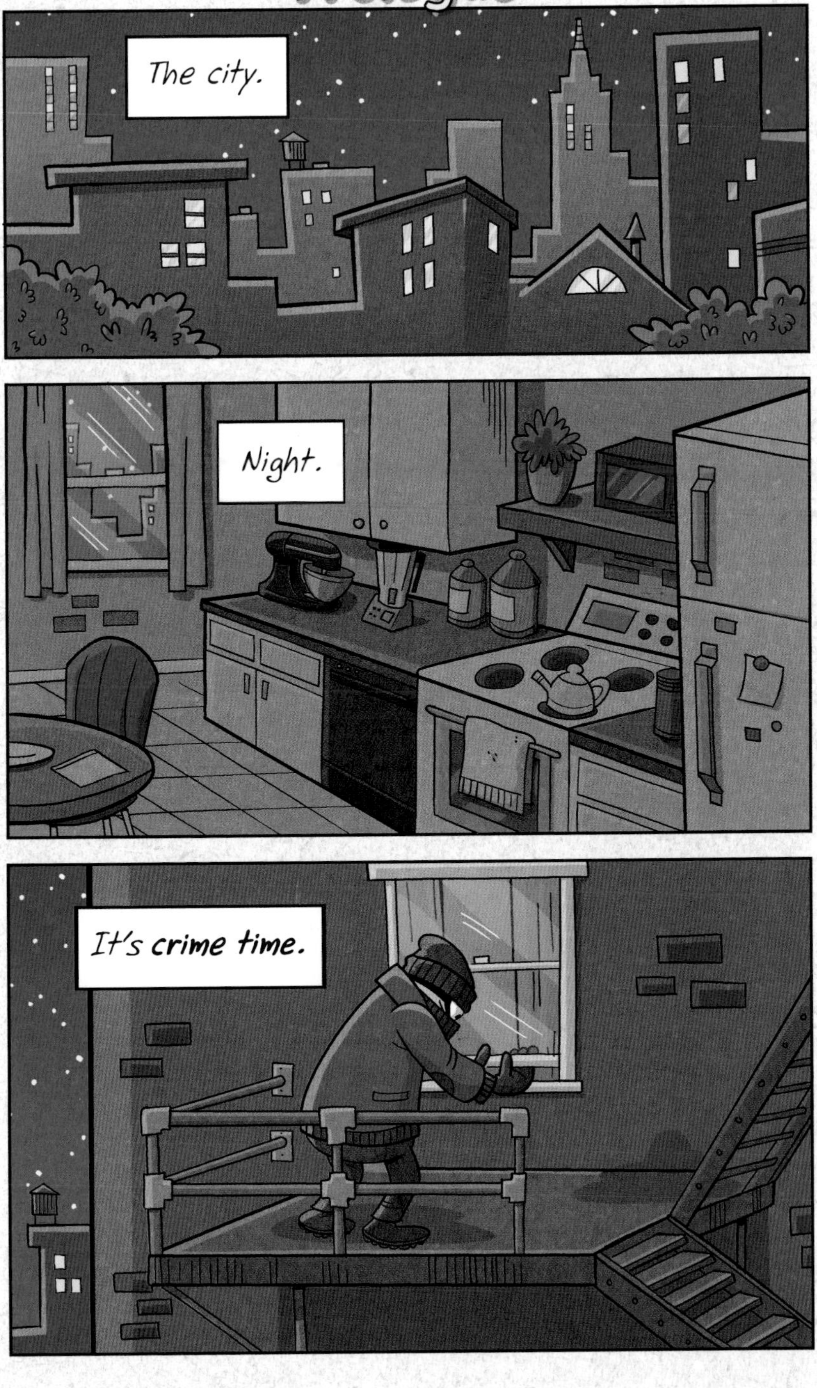
The city.
Night.
It's crime time.

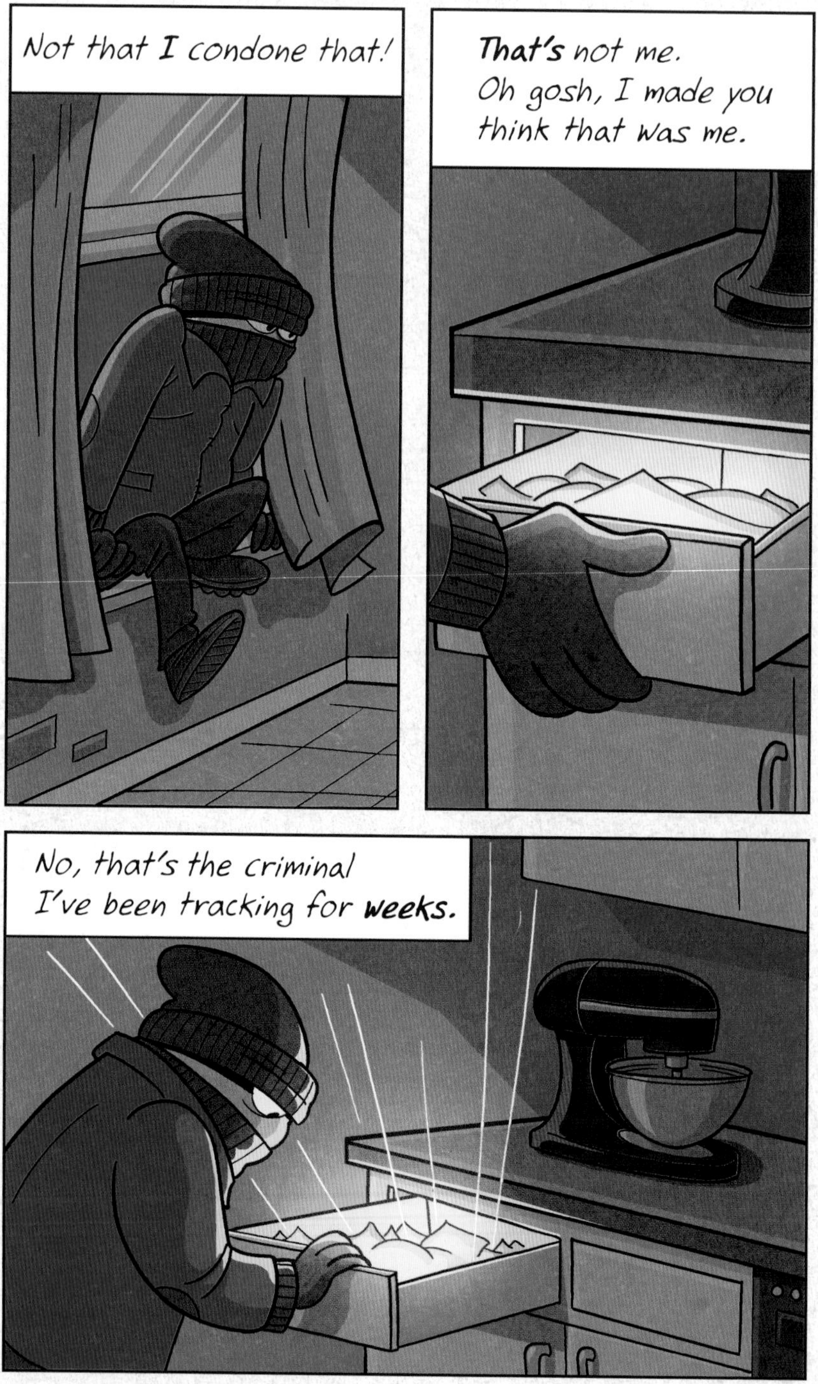
Not that I condone that!
That's not me.
Oh gosh, I made you think that was me.
No, that's the criminal I've been tracking for **weeks.**

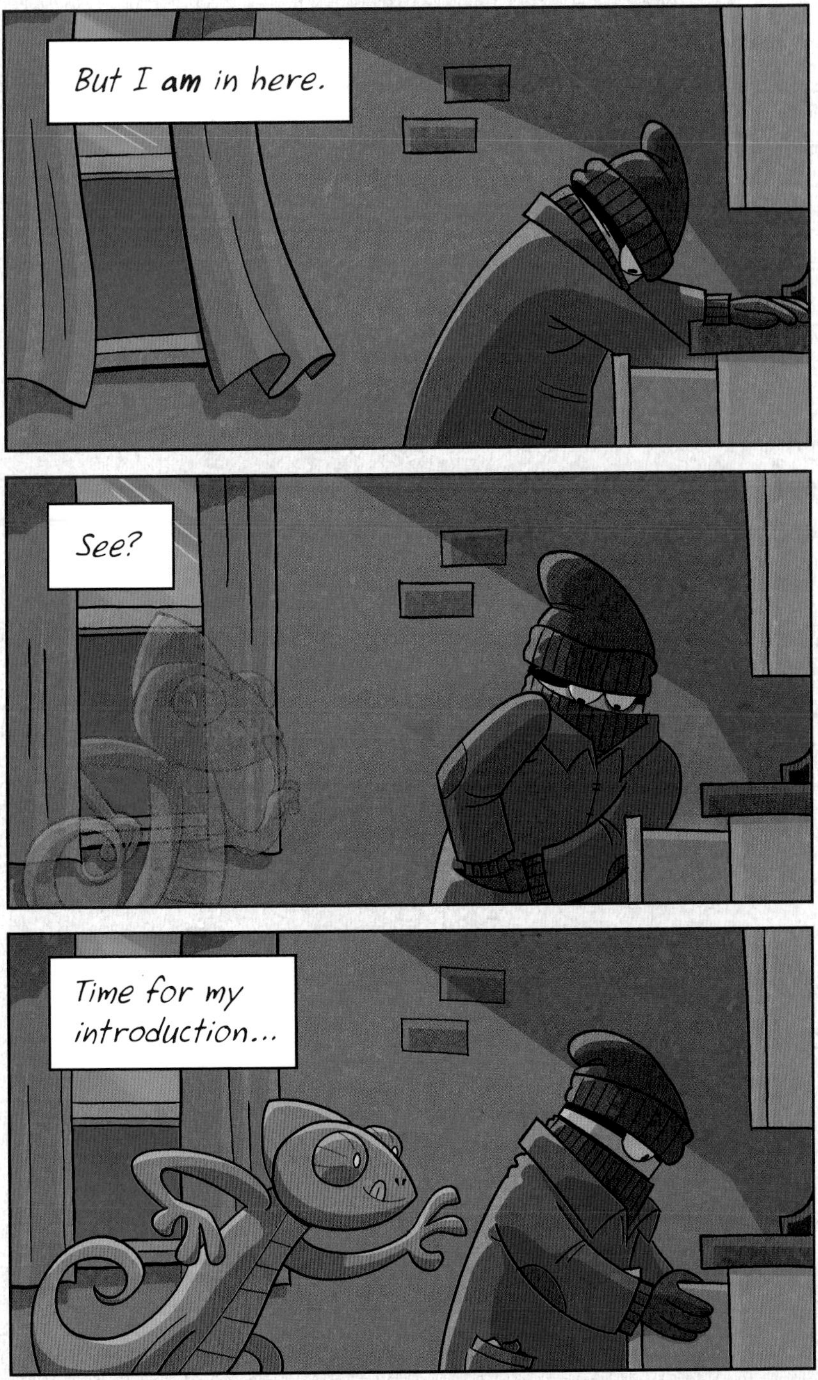
But I **am** in here.
See?
Time for my introduction...

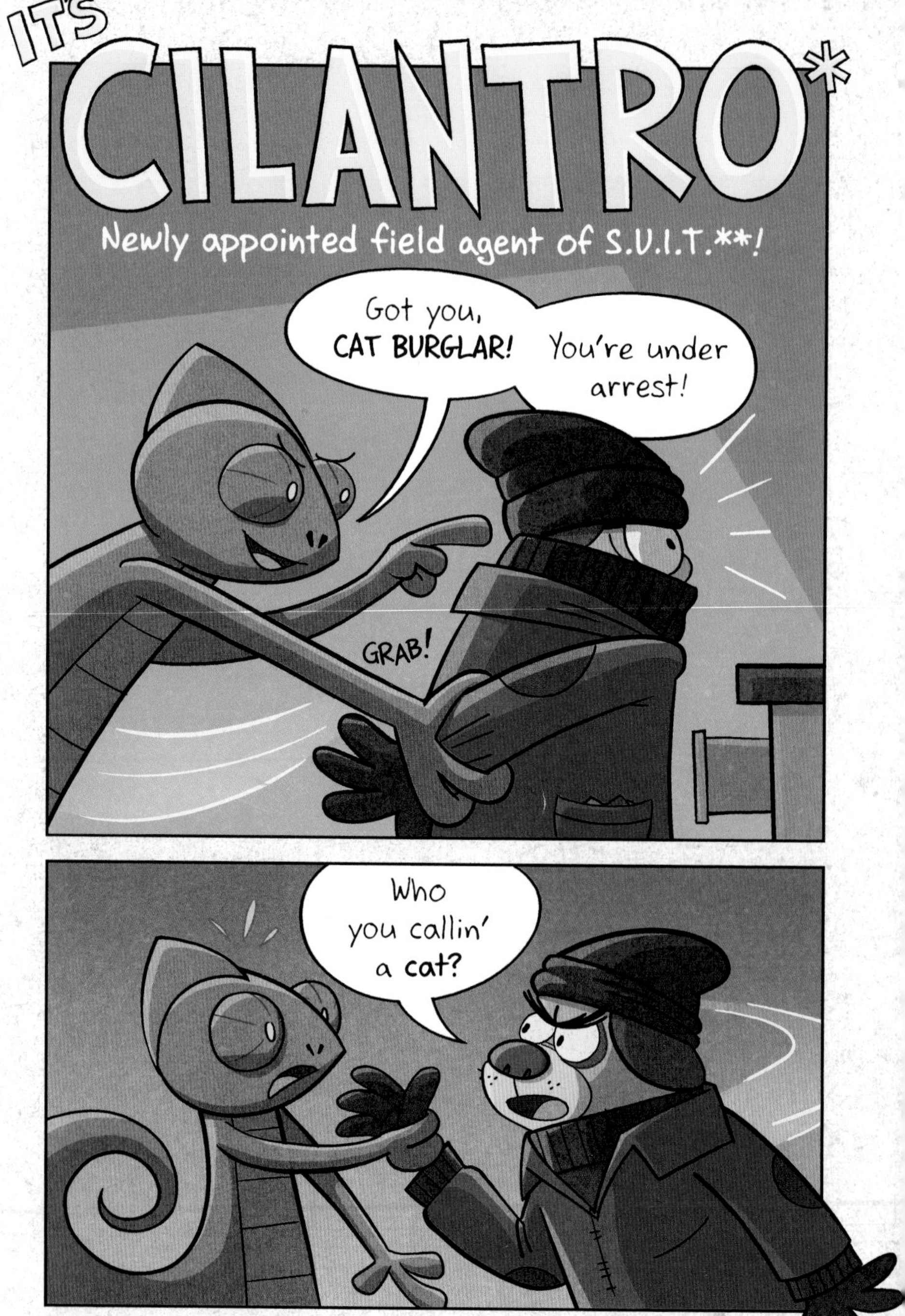
IT'S CILANTRO*
Newly appointed field agent of S.U.I.T.**!
Got you, CAT BURGLAR! You're under arrest!
GRAB!
Who you callin' a cat?

*That's the chameleon's name. We're not talking about the herb.
(Well, there *might* be some cilantro in the fridge, but we're not going to check.)

**Special Undercover Investigation Teams

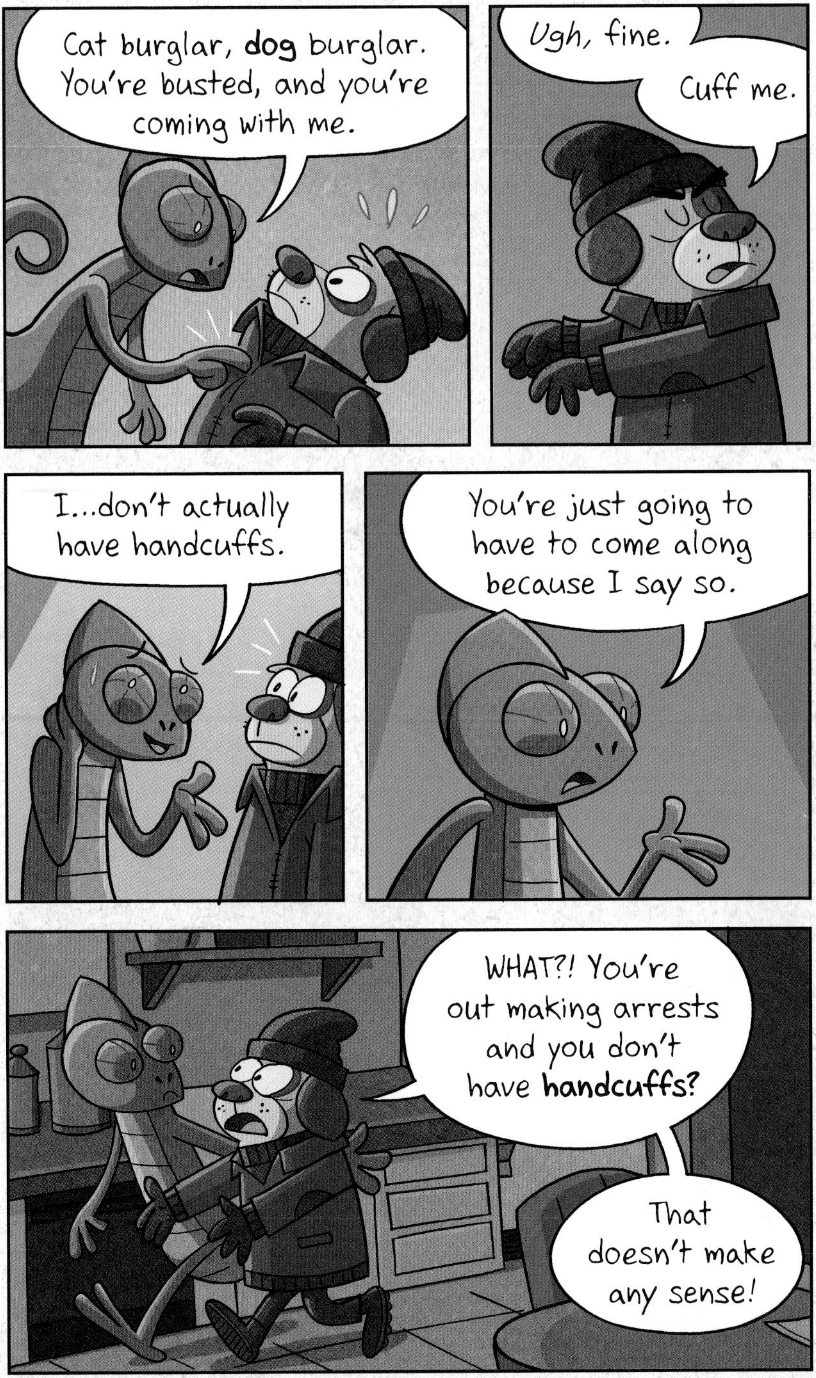

Cat burglar, **dog** burglar. You're busted, and you're coming with me.
Ugh, fine.
Cuff me.
I...don't actually have handcuffs.
You're just going to have to come along because I say so.
WHAT?! You're out making arrests and you don't have **handcuffs?**
That doesn't make any sense!

I can't carry *anything* on me when I'm on a mission, because I can only camouflage *myself*, not other stuff.

Here, I'll show you!

TA-DA!

Kind of ruins the illusion, right?

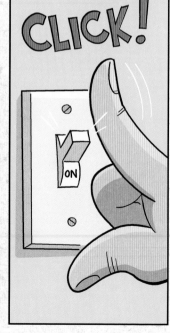

CLICK!

ON

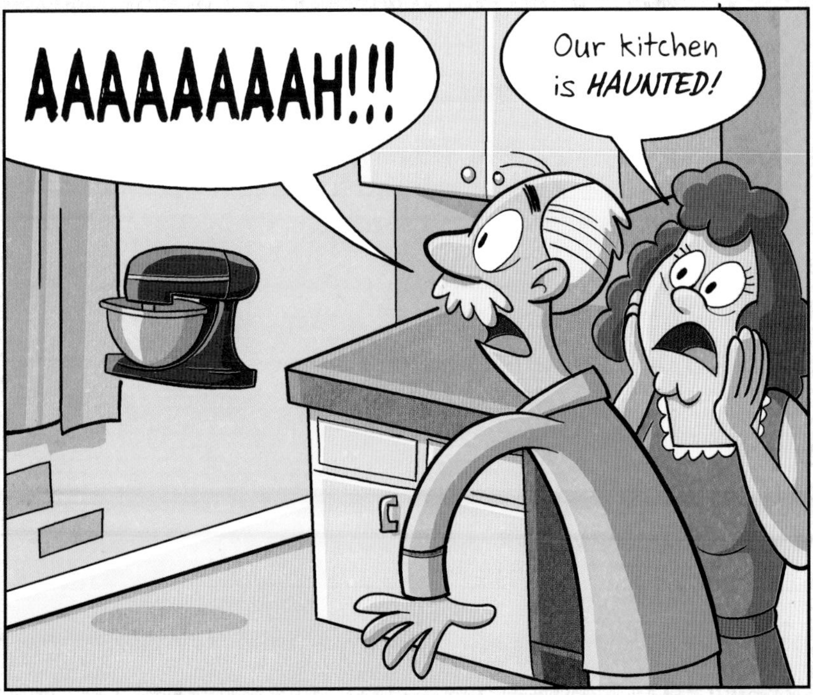
AAAAAAAAH!!!
Our kitchen is *HAUNTED!*

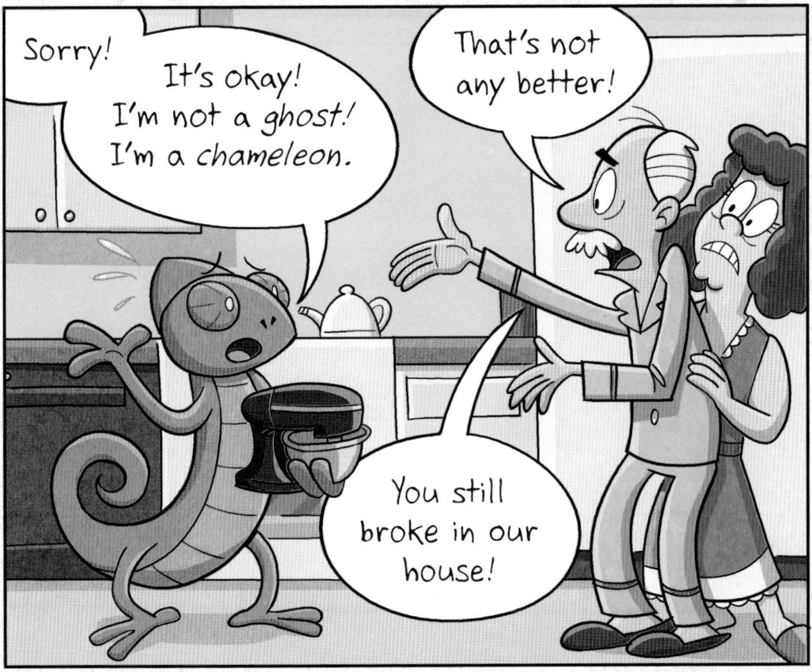
Sorry!
It's okay! I'm not a *ghost!* I'm a *chameleon.*
That's not any better!
You still broke in our house!

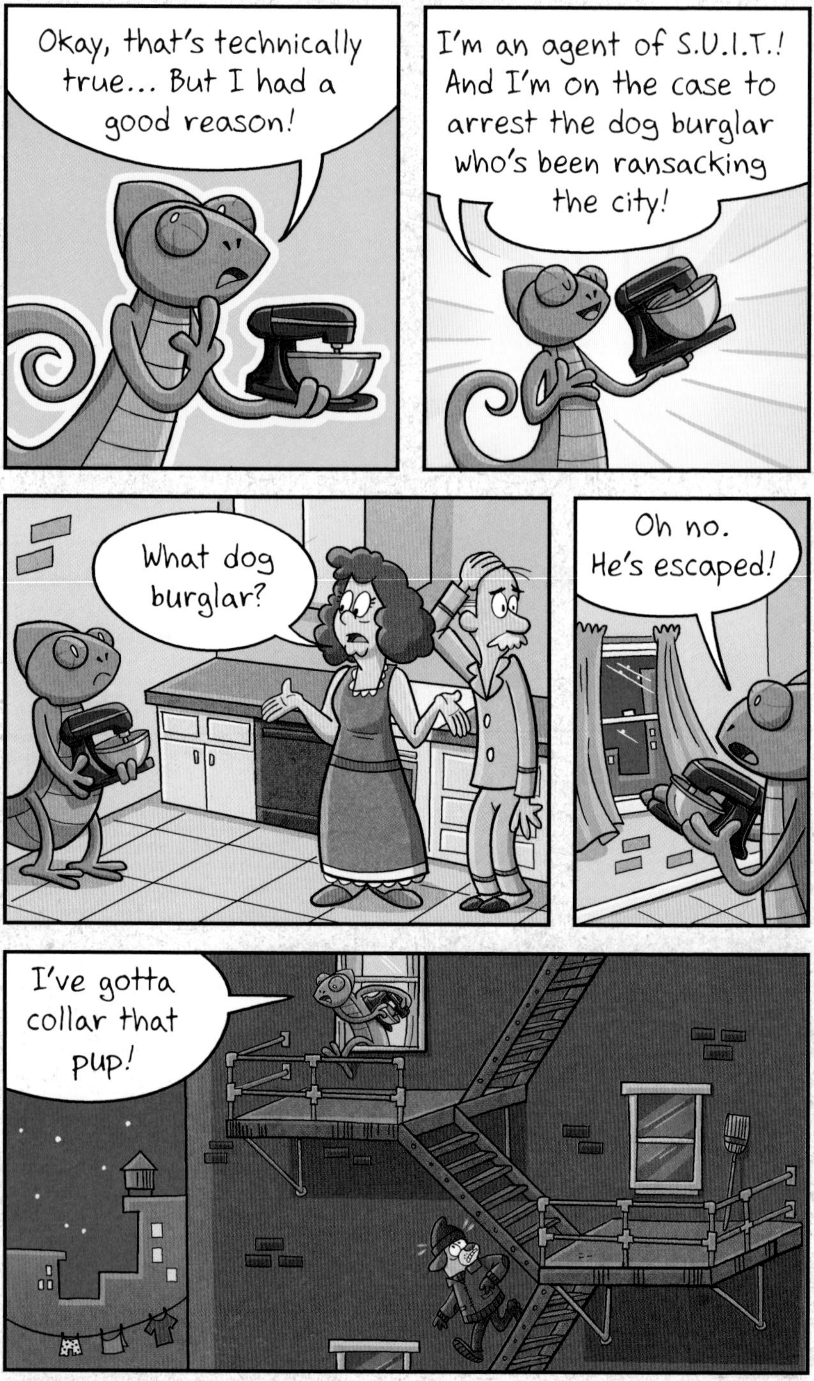
Okay, that's technically true... But I had a good reason!
I'm an agent of S.U.I.T.! And I'm on the case to arrest the dog burglar who's been ransacking the city!
What dog burglar?
Oh no. He's escaped!
I've gotta collar that pup!

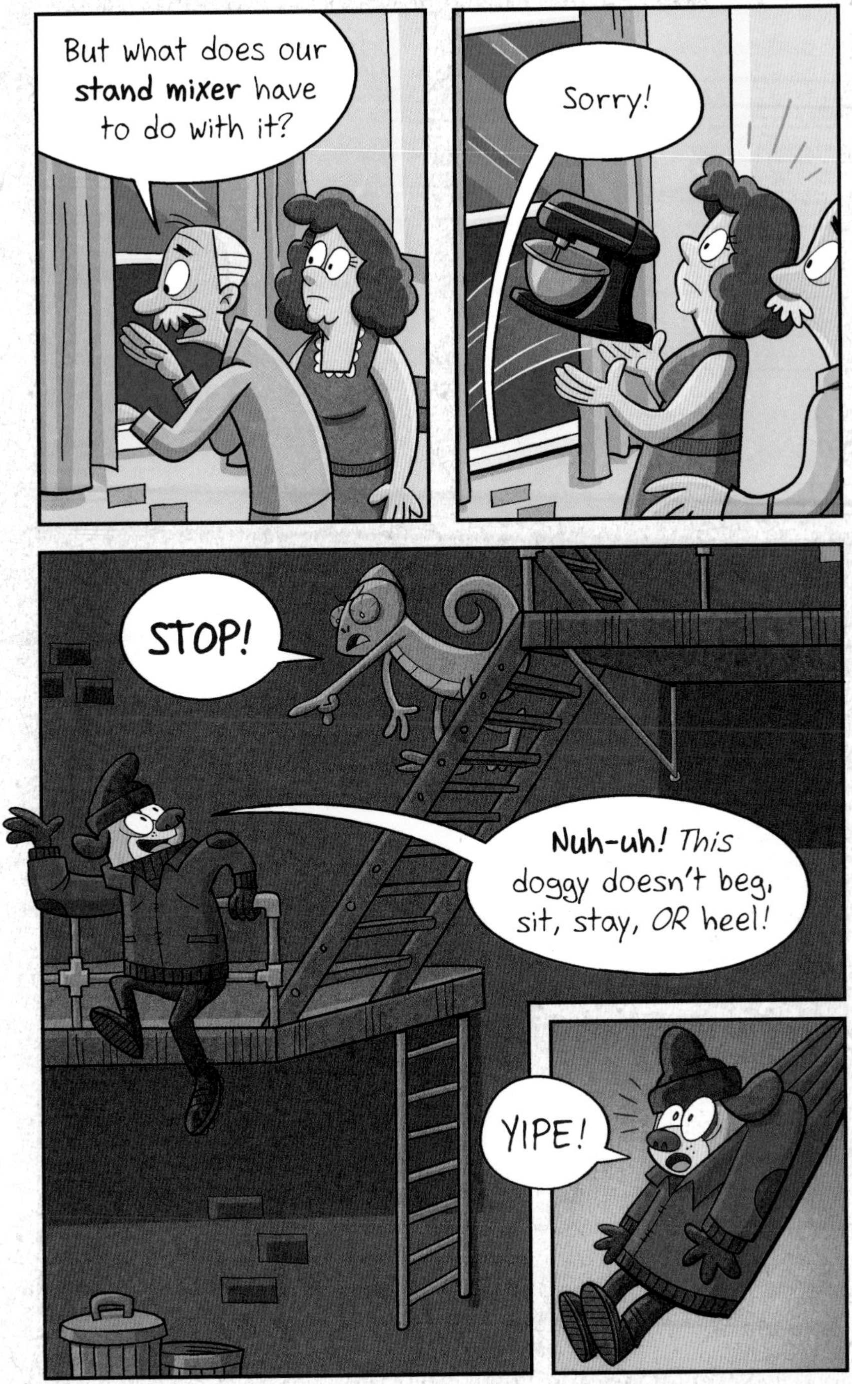
But what does our **stand mixer** have to do with it?
Sorry!
STOP!
Nuh-uh! *This* doggy doesn't beg, sit, stay, *OR* heel!
YIPE!

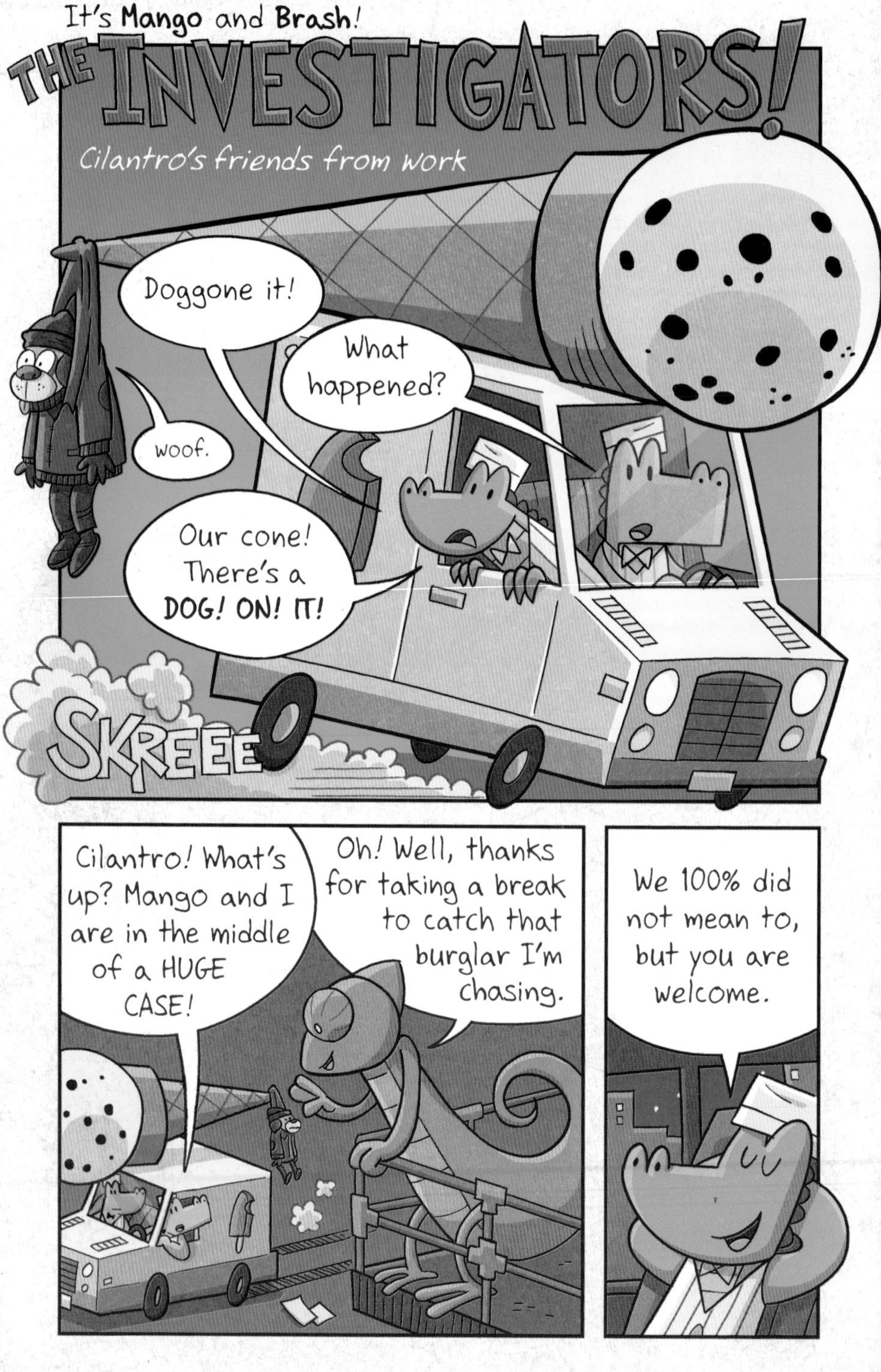
It's Mango and Brash!
THE INVESTIGATORS!
Cilantro's friends from work
Doggone it!
What happened?
woof.
Our cone! There's a DOG! ON! IT!
SKREEEE
Cilantro! What's up? Mango and I are in the middle of a HUGE CASE!
Oh! Well, thanks for taking a break to catch that burglar I'm chasing.
We 100% did not mean to, but you are welcome.

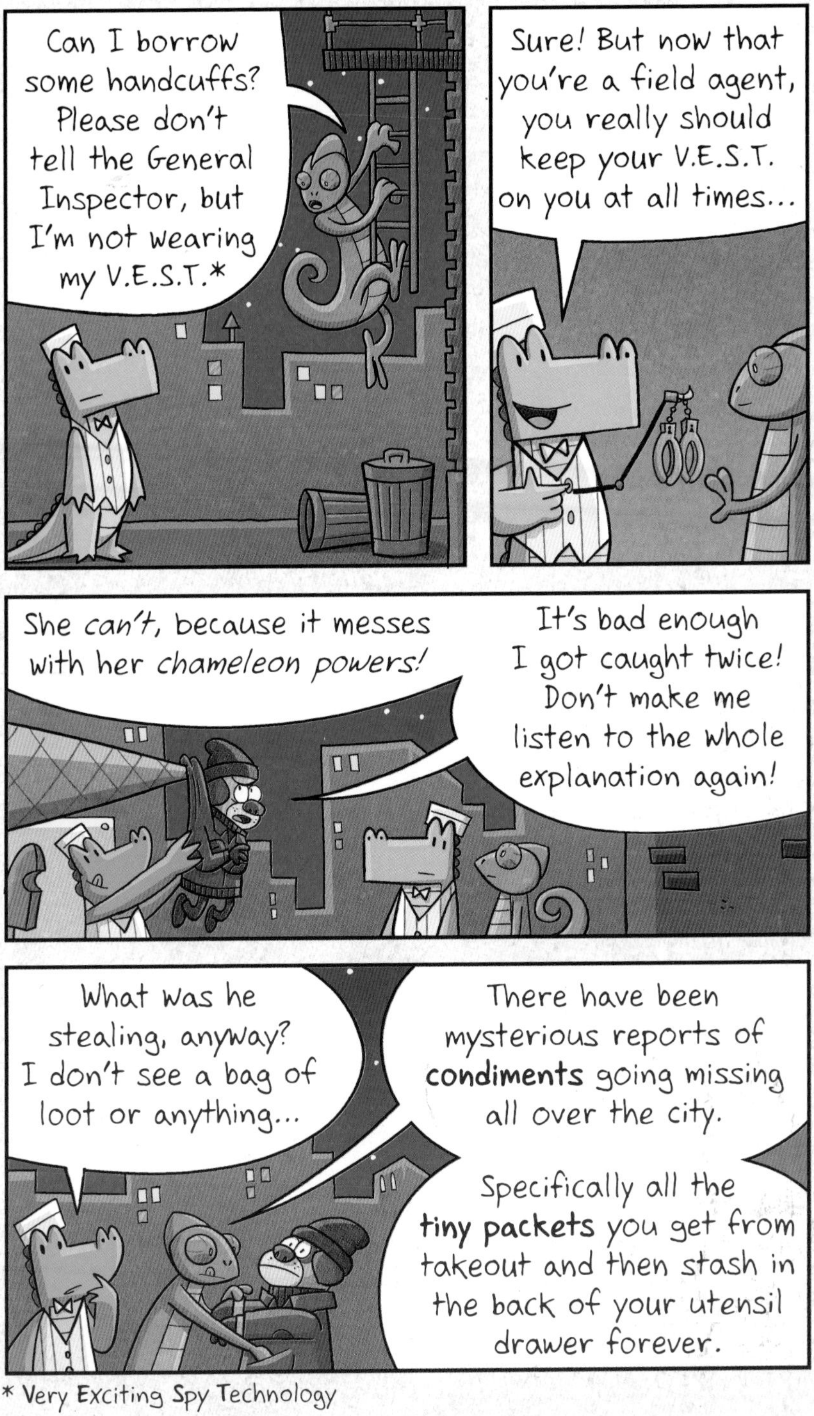
Can I borrow some handcuffs? Please don't tell the General Inspector, but I'm not wearing my V.E.S.T.*
Sure! But now that you're a field agent, you really should keep your V.E.S.T. on you at all times...
She *can't*, because it messes with her *chameleon powers!*
It's bad enough I got caught twice! Don't make me listen to the whole explanation again!
What was he stealing, anyway? I don't see a bag of loot or anything...
There have been mysterious reports of **condiments** going missing all over the city.
Specifically all the **tiny packets** you get from takeout and then stash in the back of your utensil drawer forever.

* Very Exciting Spy Technology

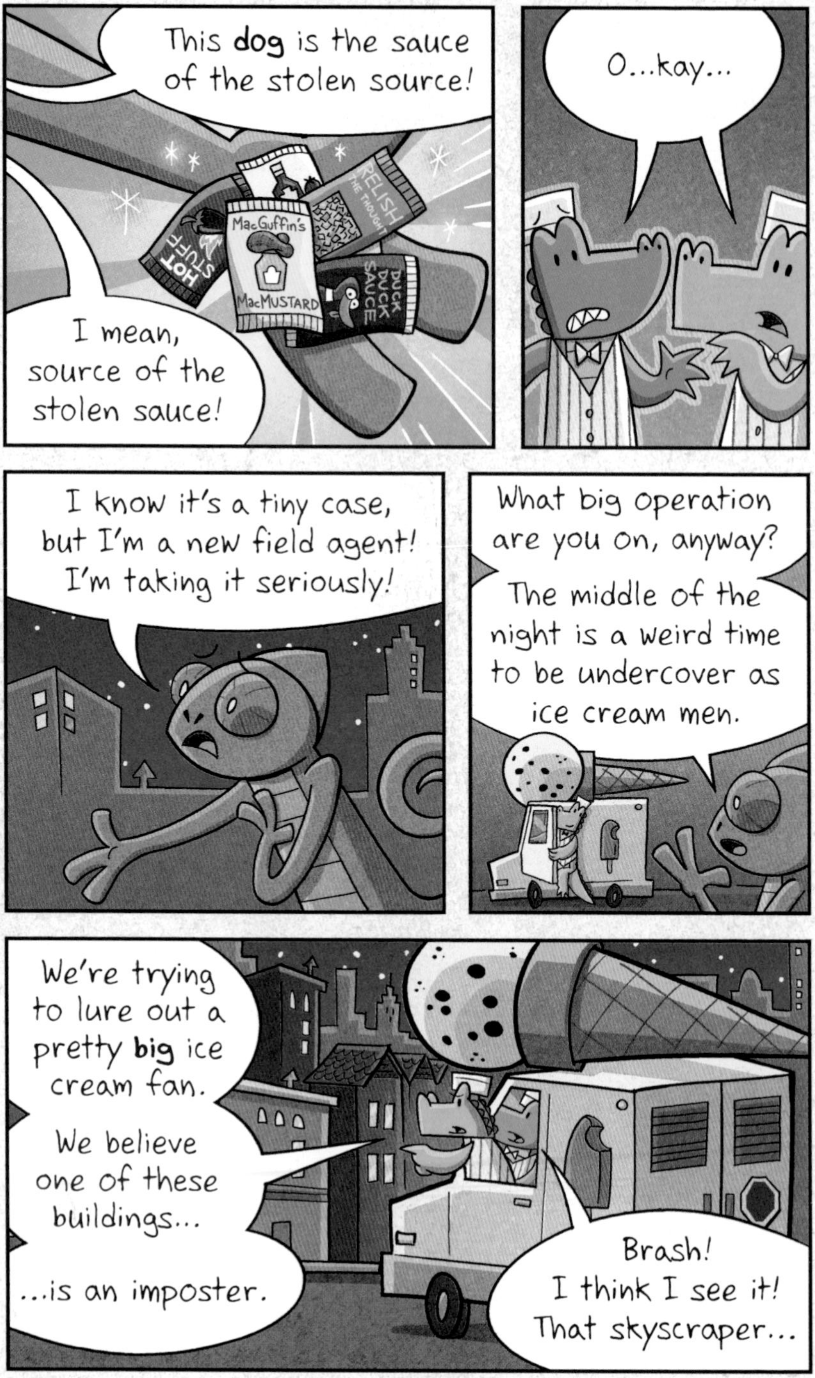
This **dog** is the sauce of the stolen source!
HOT STUFF
MacGuffin's
MacMUSTARD
RELISH THE THOUGHT
DUCK DUCK SAUCE
I mean, source of the stolen sauce!
O...kay...
I know it's a tiny case, but I'm a new field agent! I'm taking it seriously!
What big operation are you on, anyway?
The middle of the night is a weird time to be undercover as ice cream men.
We're trying to lure out a pretty **big** ice cream fan.
We believe one of these buildings...
...is an imposter.
Brash! I think I see it! That skyscraper...

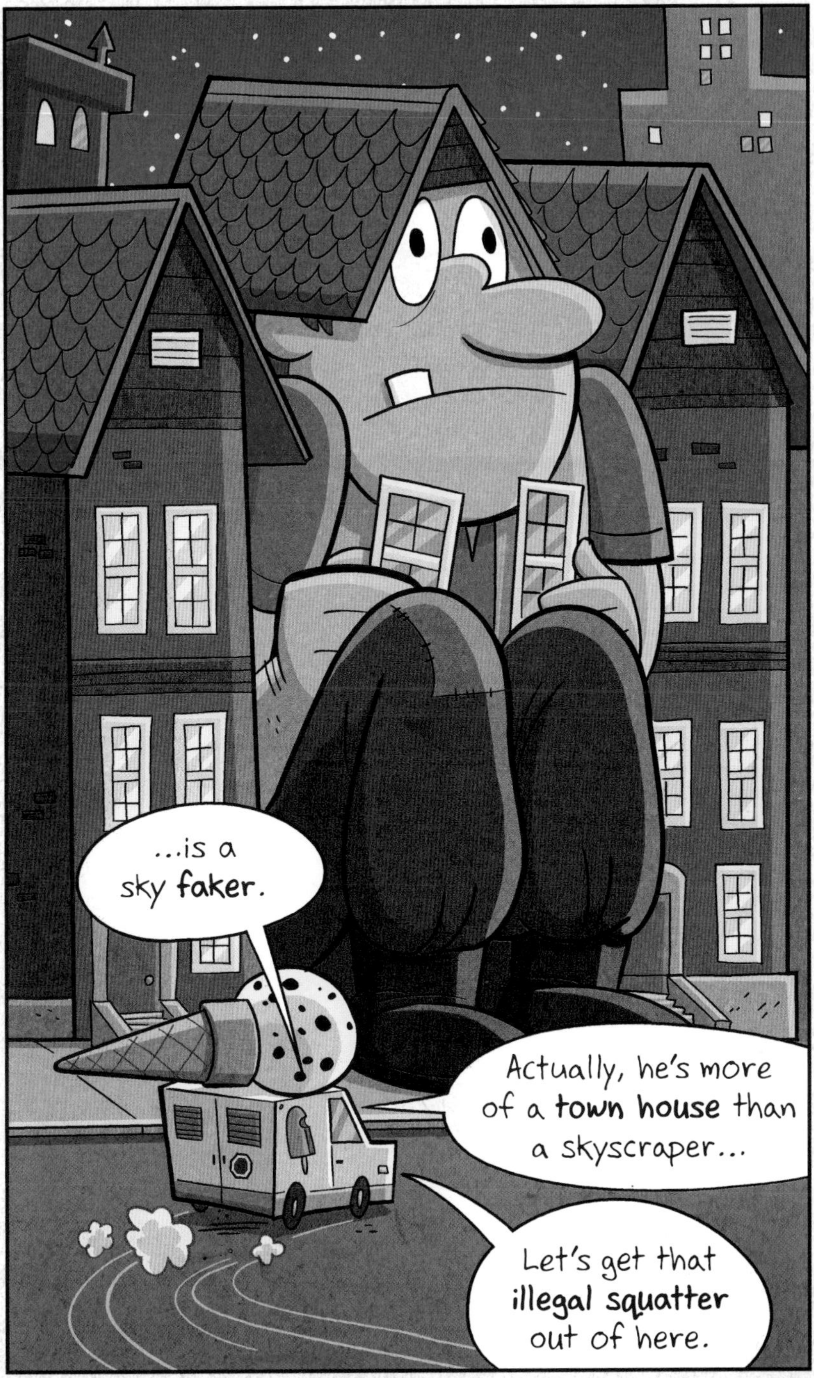
...is a sky **faker**.
Actually, he's more of a **town house** than a skyscraper...
Let's get that **illegal squatter** out of here.

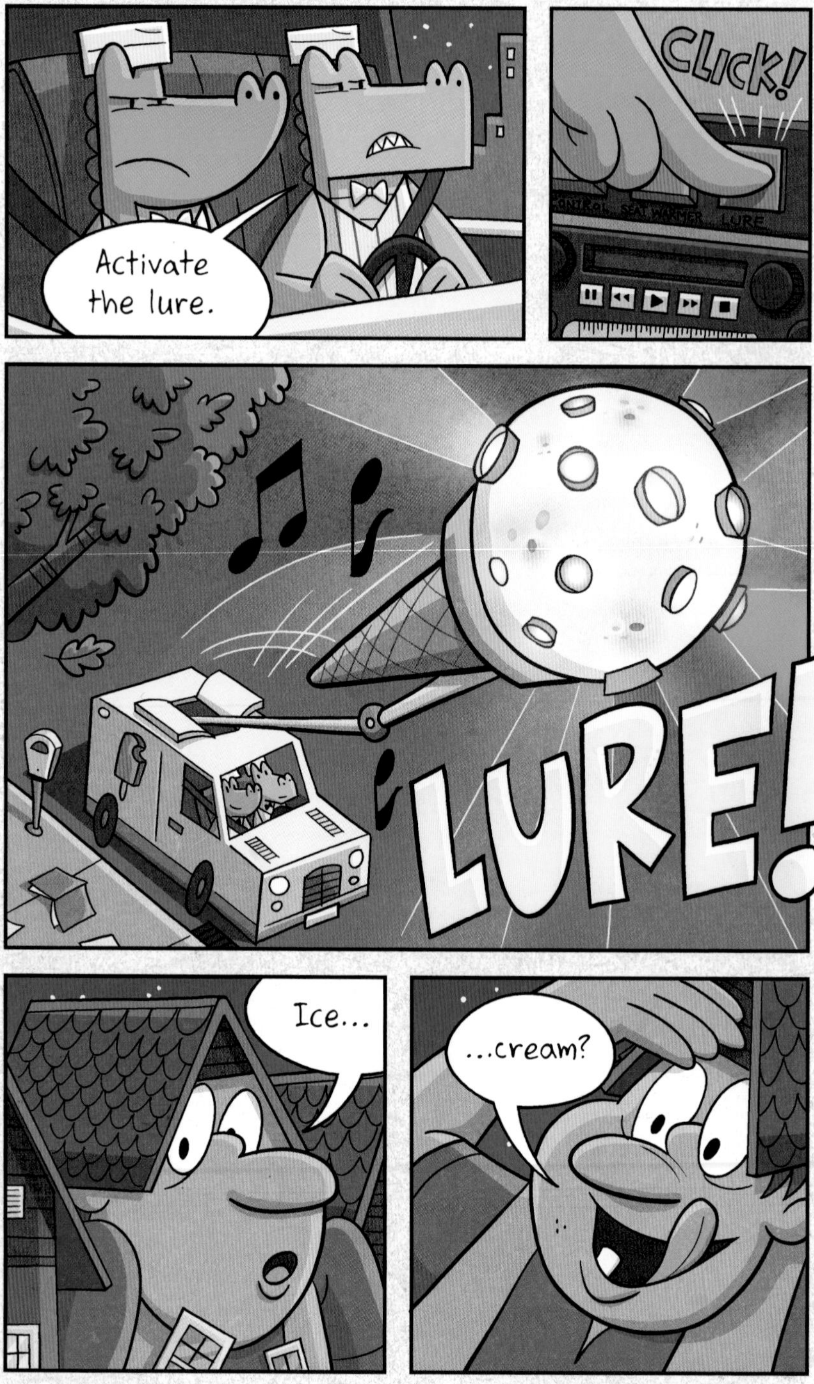
Activate the lure.
CLICK!
CONTROL
SEAT WARMER
LURE
LURE!
Ice...
...cream?

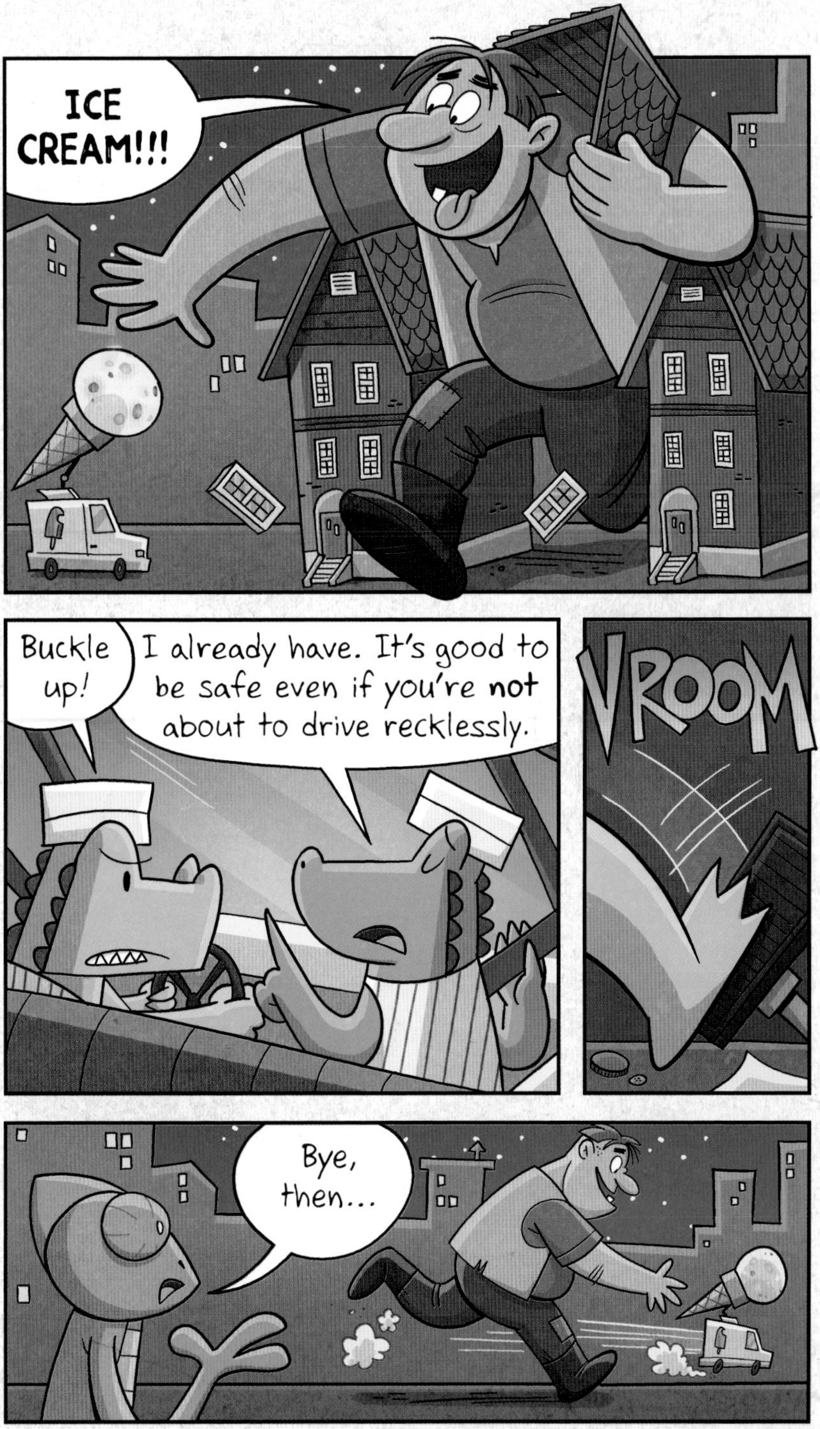
ICE CREAM!!!
Buckle up!
I already have. It's good to be safe even if you're **not** about to drive recklessly.
VROOM
Bye, then...

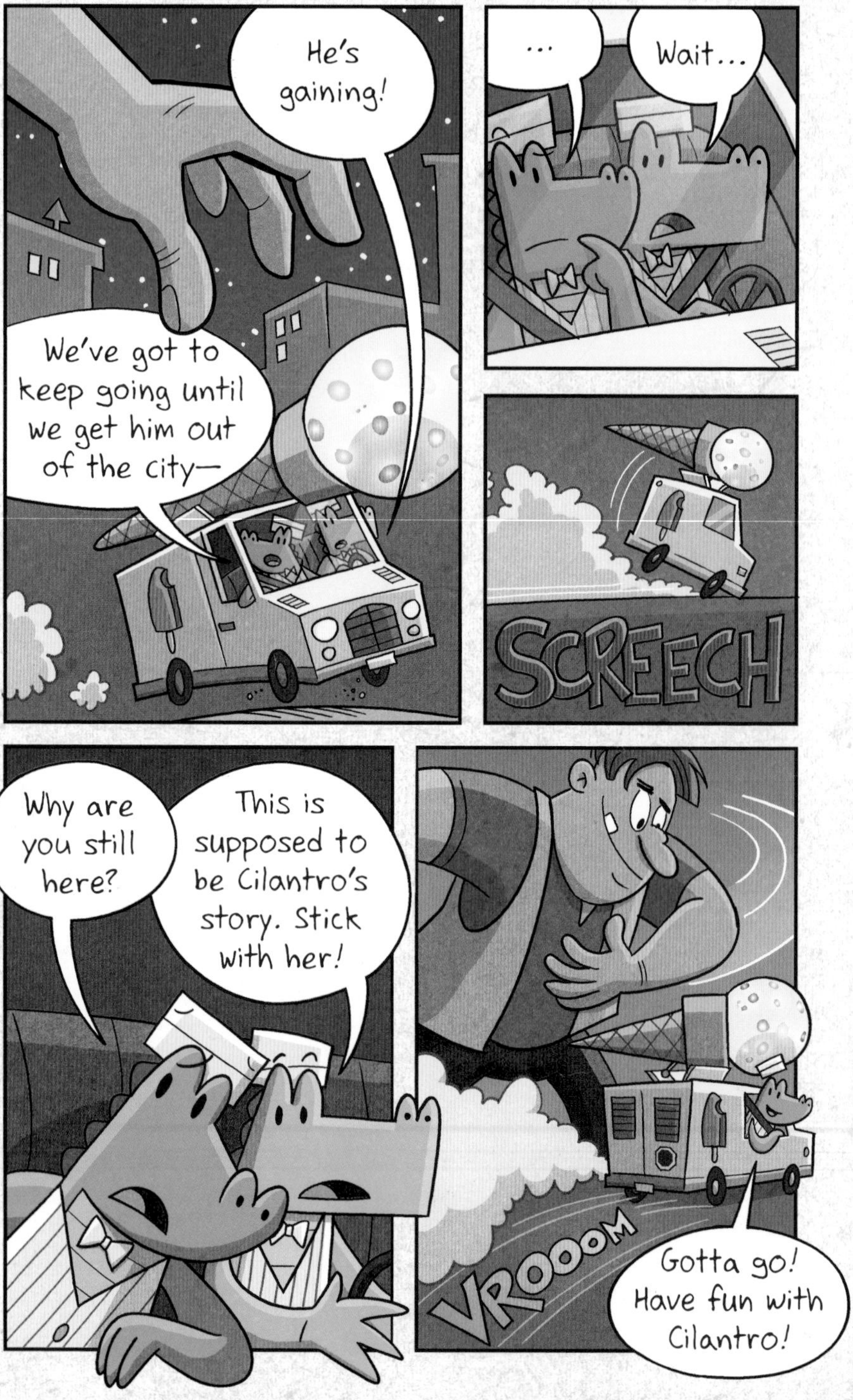
He's gaining!
We've got to keep going until we get him out of the city—
...
Wait...
SCREECH
Why are you still here?
This is supposed to be Cilantro's story. Stick with her!
VROOOM
Gotta go! Have fun with Cilantro!

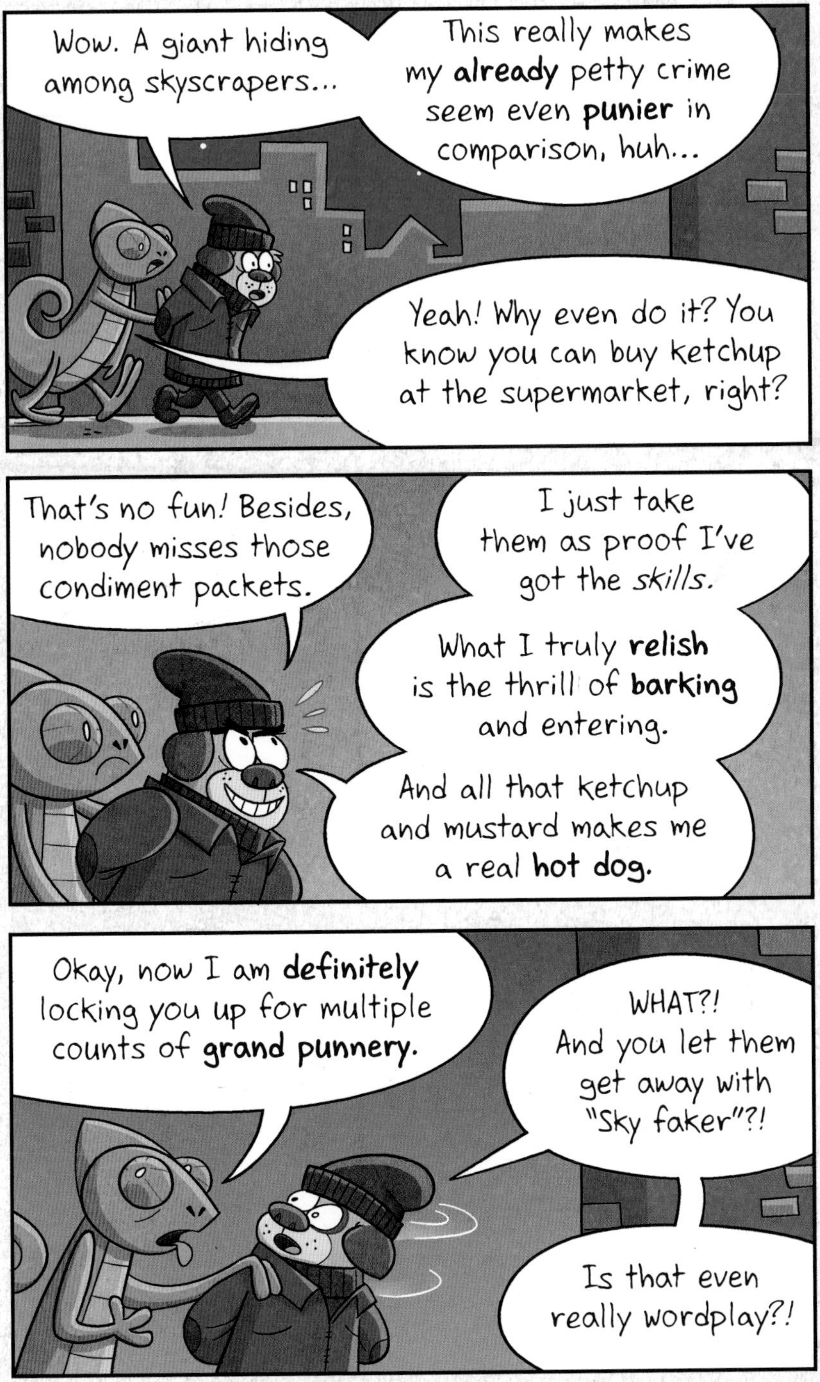
Wow. A giant hiding among skyscrapers...
This really makes my **already** petty crime seem even **punier** in comparison, huh...
Yeah! Why even do it? You know you can buy ketchup at the supermarket, right?
That's no fun! Besides, nobody misses those condiment packets.
I just take them as proof I've got the *skills.*
What I truly **relish** is the thrill of **barking** and entering.
And all that ketchup and mustard makes me a real **hot dog.**
Okay, now I am **definitely** locking you up for multiple counts of **grand punnery.**
WHAT?! And you let them get away with "Sky faker"?!
Is that even really wordplay?!

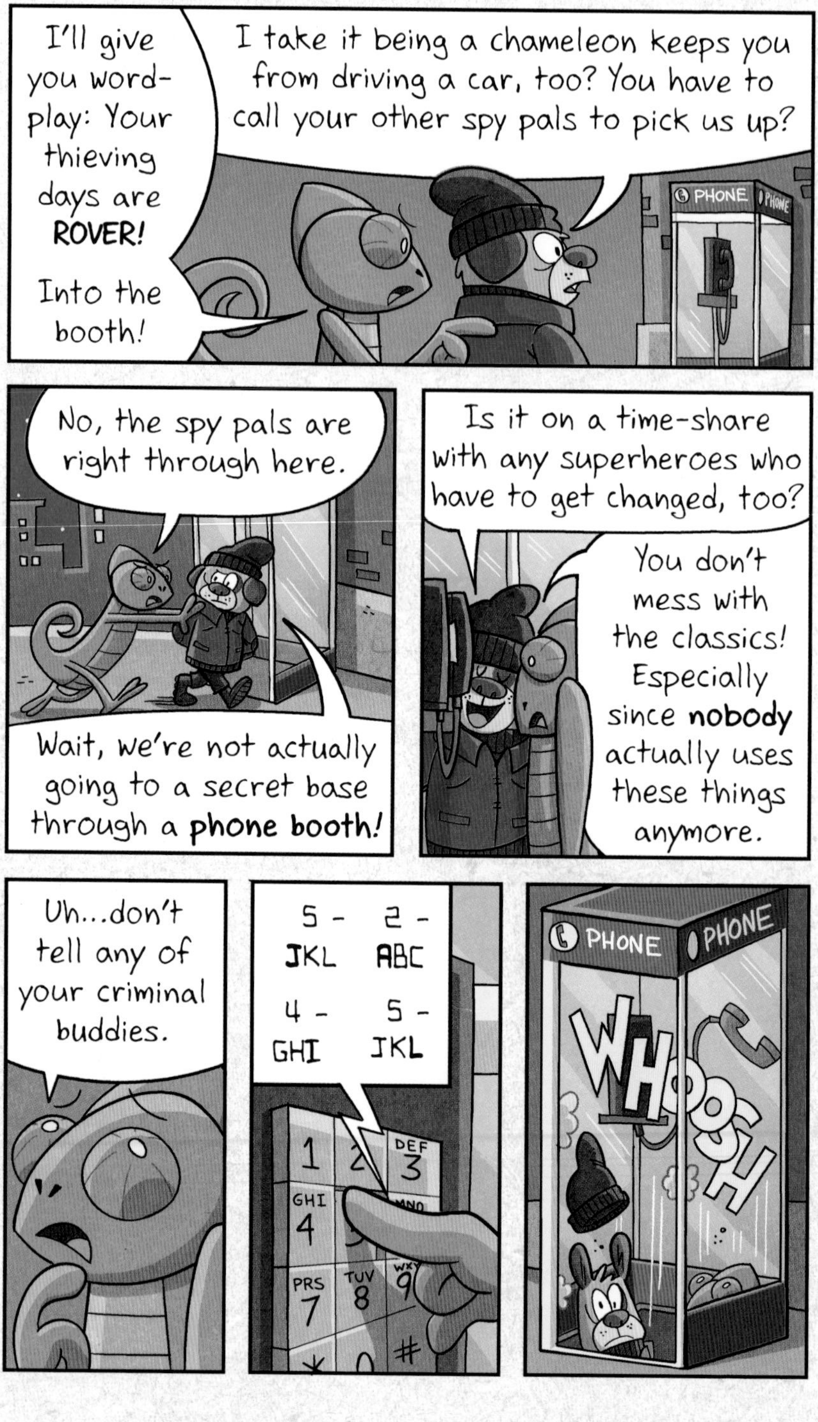
I'll give you word-play: Your thieving days are **ROVER!**
Into the booth!
I take it being a chameleon keeps you from driving a car, too? You have to call your other spy pals to pick us up?
PHONE
PHONE
No, the spy pals are right through here.
Wait, we're not actually going to a secret base through a **phone booth!**
Is it on a time-share with any superheroes who have to get changed, too?
You don't mess with the classics! Especially since **nobody** actually uses these things anymore.
Uh...don't tell any of your criminal buddies.
5 - JKL 2 - ABC 4 - GHI 5 - JKL
PHONE
PHONE
WHOOSH

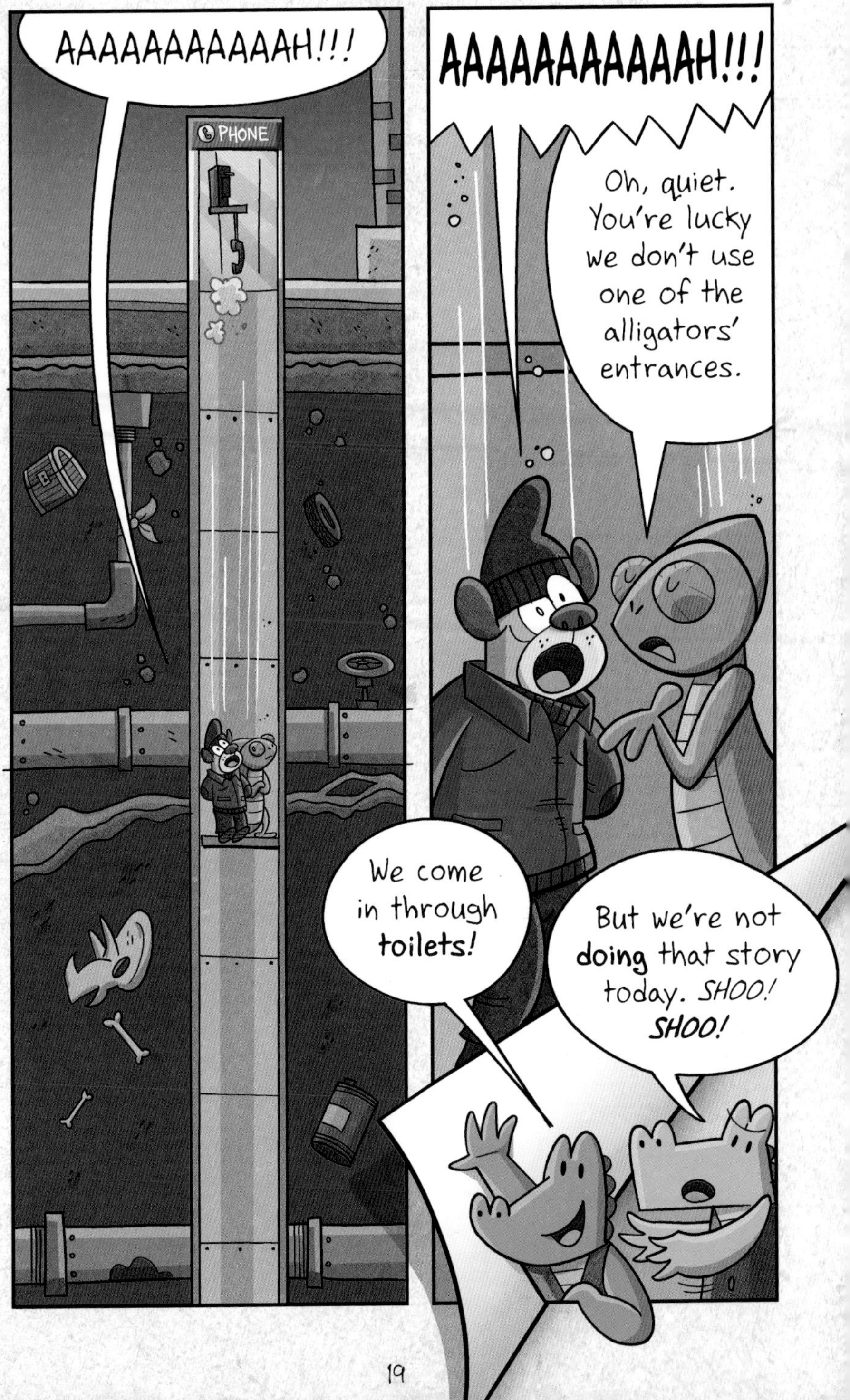
AAAAAAAAAAAH!!!
PHONE
AAAAAAAAAAAH!!!
Oh, quiet. You're lucky we don't use one of the alligators' entrances.
We come in through **toilets!**
But we're not **doing** that story today. *SHOO!* ***SHOO!***

Chapter 1

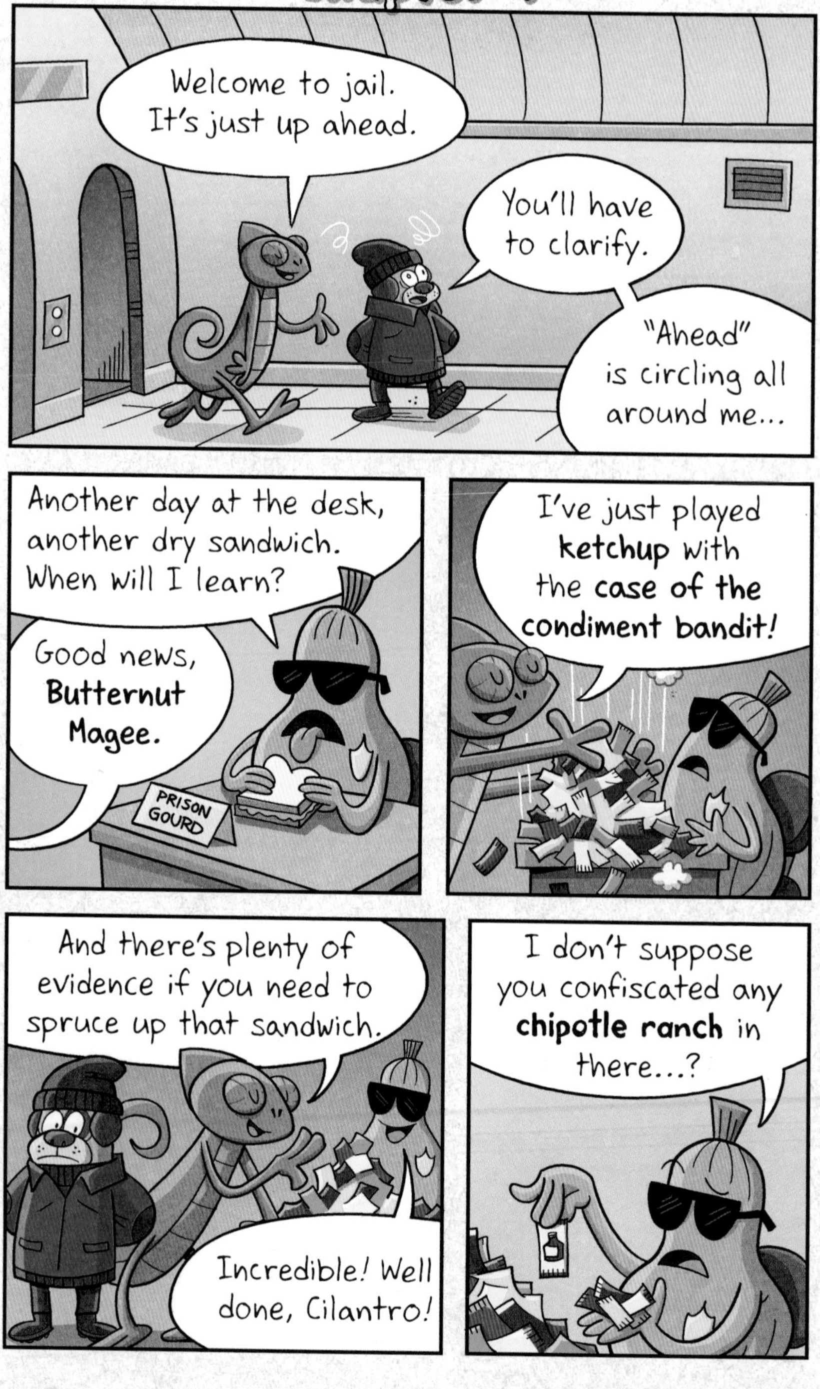
Welcome to jail. It's just up ahead.
You'll have to clarify.
"Ahead" is circling all around me...
Another day at the desk, another dry sandwich. When will I learn?
Good news, **Butternut Magee.**
PRISON GOURD
I've just played **ketchup** with the **case of the condiment bandit!**
And there's plenty of evidence if you need to spruce up that sandwich.
Incredible! Well done, Cilantro!
I don't suppose you confiscated any **chipotle ranch** in there...?

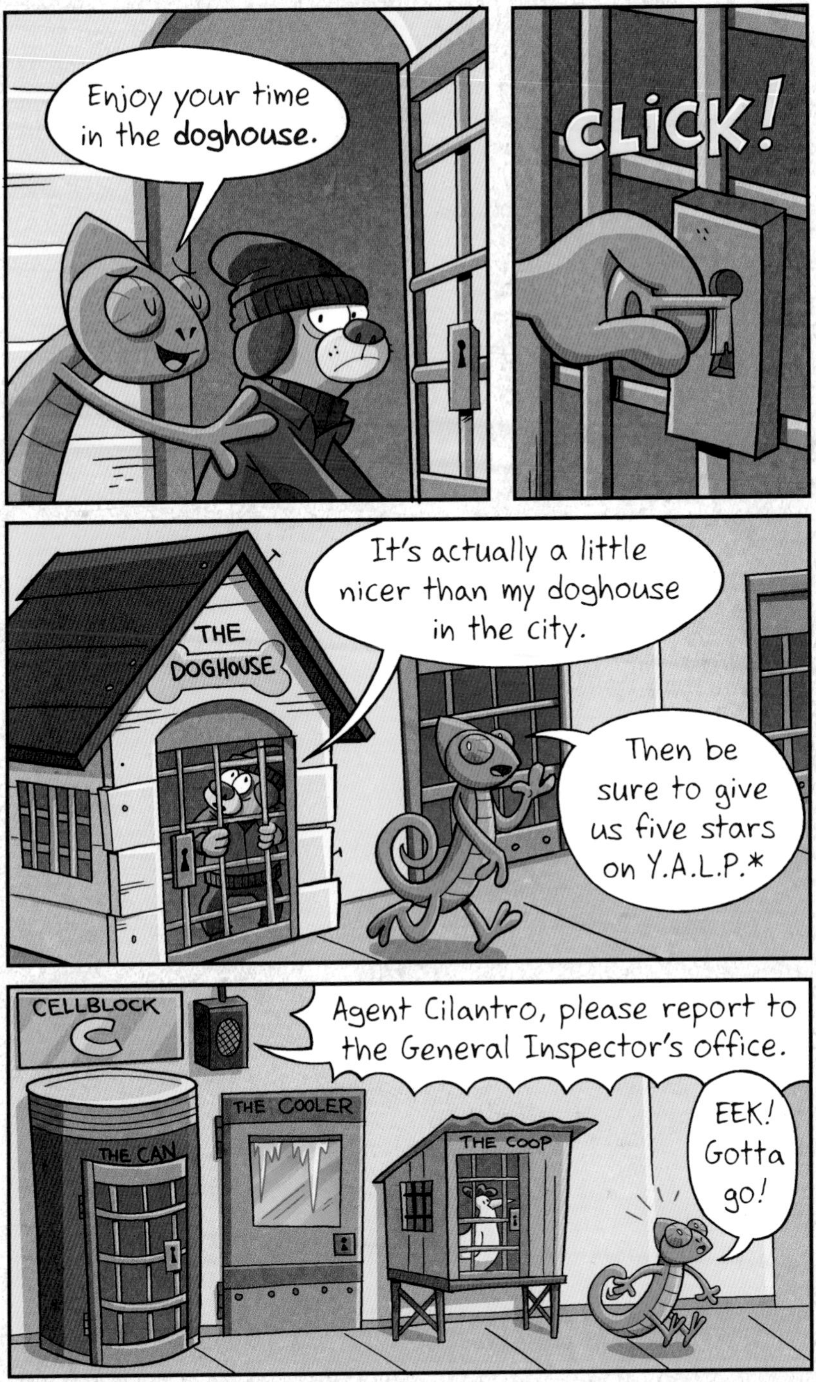
Enjoy your time in the **doghouse.**
CLICK!
THE DOGHOUSE
It's actually a little nicer than my doghouse in the city.
Then be sure to give us five stars on Y.A.L.P.*
CELLBLOCK C
Agent Cilantro, please report to the General Inspector's office.
THE CAN
THE COOLER
THE COOP
EEK! Gotta go!

*Your Appraisal of this Lovely Prison

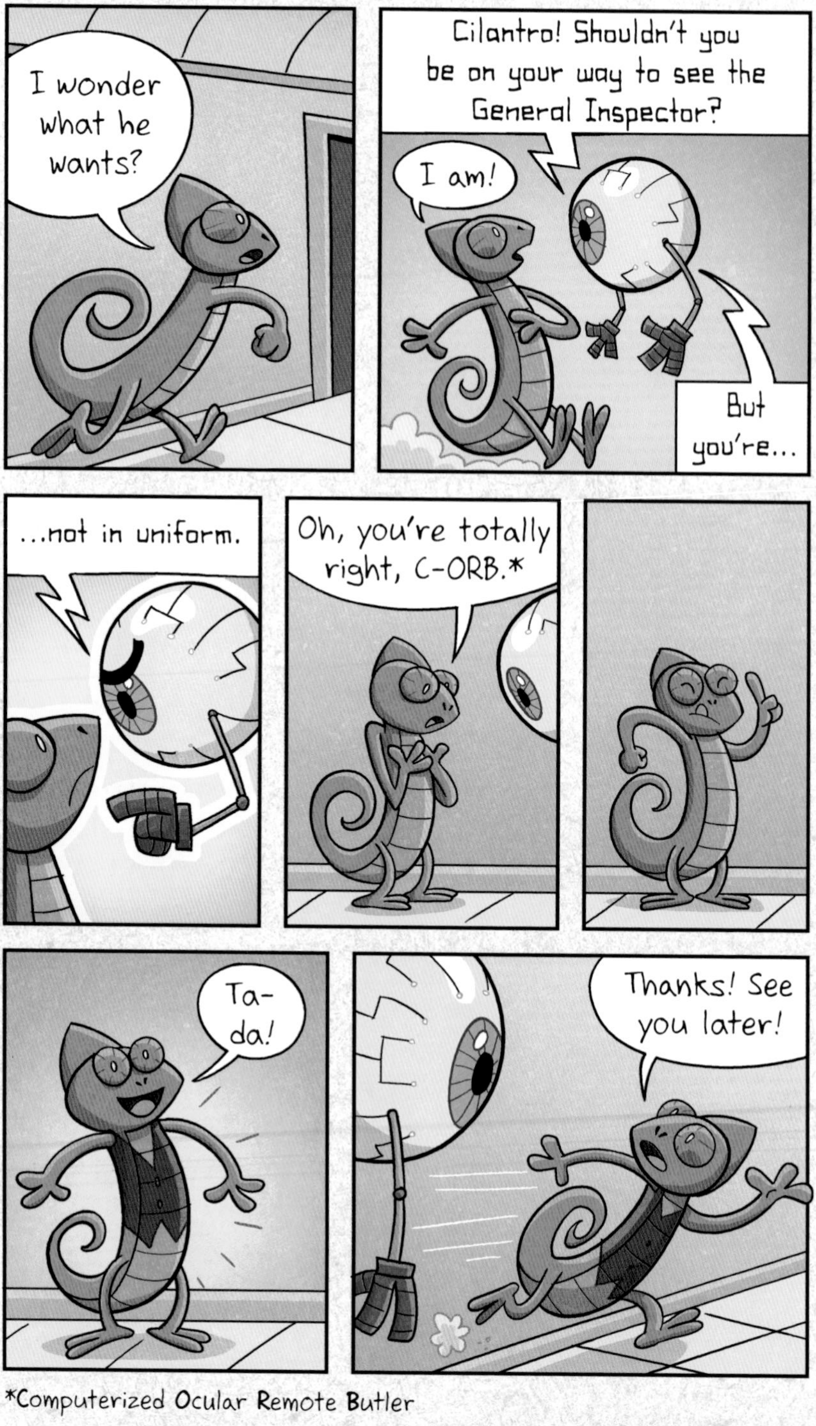
I wonder what he wants?
Cilantro! Shouldn't you be on your way to see the General Inspector?
I am!
But you're...
...not in uniform.
Oh, you're totally right, C-ORB.*
Ta-da!
Thanks! See you later!

*Computerized Ocular Remote Butler

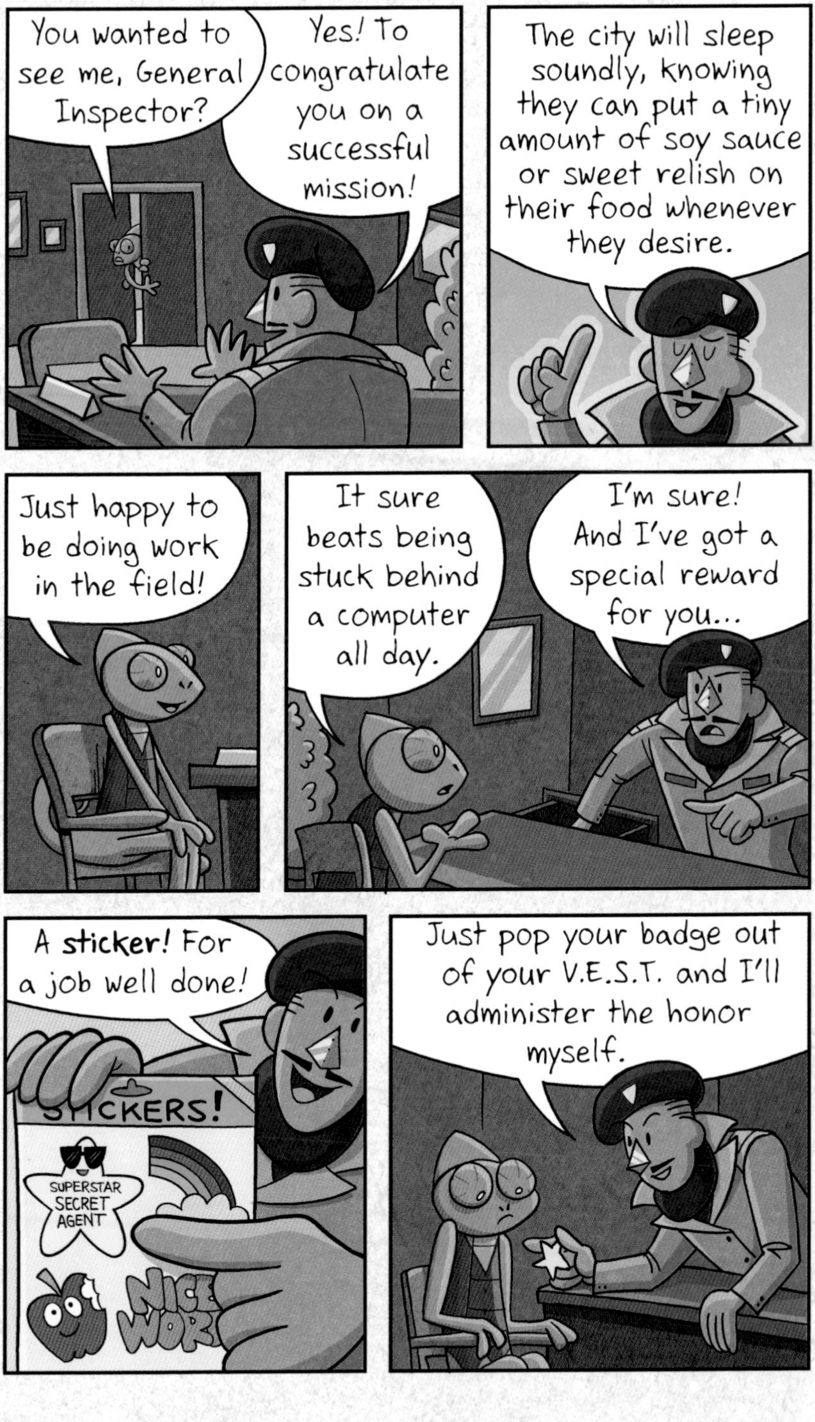
You wanted to see me, General Inspector?
Yes! To congratulate you on a successful mission!
The city will sleep soundly, knowing they can put a tiny amount of soy sauce or sweet relish on their food whenever they desire.
Just happy to be doing work in the field!
It sure beats being stuck behind a computer all day.
I'm sure! And I've got a special reward for you...
A **sticker**! For a job well done!
STICKERS!
SUPERSTAR SECRET AGENT
Just pop your badge out of your V.E.S.T. and I'll administer the honor myself.

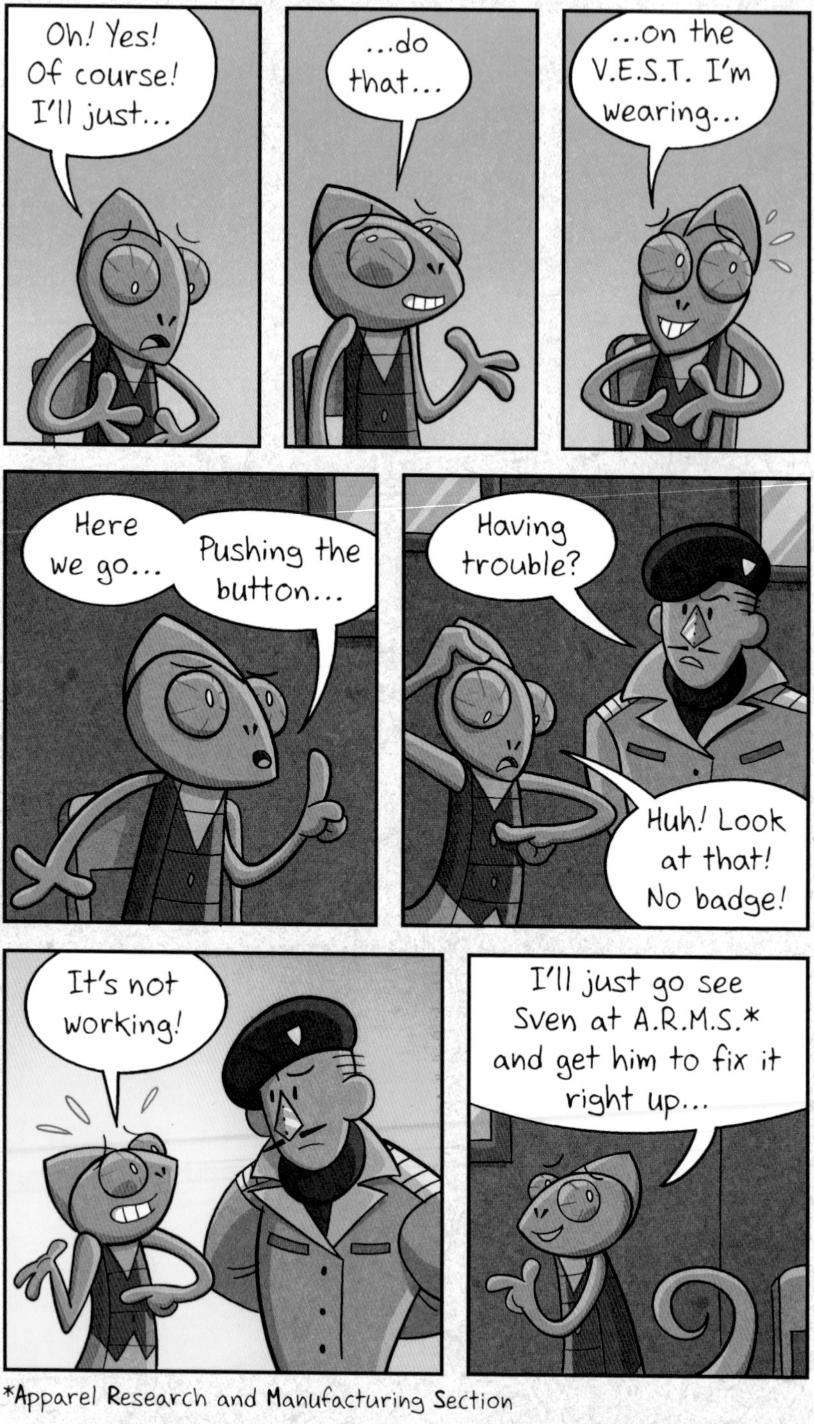
Oh! Yes! Of course! I'll just...
...do that...
...on the V.E.S.T. I'm wearing...
Here we go...
Pushing the button...
Having trouble?
Huh! Look at that! No badge!
It's not working!
I'll just go see Sven at A.R.M.S.* and get him to fix it right up...

*Apparel Research and Manufacturing Section

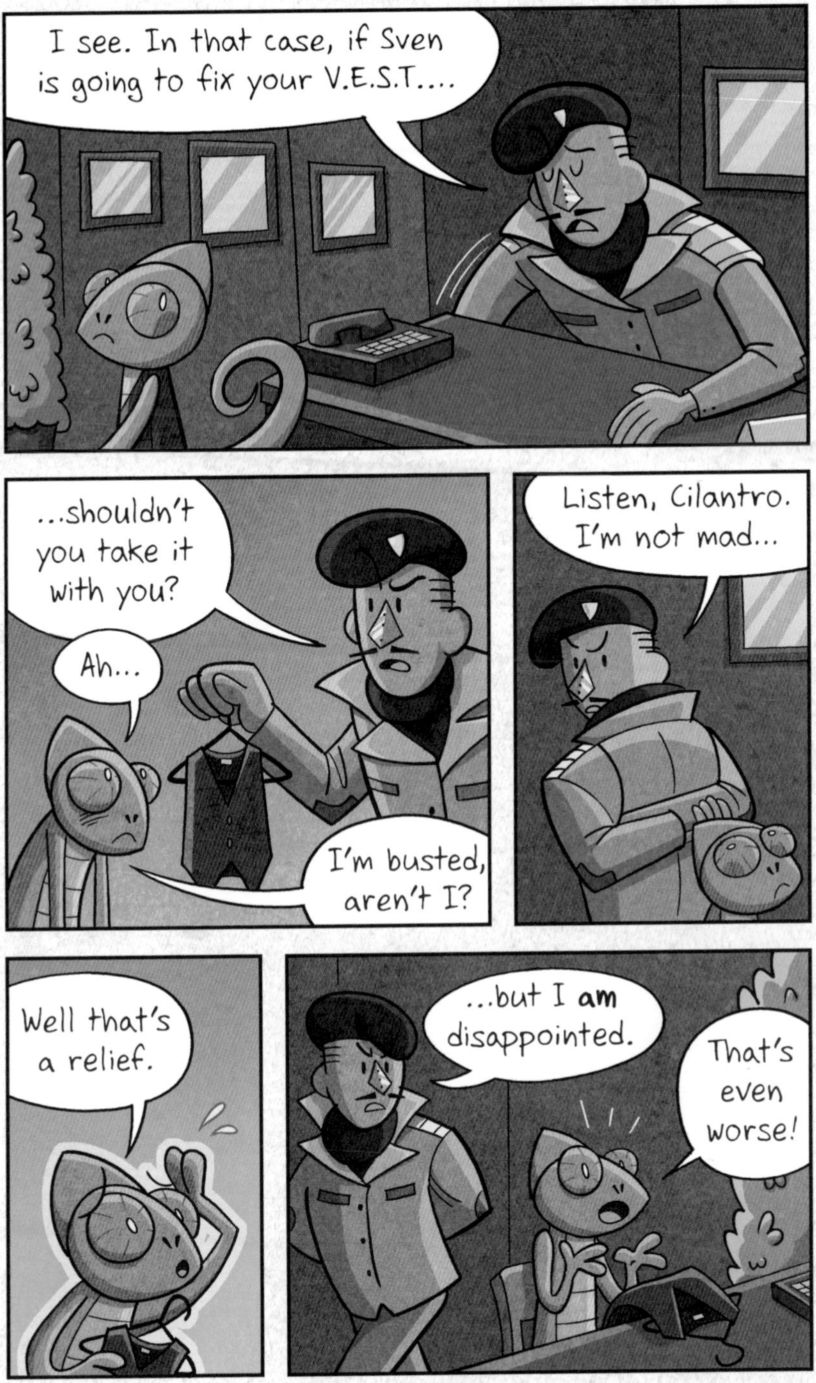
I see. In that case, if Sven is going to fix your V.E.S.T....
...shouldn't you take it with you?
Ah...
I'm busted, aren't I?
Listen, Cilantro. I'm not mad...
Well that's a relief.
...but I **am** disappointed.
That's even worse!

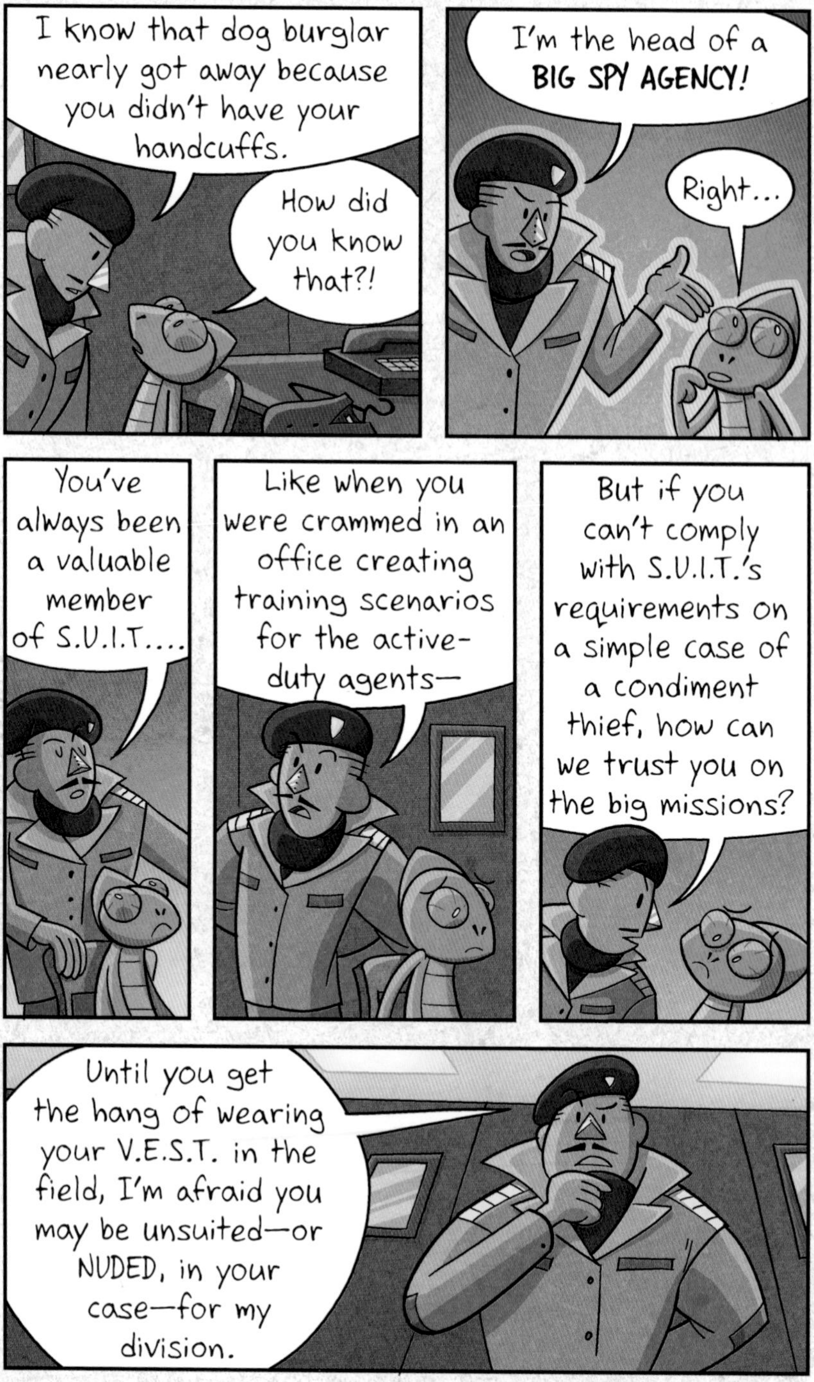
I know that dog burglar nearly got away because you didn't have your handcuffs.
How did you know that?!
I'm the head of a BIG SPY AGENCY!
Right...
You've always been a valuable member of S.U.I.T....
Like when you were crammed in an office creating training scenarios for the active-duty agents—
But if you can't comply with S.U.I.T.'s requirements on a simple case of a condiment thief, how can we trust you on the big missions?
Until you get the hang of wearing your V.E.S.T. in the field, I'm afraid you may be unsuited—or NUDED, in your case—for my division.

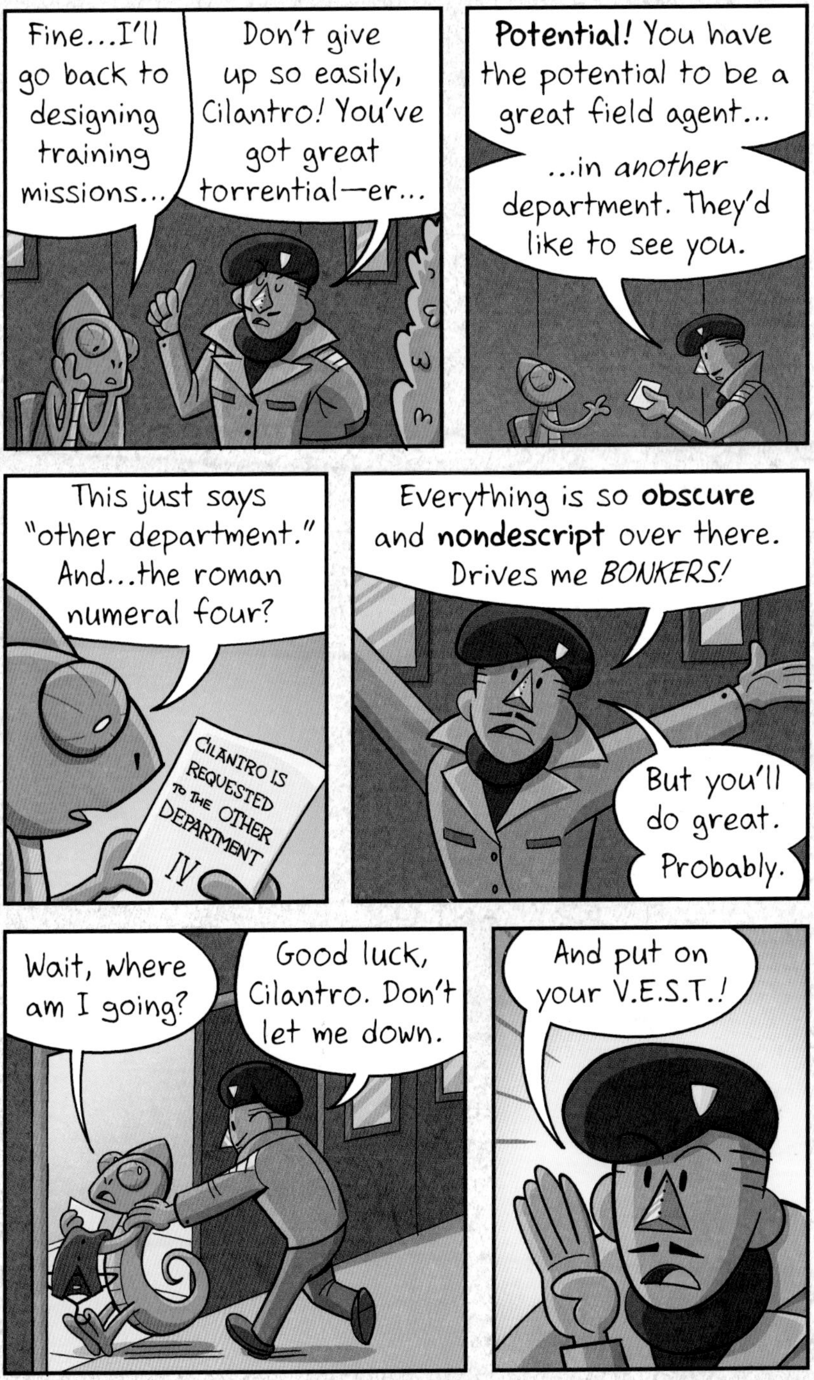
Fine...I'll go back to designing training missions...
Don't give up so easily, Cilantro! You've got great torrential—er...
Potential! You have the potential to be a great field agent...
...in *another* department. They'd like to see you.
This just says "other department." And...the roman numeral four?
CILANTRO IS REQUESTED TO THE OTHER DEPARTMENT
IV
Everything is so **obscure** and **nondescript** over there. Drives me *BONKERS!*
But you'll do great. Probably.
Wait, where am I going?
Good luck, Cilantro. Don't let me down.
And put on your V.E.S.T.!

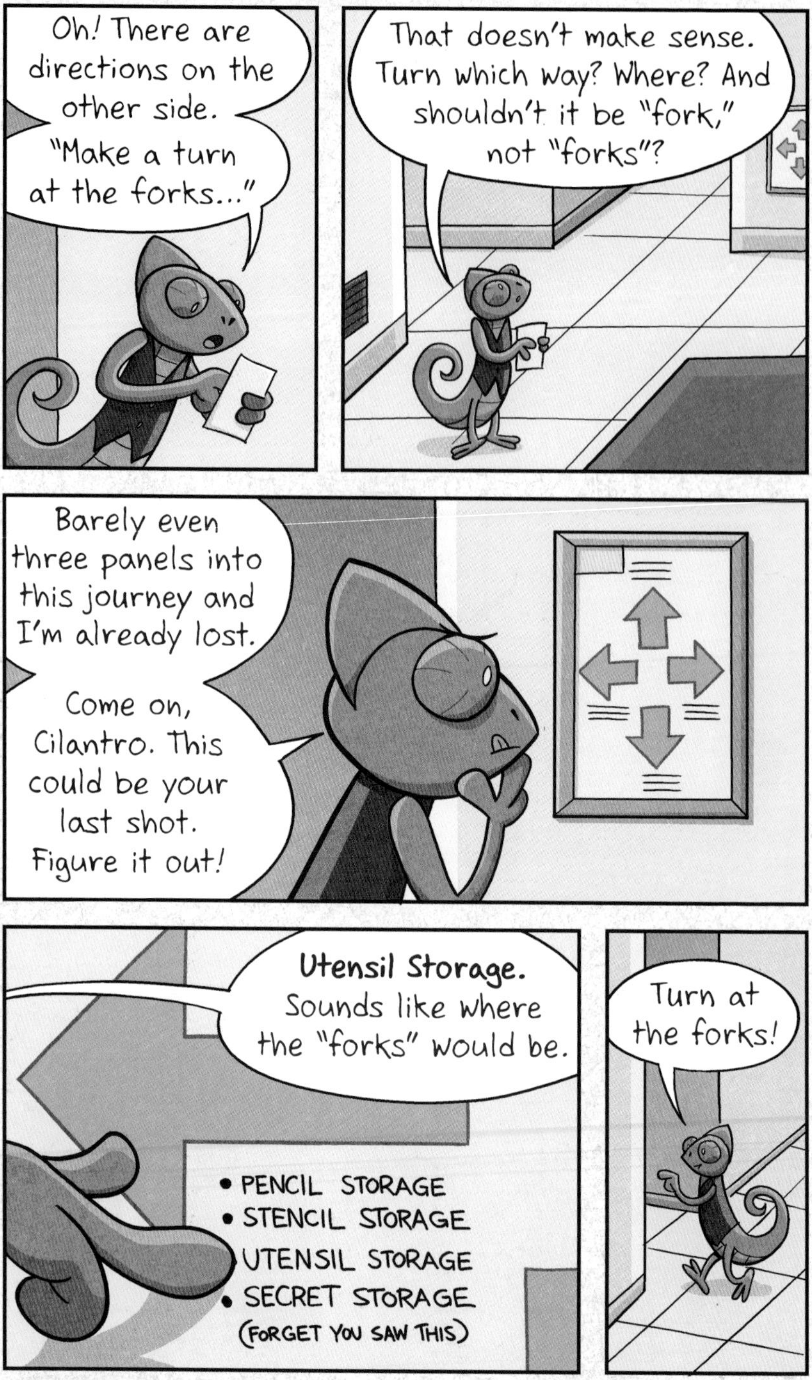
Oh! There are directions on the other side. "Make a turn at the forks..."
That doesn't make sense. Turn which way? Where? And shouldn't it be "fork," not "forks"?
Barely even three panels into this journey and I'm already lost.
Come on, Cilantro. This could be your last shot. Figure it out!
Utensil Storage. Sounds like where the "forks" would be.
• PENCIL STORAGE
• STENCIL STORAGE
UTENSIL STORAGE
• SECRET STORAGE
(FORGET YOU SAW THIS)
Turn at the forks!

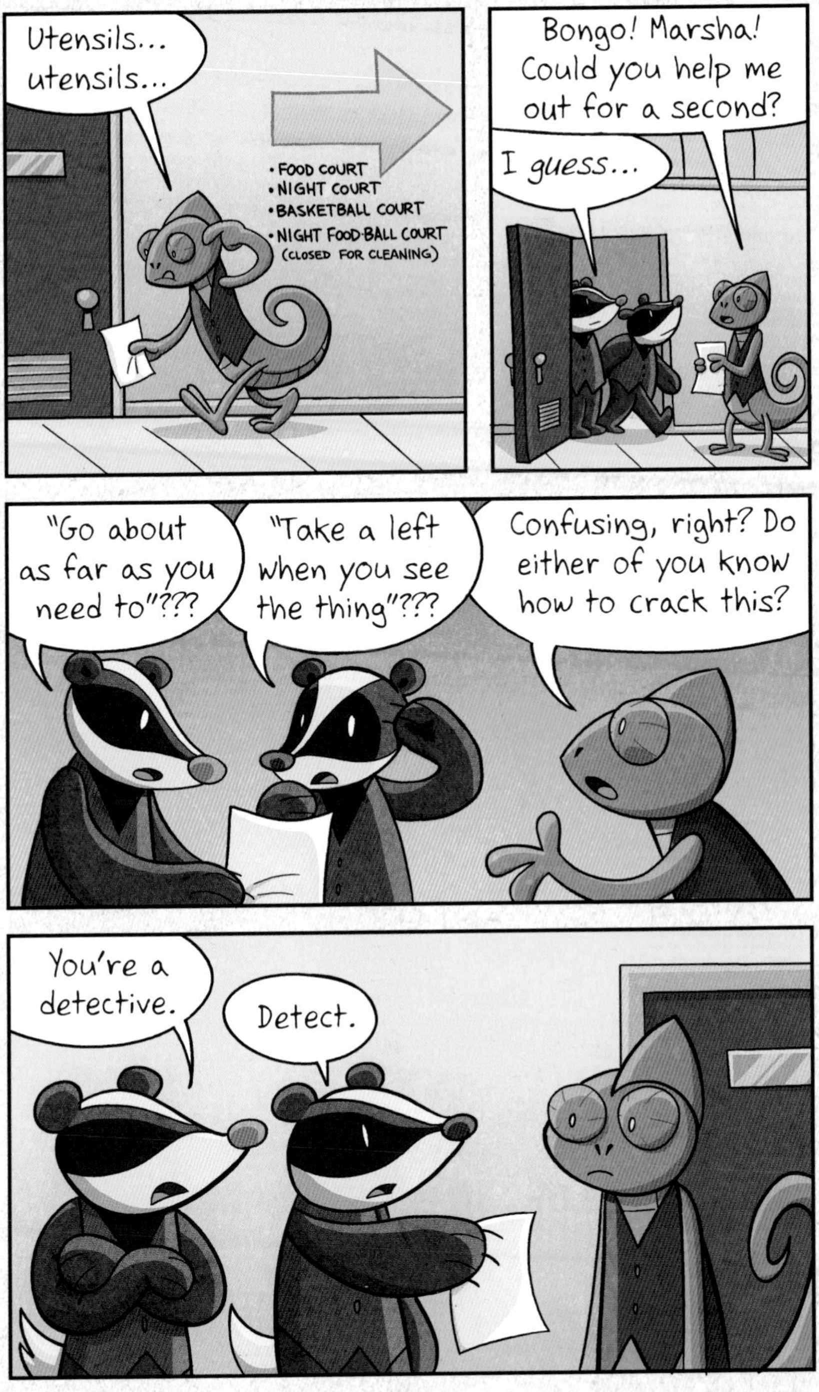

Utensils... utensils...
• FOOD COURT
• NIGHT COURT
• BASKETBALL COURT
• NIGHT FOOD-BALL COURT
(CLOSED FOR CLEANING)
Bongo! Marsha! Could you help me out for a second?
I guess...
"Go about as far as you need to"???
"Take a left when you see the thing"???
Confusing, right? Do either of you know how to crack this?
You're a detective.
Detect.

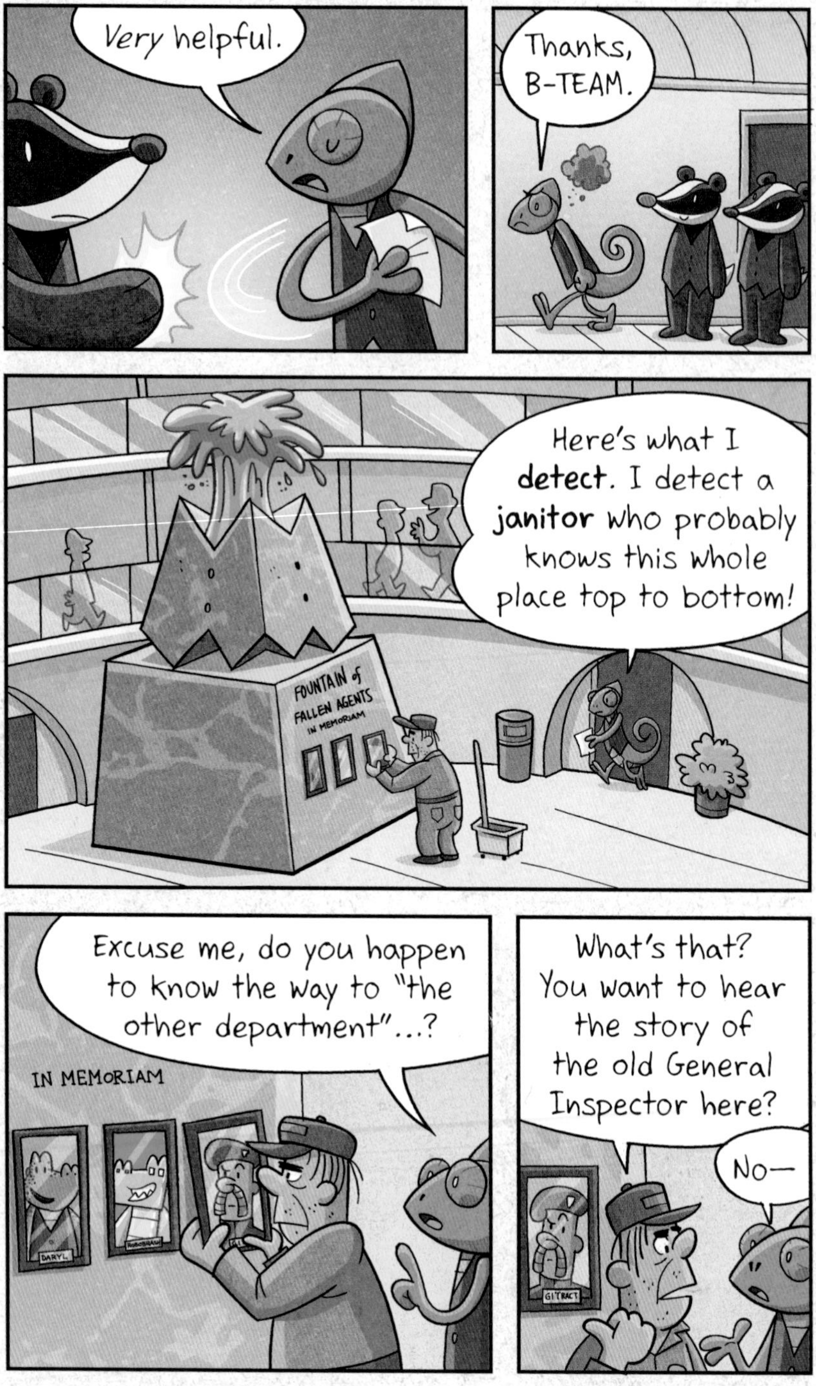
Very helpful.
Thanks, B-TEAM.
Here's what I **detect**. I detect a **janitor** who probably knows this whole place top to bottom!
FOUNTAIN of FALLEN AGENTS IN MEMORIAM
Excuse me, do you happen to know the way to "the other department"...?
IN MEMORIAM
DARYL
What's that? You want to hear the story of the old General Inspector here?
No—
GITRACT

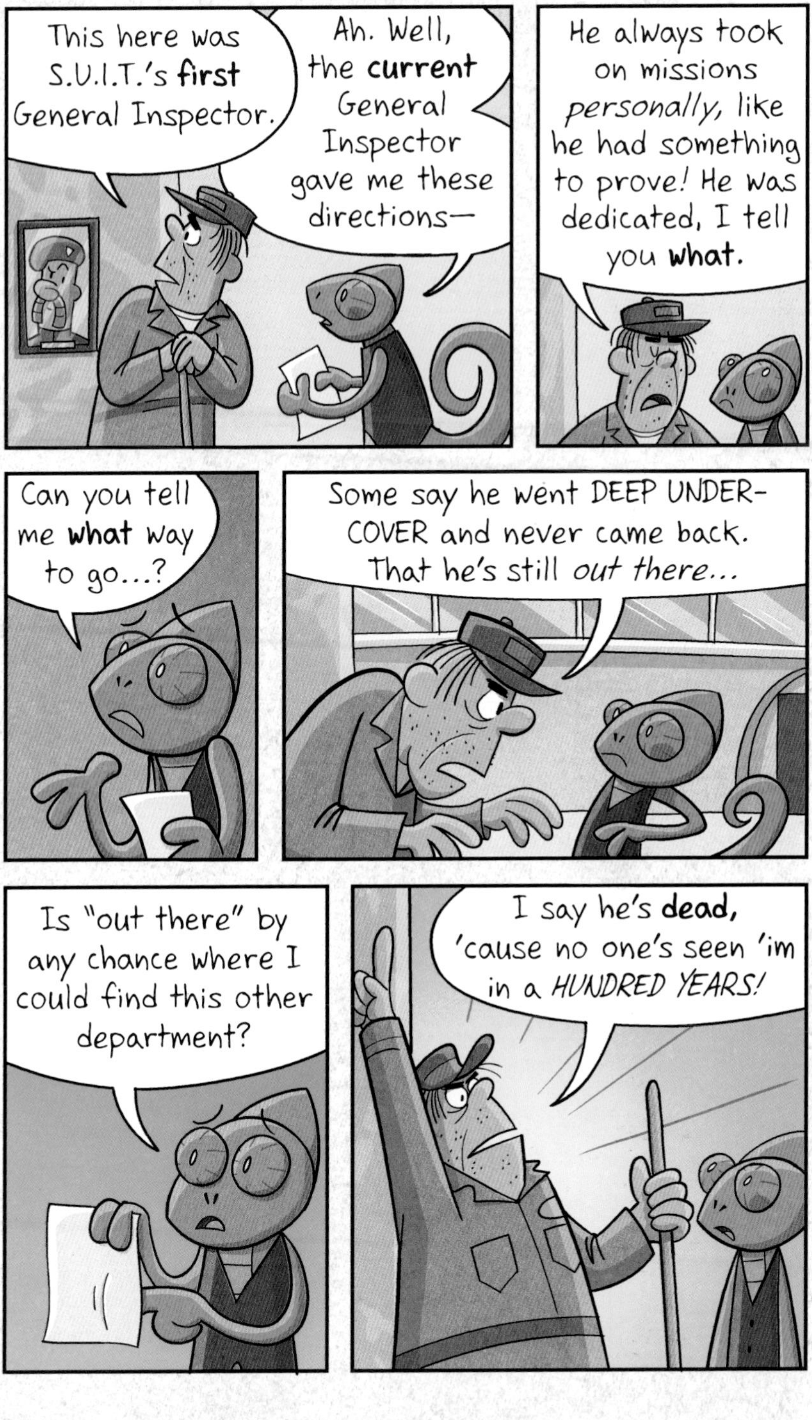
This here was S.U.I.T.'s **first** General Inspector.
Ah. Well, the **current** General Inspector gave me these directions—
He always took on missions *personally*, like he had something to prove! He was dedicated, I tell you **what.**
Can you tell me **what** way to go...?
Some say he went DEEP UNDER-COVER and never came back. That he's still *out there...*
Is "out there" by any chance where I could find this other department?
I say he's **dead,** 'cause no one's seen 'im in a *HUNDRED YEARS!*

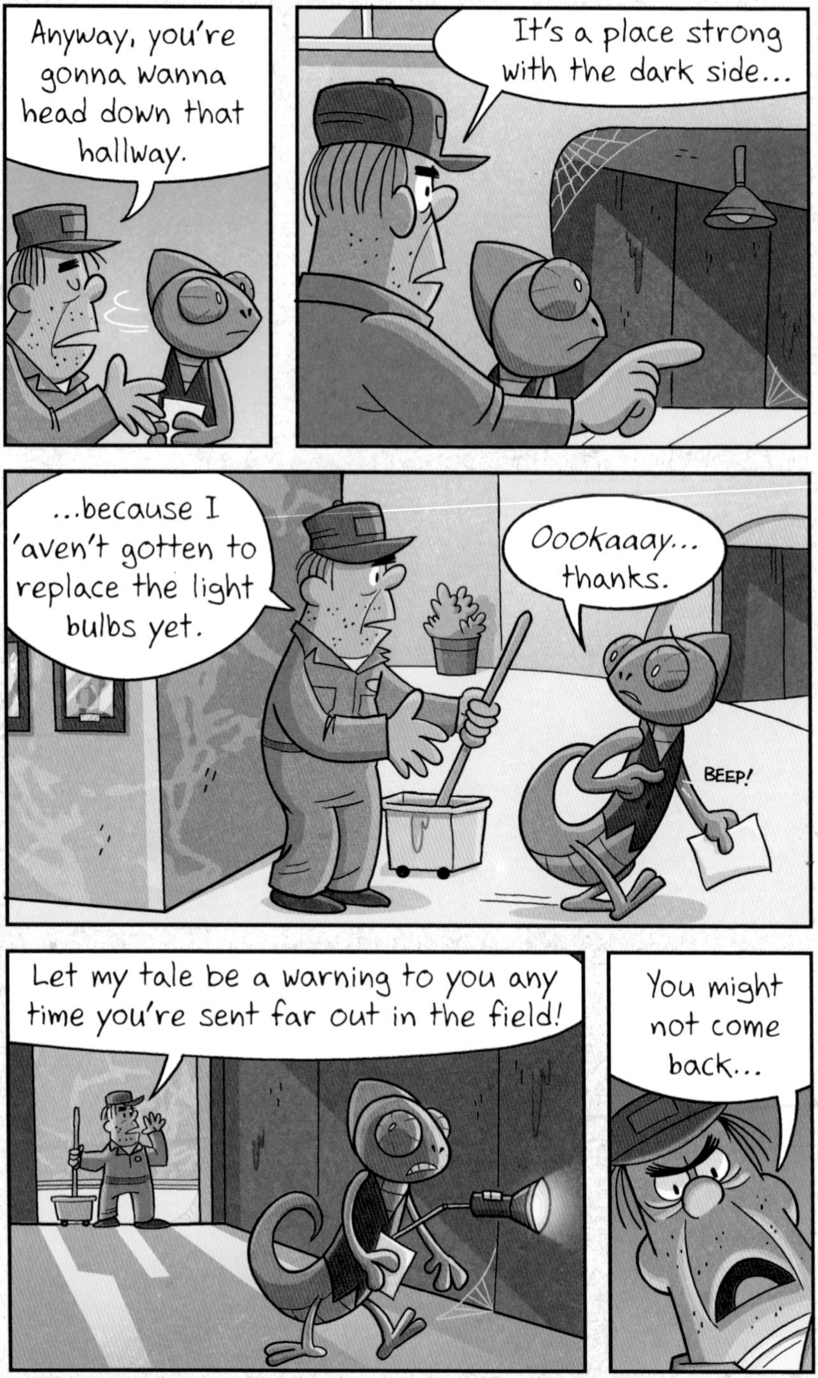
Anyway, you're gonna wanna head down that hallway.
It's a place strong with the dark side...
...because I 'aven't gotten to replace the light bulbs yet.
Oookaaay... thanks.
BEEP!
Let my tale be a warning to you any time you're sent far out in the field!
You might not come back...

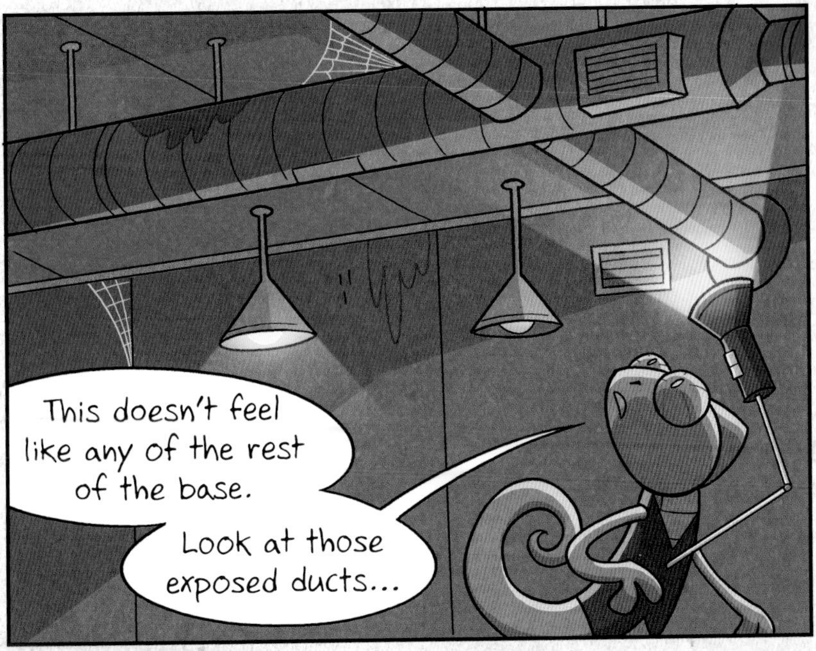
This doesn't feel like any of the rest of the base.
Look at those exposed ducts...

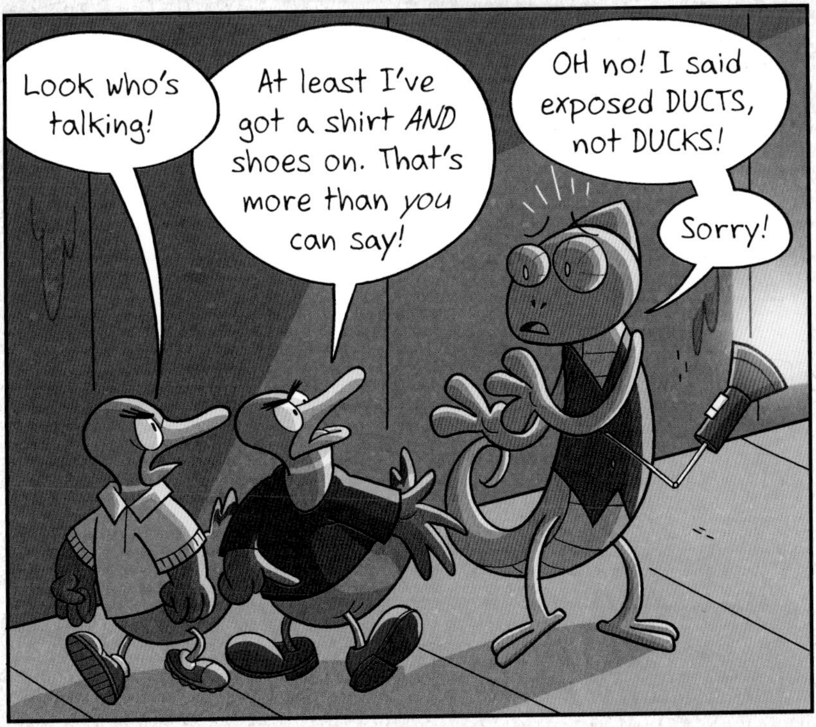
Look who's talking!
At least I've got a shirt *AND* shoes on. That's more than *you* can say!
OH no! I said exposed DUCTS, not DUCKS!
Sorry!

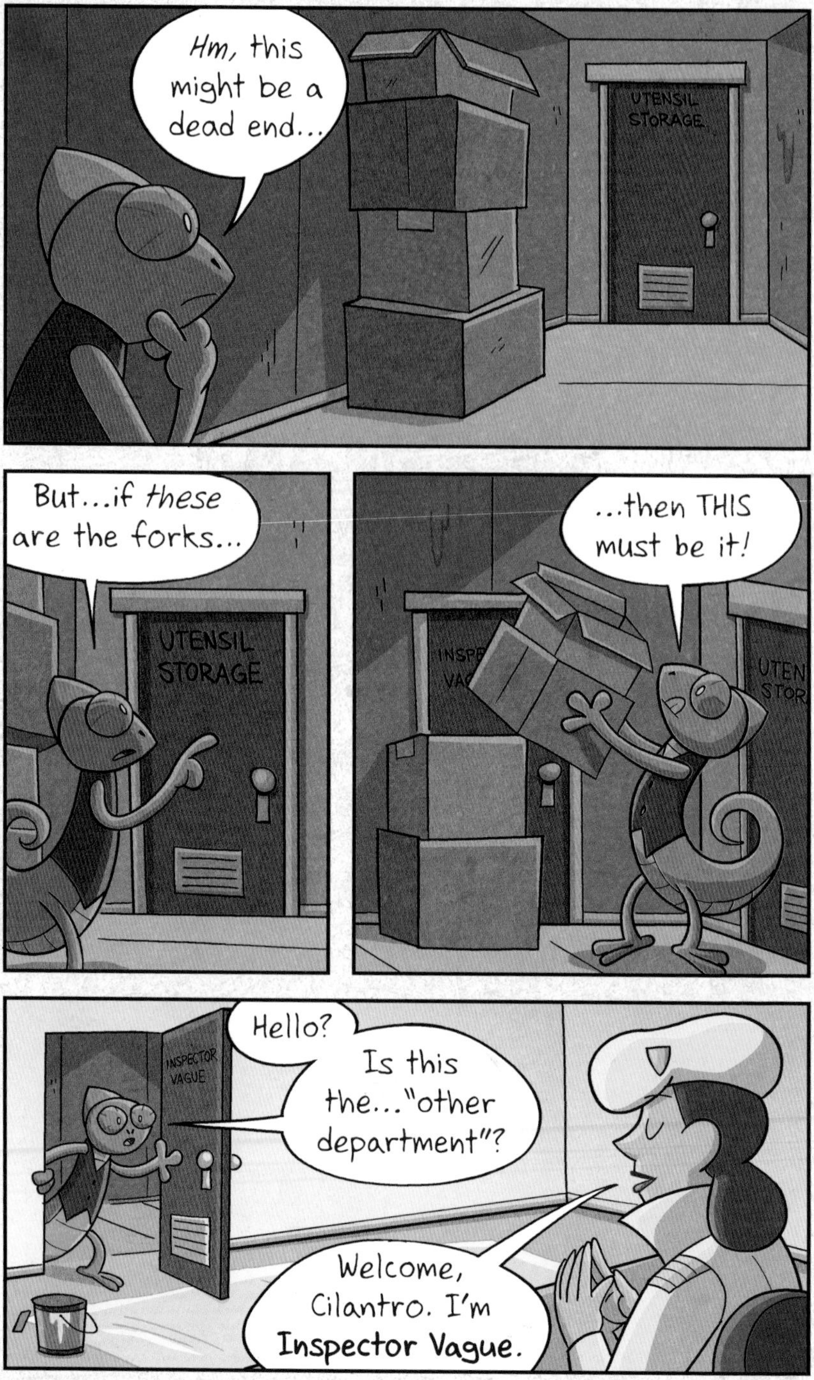
Hm, this might be a dead end...
UTENSIL STORAGE
But...if *these* are the forks...
UTENSIL STORAGE
...then THIS must be it!
Hello?
Is this the..."other department"?
INSPECTOR VAGUE
Welcome, Cilantro. I'm **Inspector Vague**.

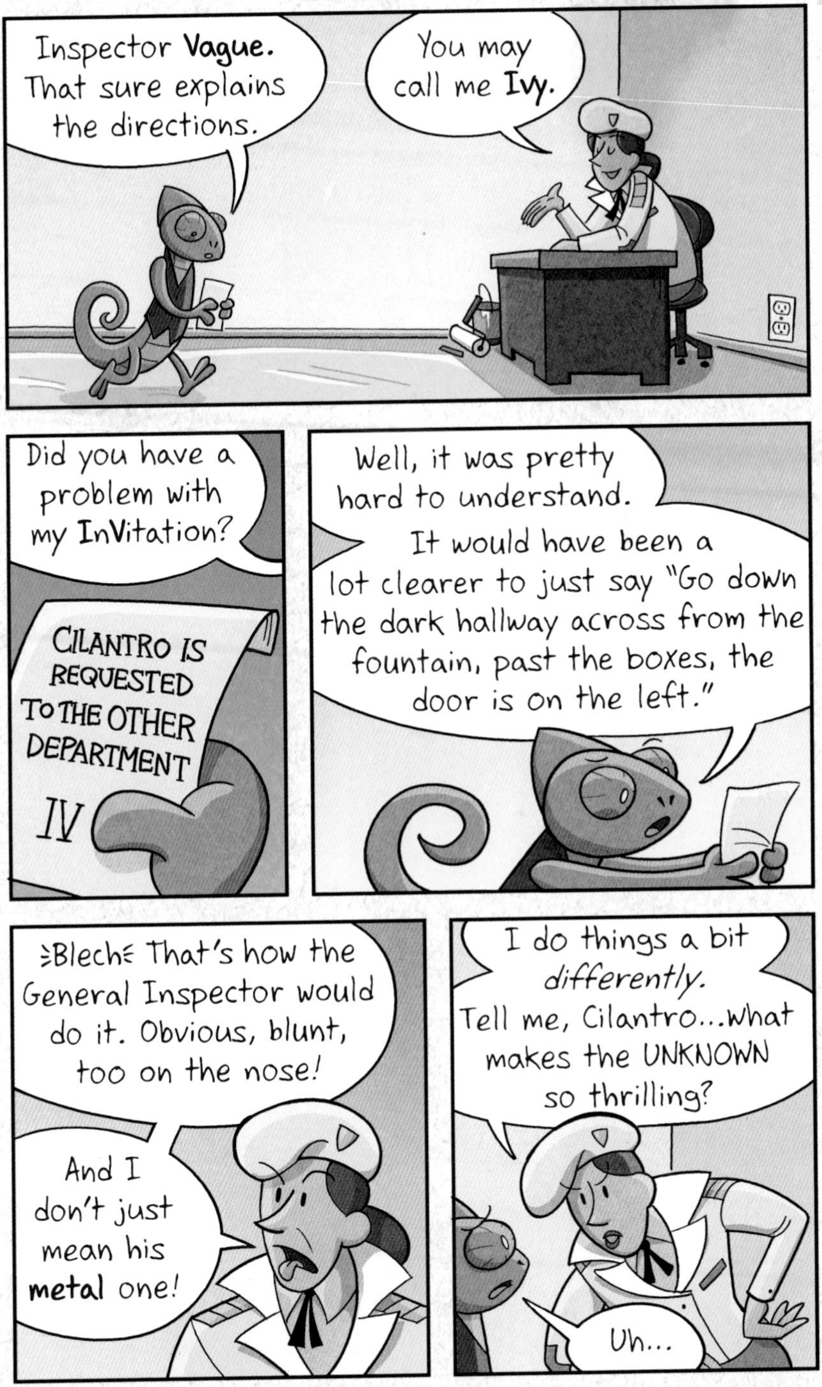
Inspector Vague. That sure explains the directions.
You may call me Ivy.
Did you have a problem with my InVitation?
CILANTRO IS REQUESTED TO THE OTHER DEPARTMENT IV
Well, it was pretty hard to understand.
It would have been a lot clearer to just say "Go down the dark hallway across from the fountain, past the boxes, the door is on the left."
Blech That's how the General Inspector would do it. Obvious, blunt, too on the nose!
And I don't just mean his metal one!
I do things a bit differently.
Tell me, Cilantro...what makes the UNKNOWN so thrilling?
Uh...

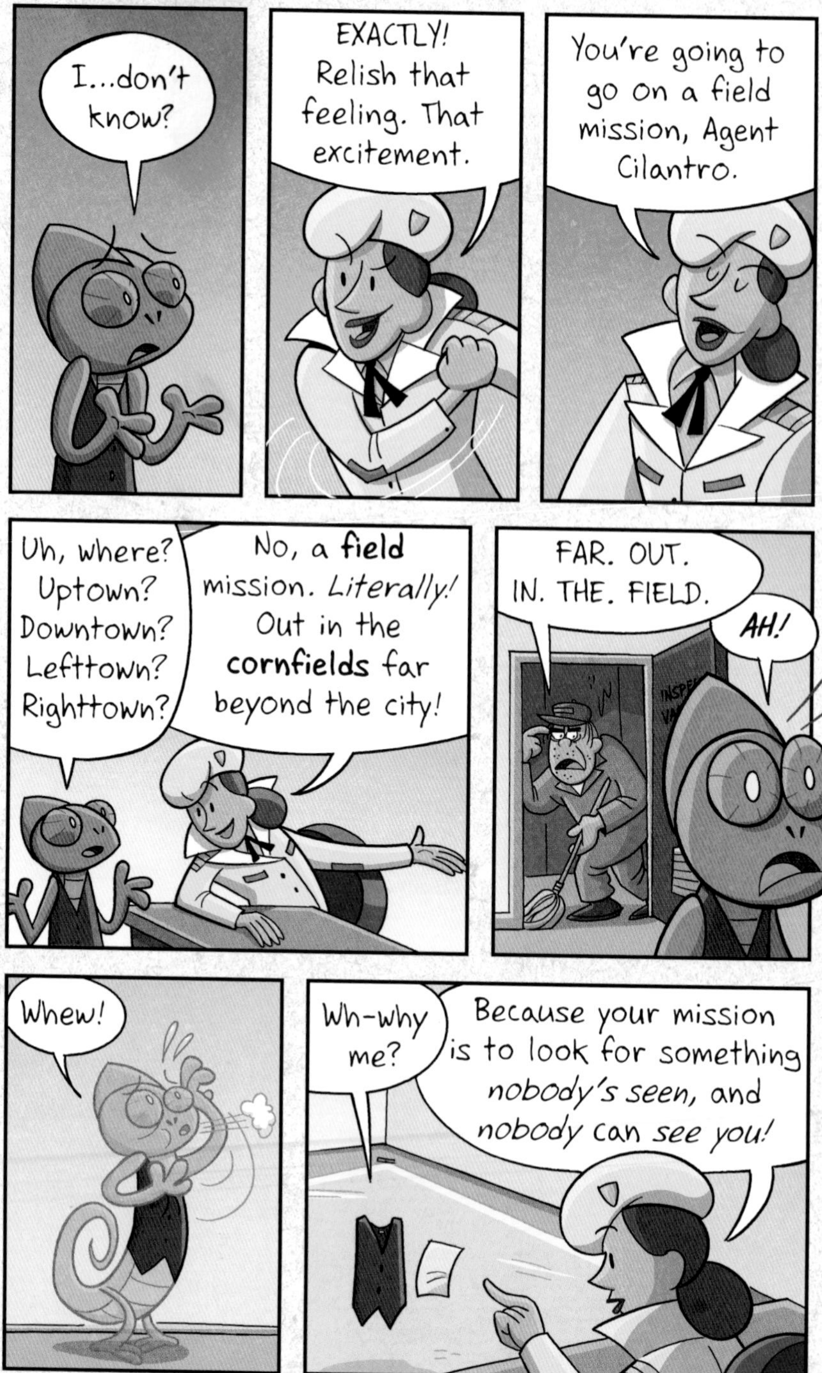
I...don't know?
EXACTLY! Relish that feeling. That excitement.
You're going to go on a field mission, Agent Cilantro.
Uh, where? Uptown? Downtown? Lefttown? Righttown?
No, a **field** mission. *Literally!* Out in the **cornfields** far beyond the city!
FAR. OUT. IN. THE. FIELD.
AH!
Whew!
Wh-why me?
Because your mission is to look for something *nobody's seen*, and *nobody* can *see you!*

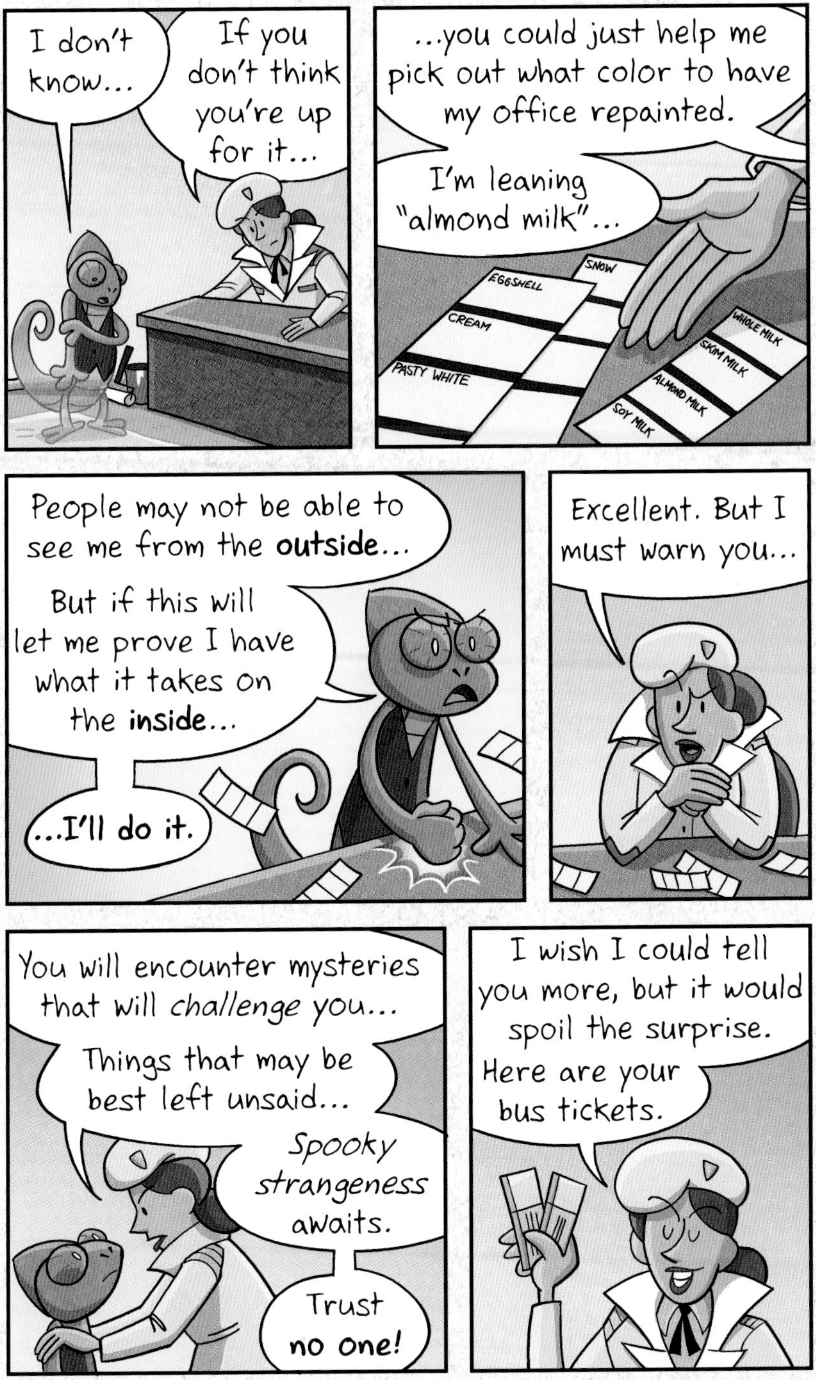

I don't know...
If you don't think you're up for it...
...you could just help me pick out what color to have my office repainted.
I'm leaning "almond milk"...
SNOW
EGGSHELL
CREAM
PASTY WHITE
WHOLE MILK
SKIM MILK
ALMOND MILK
SOY MILK
People may not be able to see me from the **outside**...
But if this will let me prove I have what it takes on the **inside**...
...I'll do it.
Excellent. But I must warn you...
You will encounter mysteries that will *challenge* you...
Things that may be best left unsaid...
Spooky strangeness awaits.
Trust **no one!**
I wish I could tell you more, but it would spoil the surprise.
Here are your bus tickets.

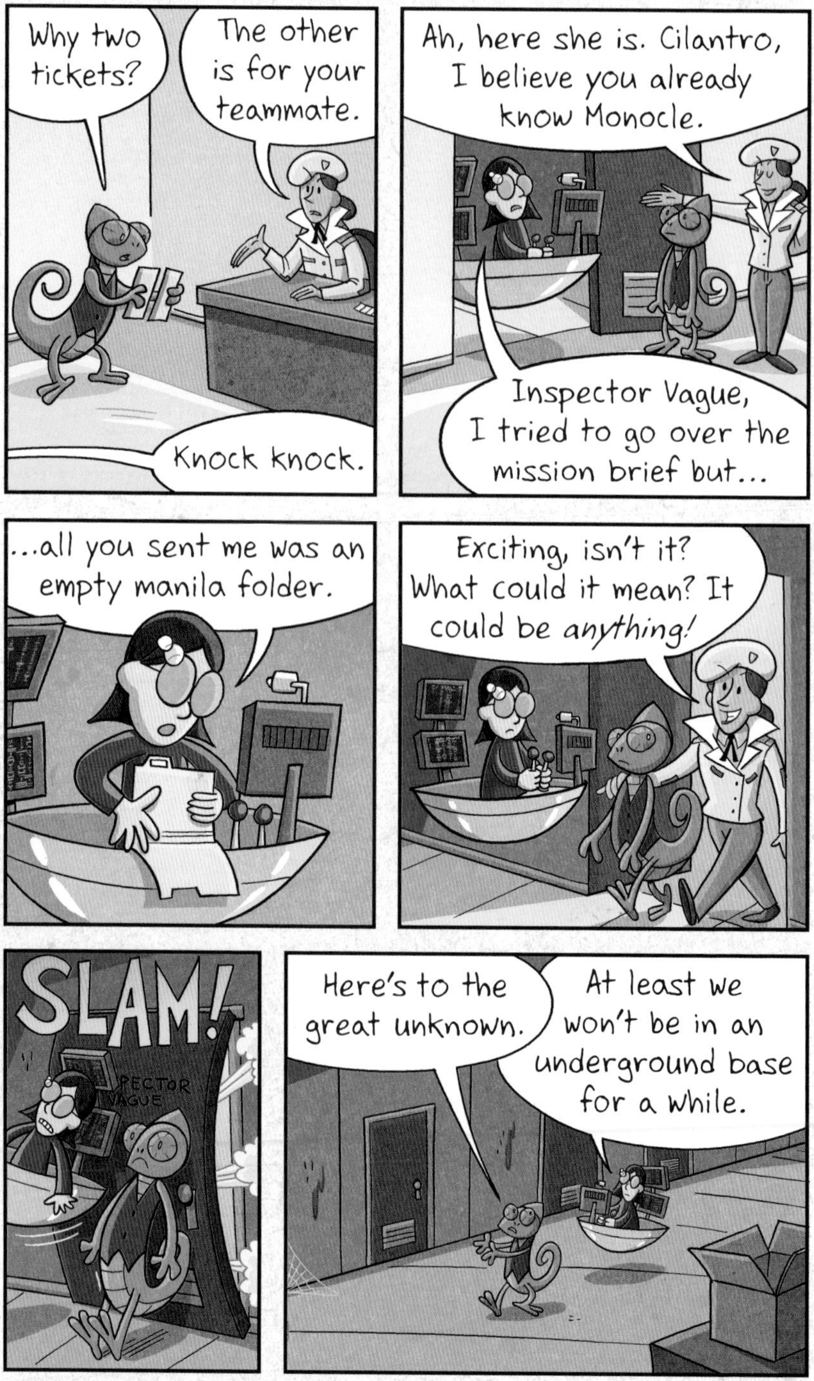
Why two tickets?
The other is for your teammate.
Knock knock.
Ah, here she is. Cilantro, I believe you already know Monocle.
Inspector Vague, I tried to go over the mission brief but...
...all you sent me was an empty manila folder.
Exciting, isn't it? What could it mean? It could be *anything!*
SLAM!
PECTOR VAGUE
Here's to the great unknown.
At least we won't be in an underground base for a while.

Chapter 2

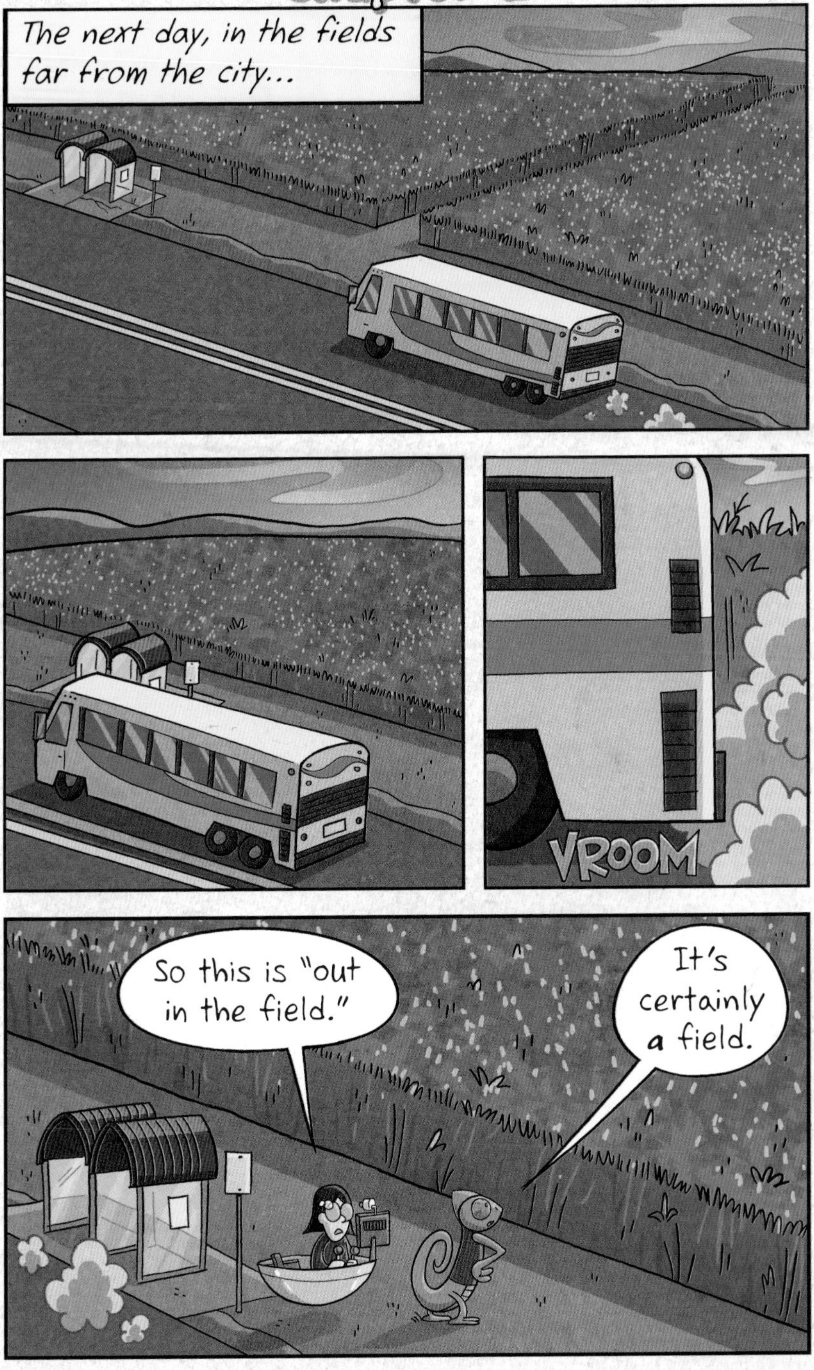
The next day, in the fields far from the city...
VROOM
So this is "out in the field."
It's certainly a field.

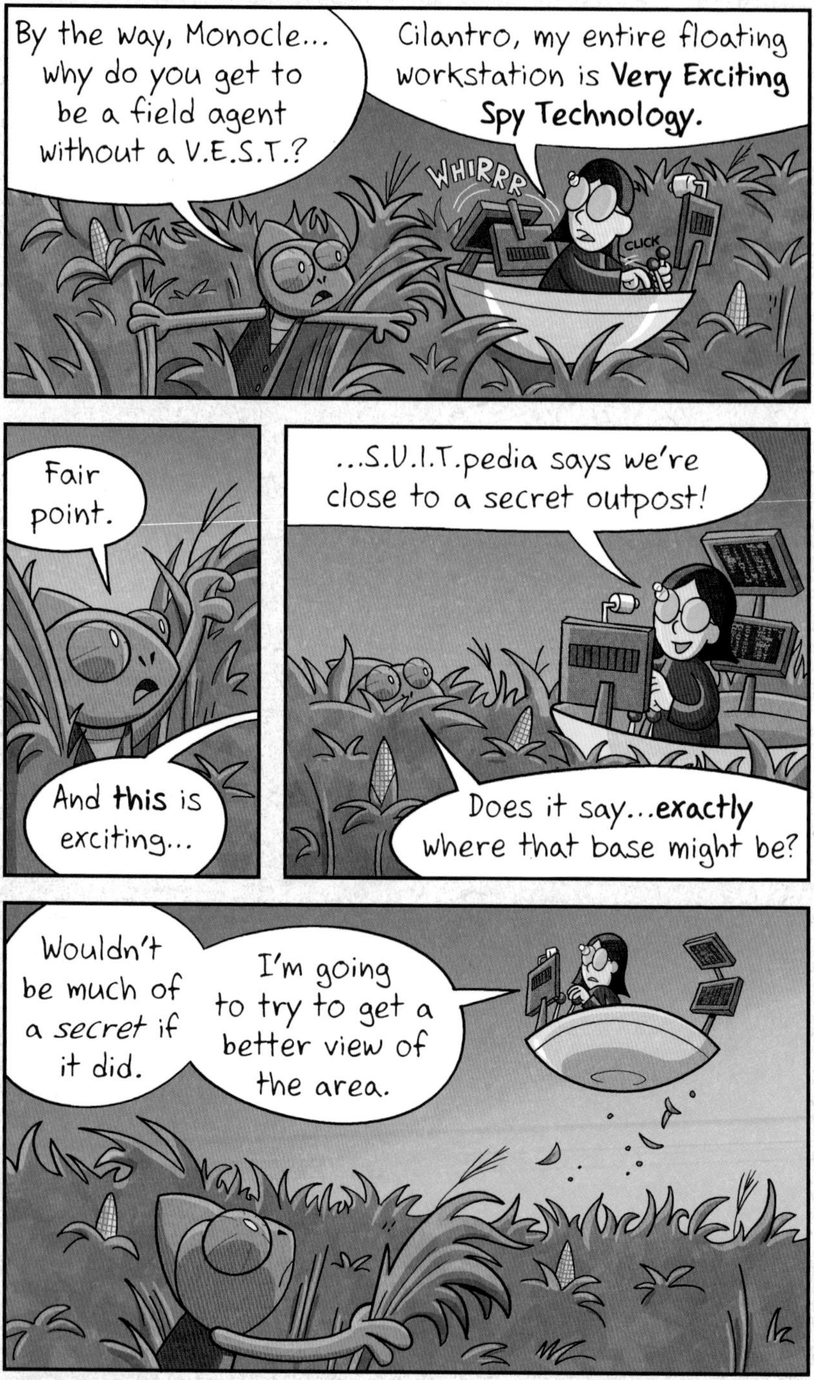
By the way, Monocle... why do you get to be a field agent without a V.E.S.T.?
Cilantro, my entire floating workstation is **Very Exciting Spy Technology.**
WHIRRR
CLICK
Fair point.
And **this** is exciting...
...S.U.I.T.pedia says we're close to a secret outpost!
Does it say...**exactly** where that base might be?
Wouldn't be much of a *secret* if it did.
I'm going to try to get a better view of the area.

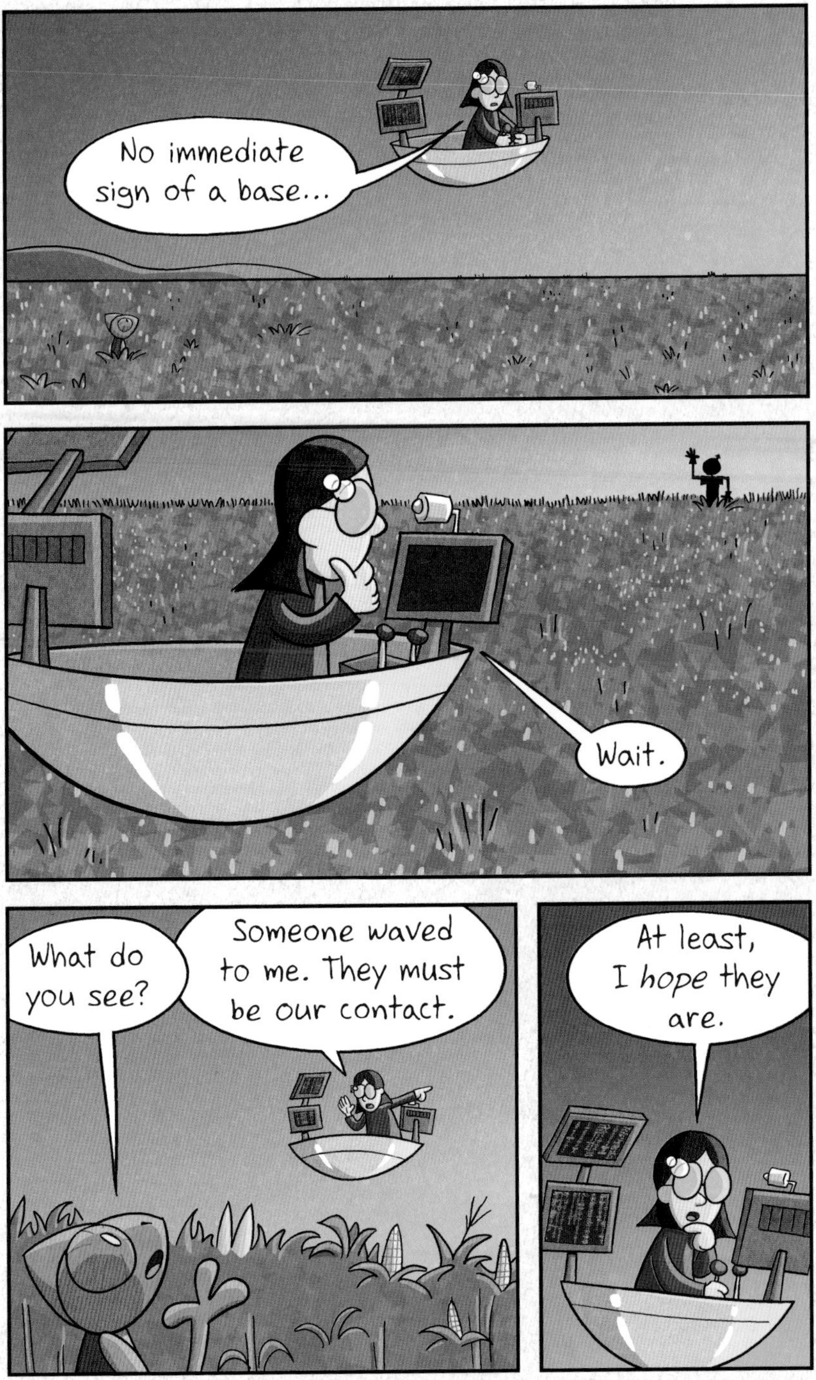
No immediate sign of a base...
Wait.
What do you see?
Someone waved to me. They must be our contact.
At least, I *hope* they are.

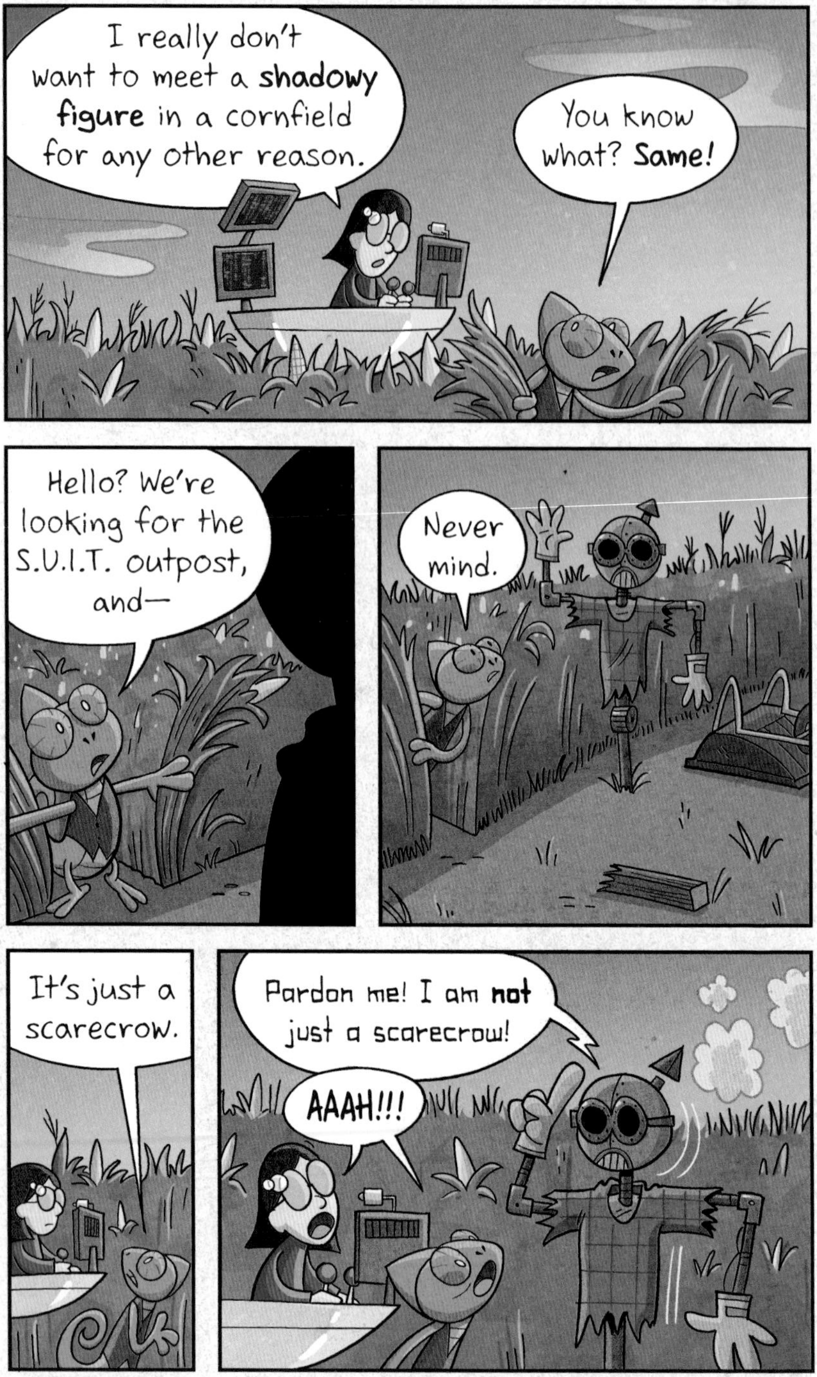

I really don't want to meet a **shadowy figure** in a cornfield for any other reason.
You know what? **Same!**
Hello? We're looking for the S.U.I.T. outpost, and—
Never mind.
It's just a scarecrow.
Pardon me! I am **not** just a scarecrow!
AAAH!!!

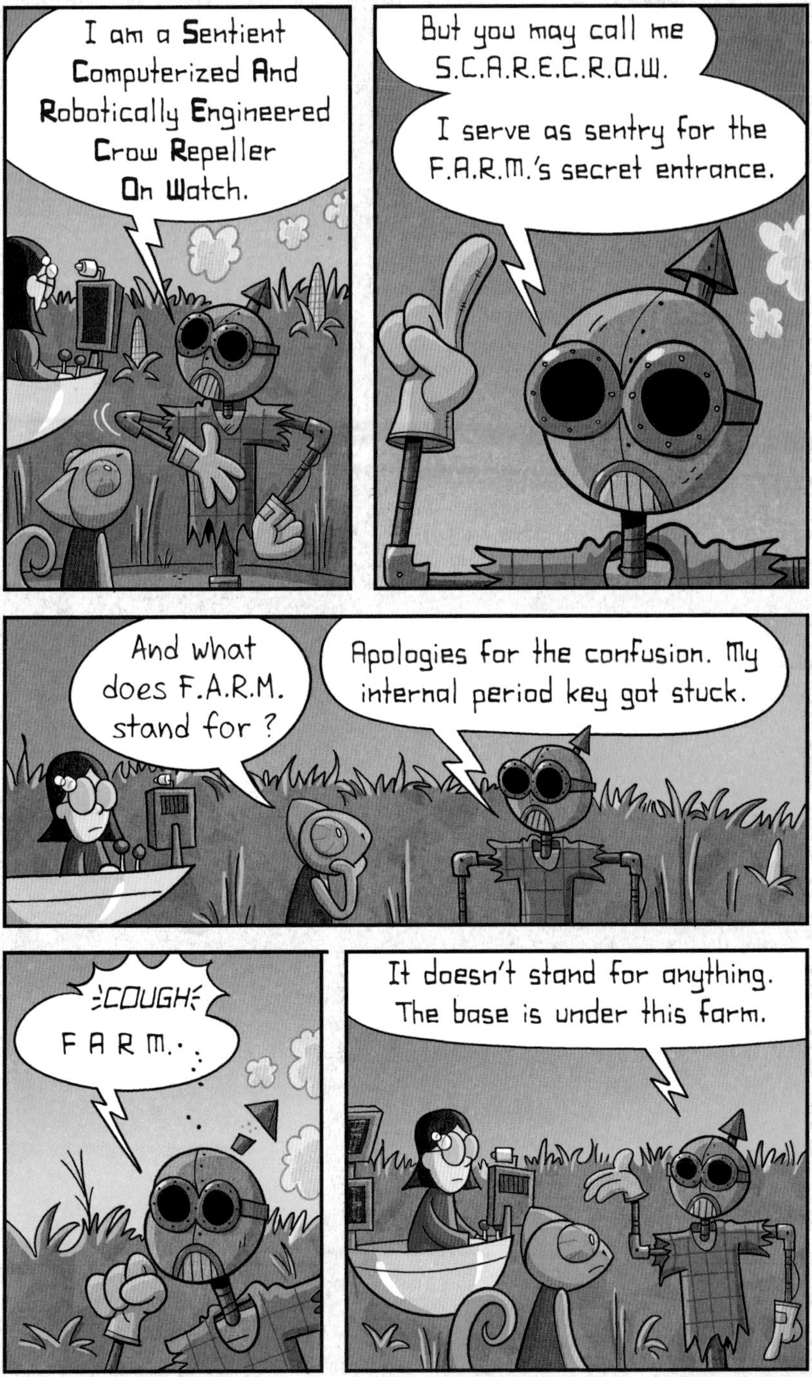
I am a Sentient Computerized And Robotically Engineered Crow Repeller On Watch.
But you may call me S.C.A.R.E.C.R.O.W.
I serve as sentry for the F.A.R.M.'s secret entrance.
And what does F.A.R.M. stand for ?
Apologies for the confusion. My internal period key got stuck.
COUGH
F A R M. . .
It doesn't stand for anything. The base is under this farm.

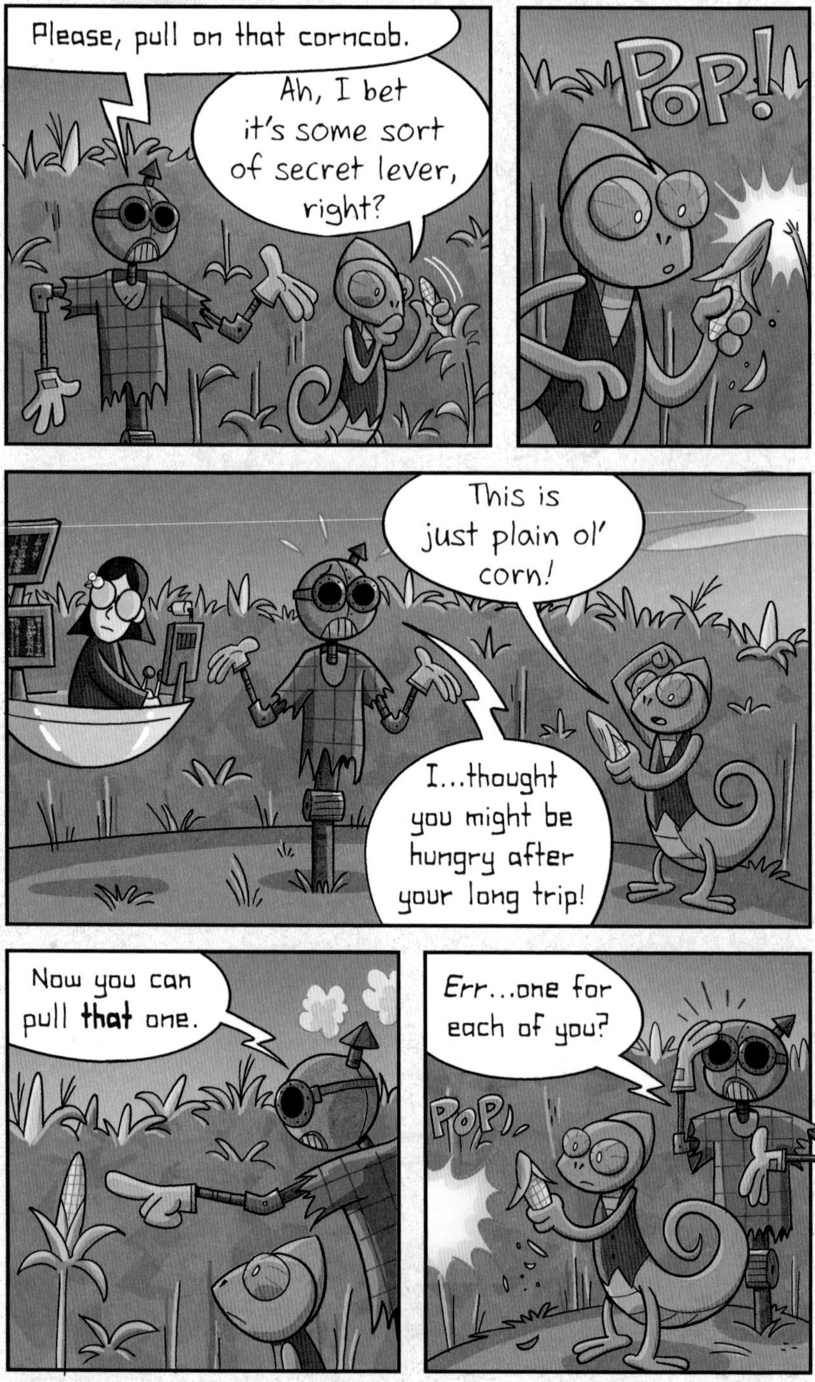
Please, pull on that corncob.
Ah, I bet it's some sort of secret lever, right?
POP!
This is just plain ol' corn!
I...thought you might be hungry after your long trip!
Now you can pull **that** one.
Err...one for each of you?
POP!

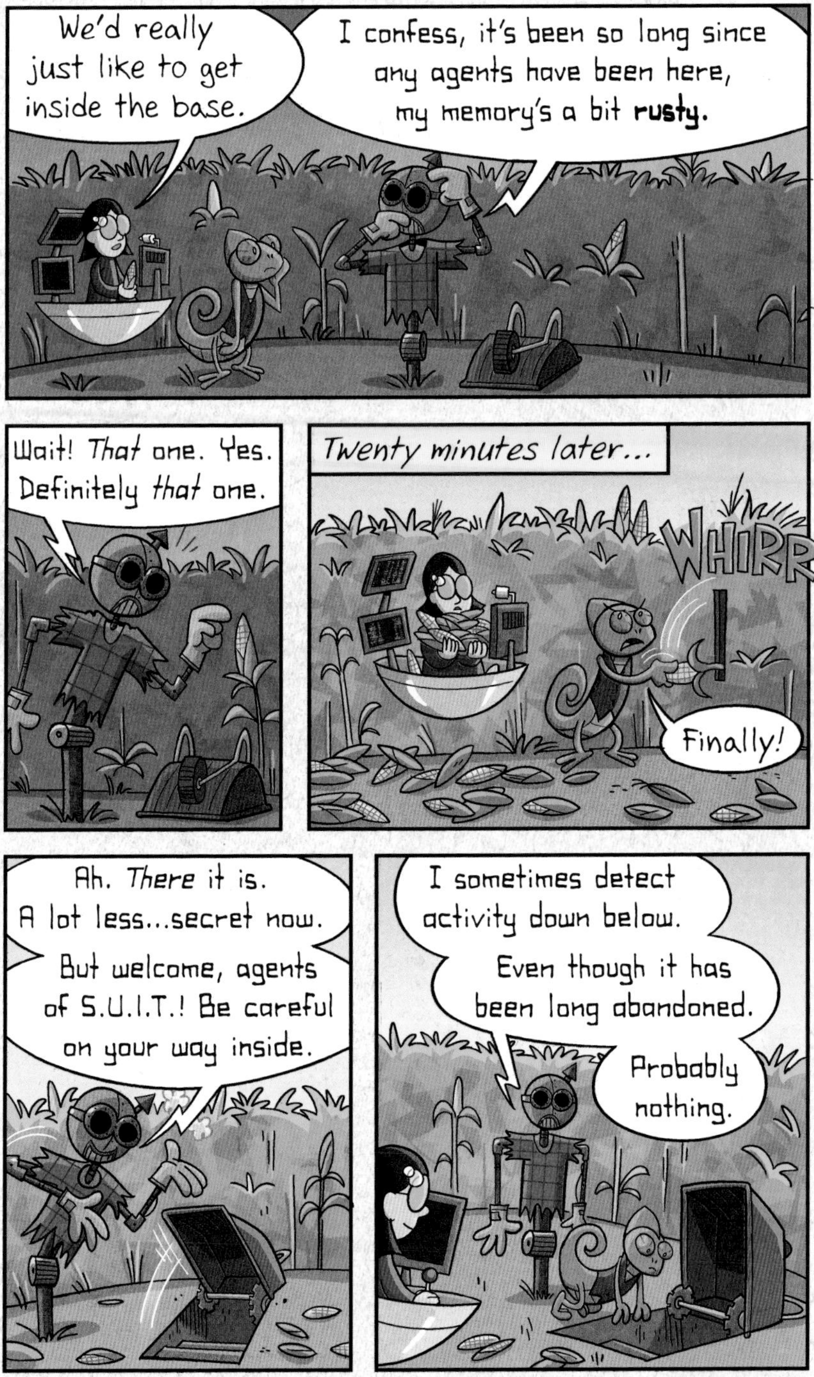
We'd really just like to get inside the base.
I confess, it's been so long since any agents have been here, my memory's a bit **rusty.**
Wait! *That* one. Yes. Definitely *that* one.
Twenty minutes later...
WHIRR
Finally!
Ah. *There* it is. A lot less...secret now.
But welcome, agents of S.U.I.T.! Be careful on your way inside.
I sometimes detect activity down below.
Even though it has been long abandoned.
Probably nothing.

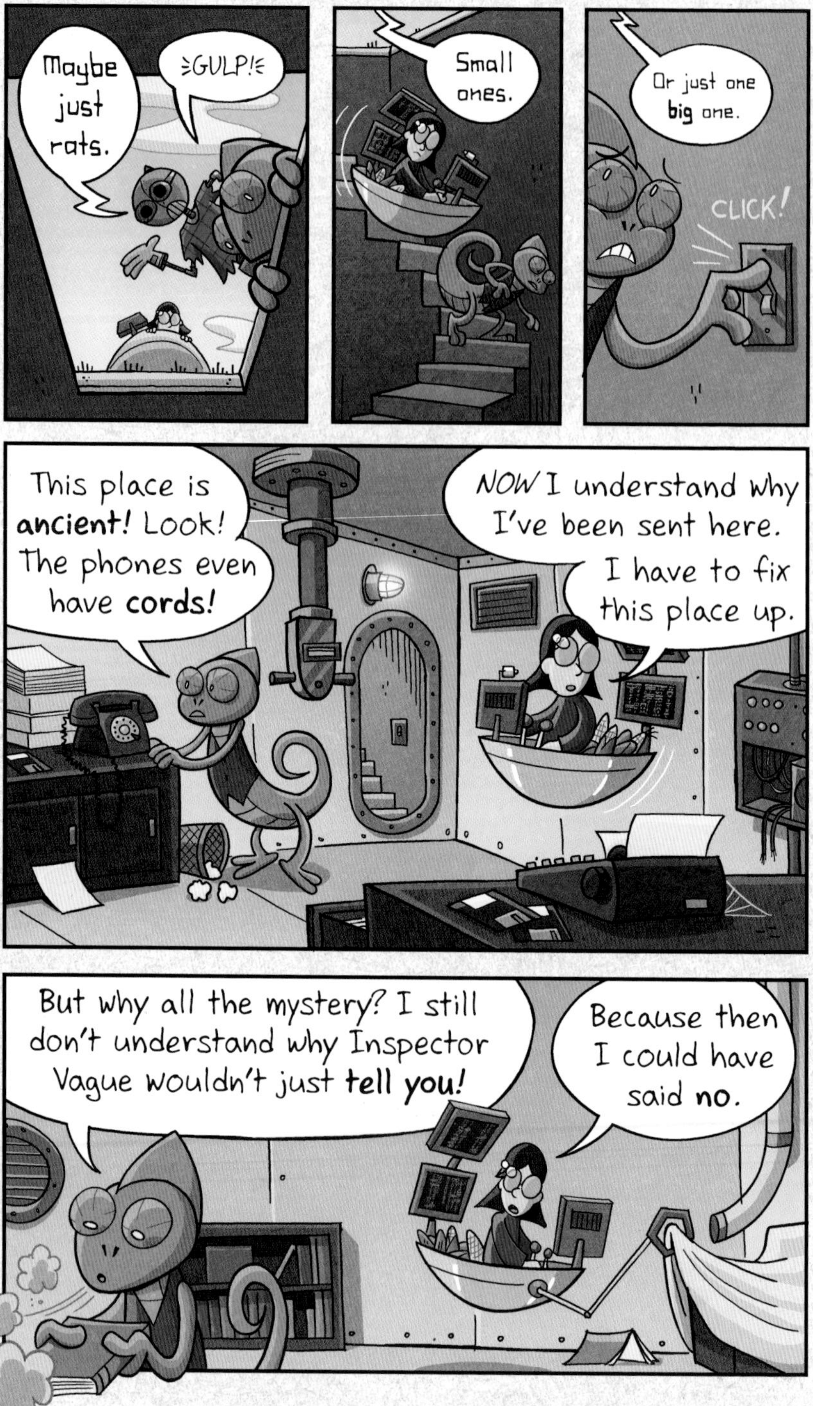
Maybe just rats.
GULP!
Small ones.
Or just one big one.
CLICK!
This place is ancient! Look! The phones even have cords!
NOW I understand why I've been sent here.
I have to fix this place up.
But why all the mystery? I still don't understand why Inspector Vague wouldn't just tell you!
Because then I could have said no.

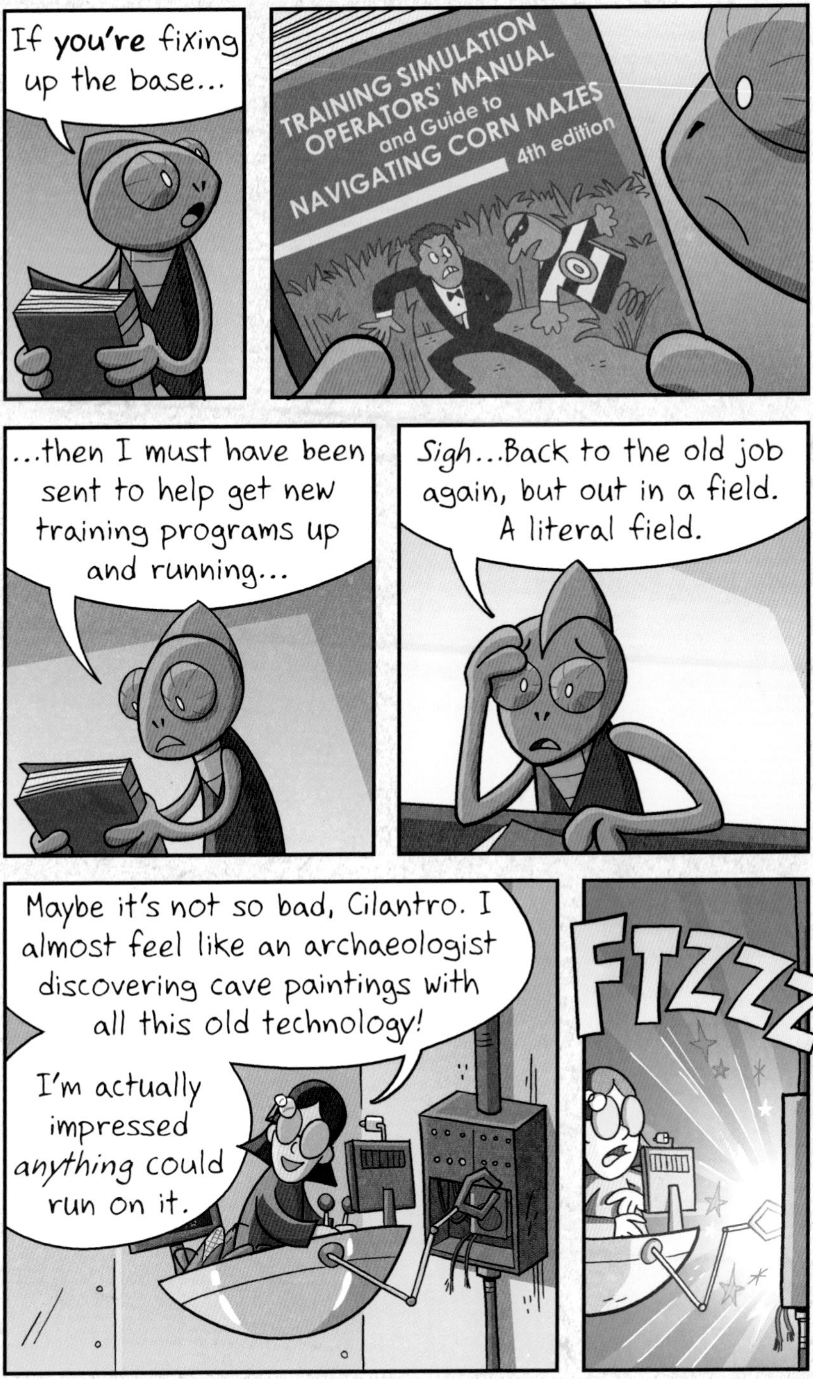
If you're fixing up the base...
TRAINING SIMULATION OPERATORS' MANUAL and Guide to NAVIGATING CORN MAZES 4th edition
...then I must have been sent to help get new training programs up and running...
Sigh...Back to the old job again, but out in a field. A literal field.
Maybe it's not so bad, Cilantro. I almost feel like an archaeologist discovering cave paintings with all this old technology!
I'm actually impressed anything could run on it.
FTZZZ!

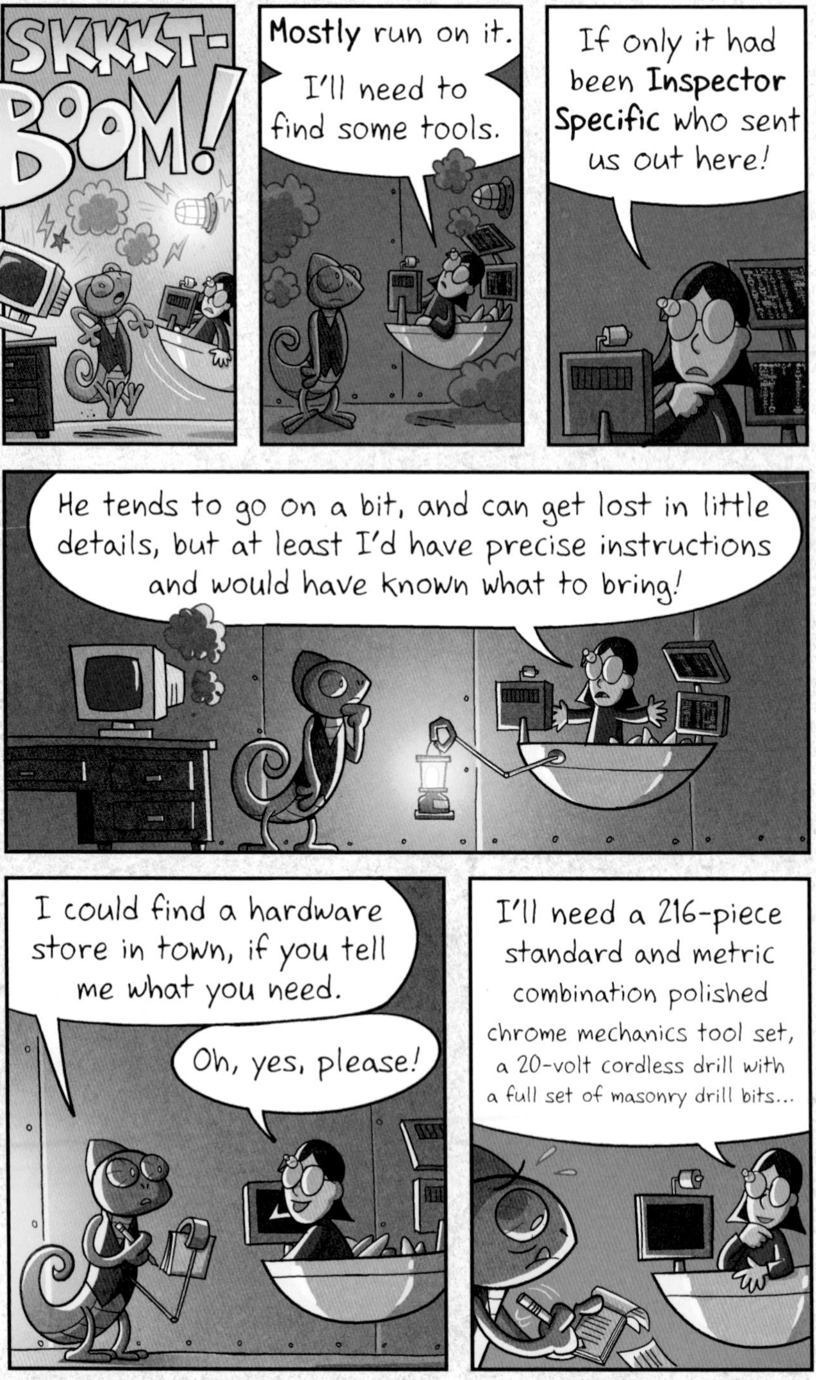
SKKKT-BOOM!
Mostly run on it.
I'll need to find some tools.
If only it had been **Inspector Specific** who sent us out here!
He tends to go on a bit, and can get lost in little details, but at least I'd have precise instructions and would have known what to bring!
I could find a hardware store in town, if you tell me what you need.
Oh, yes, please!
I'll need a 216-piece standard and metric combination polished chrome mechanics tool set, a 20-volt cordless drill with a full set of masonry drill bits...

Chapter 3

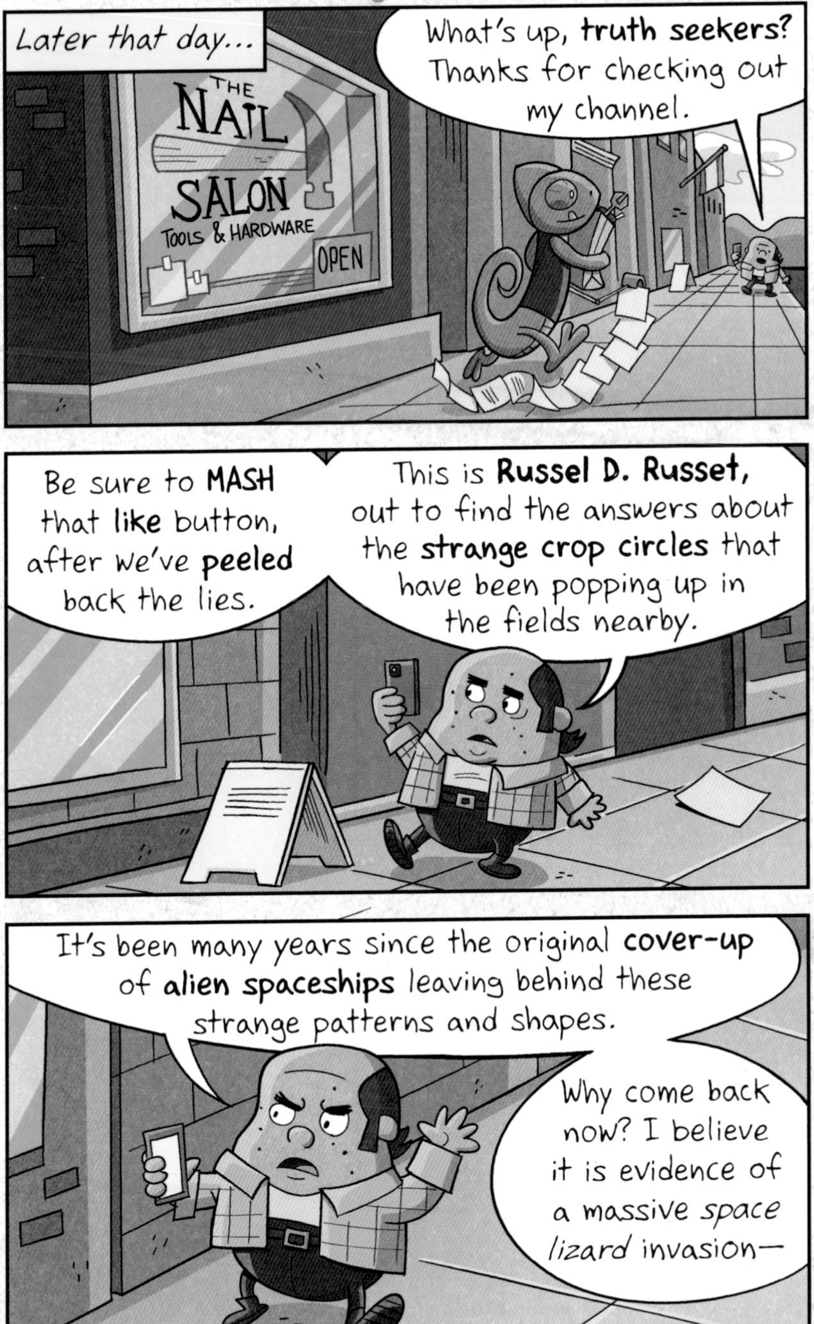
Later that day...
What's up, truth seekers? Thanks for checking out my channel.
THE NAIL SALON TOOLS & HARDWARE
OPEN
Be sure to MASH that like button, after we've peeled back the lies.
This is Russel D. Russet, out to find the answers about the strange crop circles that have been popping up in the fields nearby.
It's been many years since the original cover-up of alien spaceships leaving behind these strange patterns and shapes.
Why come back now? I believe it is evidence of a massive space lizard invasion—

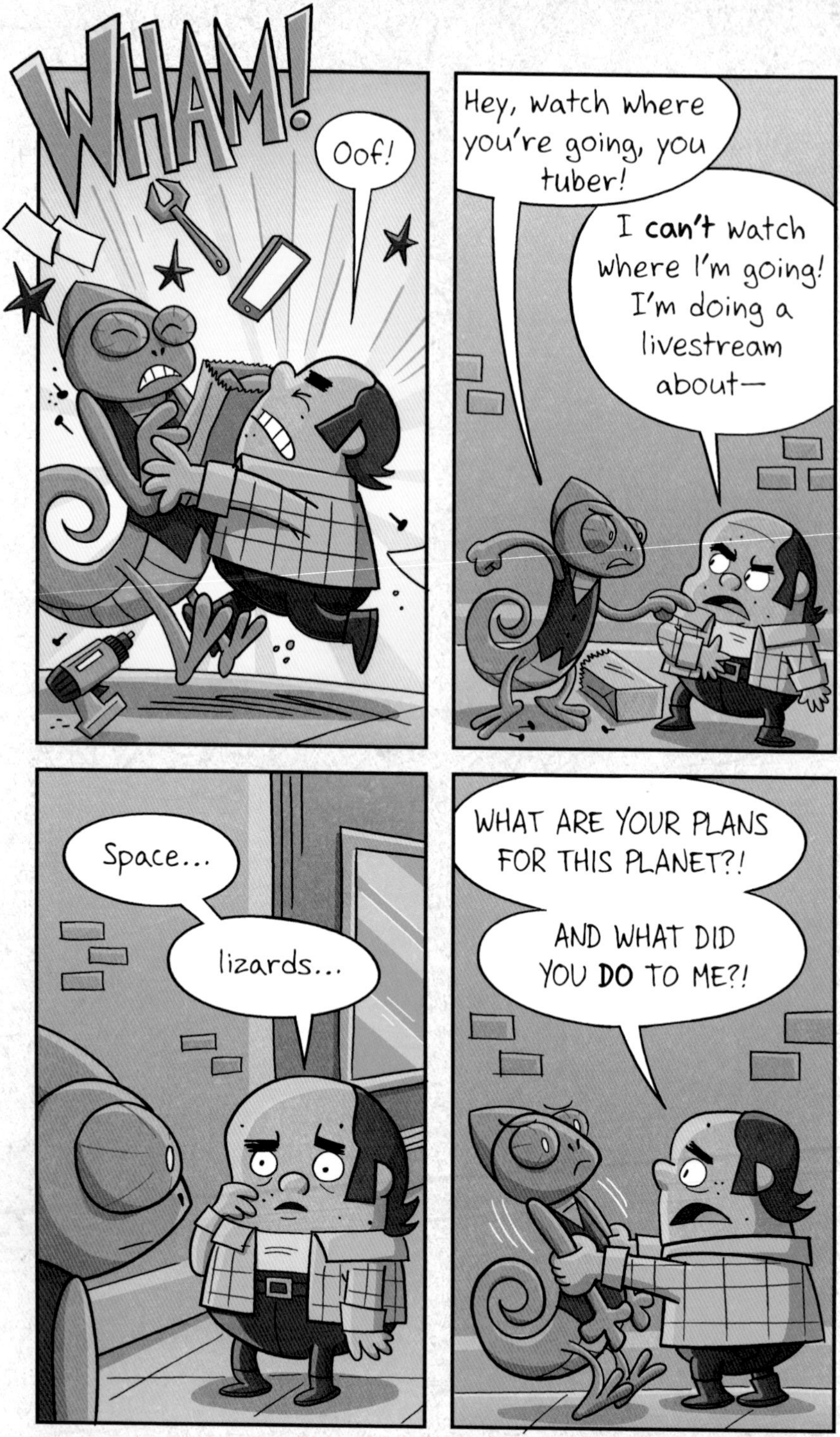
WHAM!
Oof!
Hey, watch where you're going, you tuber!
I **can't** watch where I'm going! I'm doing a livestream about—
Space...
lizards...
WHAT ARE YOUR PLANS FOR THIS PLANET?!
AND WHAT DID YOU **DO** TO ME?!

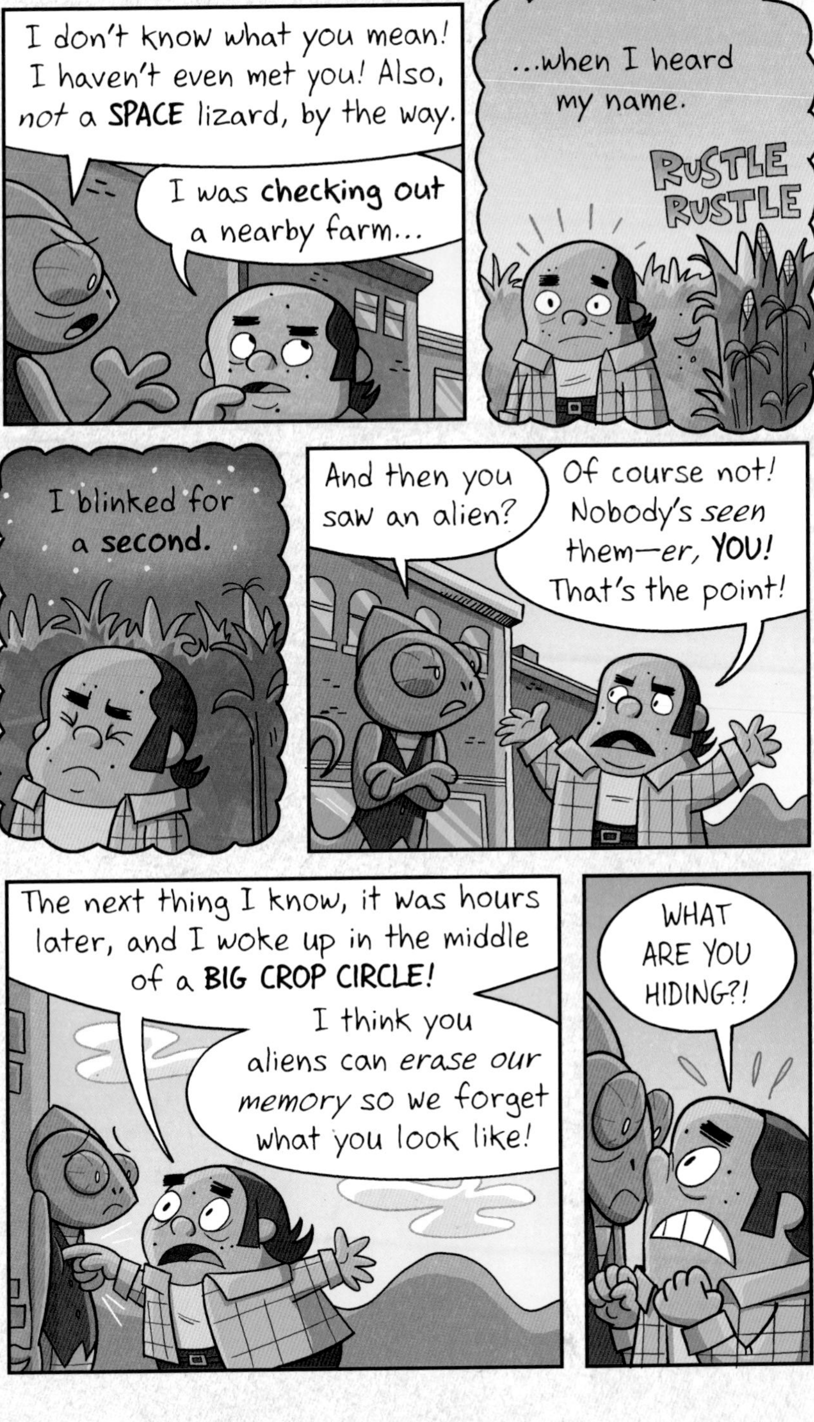
I don't know what you mean! I haven't even met you! Also, not a SPACE lizard, by the way.
I was checking out a nearby farm...
...when I heard my name.
RUSTLE RUSTLE
I blinked for a second.
And then you saw an alien?
Of course not! Nobody's seen them—er, YOU! That's the point!
The next thing I know, it was hours later, and I woke up in the middle of a BIG CROP CIRCLE!
I think you aliens can erase our memory so we forget what you look like!
WHAT ARE YOU HIDING?!

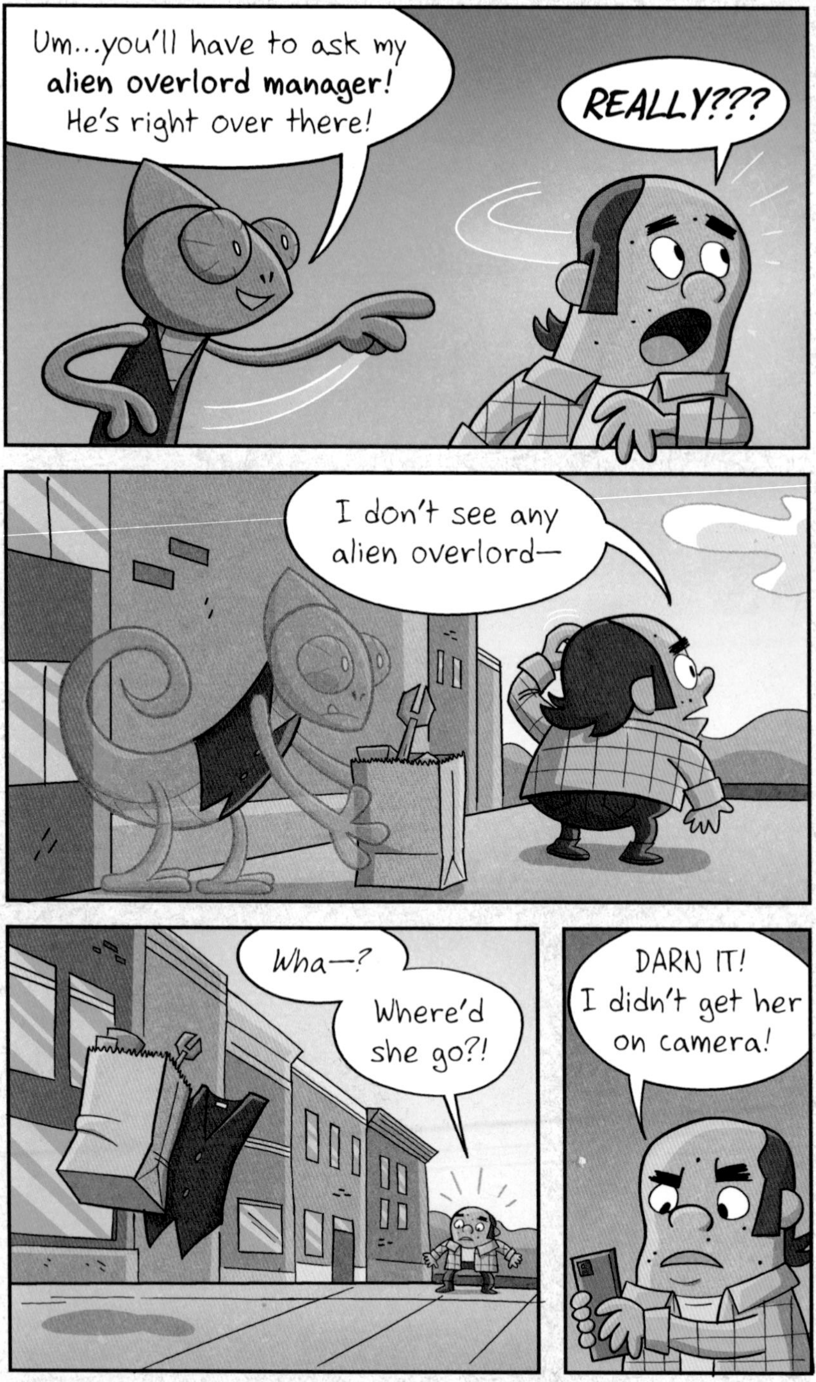
Um...you'll have to ask my **alien overlord manager!** He's right over there!
REALLY???
I don't see any alien overlord—
Wha—?
Where'd she go?!
DARN IT! I didn't get her on camera!

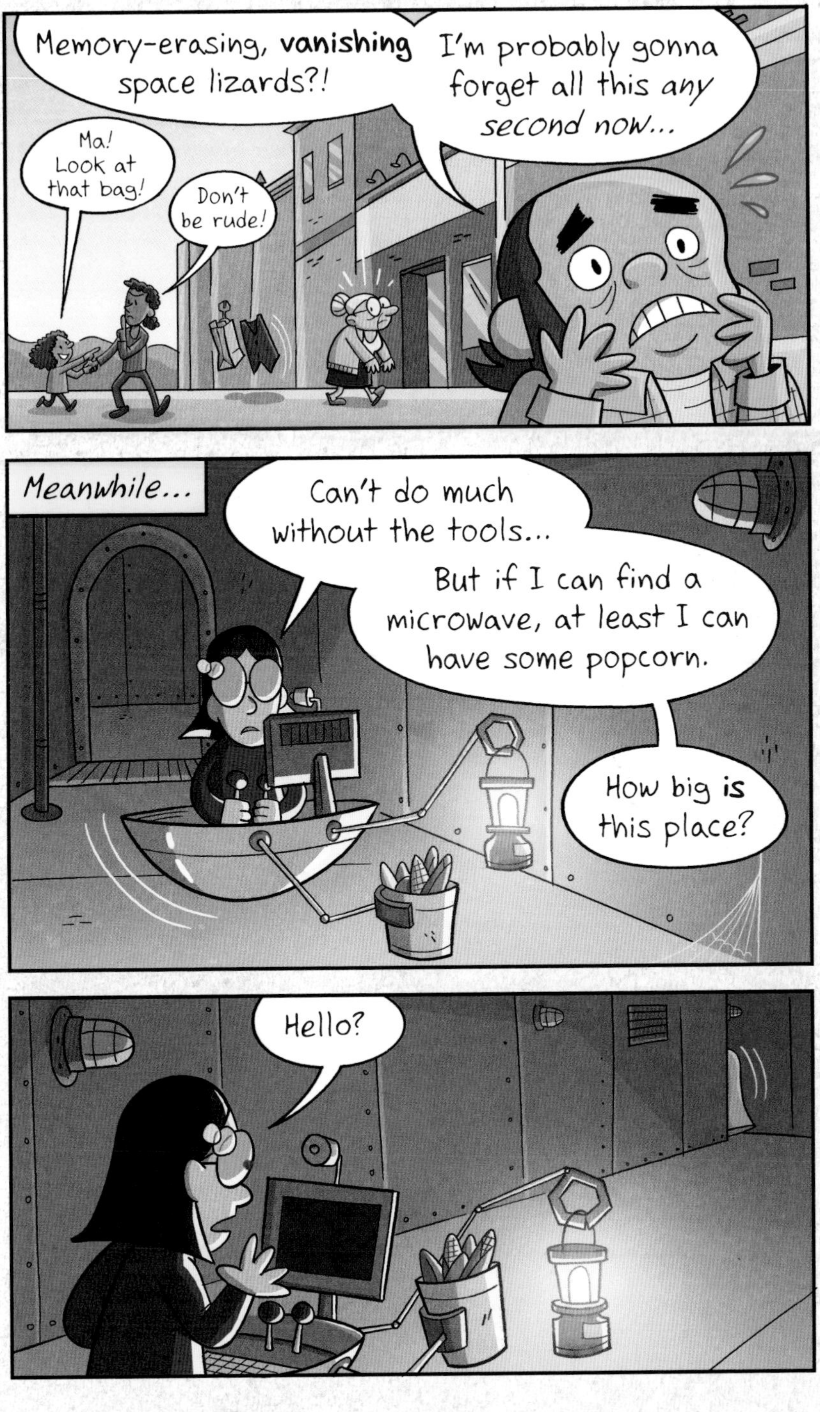
Memory-erasing, **vanishing** space lizards?!
I'm probably gonna forget all this *any second now*...
Ma! Look at that bag!
Don't be rude!
Meanwhile...
Can't do much without the tools...
But if I can find a microwave, at least I can have some popcorn.
How big **is** this place?
Hello?

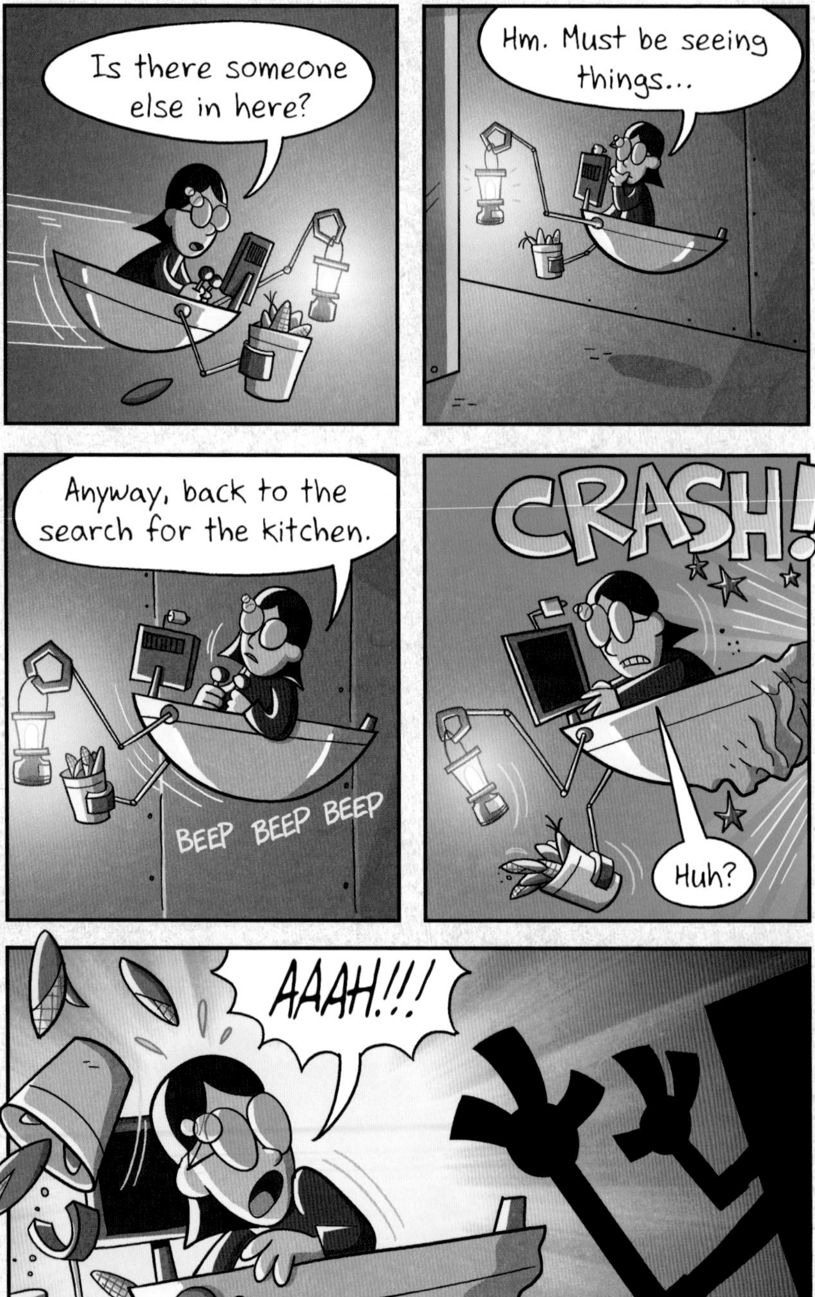
Is there someone else in here?
Hm. Must be seeing things...
Anyway, back to the search for the kitchen.
BEEP BEEP BEEP
CRASH!
Huh?
AAAH!!!

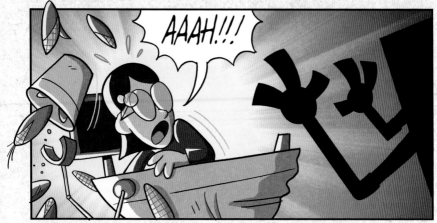

Chapter 4

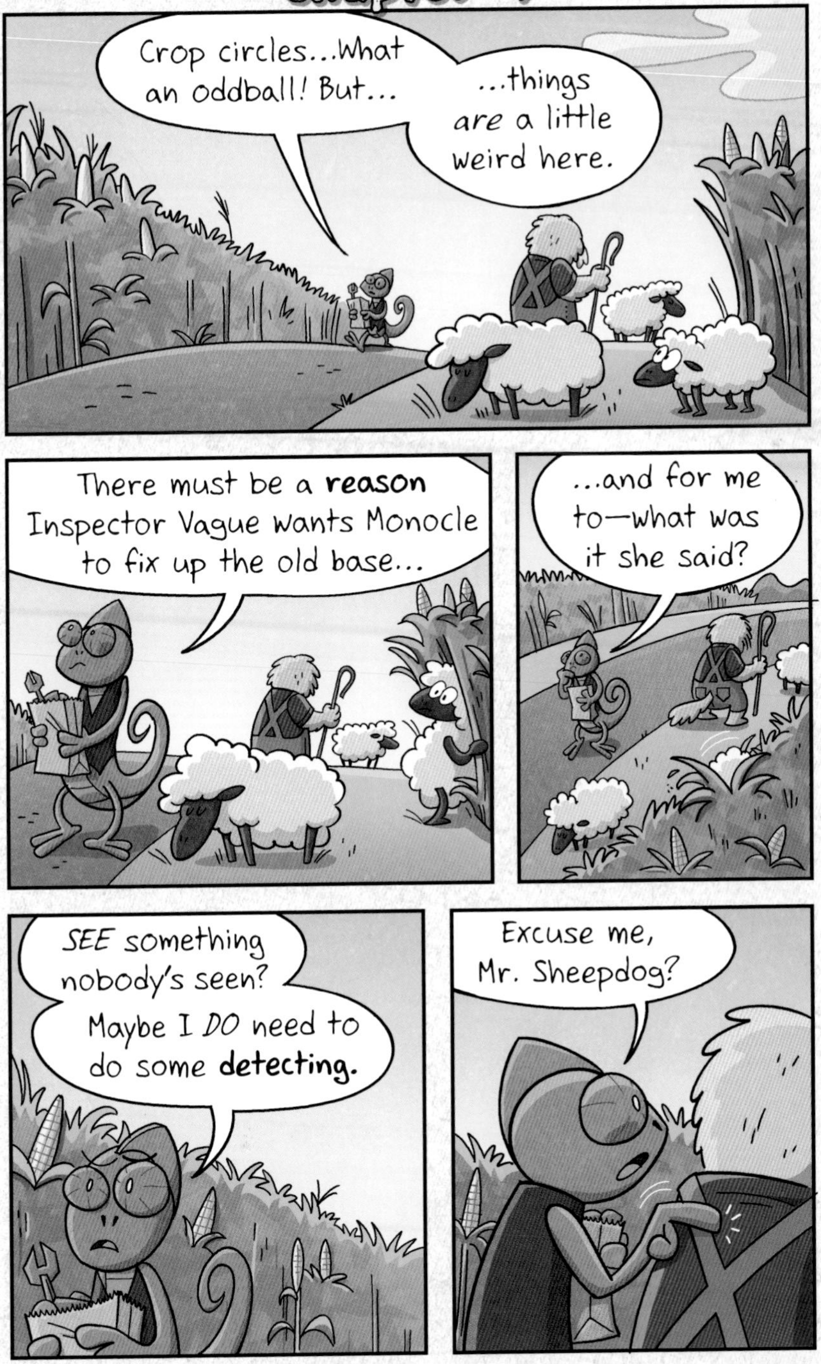
Crop circles...What an oddball! But...
...things are a little weird here.
There must be a **reason** Inspector Vague wants Monocle to fix up the old base...
...and for me to—what was it she said?
SEE something nobody's seen?
Maybe I *DO* need to do some **detecting.**
Excuse me, Mr. Sheepdog?

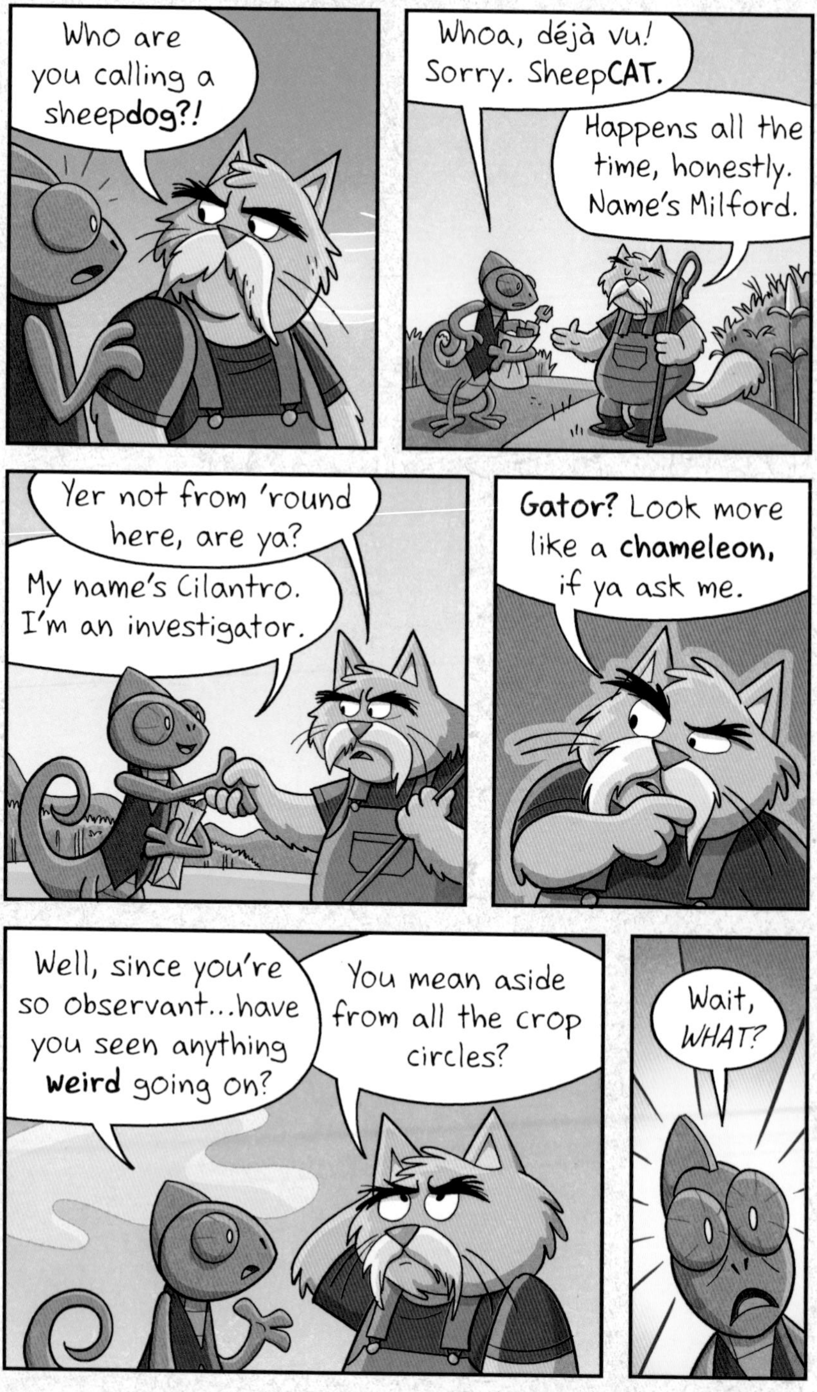
Who are you calling a sheep**dog**?!
Whoa, déjà vu! Sorry. Sheep**CAT**.
Happens all the time, honestly. Name's Milford.
Yer not from 'round here, are ya?
My name's Cilantro. I'm an investigator.
Gator? Look more like a **chameleon,** if ya ask me.
Well, since you're so observant...have you seen anything **weird** going on?
You mean aside from all the crop circles?
Wait, *WHAT?*

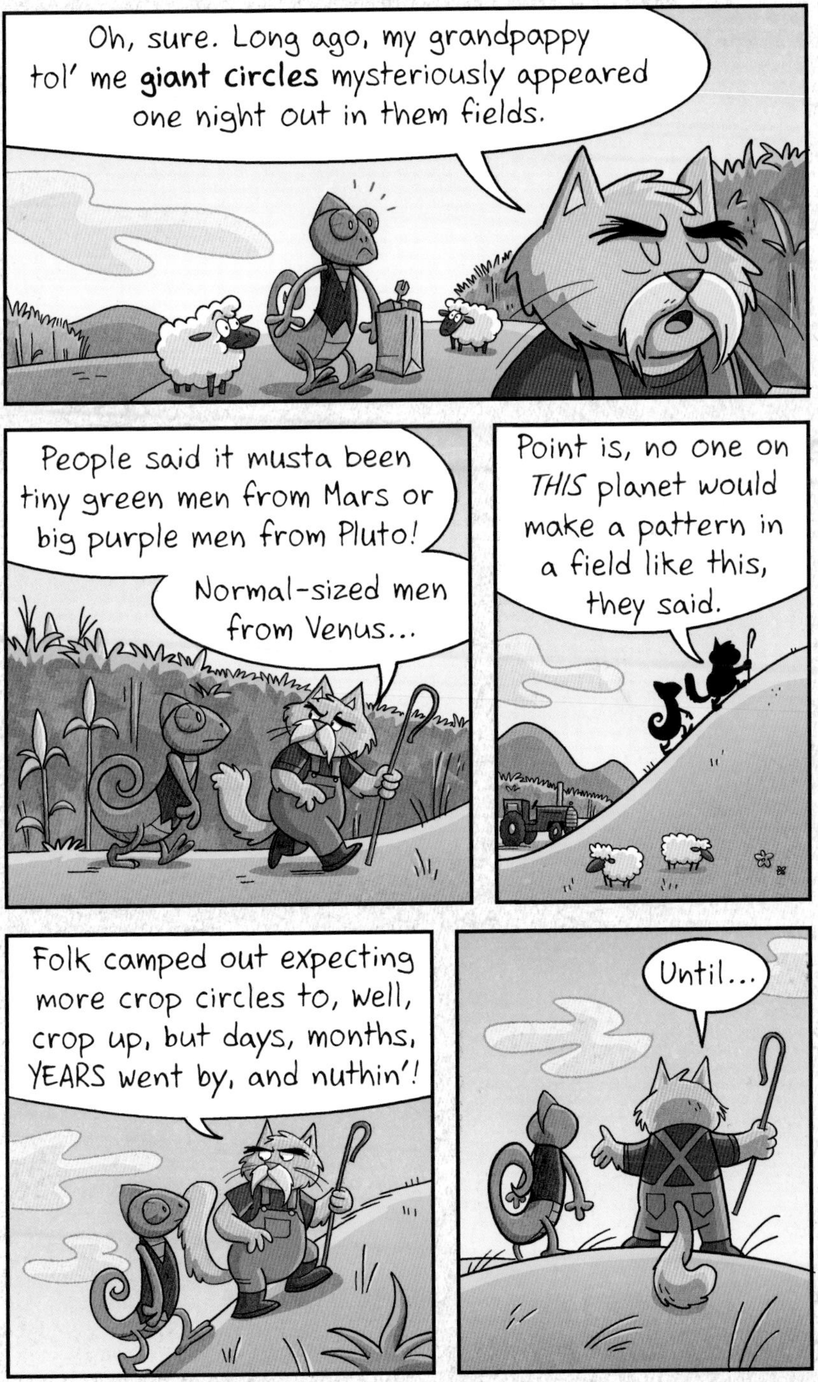
Oh, sure. Long ago, my grandpappy tol' me **giant circles** mysteriously appeared one night out in them fields.
People said it musta been tiny green men from Mars or big purple men from Pluto!
Normal-sized men from Venus...
Point is, no one on *THIS* planet would make a pattern in a field like this, they said.
Folk camped out expecting more crop circles to, well, crop up, but days, months, YEARS went by, and nuthin'!
Until...

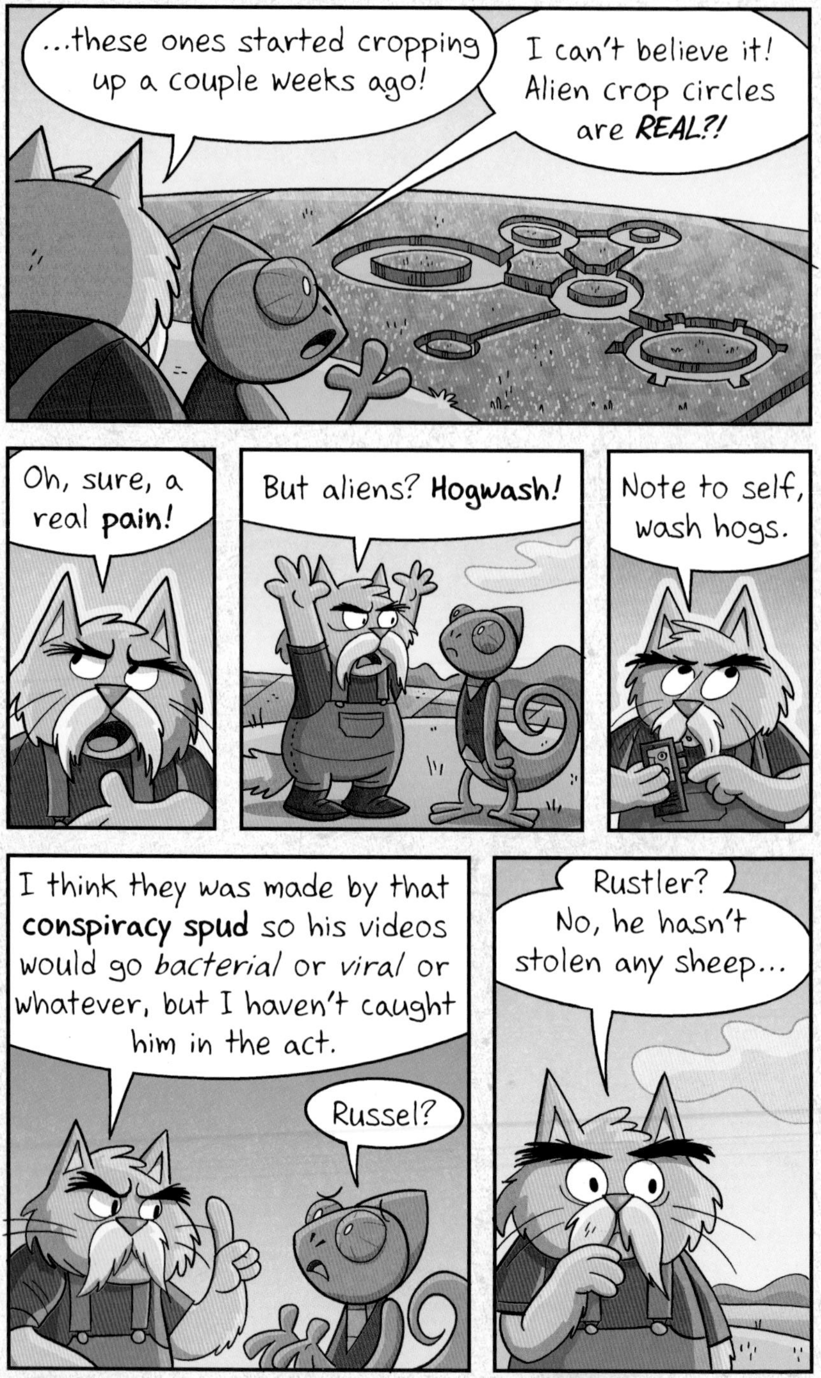
...these ones started cropping up a couple weeks ago!
I can't believe it! Alien crop circles are ***REAL?!***
Oh, sure, a real **pain!**
But aliens? **Hogwash!**
Note to self, wash hogs.
I think they was made by that **conspiracy spud** so his videos would go *bacterial* or *viral* or whatever, but I haven't caught him in the act.
Russel?
Rustler? No, he hasn't stolen any sheep...

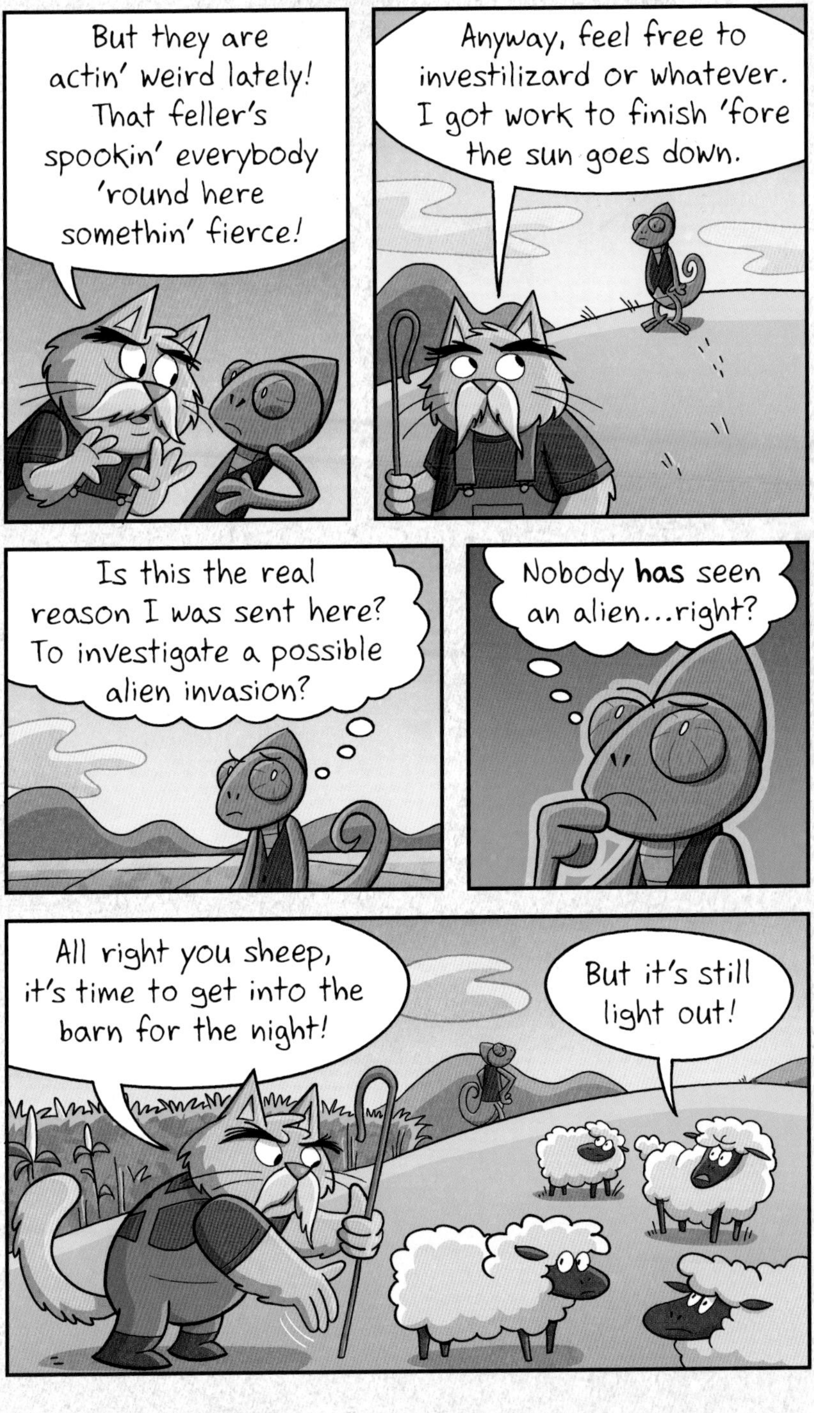
But they are actin' weird lately! That feller's spookin' everybody 'round here somethin' fierce!
Anyway, feel free to investilizard or whatever. I got work to finish 'fore the sun goes down.
Is this the real reason I was sent here? To investigate a possible alien invasion?
Nobody **has** seen an alien...right?
All right you sheep, it's time to get into the barn for the night!
But it's still light out!

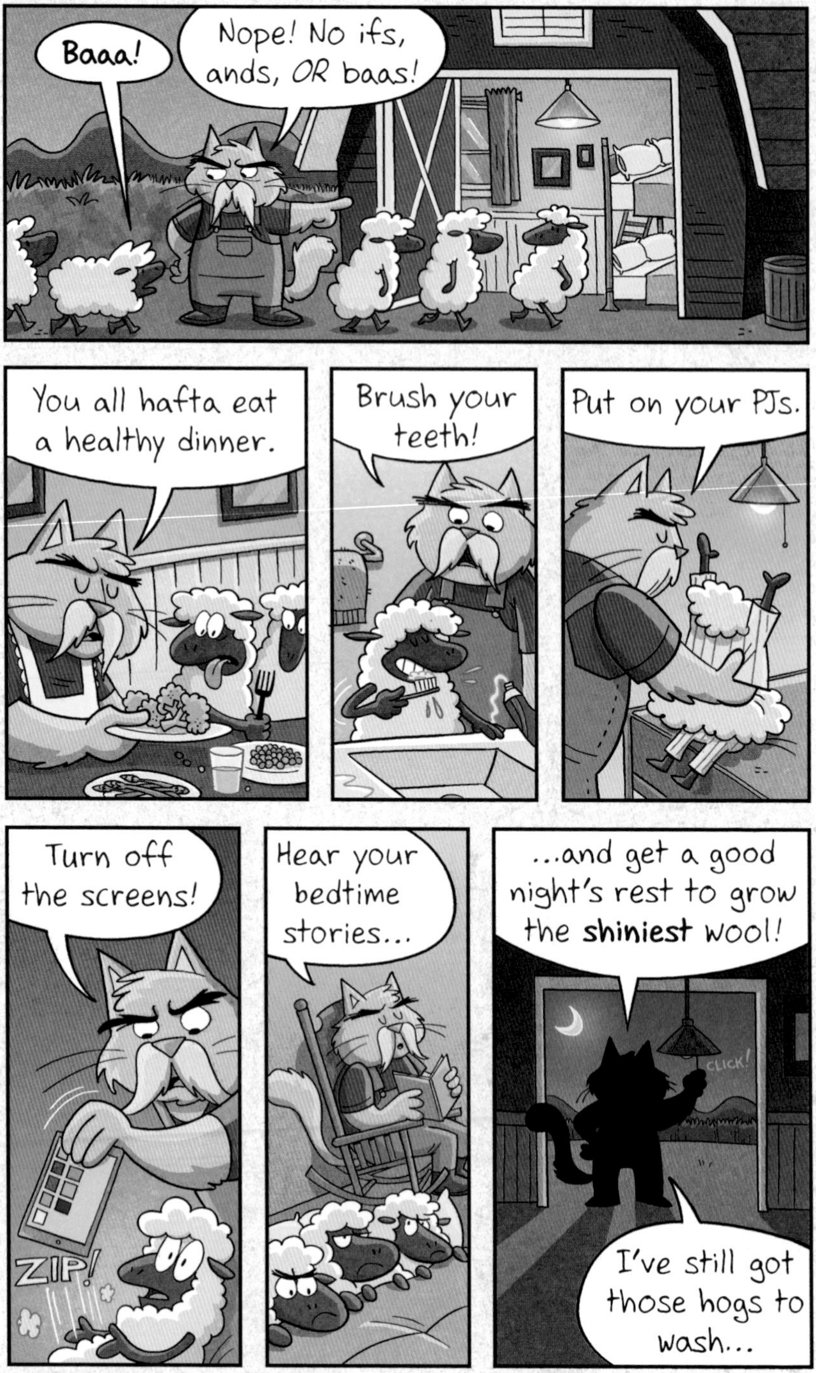
Baaa!
Nope! No ifs, ands, OR baas!
You all hafta eat a healthy dinner.
Brush your teeth!
Put on your PJs.
Turn off the screens!
ZIP!
Hear your bedtime stories...
...and get a good night's rest to grow the **shiniest** wool!
CLICK!
I've still got those hogs to wash...

Chapter 5

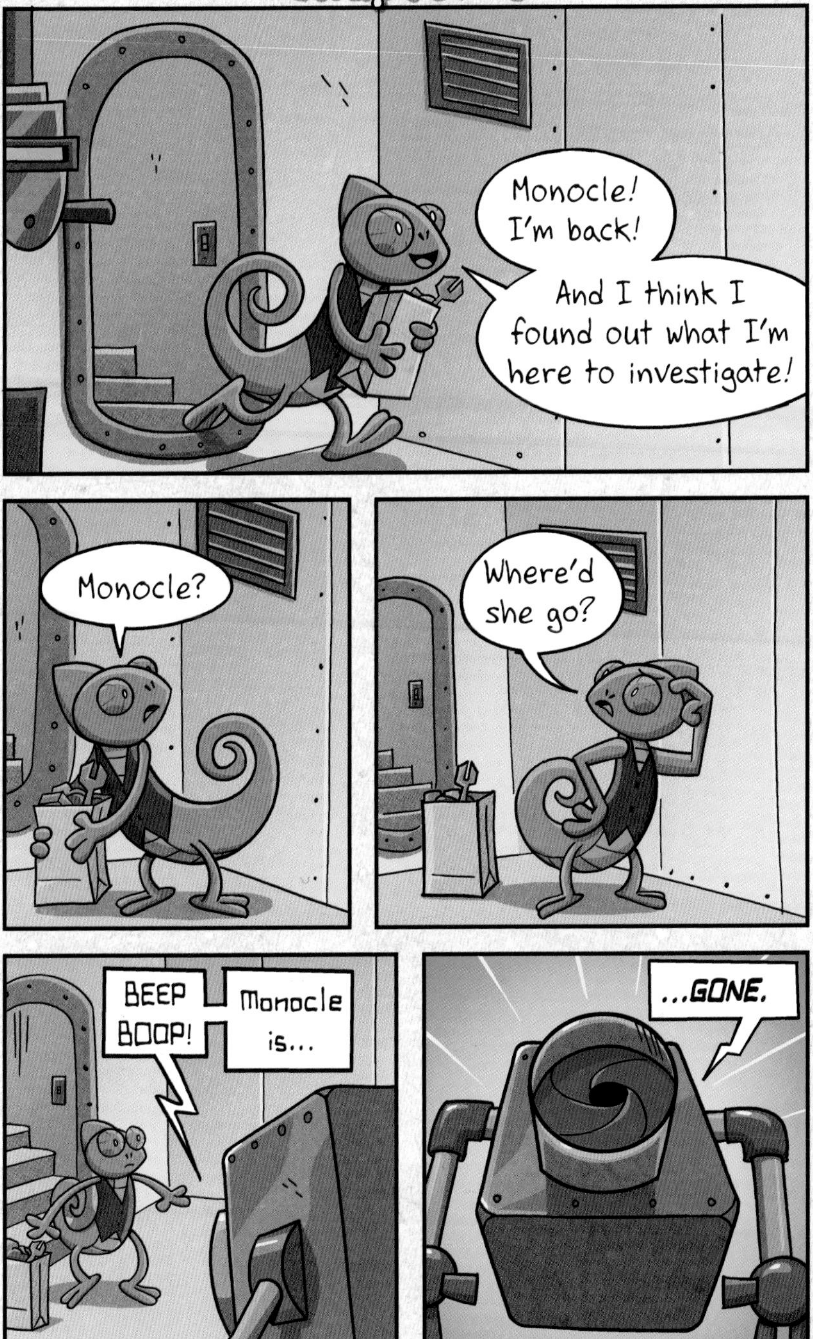
Monocle! I'm back!
And I think I found out what I'm here to investigate!
Monocle?
Where'd she go?
BEEP BOOP!
Monocle is...
...GONE.

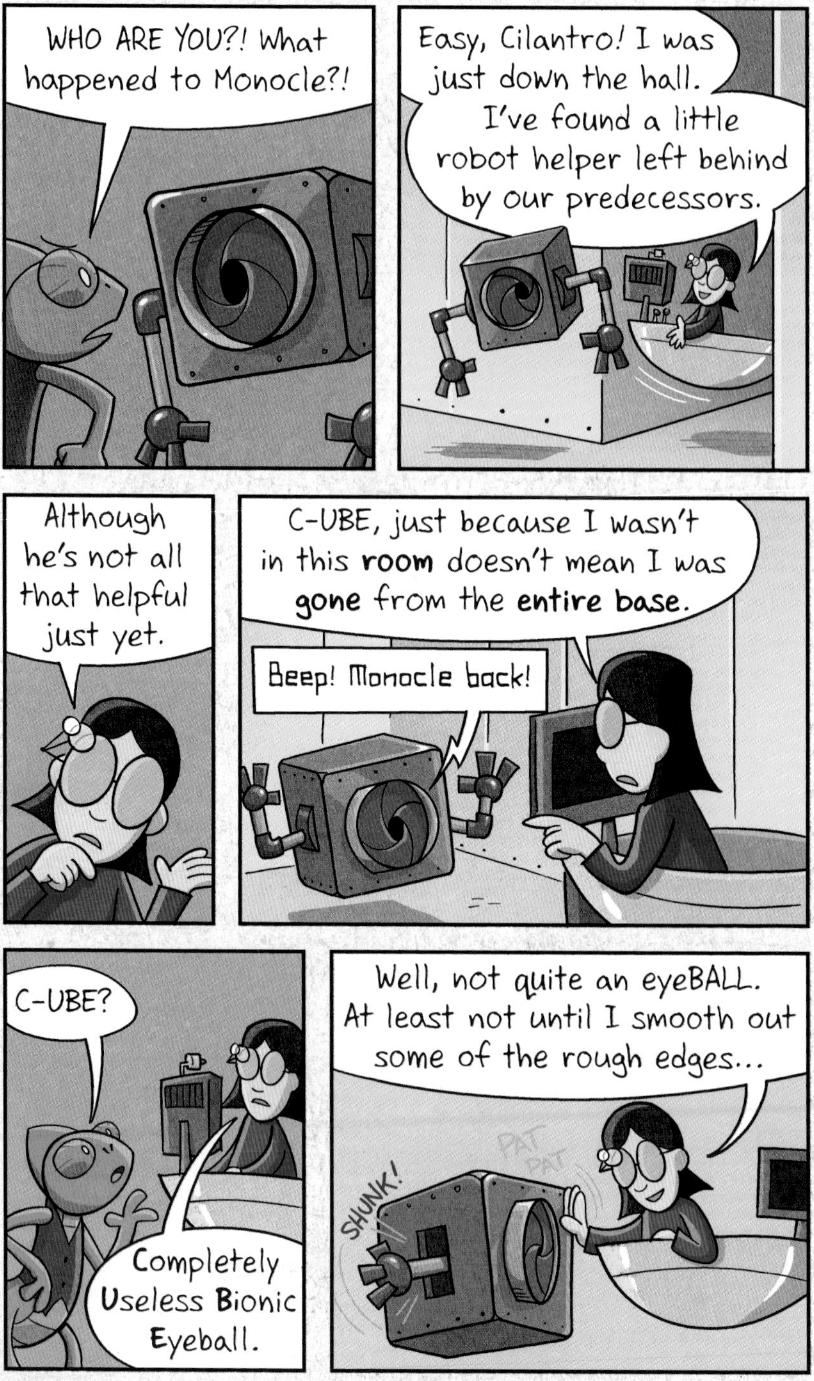
WHO ARE YOU?! What happened to Monocle?!
Easy, Cilantro! I was just down the hall. I've found a little robot helper left behind by our predecessors.
Although he's not all that helpful just yet.
C-UBE, just because I wasn't in this **room** doesn't mean I was **gone** from the **entire base**.
Beep! Monocle back!
C-UBE?
Completely Useless Bionic Eyeball.
Well, not quite an eyeBALL. At least not until I smooth out some of the rough edges...
PAT PAT
SHUNK!

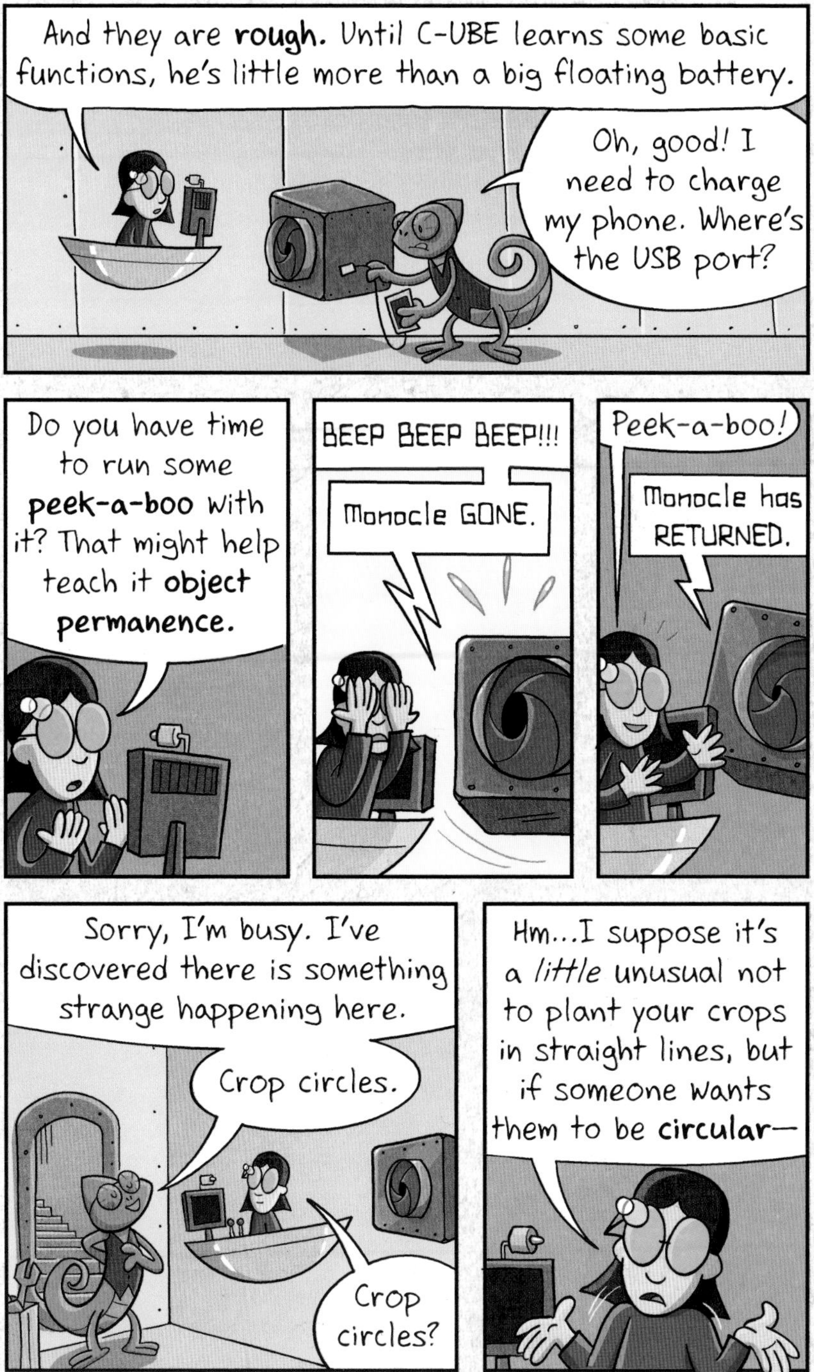
And they are **rough.** Until C-UBE learns some basic functions, he's little more than a big floating battery.
Oh, good! I need to charge my phone. Where's the USB port?
Do you have time to run some **peek-a-boo** with it? That might help teach it **object permanence.**
BEEP BEEP BEEP!!!
Monocle GONE.
Peek-a-boo!
Monocle has RETURNED.
Sorry, I'm busy. I've discovered there is something strange happening here.
Crop circles.
Crop circles?
Hm...I suppose it's a *little* unusual not to plant your crops in straight lines, but if someone wants them to be **circular**—

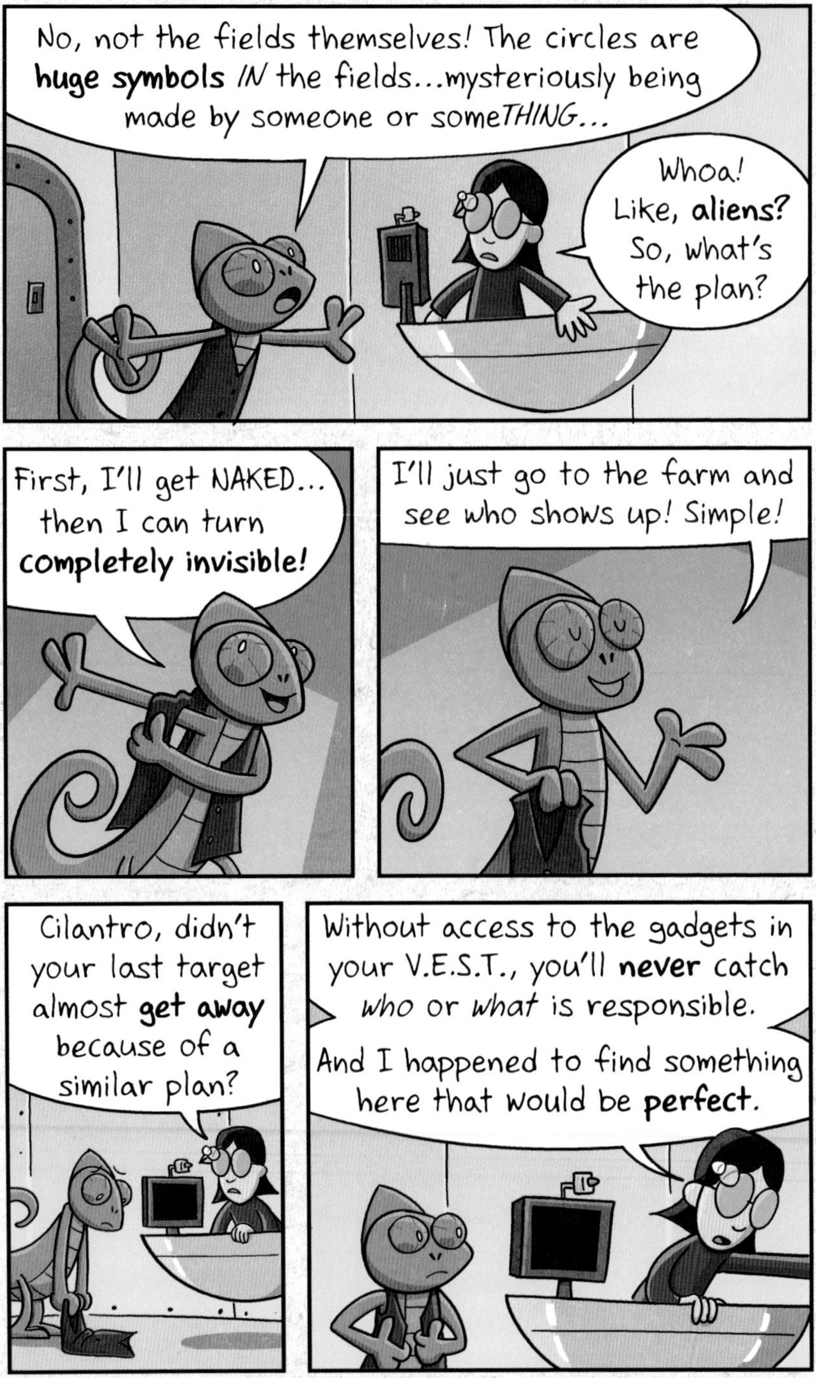
No, not the fields themselves! The circles are **huge symbols** *IN* the fields...mysteriously being made by someone or some*THING*...
Whoa! Like, **aliens?** So, what's the plan?
First, I'll get NAKED... then I can turn **completely invisible!**
I'll just go to the farm and see who shows up! Simple!
Cilantro, didn't your last target almost **get away** because of a similar plan?
Without access to the gadgets in your V.E.S.T., you'll **never** catch *who* or *what* is responsible.
And I happened to find something here that would be **perfect**.

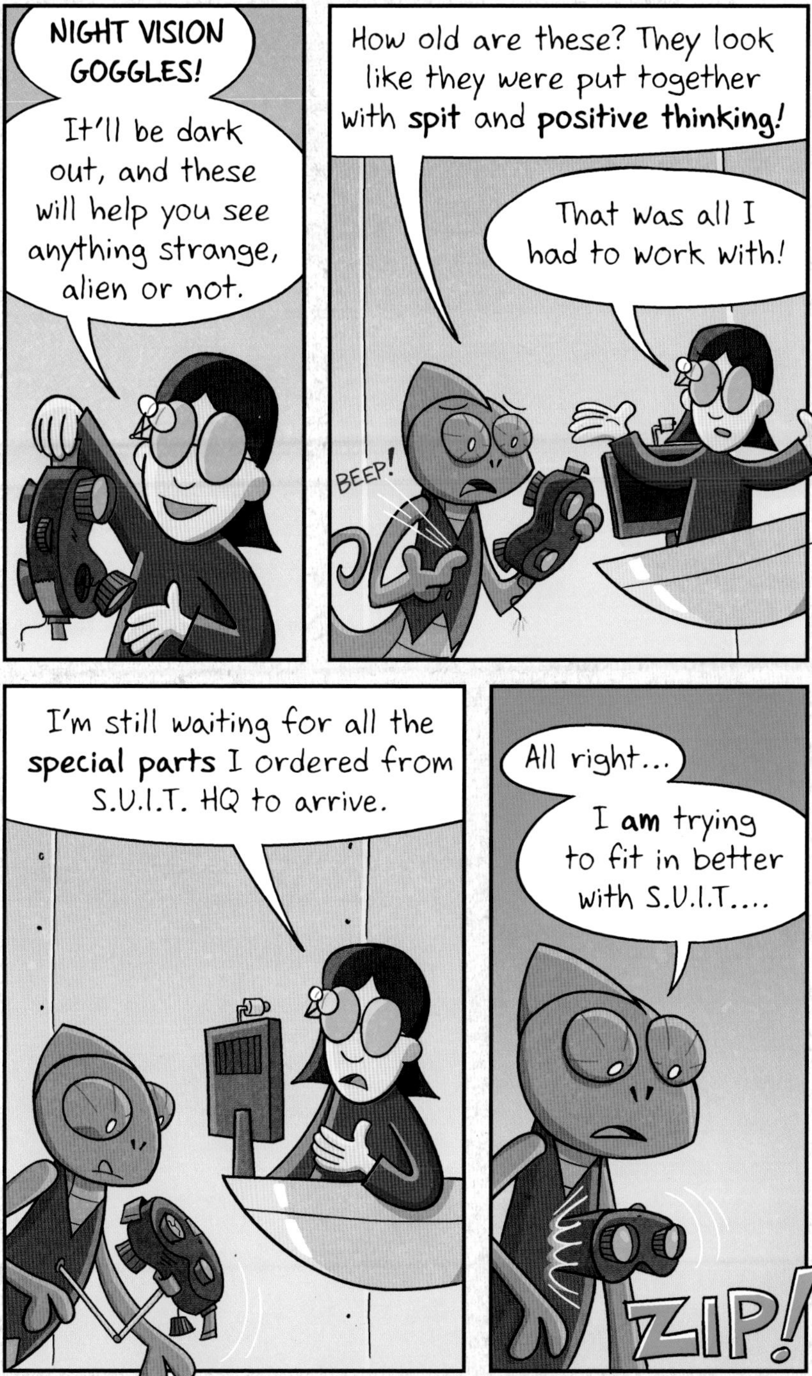
NIGHT VISION GOGGLES!
It'll be dark out, and these will help you see anything strange, alien or not.
How old are these? They look like they were put together with **spit** and **positive thinking!**
BEEP!
That was all I had to work with!
I'm still waiting for all the **special parts** I ordered from S.U.I.T. HQ to arrive.
All right...
I **am** trying to fit in better with S.U.I.T....
ZIP!

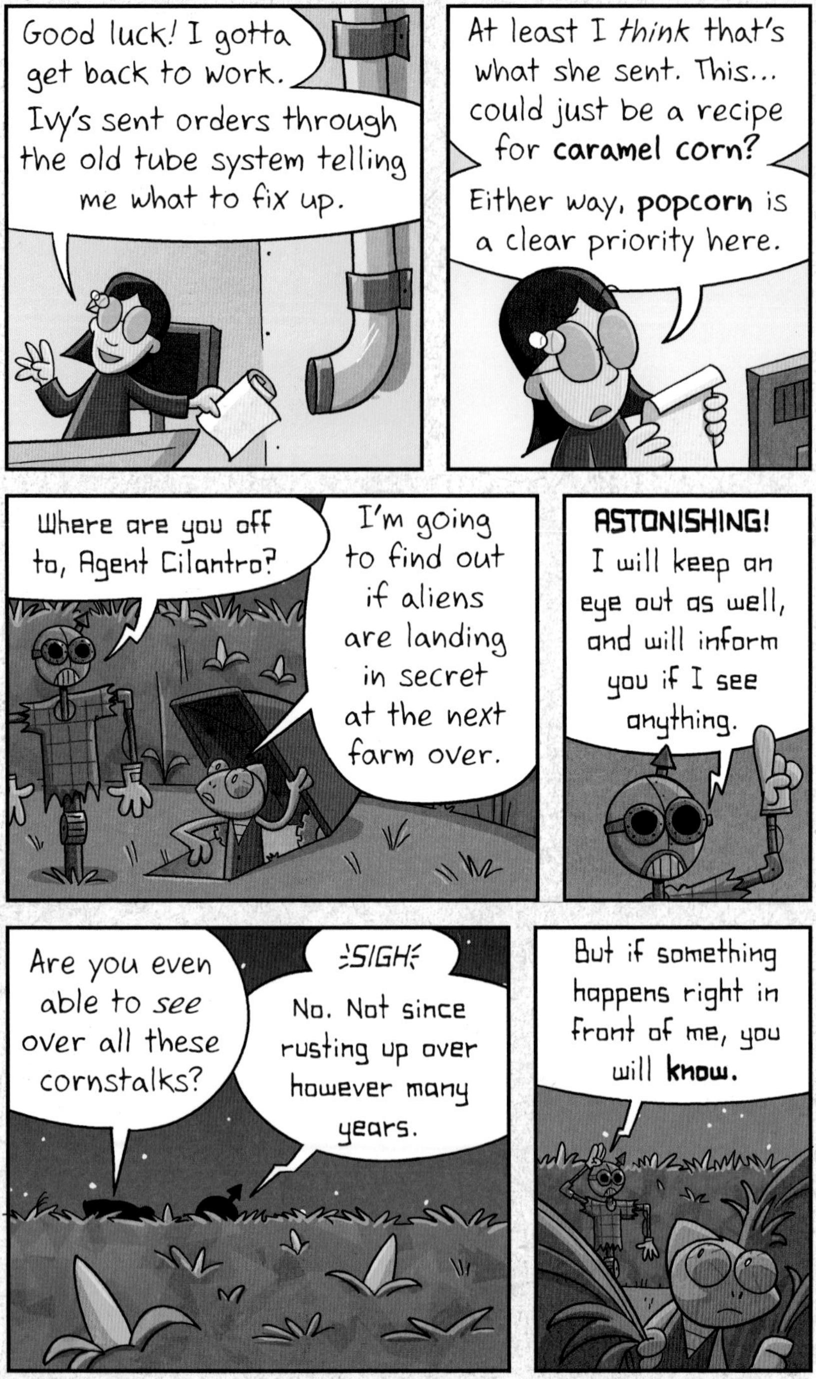
Good luck! I gotta get back to work.
Ivy's sent orders through the old tube system telling me what to fix up.
At least I *think* that's what she sent. This... could just be a recipe for **caramel corn?**
Either way, **popcorn** is a clear priority here.
Where are you off to, Agent Cilantro?
I'm going to find out if aliens are landing in secret at the next farm over.
ASTONISHING!
I will keep an eye out as well, and will inform you if I see anything.
Are you even able to *see* over all these cornstalks?
SIGH
No. Not since rusting up over however many years.
But if something happens right in front of me, you will **know.**

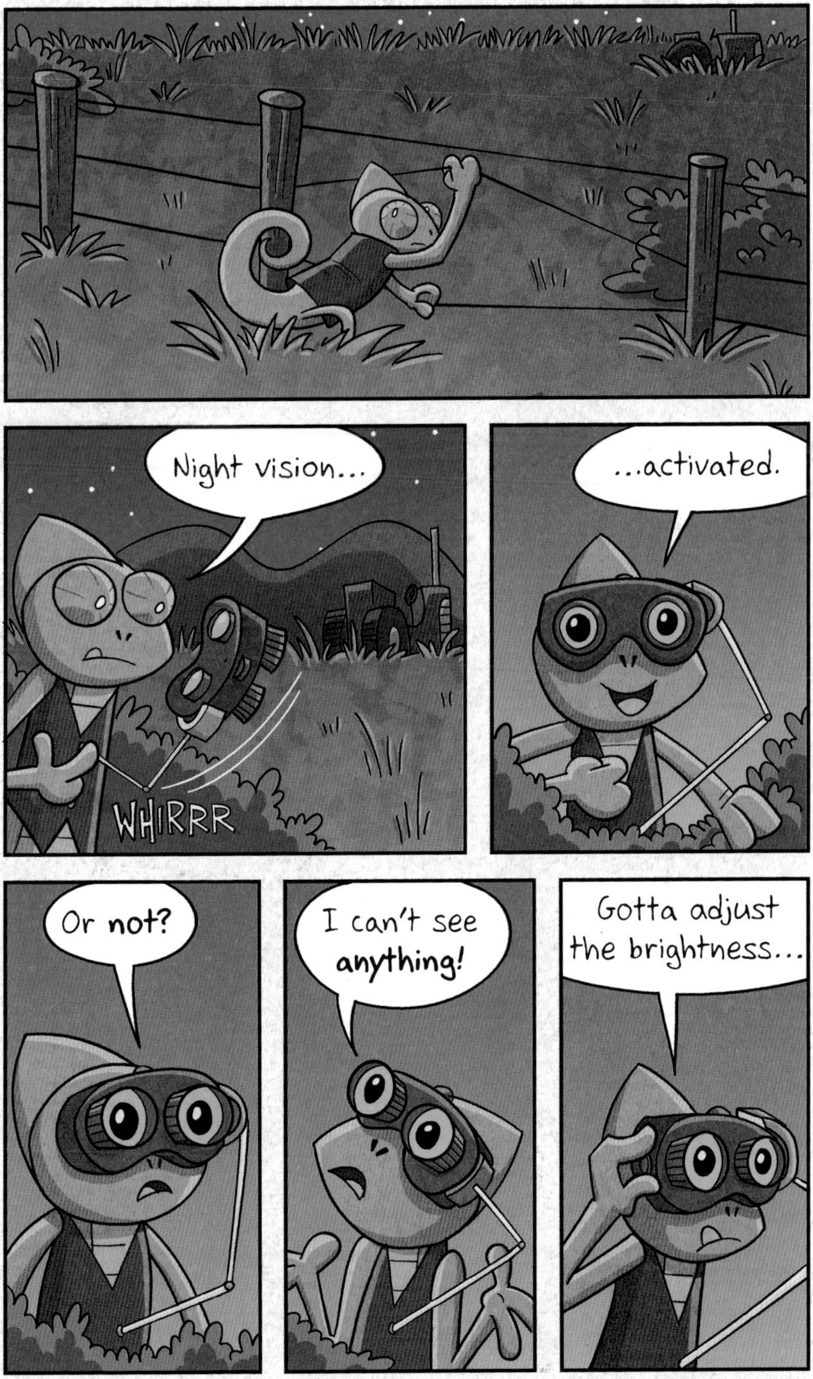
Night vision...
WHIRRR
...activated.
Or not?
I can't see anything!
Gotta adjust the brightness...

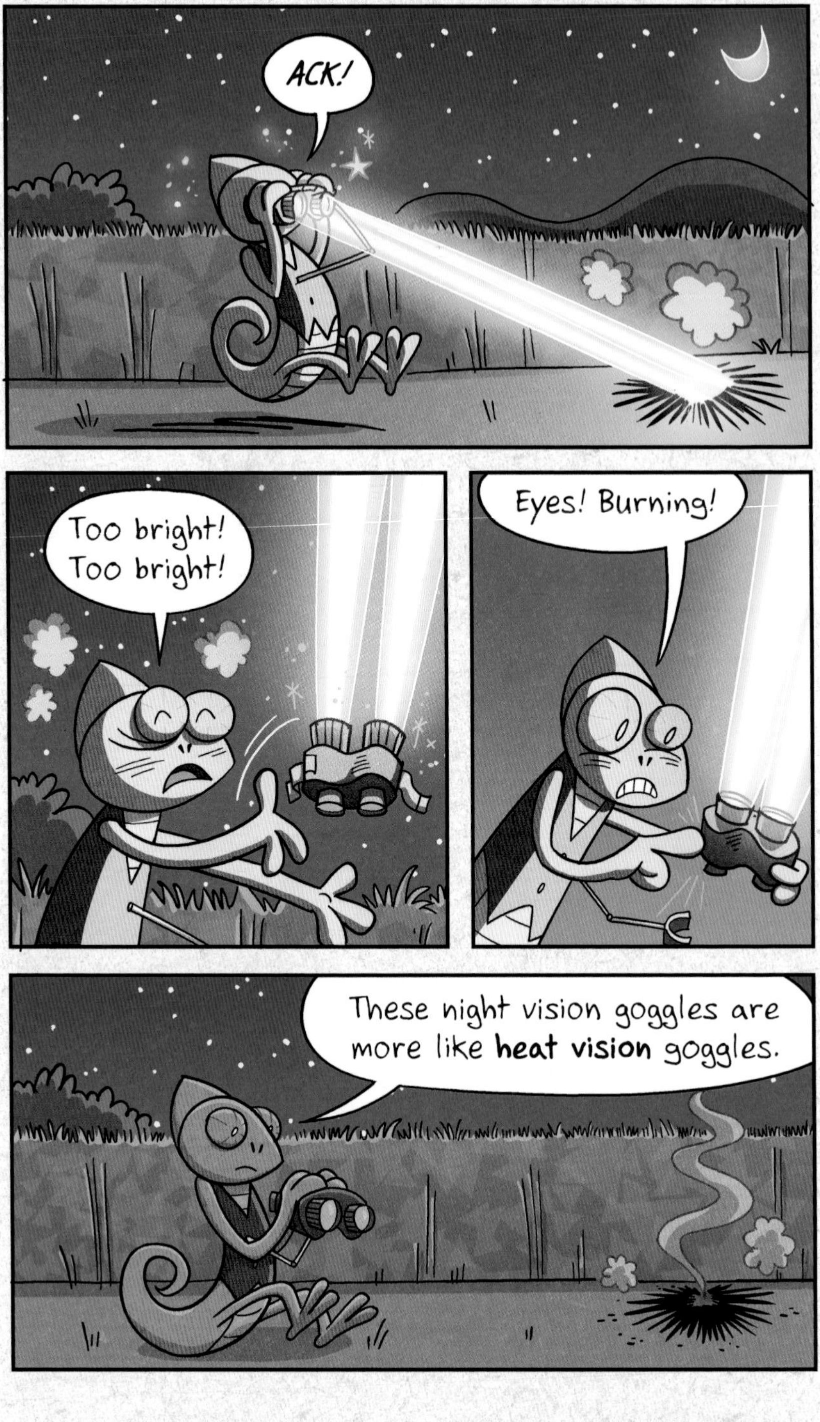
ACK!
Too bright! Too bright!
Eyes! Burning!
These night vision goggles are more like **heat vision** goggles.

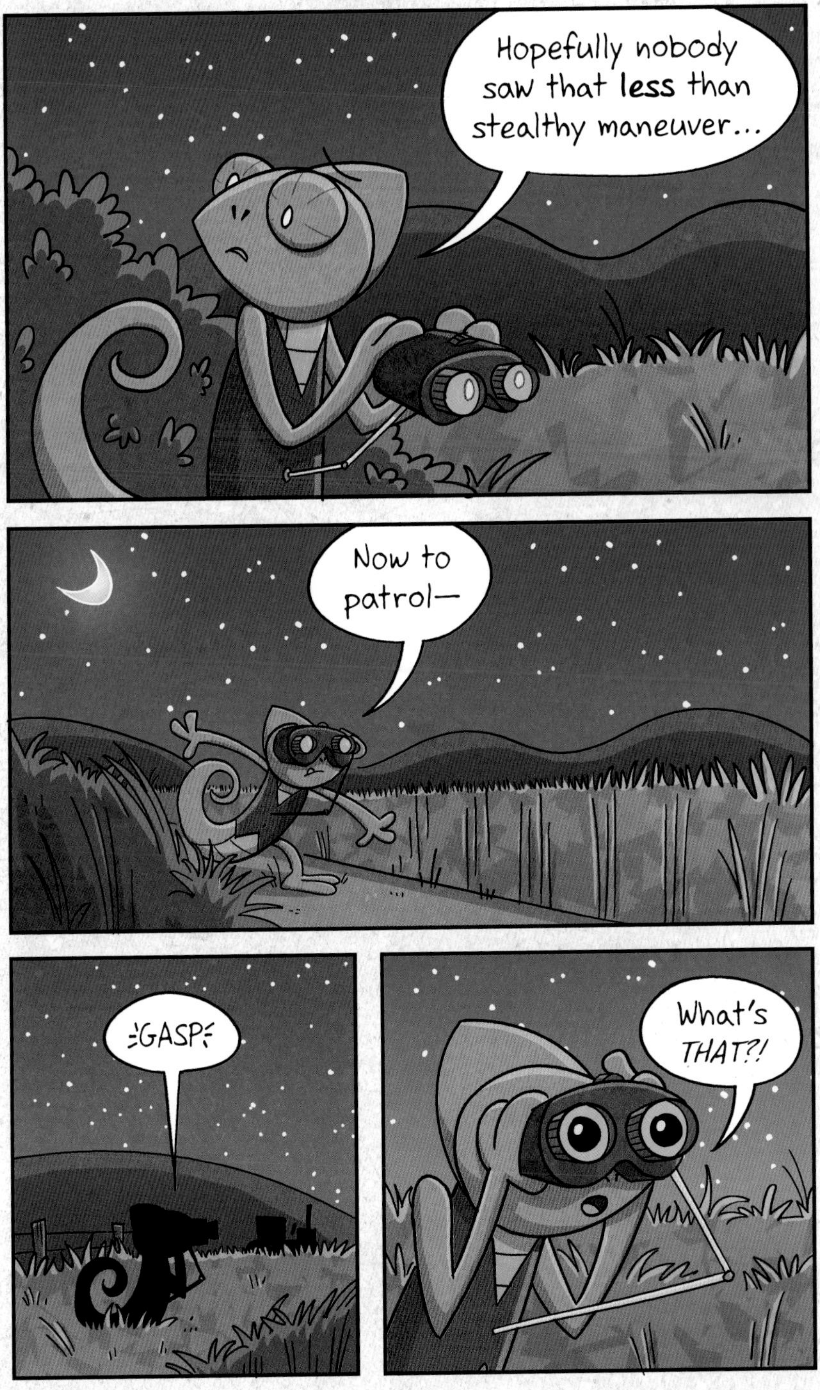
Hopefully nobody saw that **less** than stealthy maneuver...
Now to patrol—
GASP
What's THAT?!

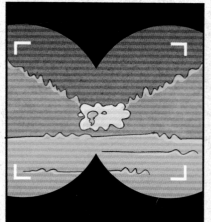

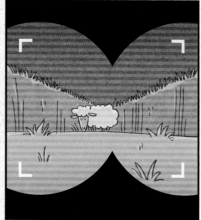

Oh. Just a sheep.

All right, keep focused.

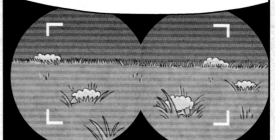

Wow, I thought that farmer was pretty strict about getting all the sheep to bed, but there must be...

...five? Six... sheep out there?

Wait, there's more. Seven—

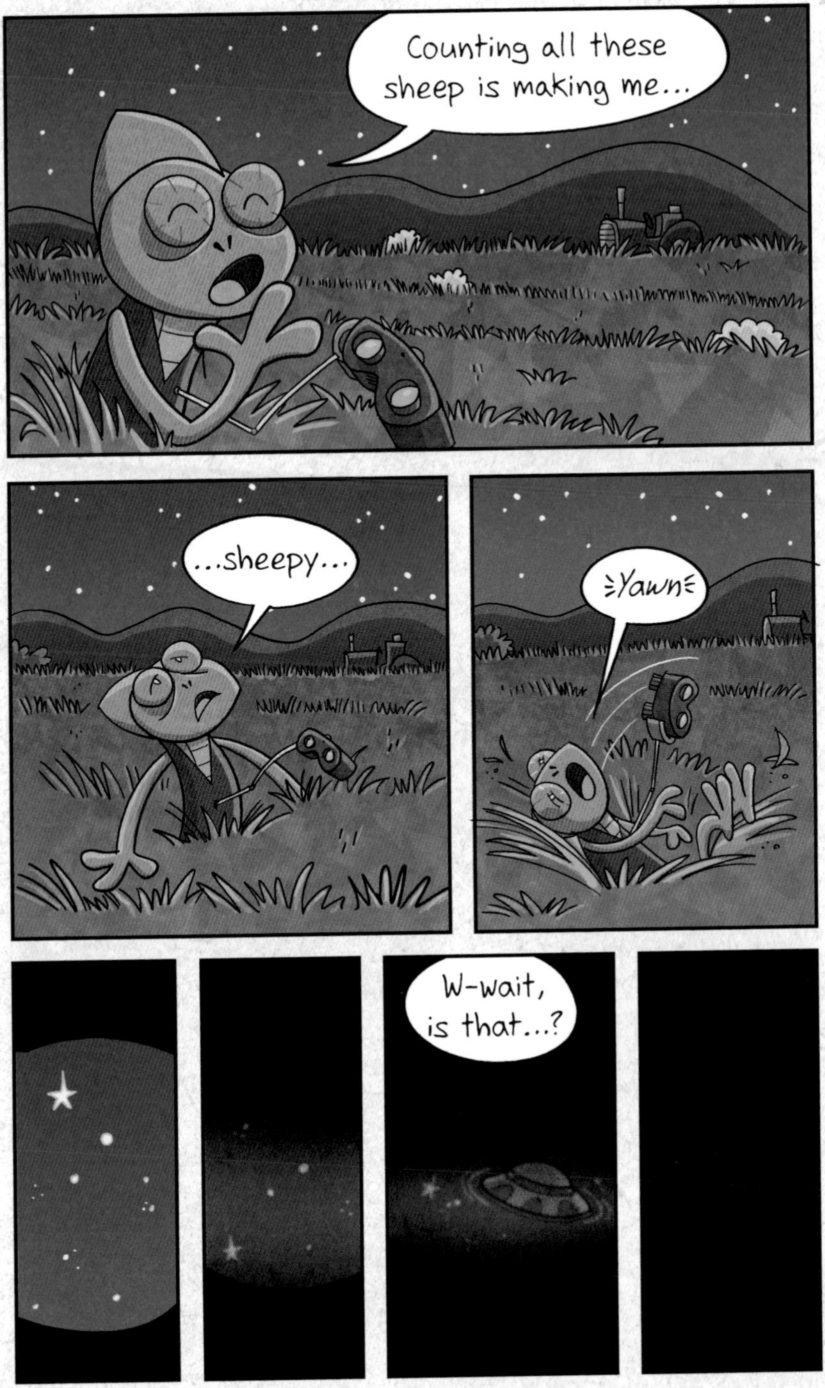
Counting all these sheep is making me...
...sheepy...
Yawn
W-wait, is that...?

Chapter 6

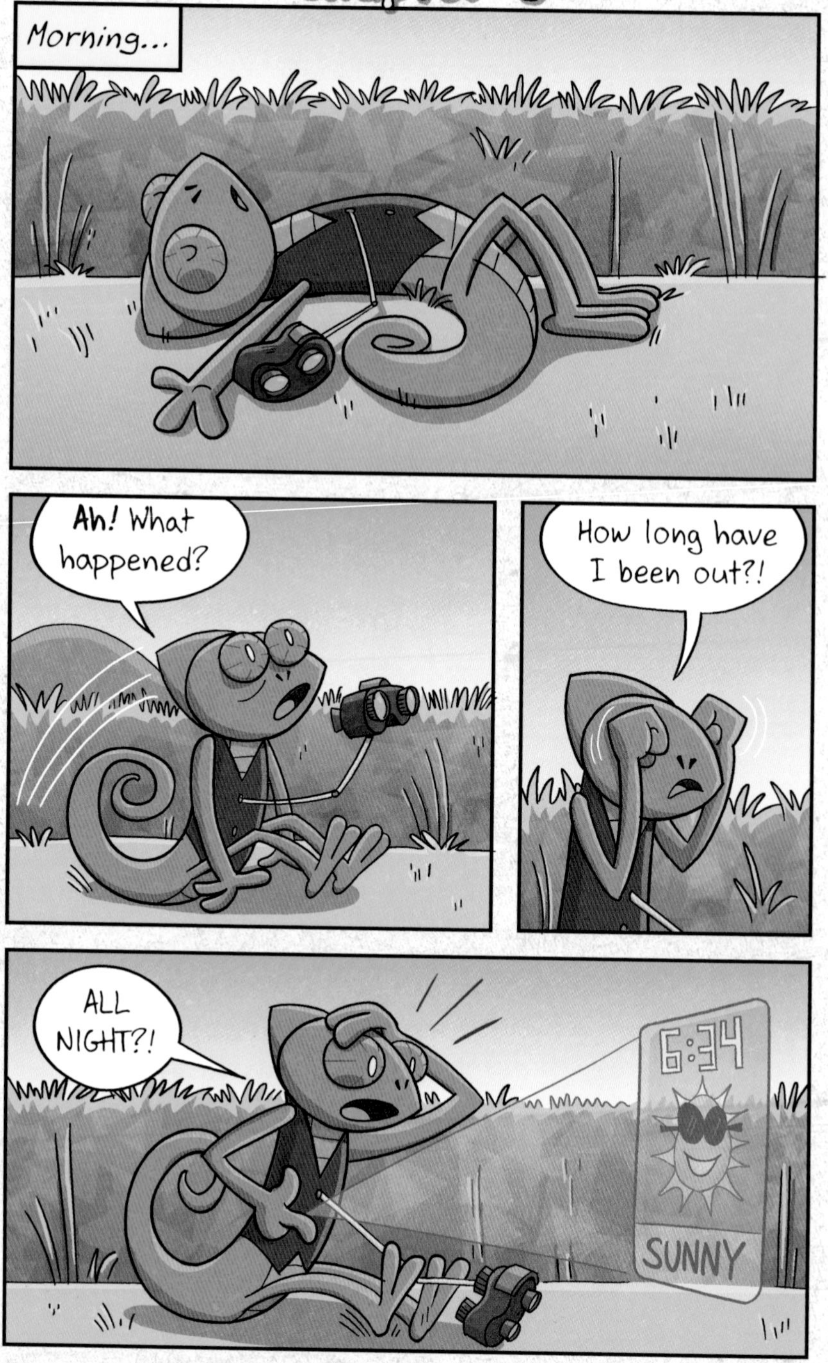
Morning...
Ah! What happened?
How long have I been out?!
ALL NIGHT?!
6:34
SUNNY

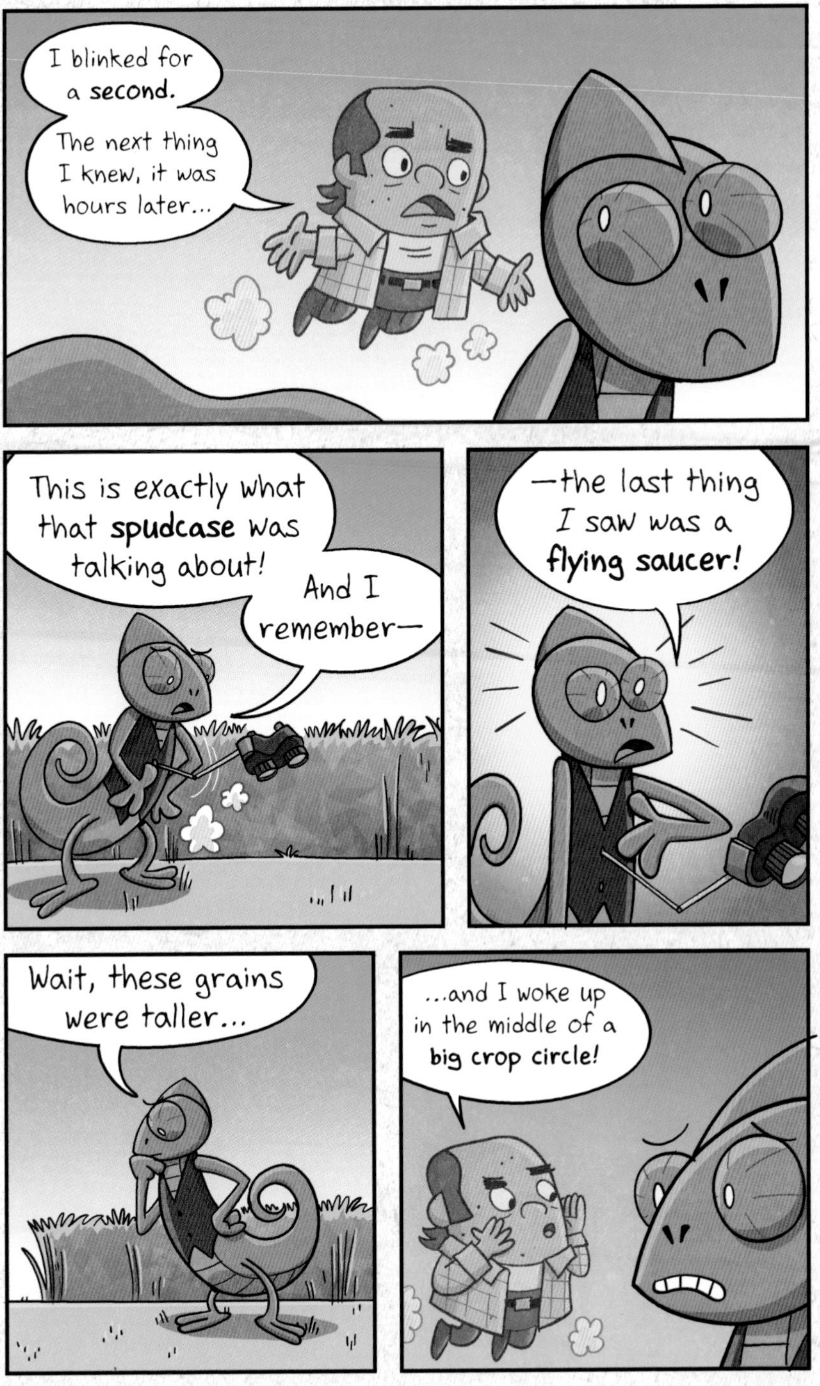
I blinked for a **second.**
The next thing I knew, it was hours later...
This is exactly what that **spudcase** was talking about!
And I remember—
—the last thing I saw was a **flying saucer!**
Wait, these grains were taller...
...and I woke up in the middle of a **big crop circle!**

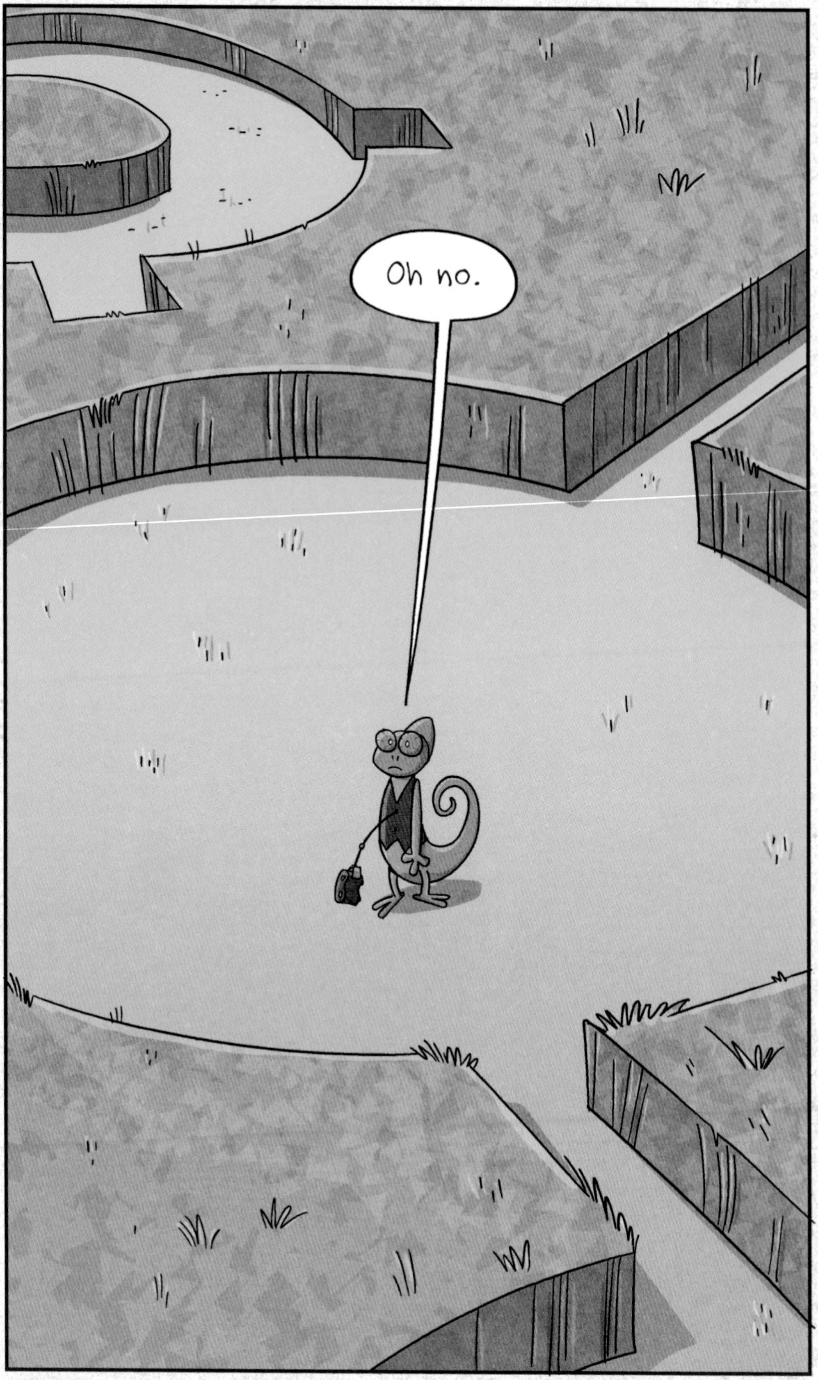
Oh no.

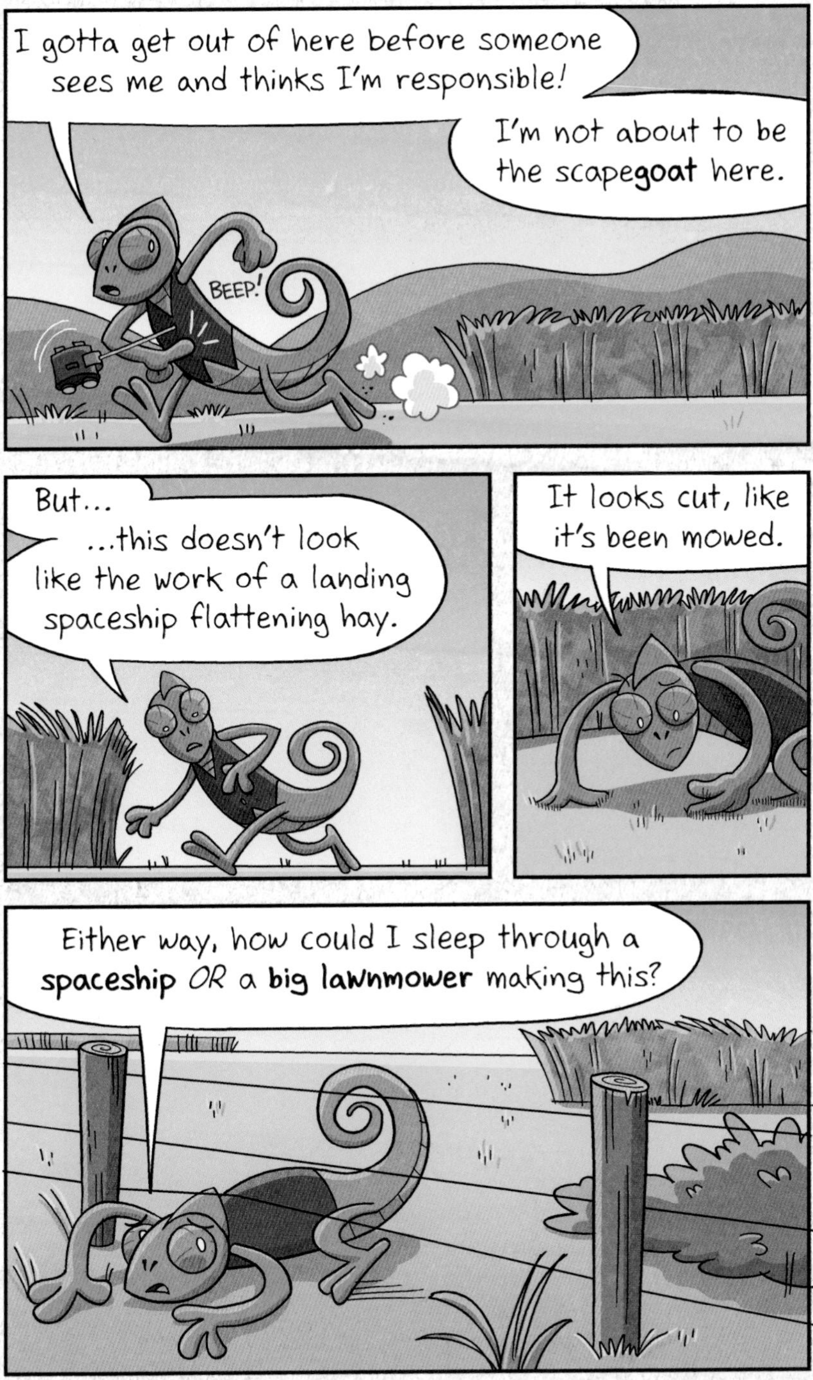
I gotta get out of here before someone sees me and thinks I'm responsible!
I'm not about to be the scapegoat here.
BEEP!
But...
...this doesn't look like the work of a landing spaceship flattening hay.
It looks cut, like it's been mowed.
Either way, how could I sleep through a spaceship OR a big lawnmower making this?

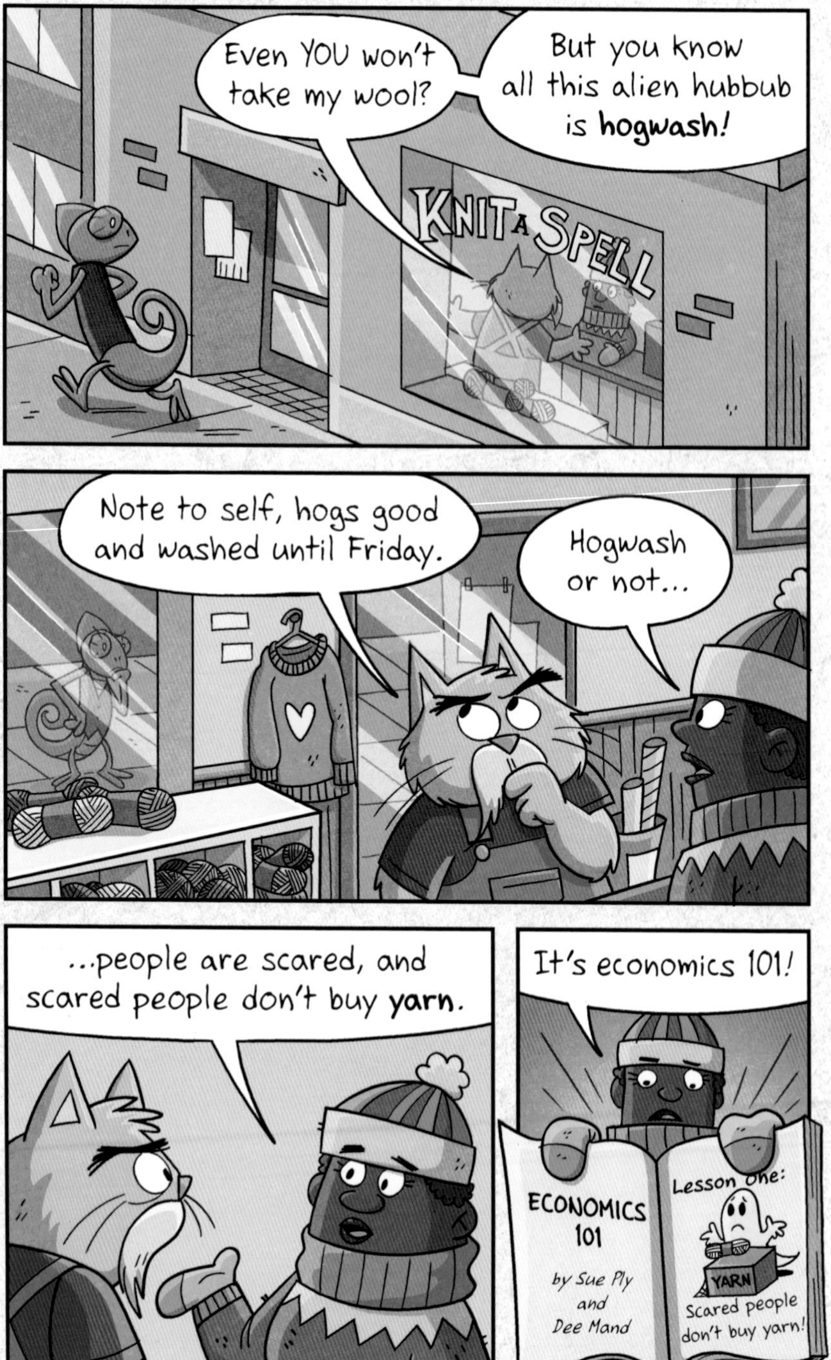
Even YOU won't take my wool?
But you know all this alien hubbub is hogwash!
KNIT A SPELL
Note to self, hogs good and washed until Friday.
Hogwash or not...
...people are scared, and scared people don't buy yarn.
It's economics 101!
ECONOMICS 101
by Sue Ply and Dee Mand
Lesson One:
YARN
Scared people don't buy yarn!

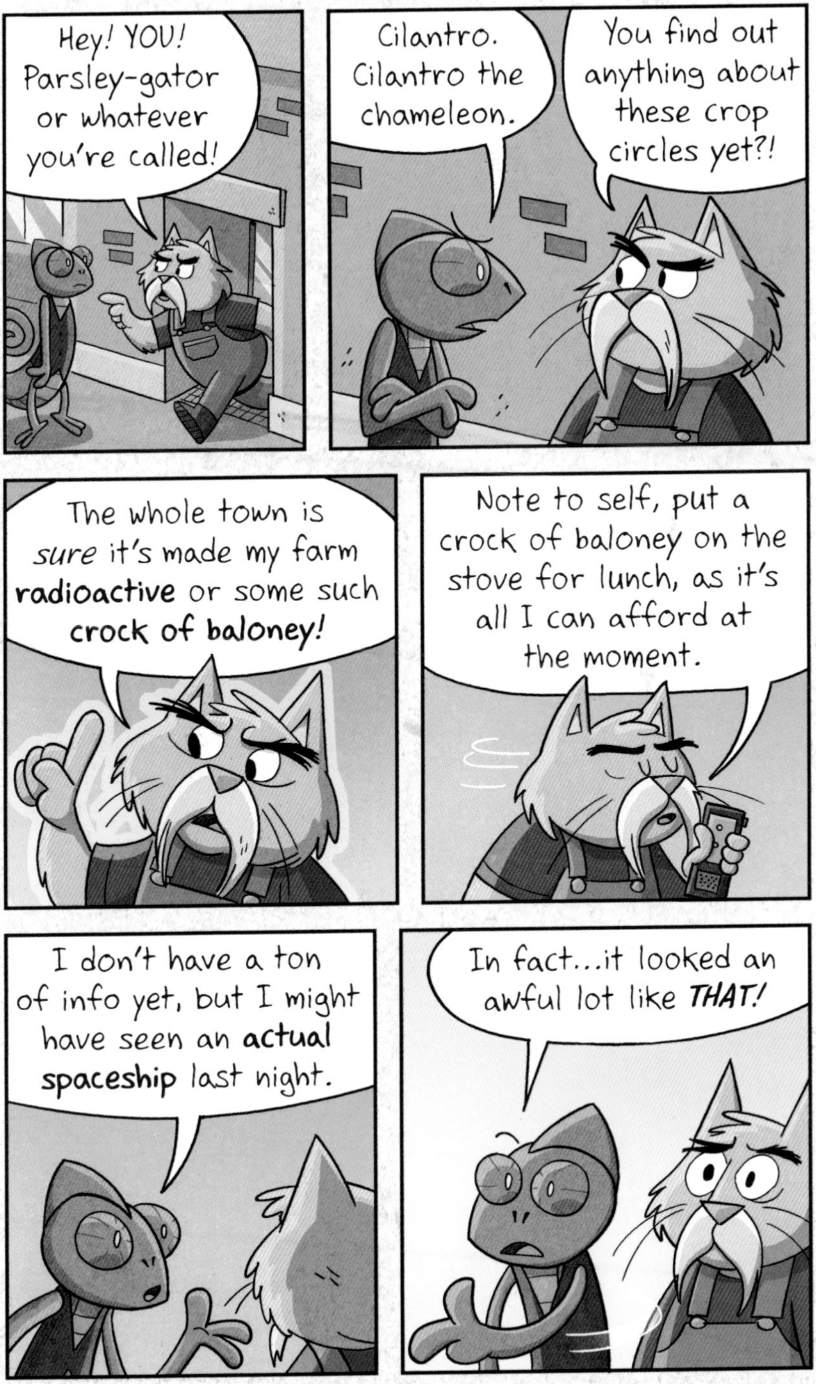
Hey! YOU! Parsley-gator or whatever you're called!
Cilantro. Cilantro the chameleon.
You find out anything about these crop circles yet?!
The whole town is *sure* it's made my farm **radioactive** or some such **crock of baloney!**
Note to self, put a crock of baloney on the stove for lunch, as it's all I can afford at the moment.
I don't have a ton of info yet, but I might have seen an **actual spaceship** last night.
In fact...it looked an awful lot like ***THAT!***

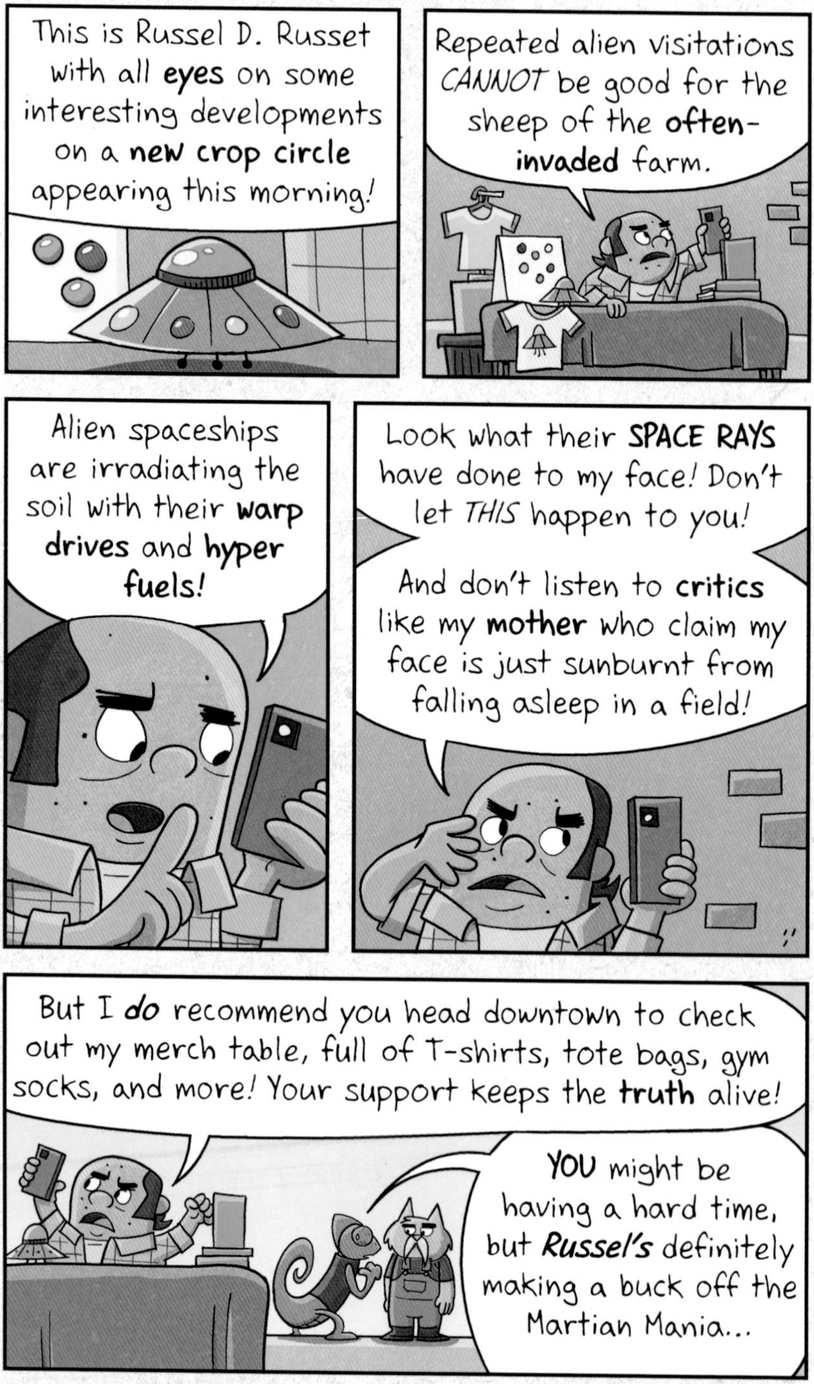
This is Russel D. Russet with all **eyes** on some interesting developments on a **new crop circle** appearing this morning!
Repeated alien visitations *CANNOT* be good for the sheep of the **often-invaded** farm.
Alien spaceships are irradiating the soil with their **warp drives** and **hyper fuels**!
Look what their **SPACE RAYS** have done to my face! Don't let *THIS* happen to you!
And don't listen to **critics** like my **mother** who claim my face is just sunburnt from falling asleep in a field!
But I *do* recommend you head downtown to check out my merch table, full of T-shirts, tote bags, gym socks, and more! Your support keeps the **truth** alive!
YOU might be having a hard time, but ***Russel's*** definitely making a buck off the Martian Mania...

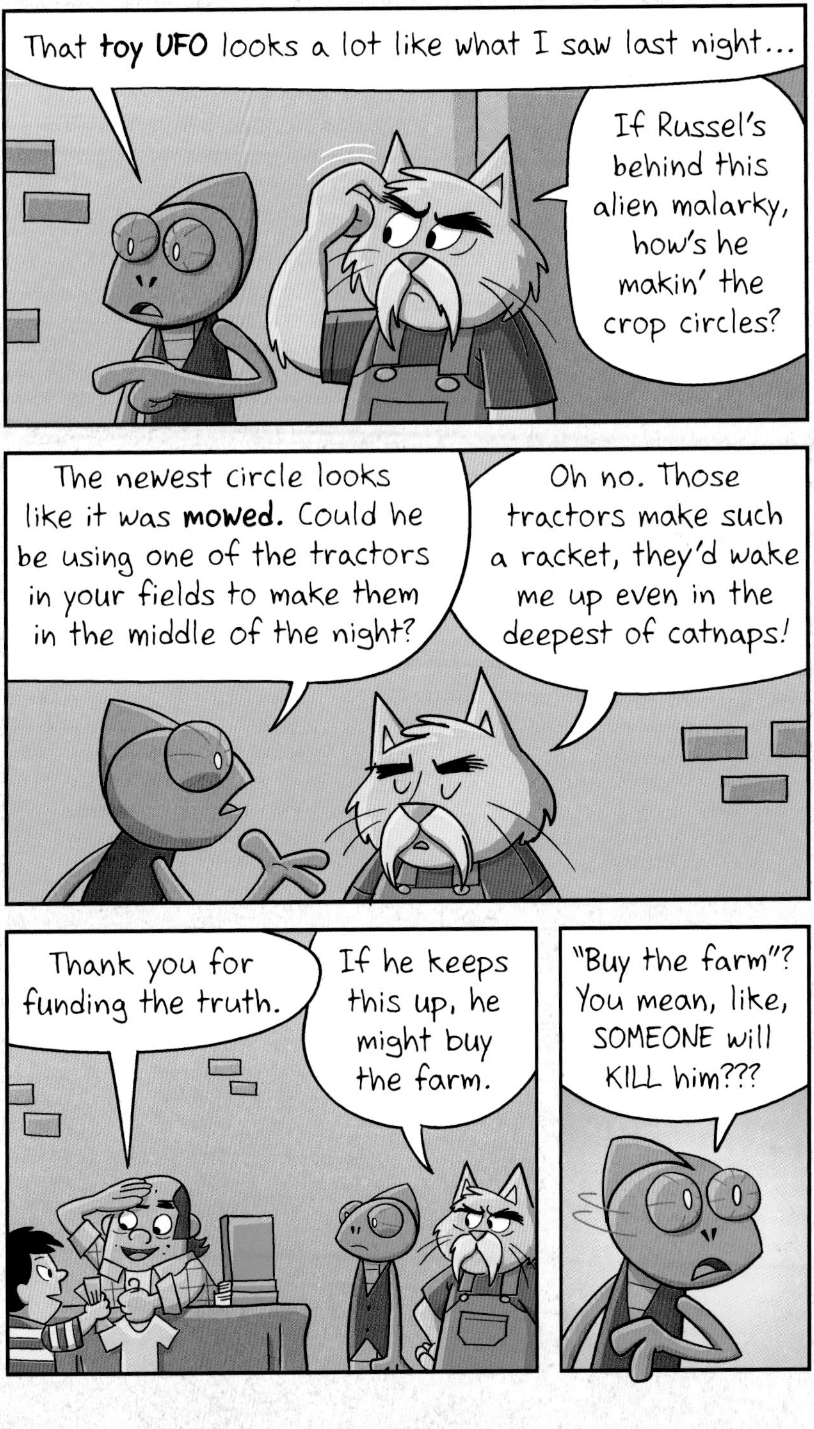
That **toy UFO** looks a lot like what I saw last night...
If Russel's behind this alien malarky, how's he makin' the crop circles?
The newest circle looks like it was **mowed.** Could he be using one of the tractors in your fields to make them in the middle of the night?
Oh no. Those tractors make such a racket, they'd wake me up even in the deepest of catnaps!
Thank you for funding the truth.
If he keeps this up, he might buy the farm.
"Buy the farm"? You mean, like, SOMEONE will KILL him???

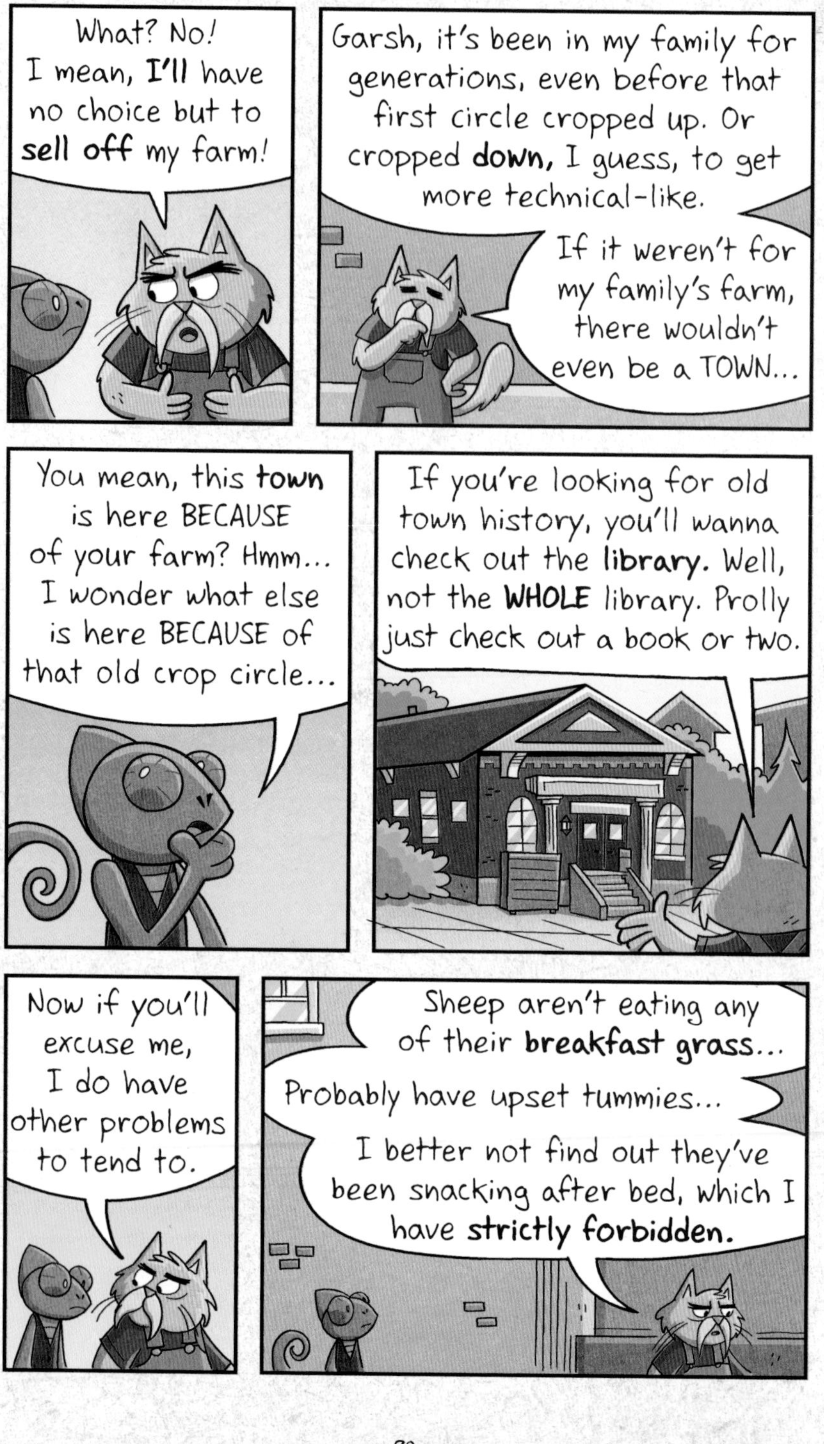
What? No! I mean, I'll have no choice but to sell off my farm!
Garsh, it's been in my family for generations, even before that first circle cropped up. Or cropped down, I guess, to get more technical-like.
If it weren't for my family's farm, there wouldn't even be a TOWN...
You mean, this town is here BECAUSE of your farm? Hmm... I wonder what else is here BECAUSE of that old crop circle...
If you're looking for old town history, you'll wanna check out the library. Well, not the WHOLE library. Prolly just check out a book or two.
Now if you'll excuse me, I do have other problems to tend to.
Sheep aren't eating any of their breakfast grass...
Probably have upset tummies...
I better not find out they've been snacking after bed, which I have strictly forbidden.

Not the most exciting read...

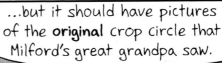

...but it should have pictures of the **original** crop circle that Milford's great grandpa saw.

A VISUAL HISTORY OF LOCAL FARMS: PICTURES OF GRASS, WHEAT, CORN, AND MORE FOR THE LAST 50 YEARS.

THUNK!

There it is!

Hm... not quite the same as the recent crop circles...

And...ah–HA! S.U.I.T. agents, **here!** Years ago.

The outpost *WAS* set up in case aliens made that crop circle! But when no additional circles appeared, the case was closed, along with the base...

Until now.

Inspector Vague sent Monocle and me here to revive a decades-old investigation!

But why would aliens come back **NOW** to make more crop circles after so long?

Unless... Who **else** might be looking up crop circles?

Not a very popular book. A few check-outs forty, fifty years ago, and then nothing...

...until last month.

8/24/1968	✓
11/16/1977	✓
6/11/1982	✓
7/18/1986	✓
6/7/2023	✓

Just **days** before the first **new** crop circle popped up!

Did somebody check this out to **copy** the old one?

Buy my shirts! Buy my bumper stickers! Aliens are real and you should give me money!

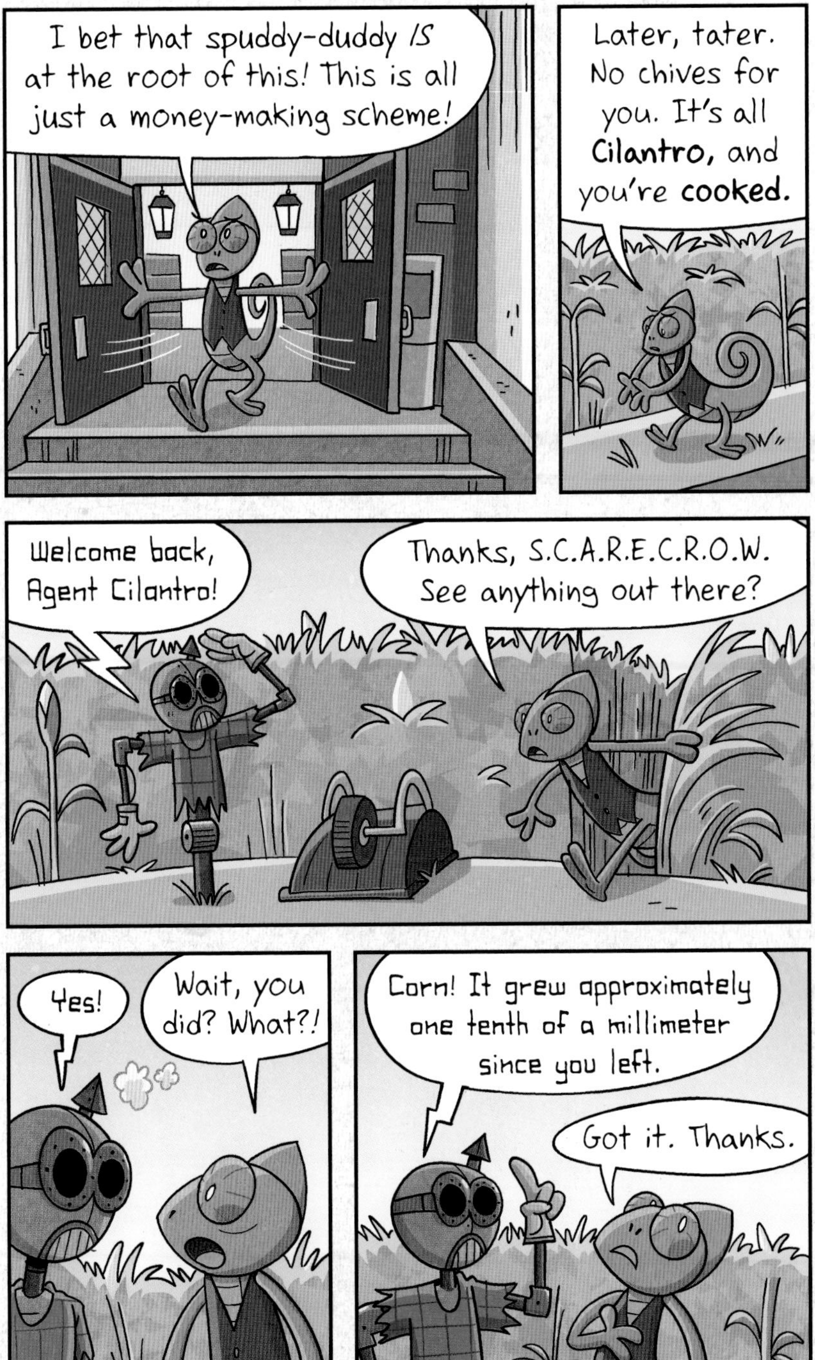
I bet that spuddy-duddy *IS* at the root of this! This is all just a money-making scheme!
Later, tater. No chives for you. It's all **Cilantro,** and you're **cooked.**
Welcome back, Agent Cilantro!
Thanks, S.C.A.R.E.C.R.O.W. See anything out there?
Yes!
Wait, you did? What?!
Corn! It grew approximately one tenth of a millimeter since you left.
Got it. Thanks.

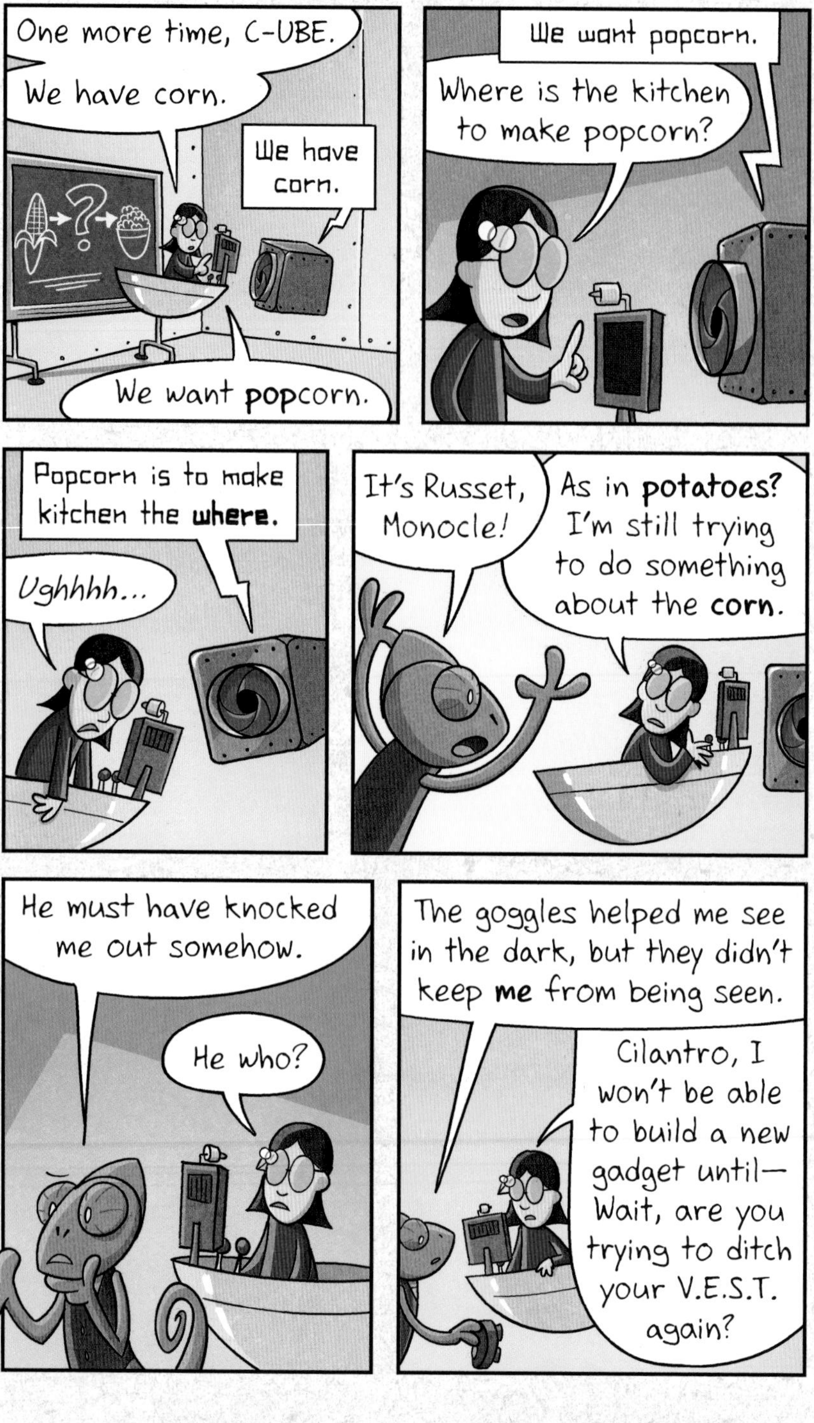
One more time, C-UBE.
We have corn.
We have corn.
We want **popcorn**.
We want popcorn.
Where is the kitchen to make popcorn?
Popcorn is to make kitchen the **where**.
Ughhhh...
It's Russet, Monocle!
As in **potatoes**? I'm still trying to do something about the **corn**.
He must have knocked me out somehow.
He who?
The goggles helped me see in the dark, but they didn't keep **me** from being seen.
Cilantro, I won't be able to build a new gadget until— Wait, are you trying to ditch your V.E.S.T. again?

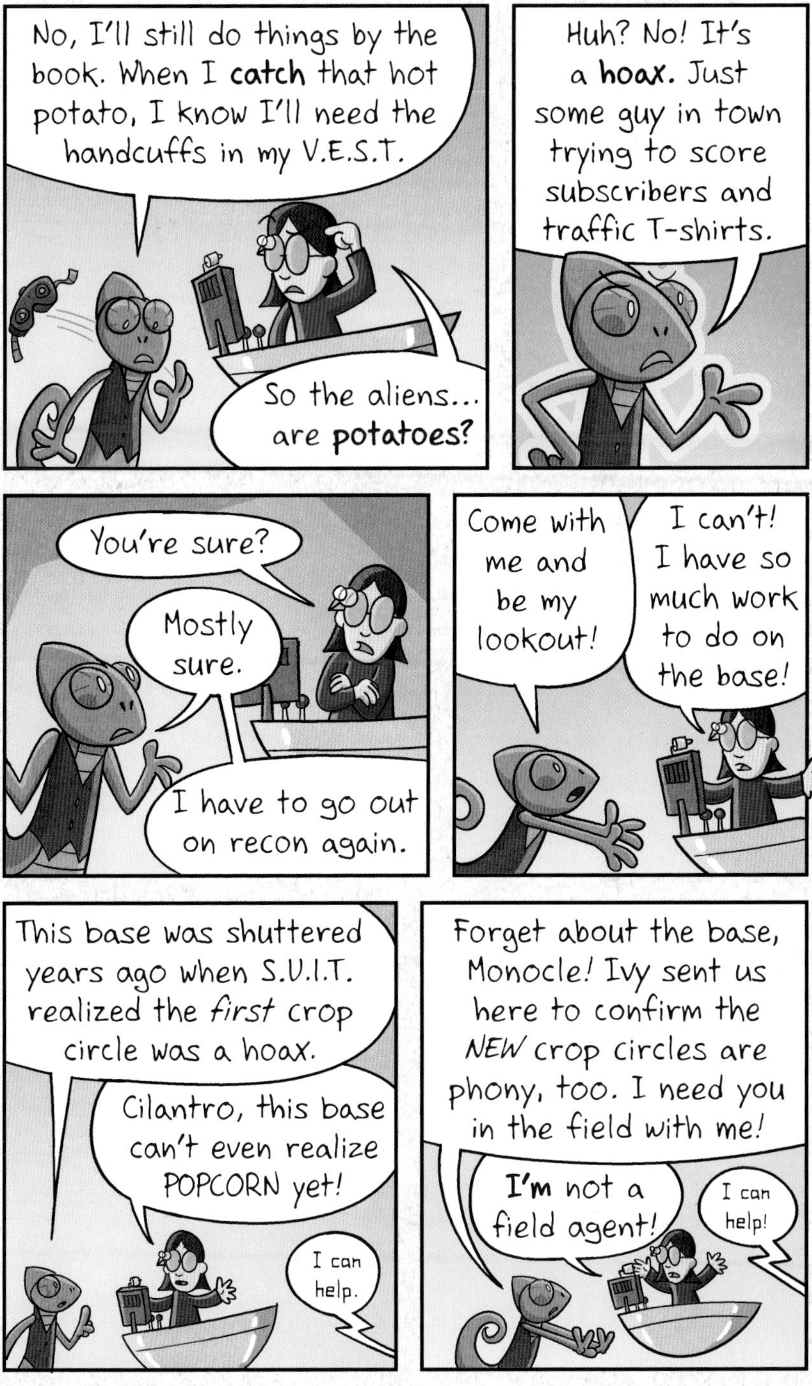

No, I'll still do things by the book. When I **catch** that hot potato, I know I'll need the handcuffs in my V.E.S.T.
So the aliens... are **potatoes?**
Huh? No! It's a **hoax.** Just some guy in town trying to score subscribers and traffic T-shirts.
You're sure?
Mostly sure.
I have to go out on recon again.
Come with me and be my lookout!
I can't! I have so much work to do on the base!
This base was shuttered years ago when S.U.I.T. realized the *first* crop circle was a hoax.
Cilantro, this base can't even realize POPCORN yet!
I can help.
Forget about the base, Monocle! Ivy sent us here to confirm the *NEW* crop circles are phony, too. I need you in the field with me!
I'm not a field agent!
I can help!

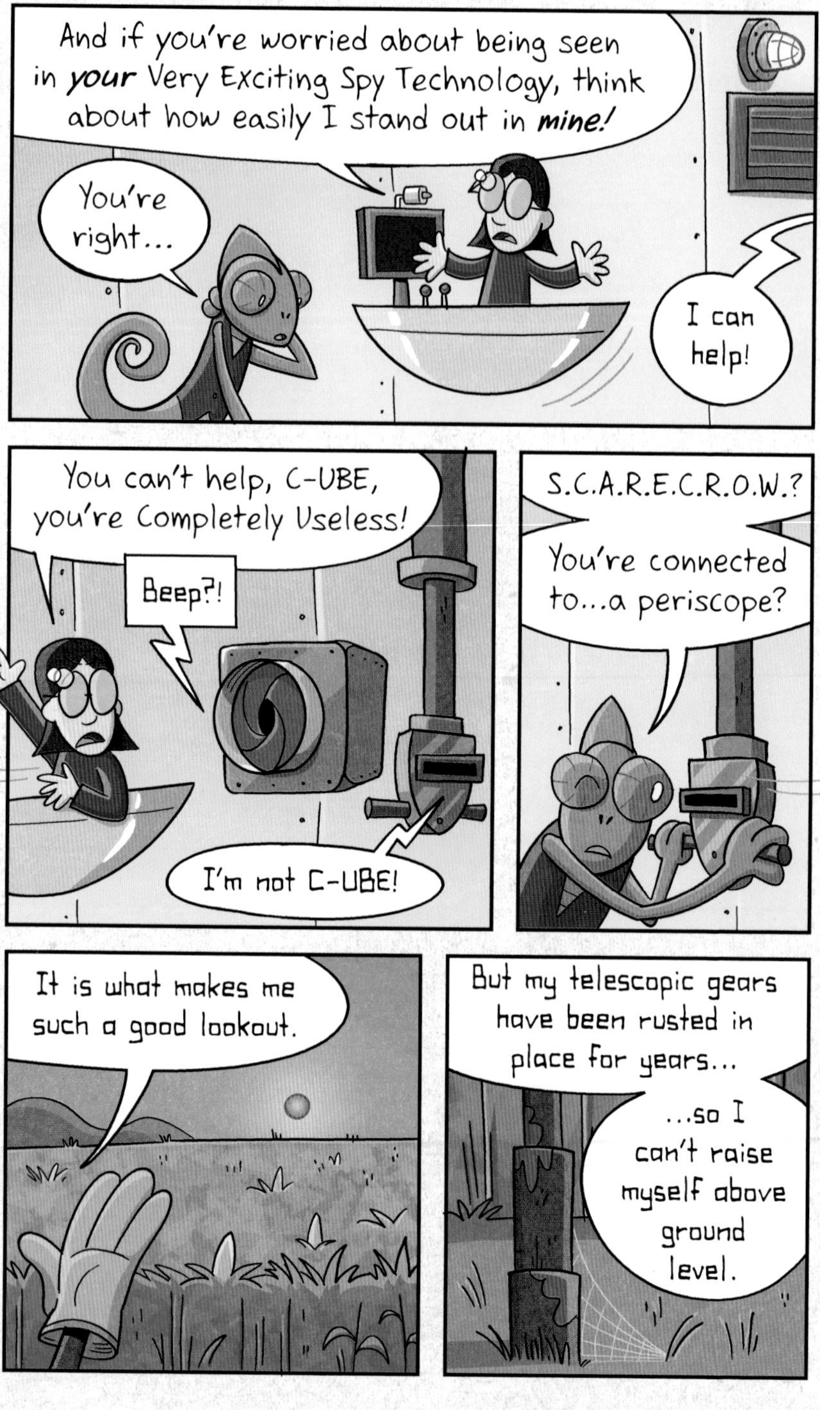
And if you're worried about being seen in *your* Very Exciting Spy Technology, think about how easily I stand out in *mine!*
You're right...
I can help!
You can't help, C-UBE, you're Completely Useless!
Beep?!
I'm not C-UBE!
S.C.A.R.E.C.R.O.W.?
You're connected to...a periscope?
It is what makes me such a good lookout.
But my telescopic gears have been rusted in place for years...
...so I can't raise myself above ground level.

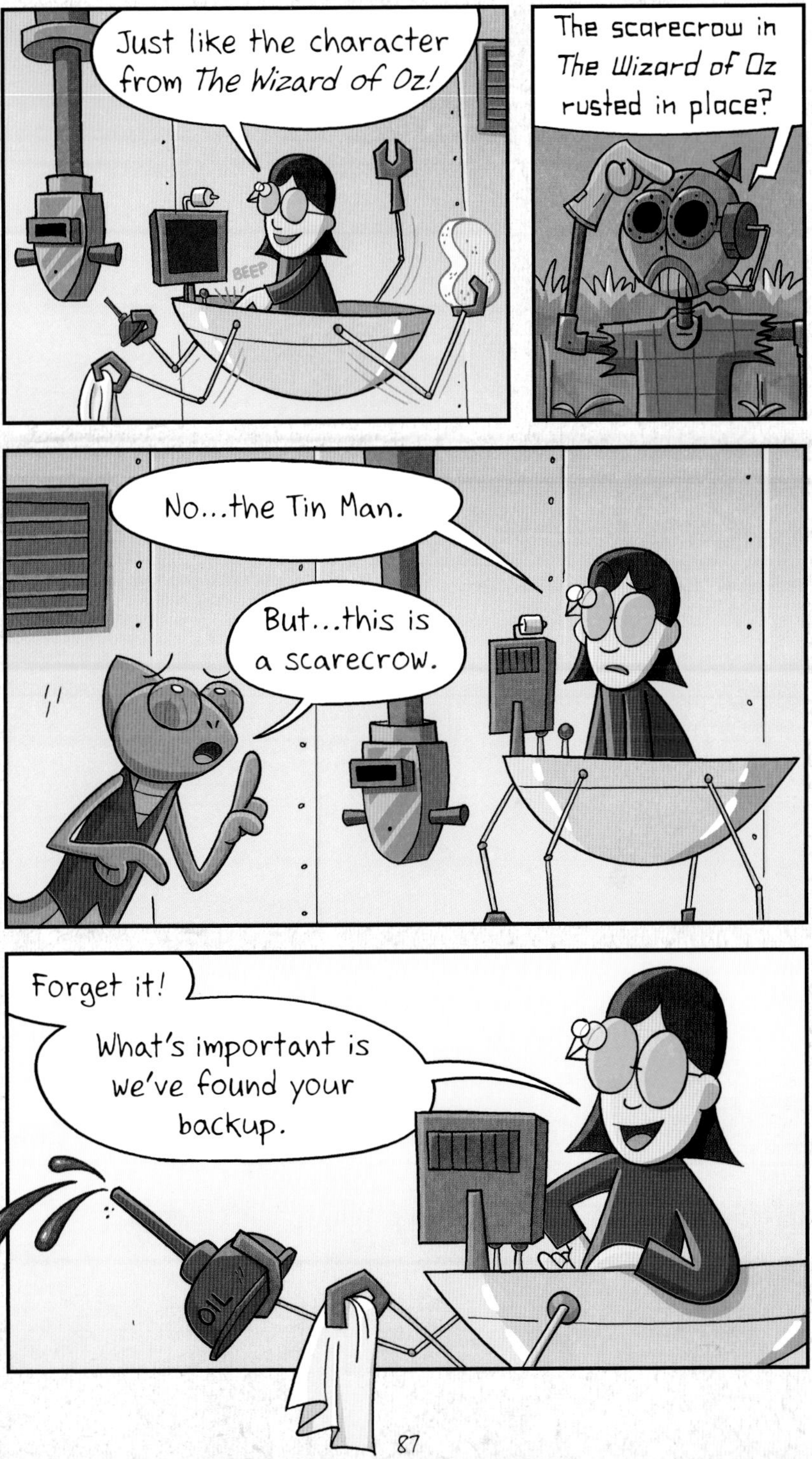
Just like the character from *The Wizard of Oz*!
BEEP
The scarecrow in *The Wizard of Oz* rusted in place?
No...the Tin Man.
But...this is a scarecrow.
Forget it!
What's important is we've found your backup.
OIL

Chapter 7

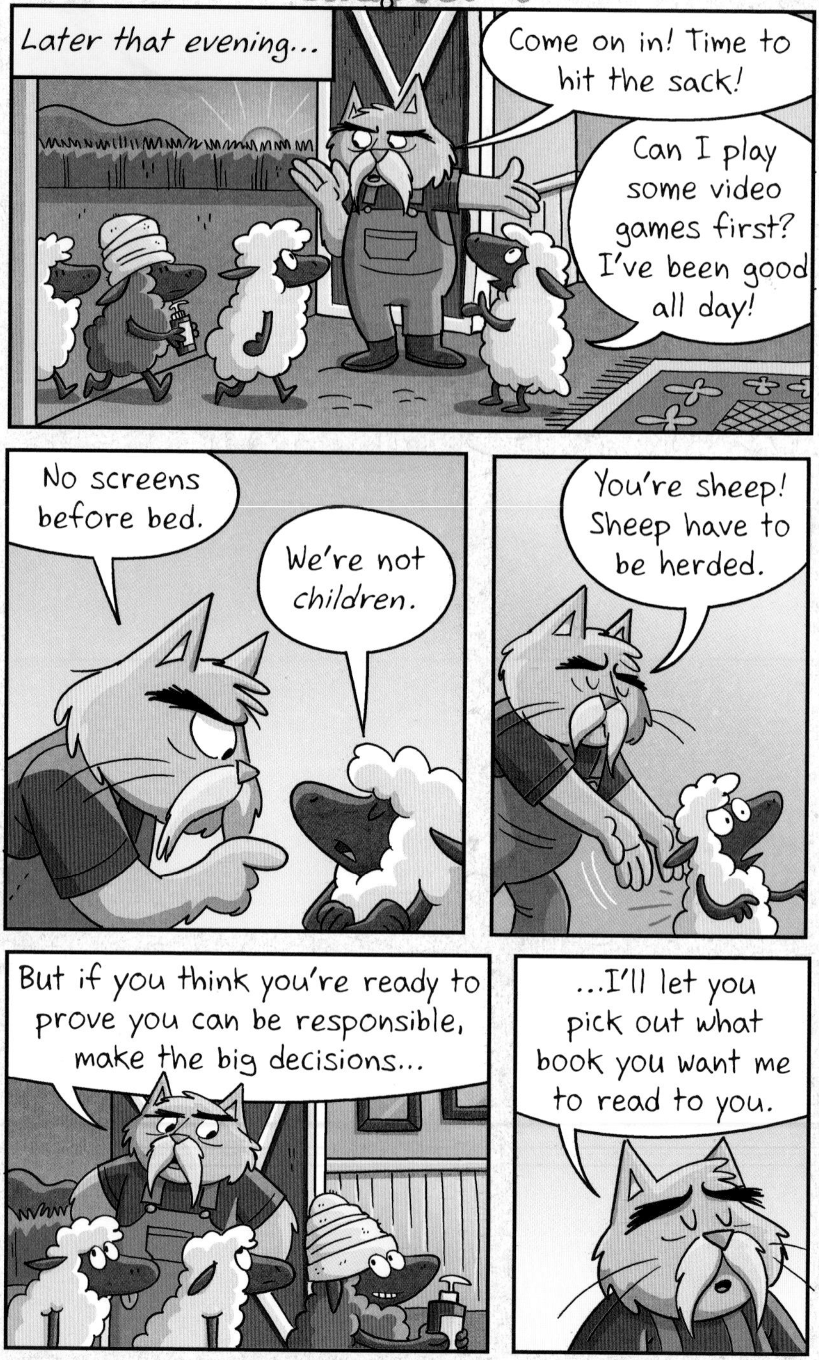
Later that evening...
Come on in! Time to hit the sack!
Can I play some video games first? I've been good all day!
No screens before bed.
We're not children.
You're sheep! Sheep have to be herded.
But if you think you're ready to prove you can be responsible, make the big decisions...
...I'll let you pick out what book you want me to read to you.

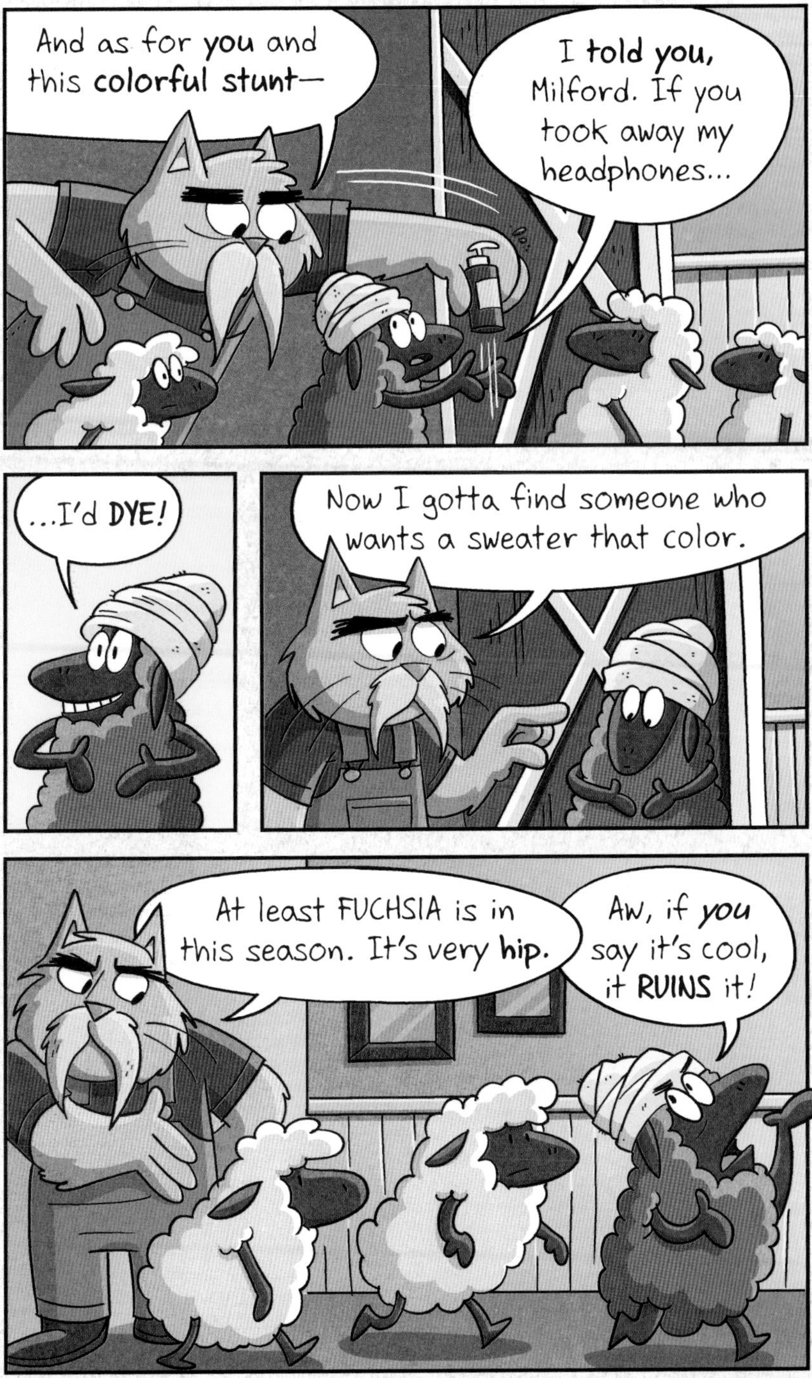
And as for you and this colorful stunt—
I told you, Milford. If you took away my headphones...
...I'd DYE!
Now I gotta find someone who wants a sweater that color.
At least FUCHSIA is in this season. It's very hip.
Aw, if you say it's cool, it RUINS it!

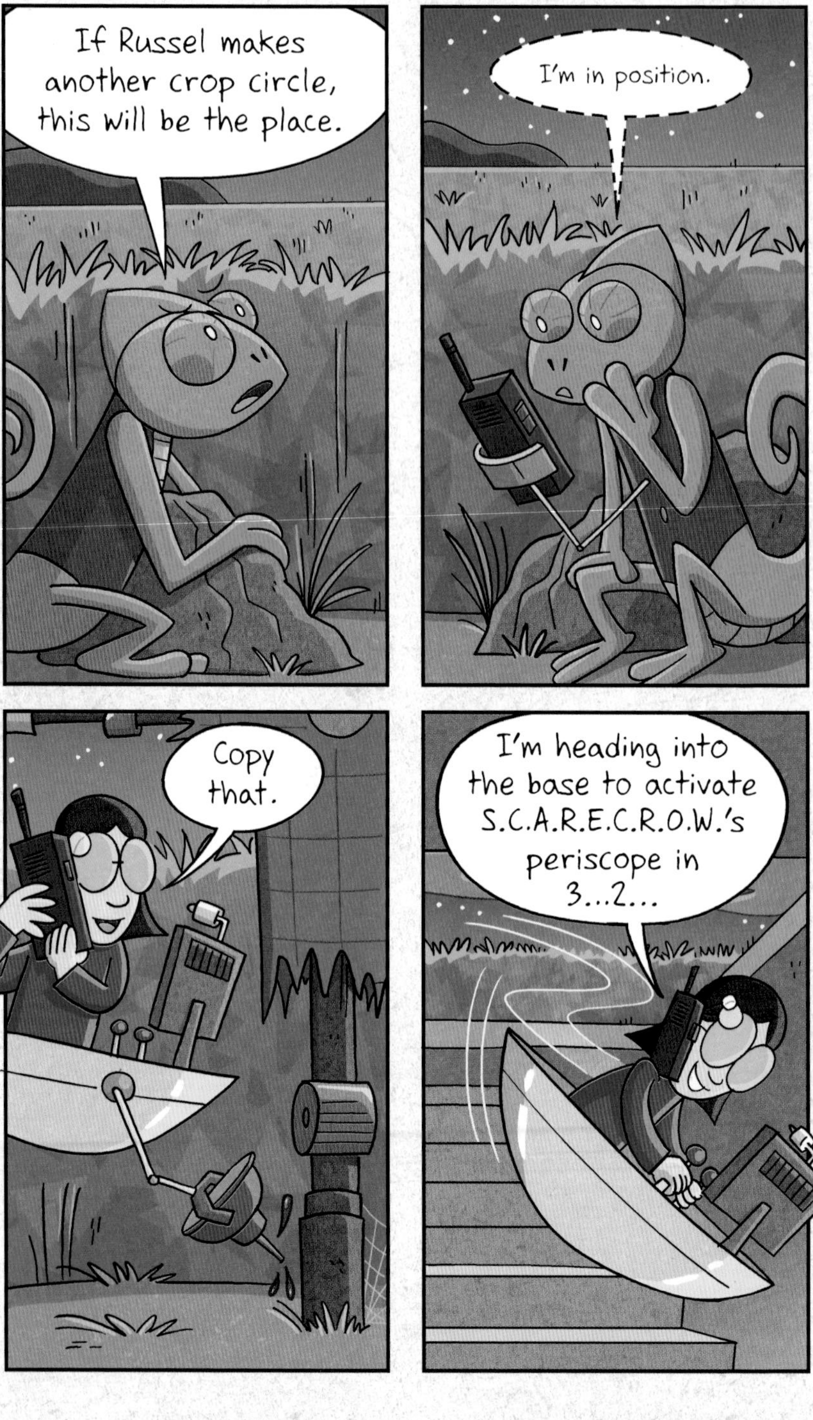
If Russel makes another crop circle, this will be the place.
I'm in position.
Copy that.
I'm heading into the base to activate S.C.A.R.E.C.R.O.W.'s periscope in 3...2...

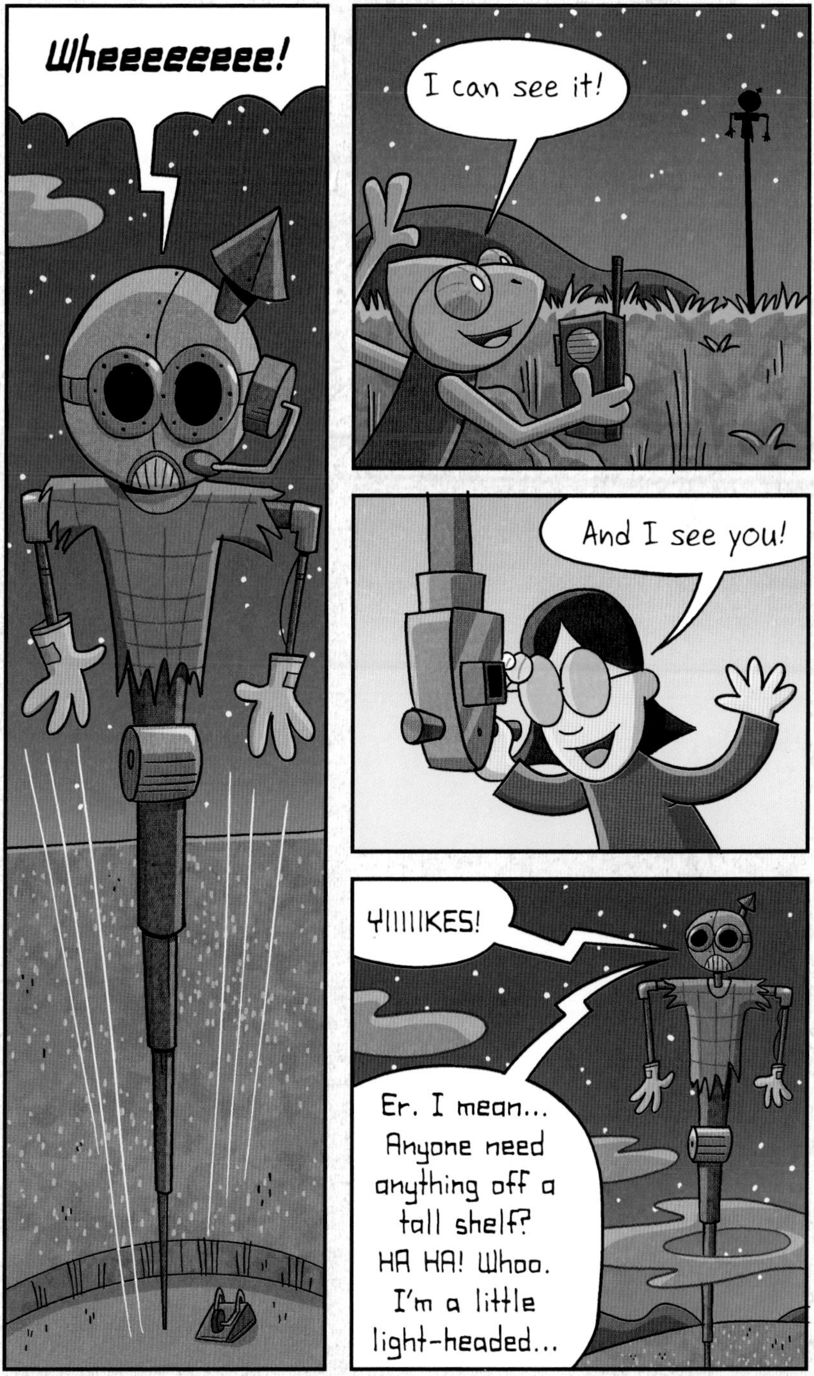
Wheeeeeeee!
I can see it!
And I see you!
YIIIIIKES!
Er. I mean... Anyone need anything off a tall shelf? HA HA! Whoo. I'm a little light-headed...

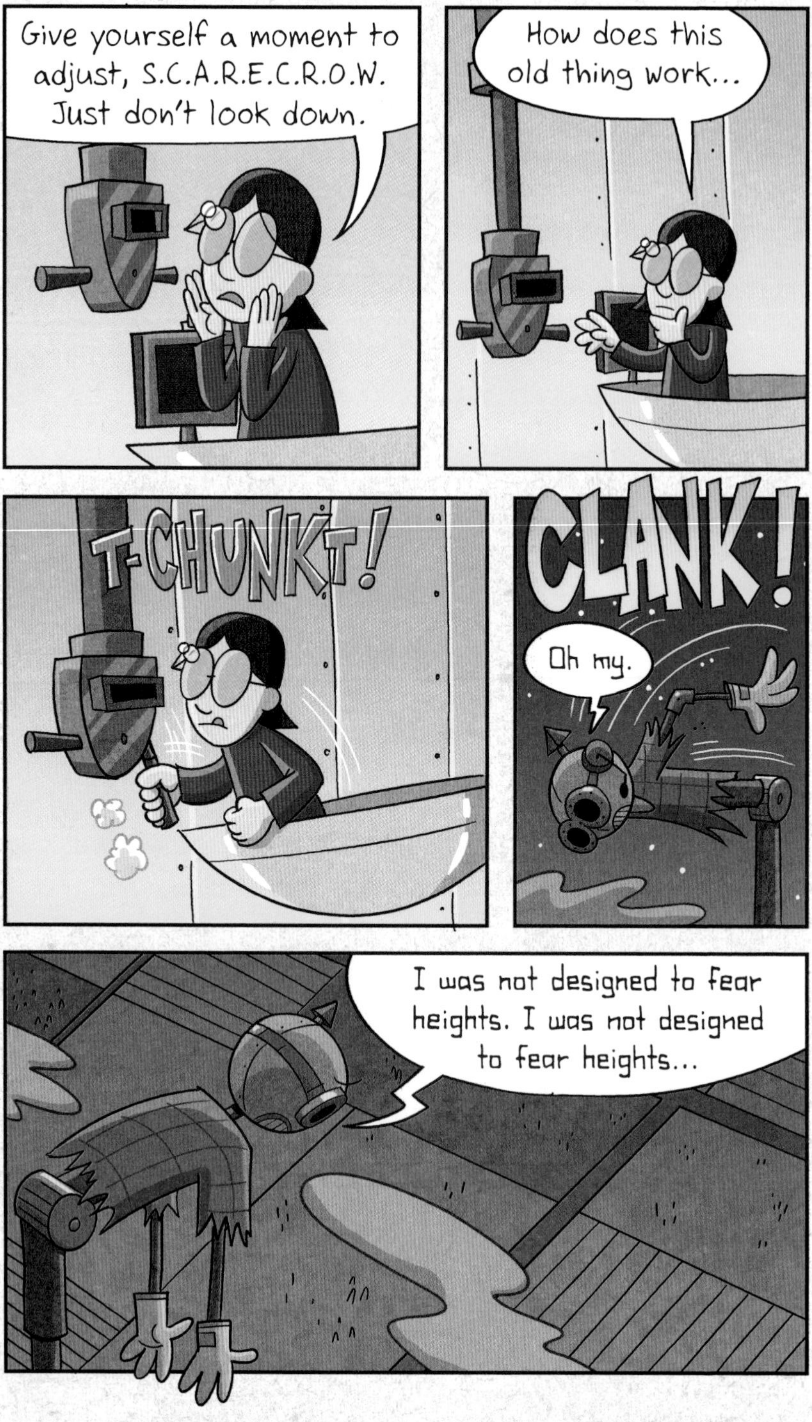
Give yourself a moment to adjust, S.C.A.R.E.C.R.O.W. Just don't look down.
How does this old thing work...
T-CHUNKT!
CLANK!
Oh my.
I was not designed to fear heights. I was not designed to fear heights...

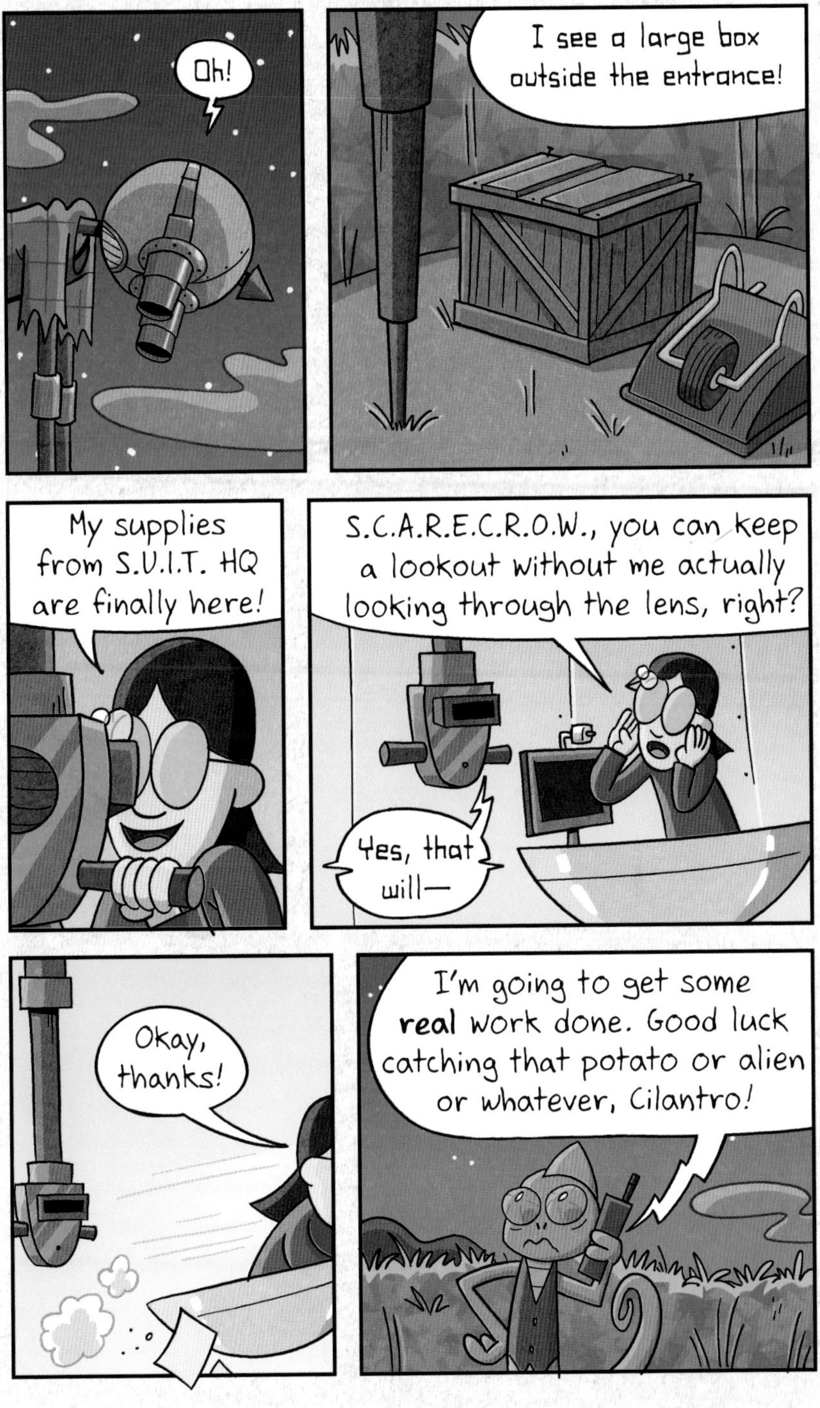
Oh!
I see a large box outside the entrance!
My supplies from S.U.I.T. HQ are finally here!
S.C.A.R.E.C.R.O.W., you can keep a lookout without me actually looking through the lens, right?
Yes, that will—
Okay, thanks!
I'm going to get some **real** work done. Good luck catching that potato or alien or whatever, Cilantro!

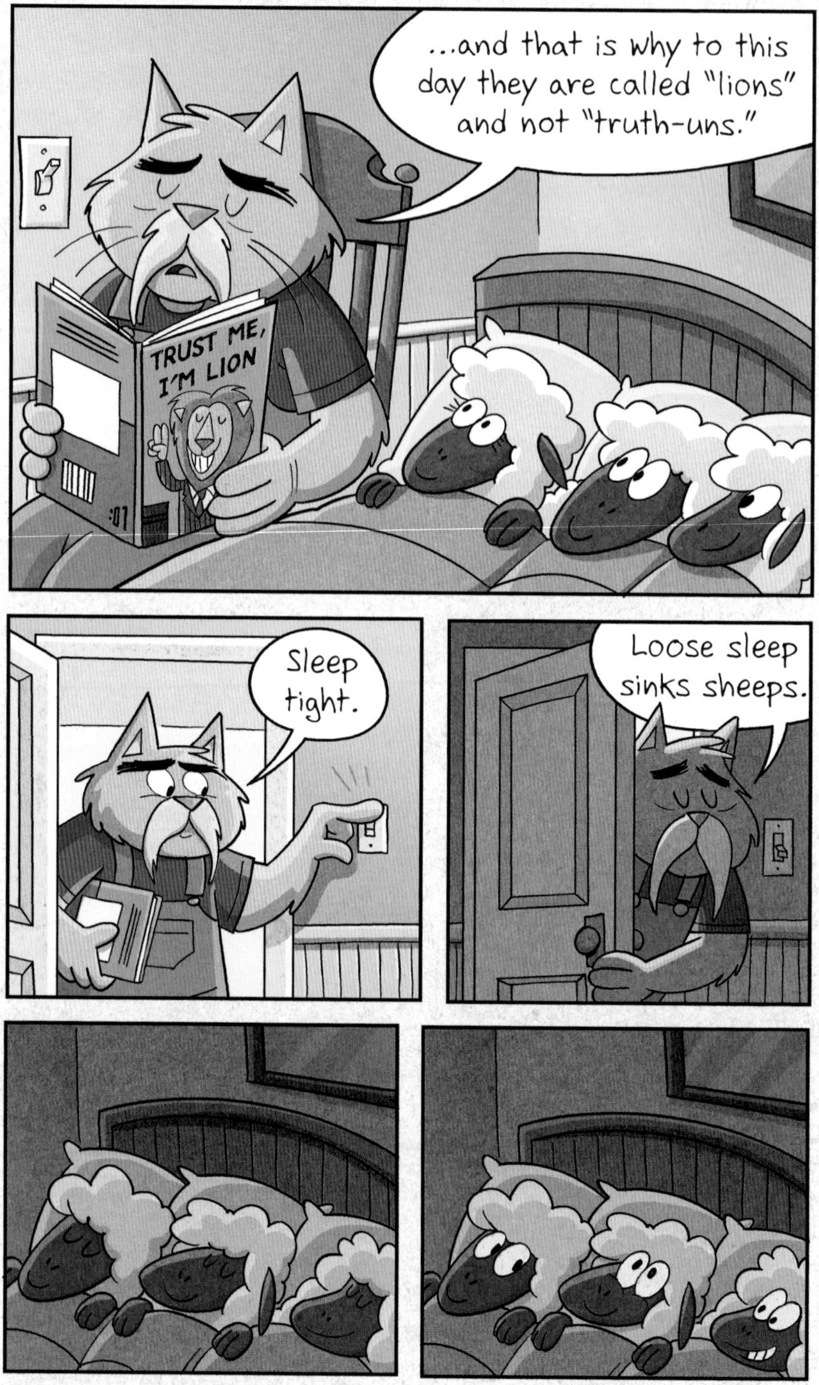
...and that is why to this day they are called "lions" and not "truth-uns."
TRUST ME, I'M LION
Sleep tight.
Loose sleep sinks sheeps.

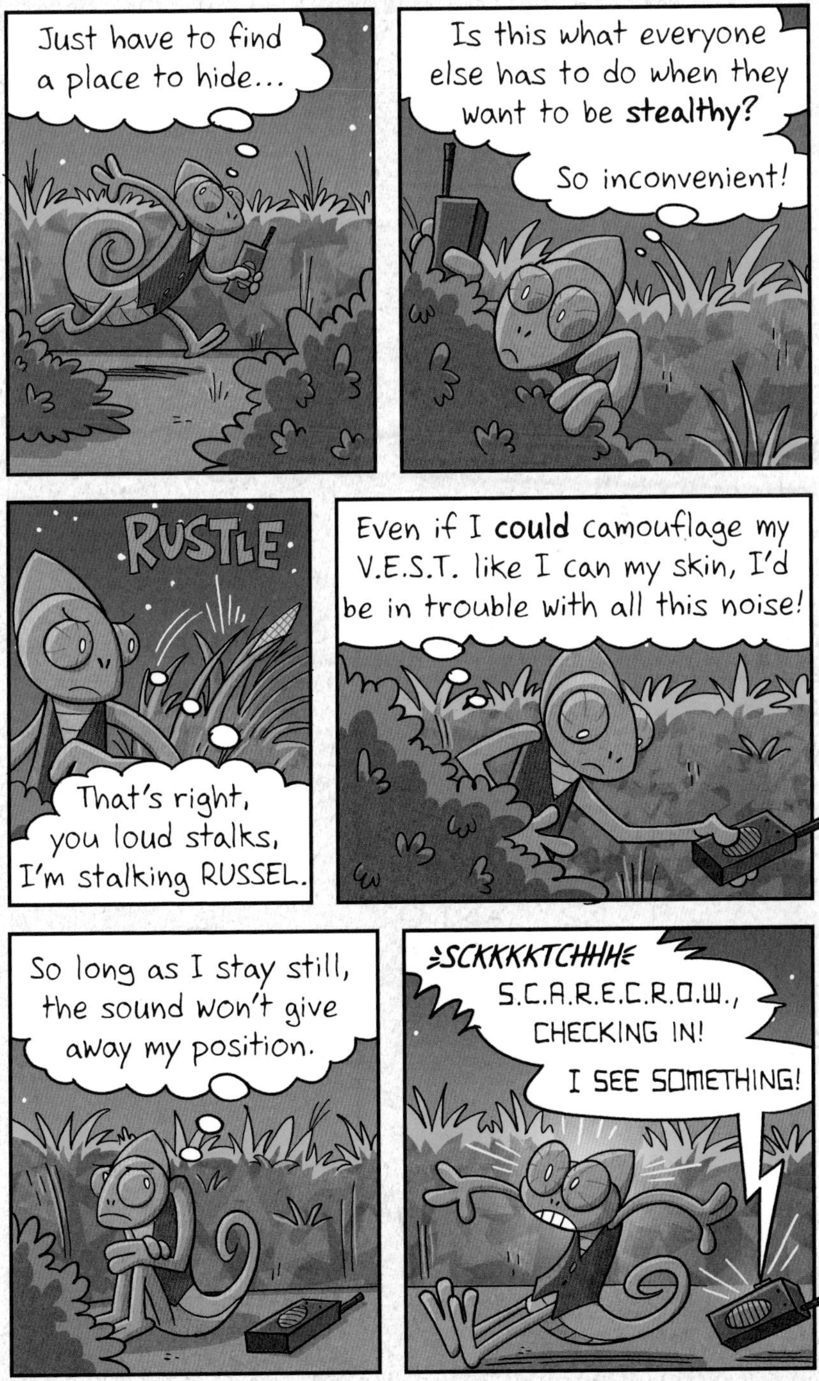
Just have to find a place to hide...
Is this what everyone else has to do when they want to be **stealthy?**
So inconvenient!
RUSTLE
That's right, you loud stalks, I'm stalking RUSSEL.
Even if I **could** camouflage my V.E.S.T. like I can my skin, I'd be in trouble with all this noise!
So long as I stay still, the sound won't give away my position.
SCKKKKTCHHH
S.C.A.R.E.C.R.O.W., CHECKING IN!
I SEE SOMETHING!

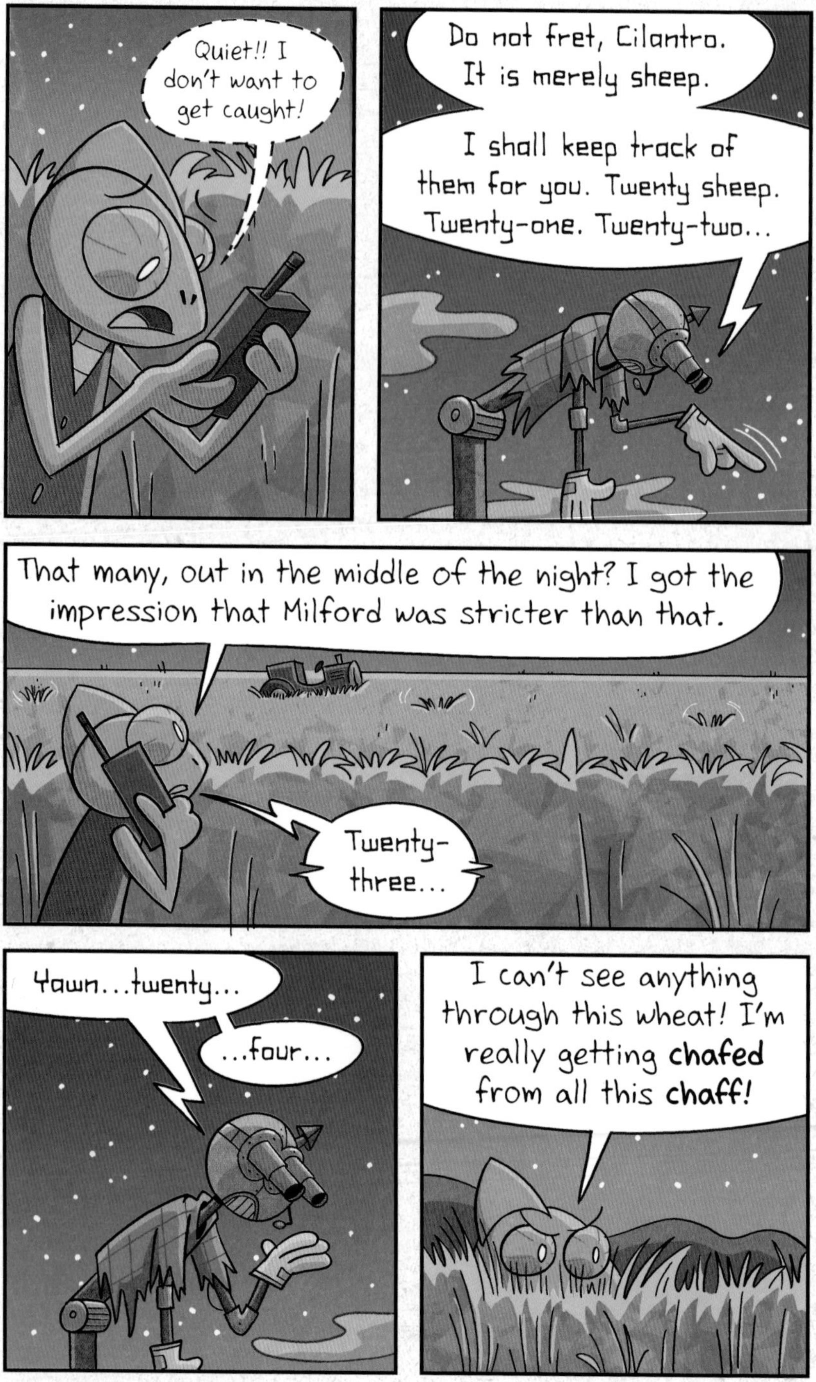
Quiet!! I don't want to get caught!
Do not fret, Cilantro. It is merely sheep.
I shall keep track of them for you. Twenty sheep. Twenty-one. Twenty-two...
That many, out in the middle of the night? I got the impression that Milford was stricter than that.
Twenty-three...
Yawn...twenty...
...four...
I can't see anything through this wheat! I'm really getting **chafed** from all this **chaff**!

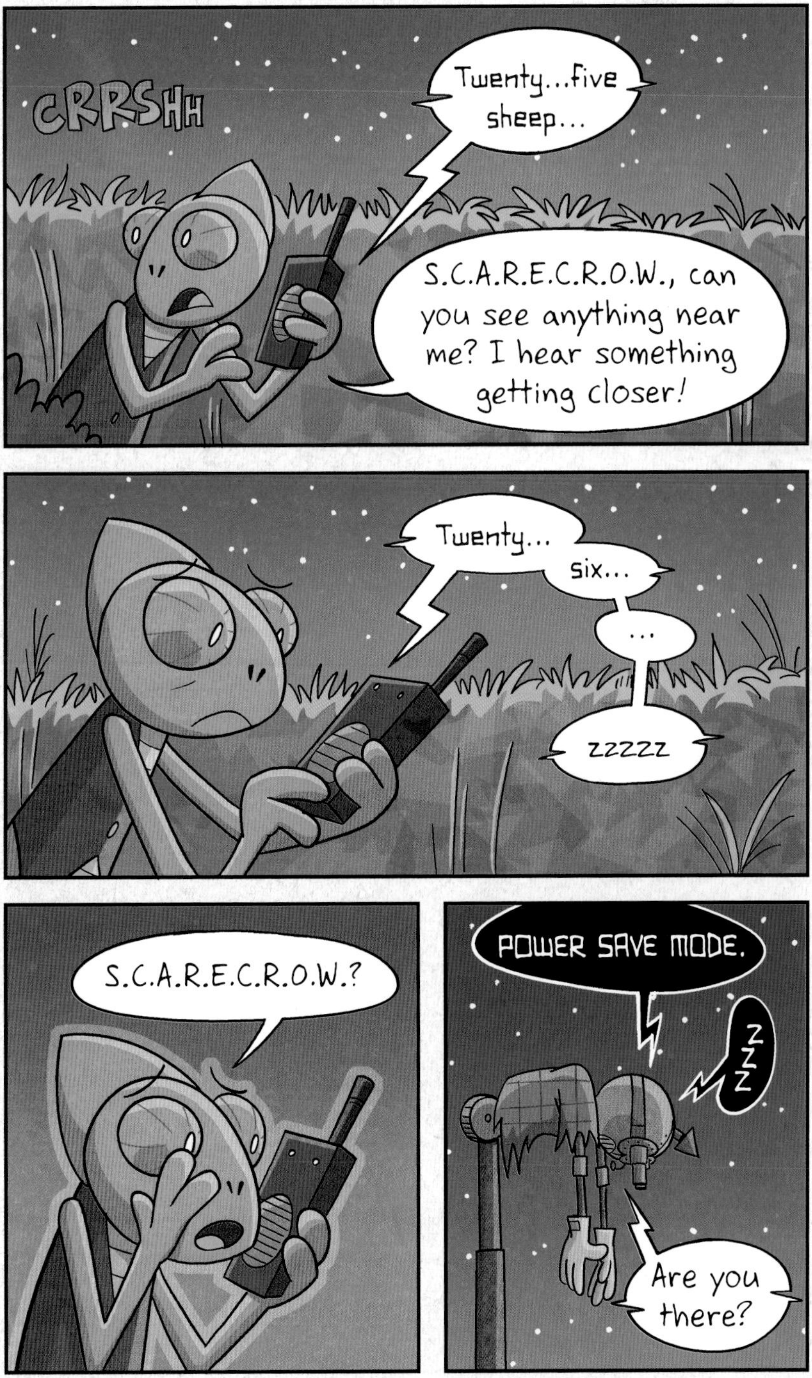
CRRSHH
Twenty...five sheep...
S.C.A.R.E.C.R.O.W., can you see anything near me? I hear something getting closer!
Twenty...
six...
...
zzzzz
S.C.A.R.E.C.R.O.W.?
POWER SAVE MODE.
ZZZ
Are you there?

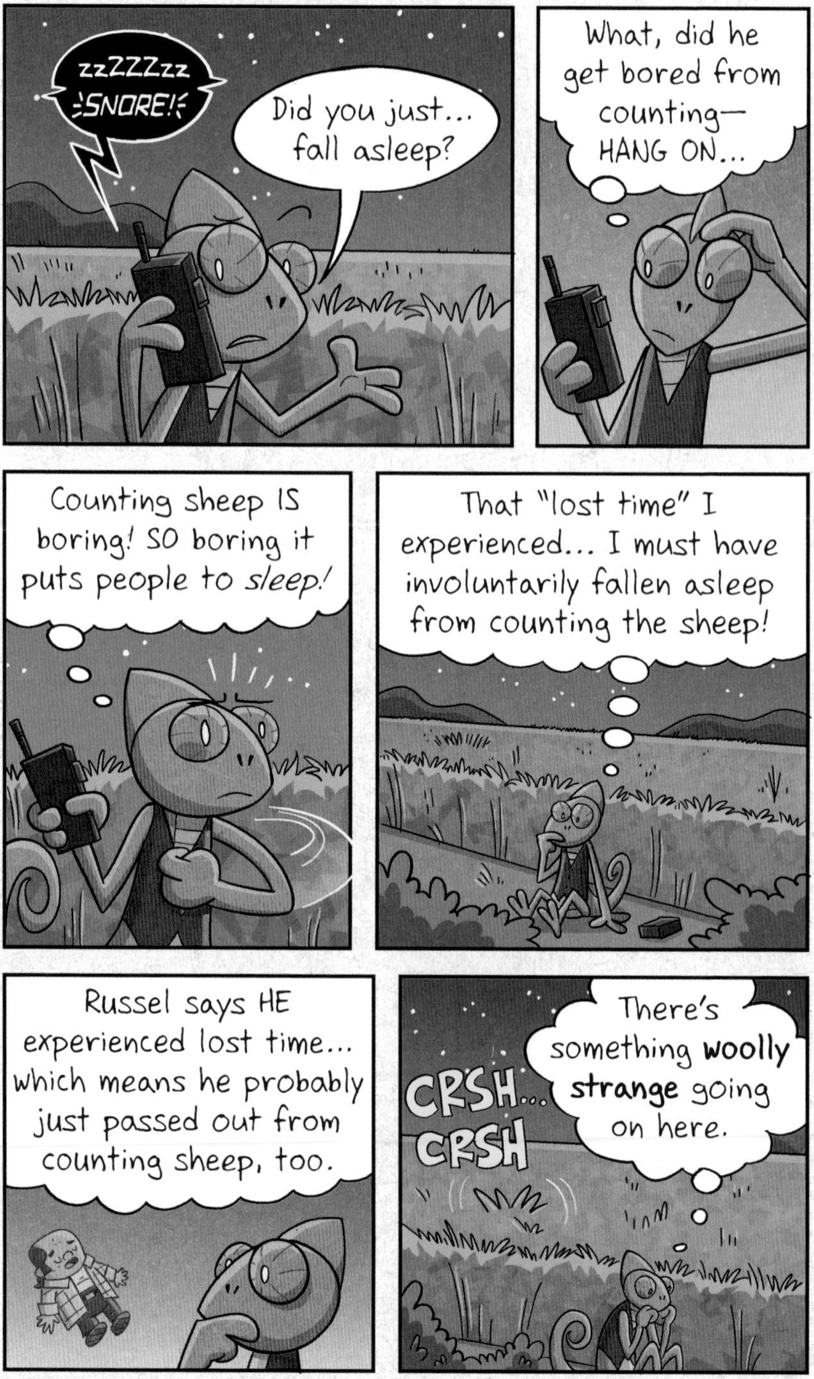
zzZZZzz
SNORE!
Did you just... fall asleep?
What, did he get bored from counting— HANG ON...
Counting sheep IS boring! SO boring it puts people to *sleep!*
That "lost time" I experienced... I must have involuntarily fallen asleep from counting the sheep!
Russel says HE experienced lost time... which means he probably just passed out from counting sheep, too.
CRSH... CRSH
There's something **woolly strange** going on here.

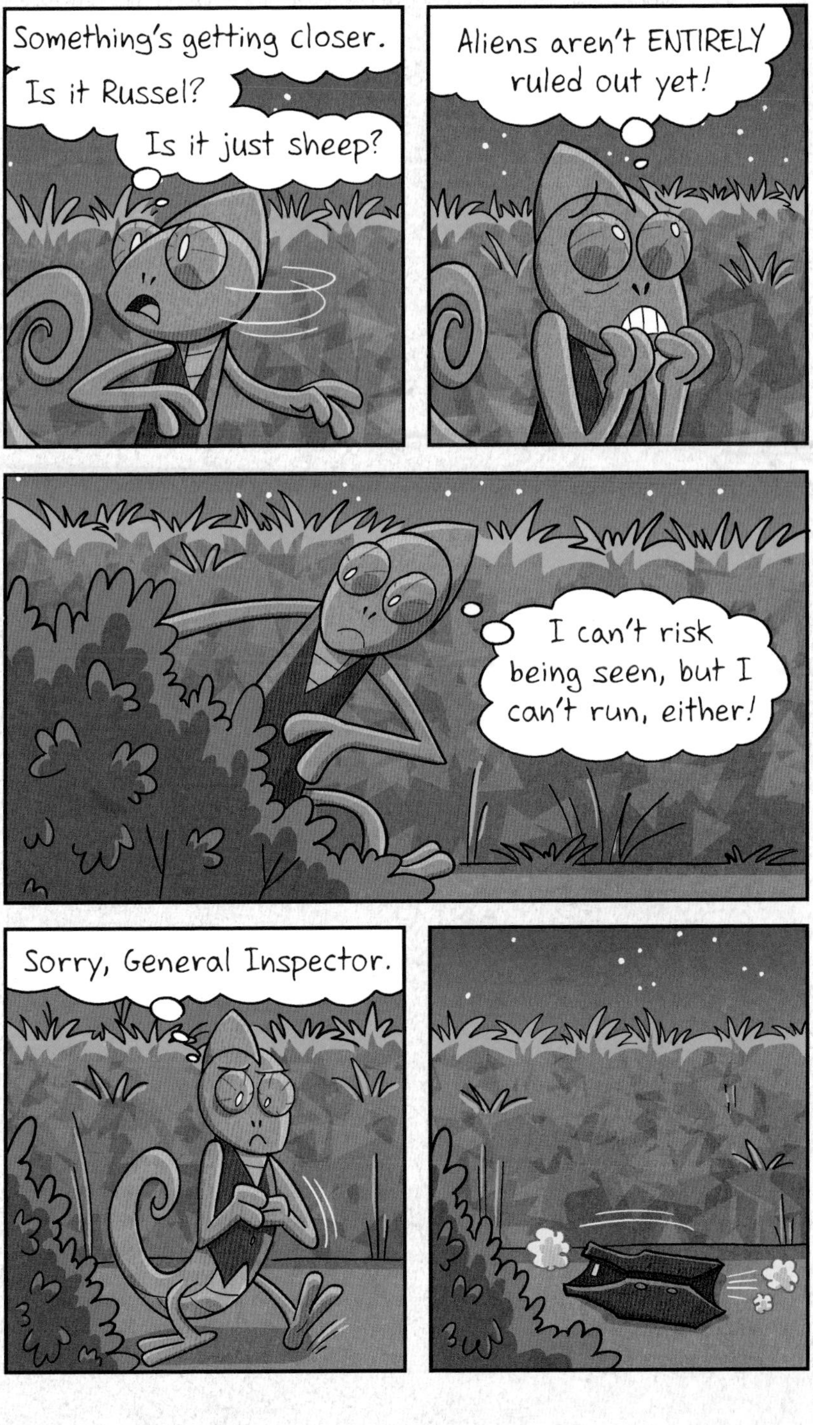
Something's getting closer.
Is it Russel?
Is it just sheep?
Aliens aren't ENTIRELY ruled out yet!
I can't risk being seen, but I can't run, either!
Sorry, General Inspector.

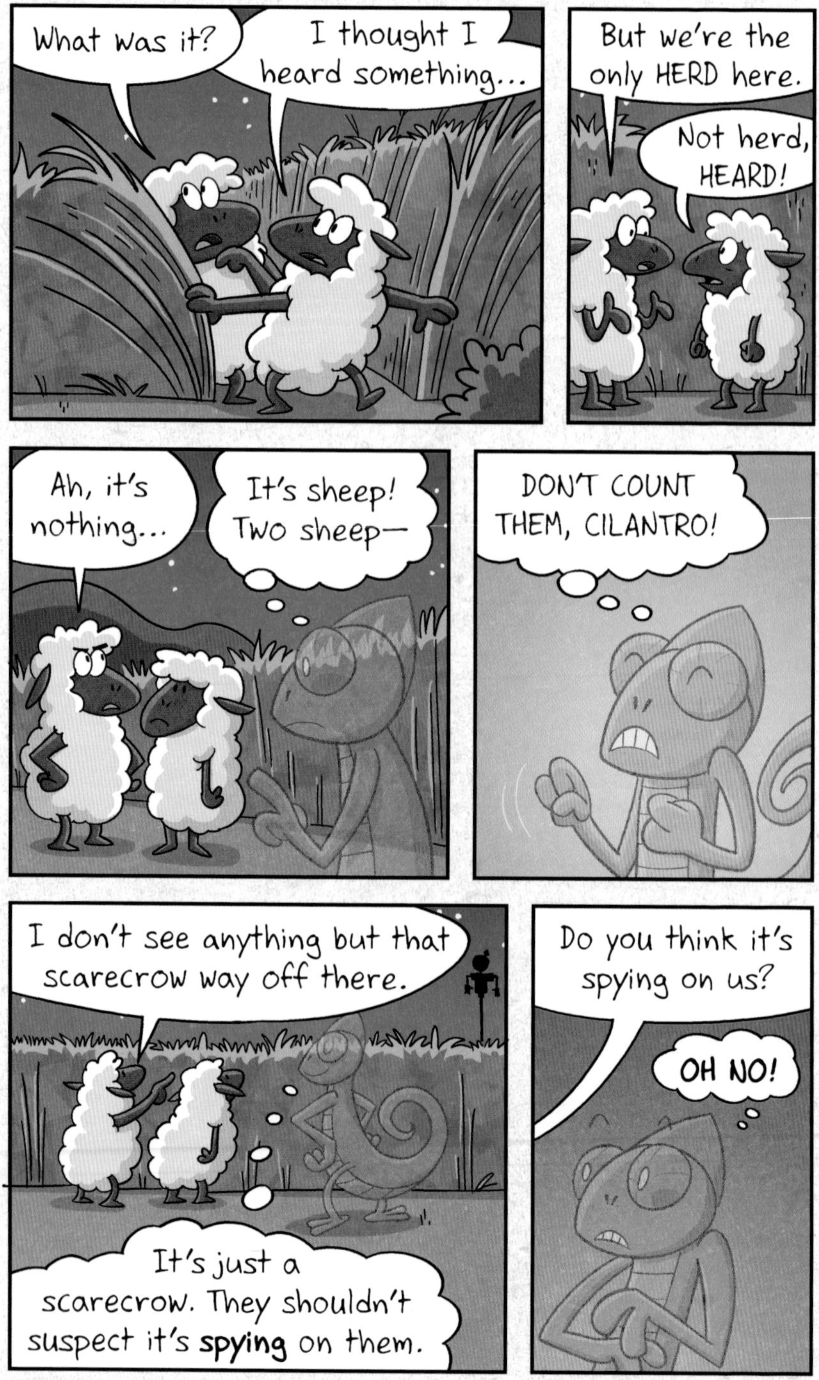

What was it?
I thought I heard something...
But we're the only HERD here.
Not herd, HEARD!
Ah, it's nothing...
It's sheep! Two sheep—
DON'T COUNT THEM, CILANTRO!
I don't see anything but that scarecrow way off there.
It's just a scarecrow. They shouldn't suspect it's **spying** on them.
Do you think it's spying on us?
OH NO!

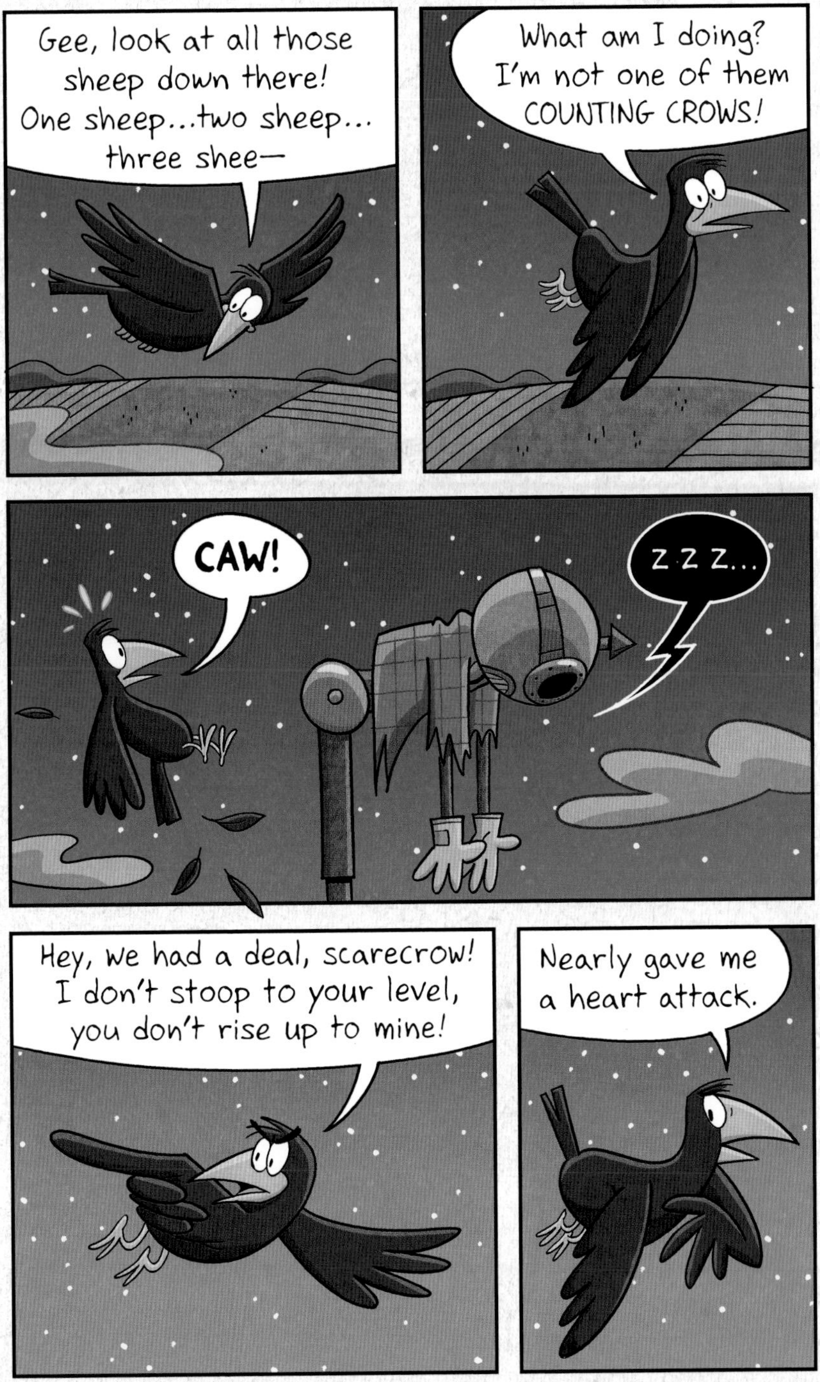
Gee, look at all those sheep down there! One sheep...two sheep... three shee—
What am I doing? I'm not one of them COUNTING CROWS!
CAW!
Z Z Z...
Hey, we had a deal, scarecrow! I don't stoop to your level, you don't rise up to mine!
Nearly gave me a heart attack.

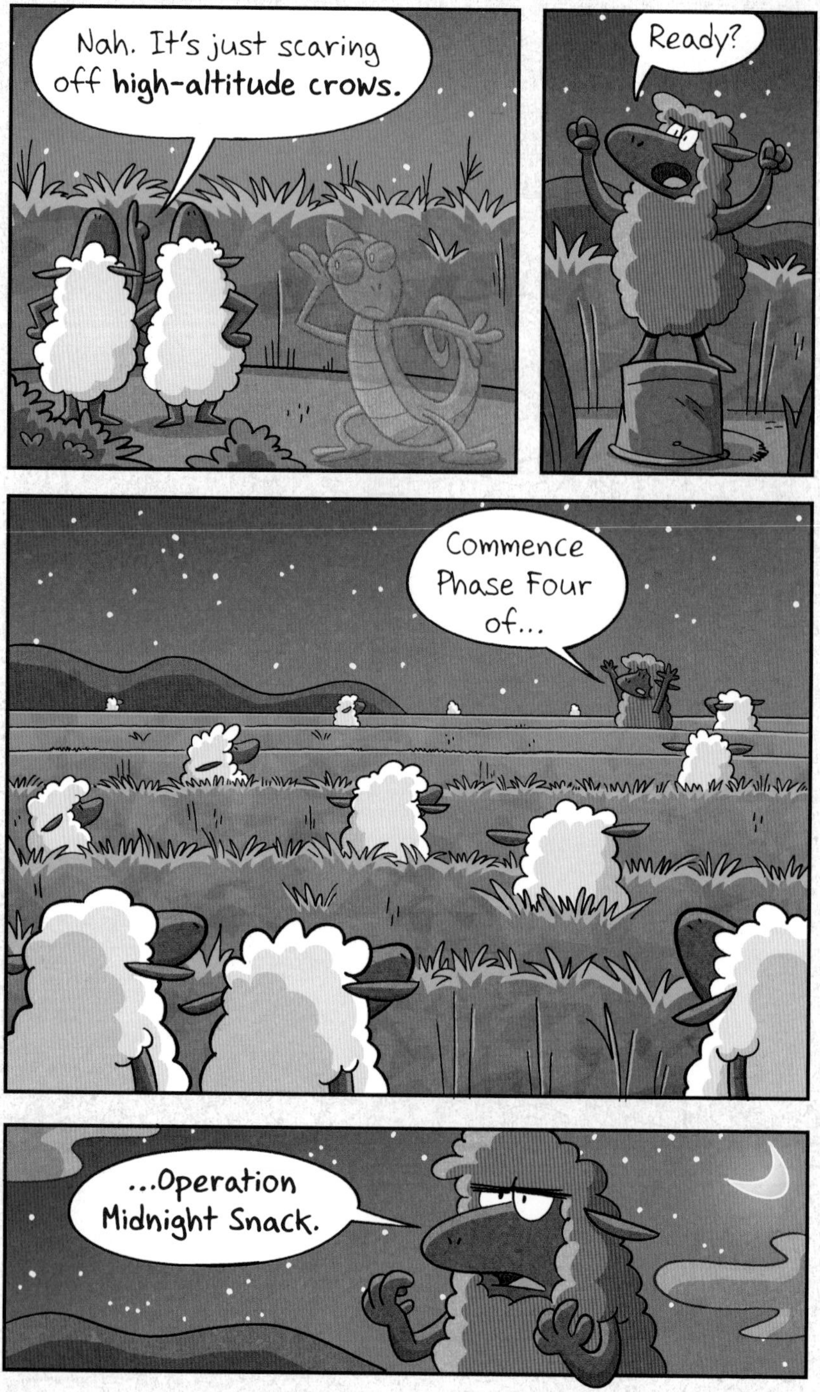
Nah. It's just scaring off **high-altitude crows.**
Ready?
Commence Phase Four of...
...Operation Midnight Snack.

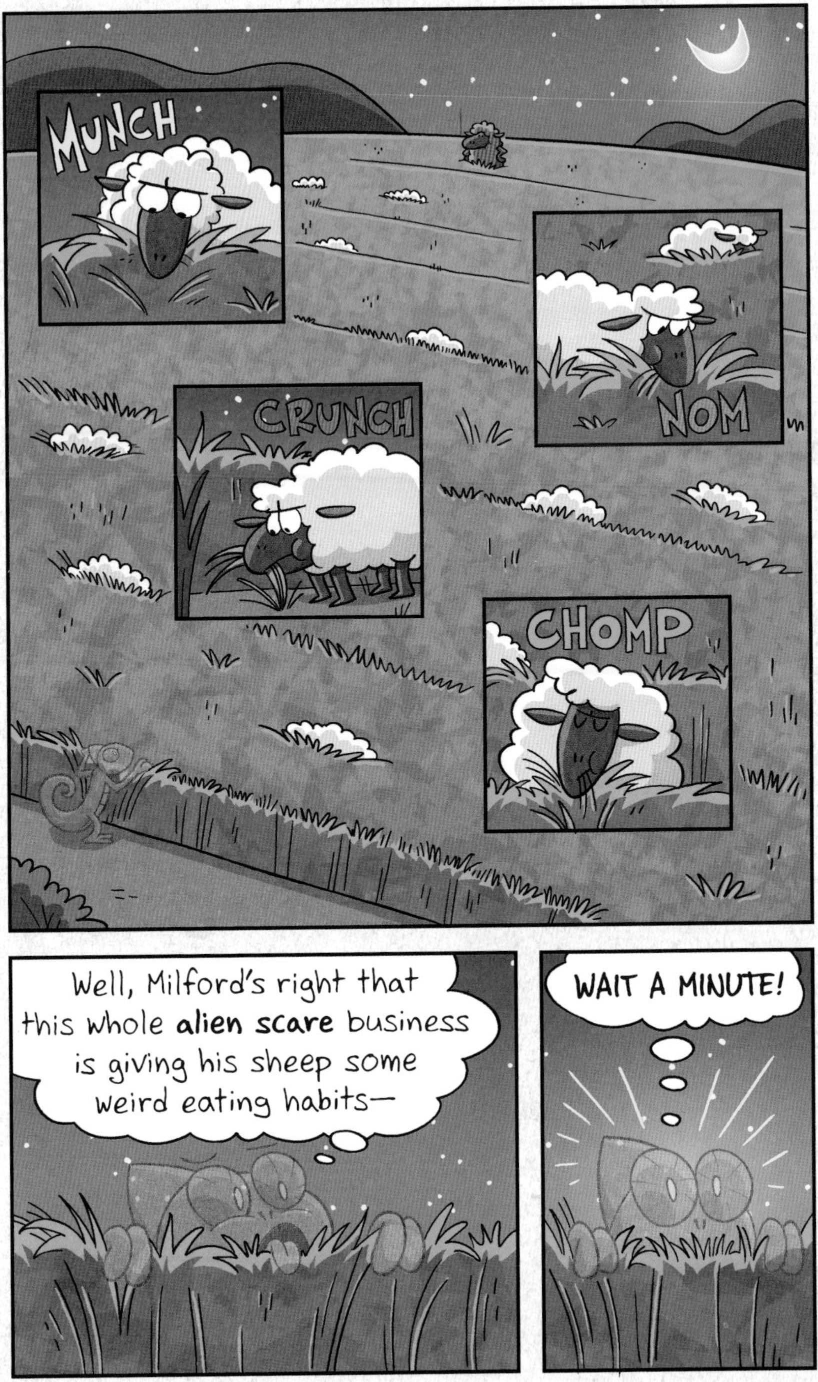
MUNCH
NOM
CRUNCH
CHOMP
Well, Milford's right that this whole **alien scare** business is giving his sheep some weird eating habits—
WAIT A MINUTE!

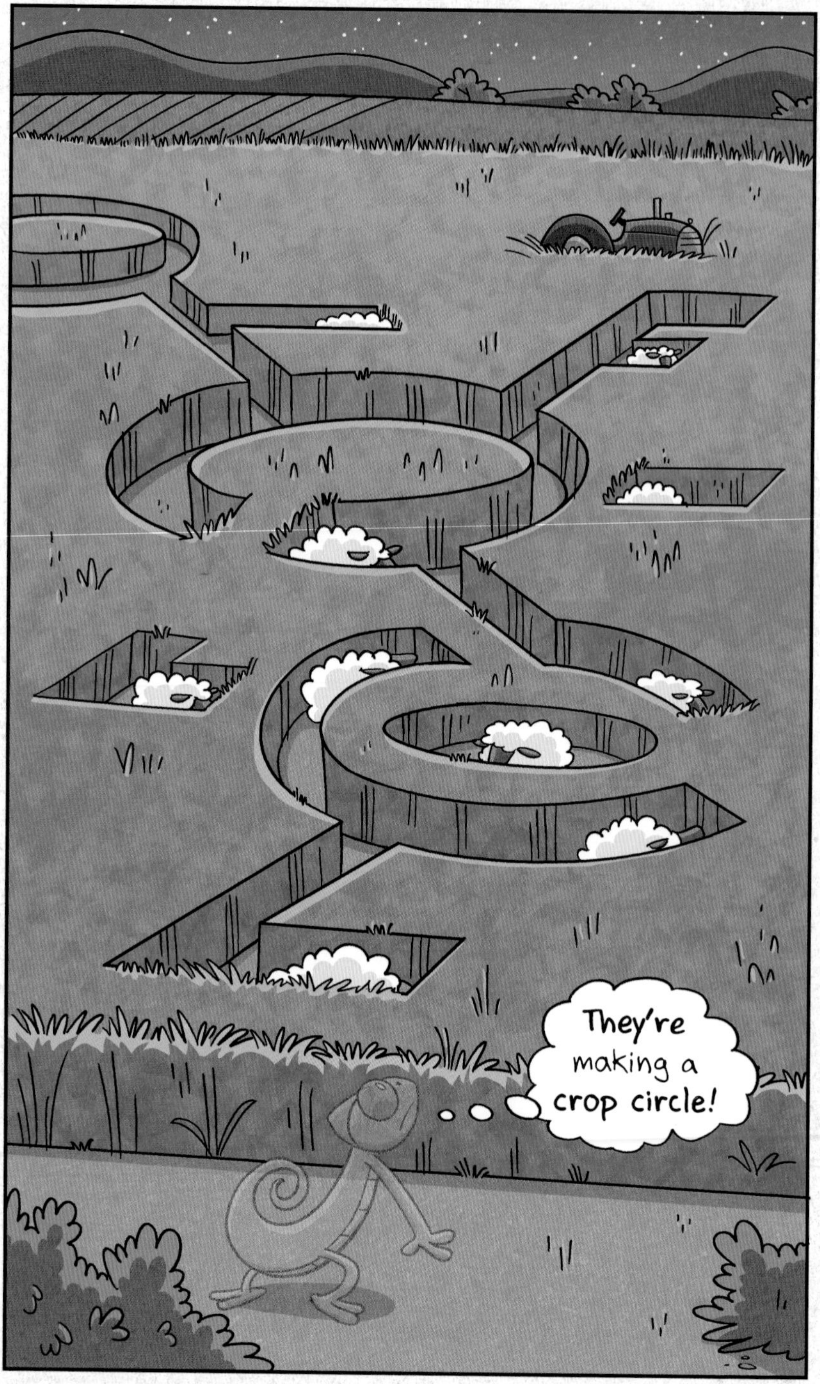
They're making a crop circle!

Chapter 8

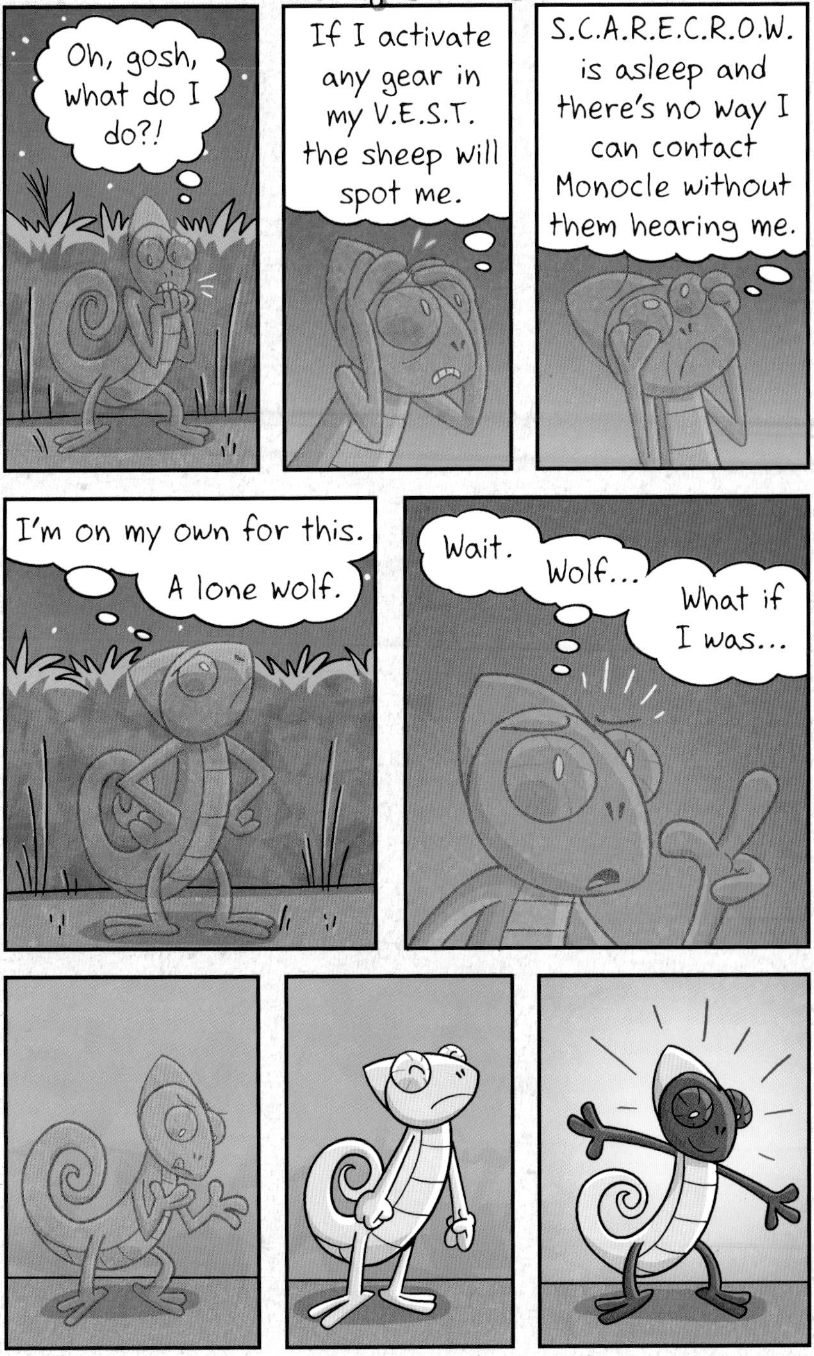
Oh, gosh, what do I do?!
If I activate any gear in my V.E.S.T. the sheep will spot me.
S.C.A.R.E.C.R.O.W. is asleep and there's no way I can contact Monocle without them hearing me.
I'm on my own for this.
A lone wolf.
Wait.
Wolf...
What if I was...

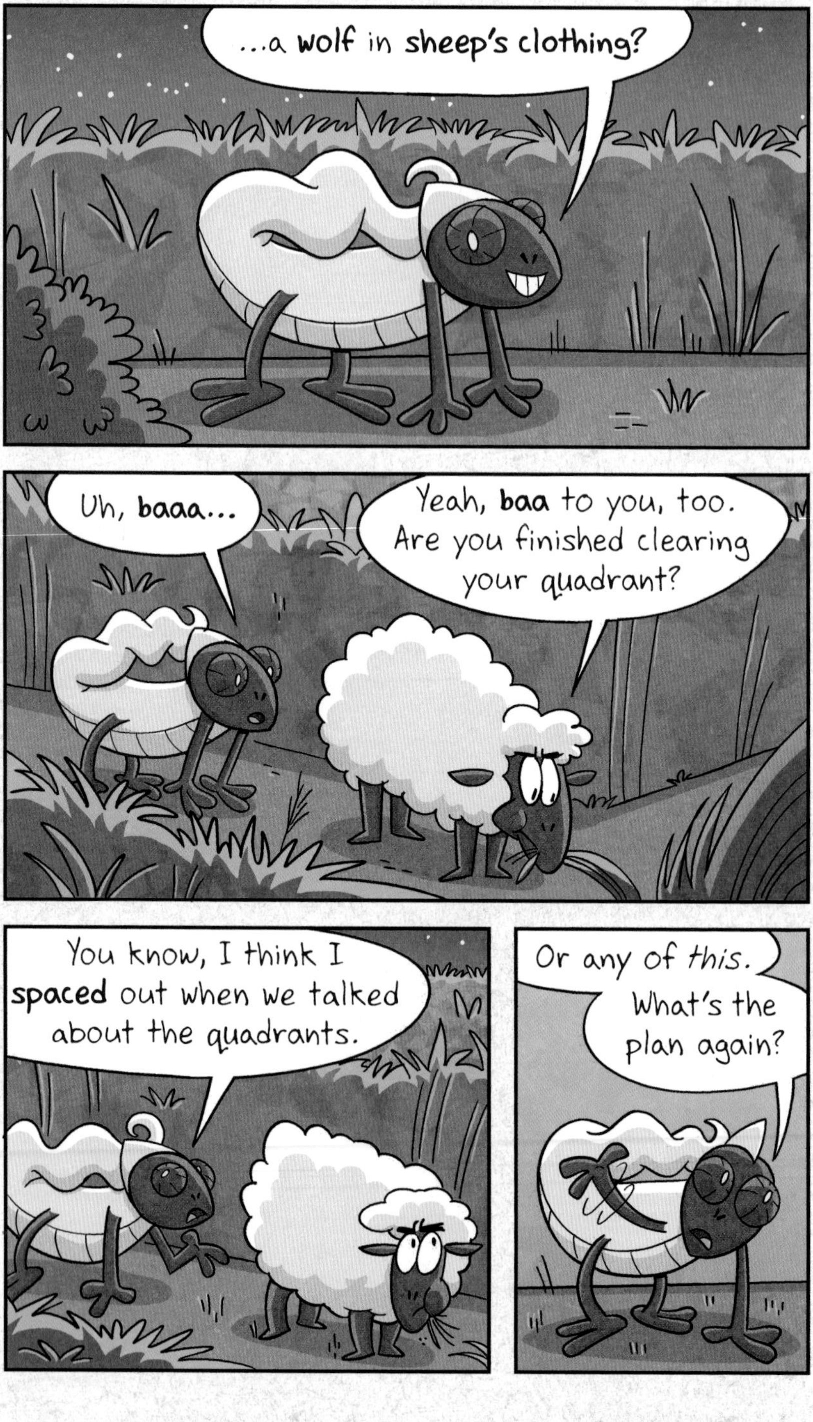
...a wolf in sheep's clothing?
Uh, baaa...
Yeah, baa to you, too. Are you finished clearing your quadrant?
You know, I think I spaced out when we talked about the quadrants.
Or any of this.
What's the plan again?

The **plan** is to craft large, strange patterns and circles in the fields, with each sheep tending to a small portion of an impressive whole.

No sheep has **ever** done **anything** like this before. No one would ever suspect US.

"SHEEP are nothing but FOLLOWERS," they say.

And with no other way for them to explain where these came from, they assume it must be ALIENS!

And then they freak out.

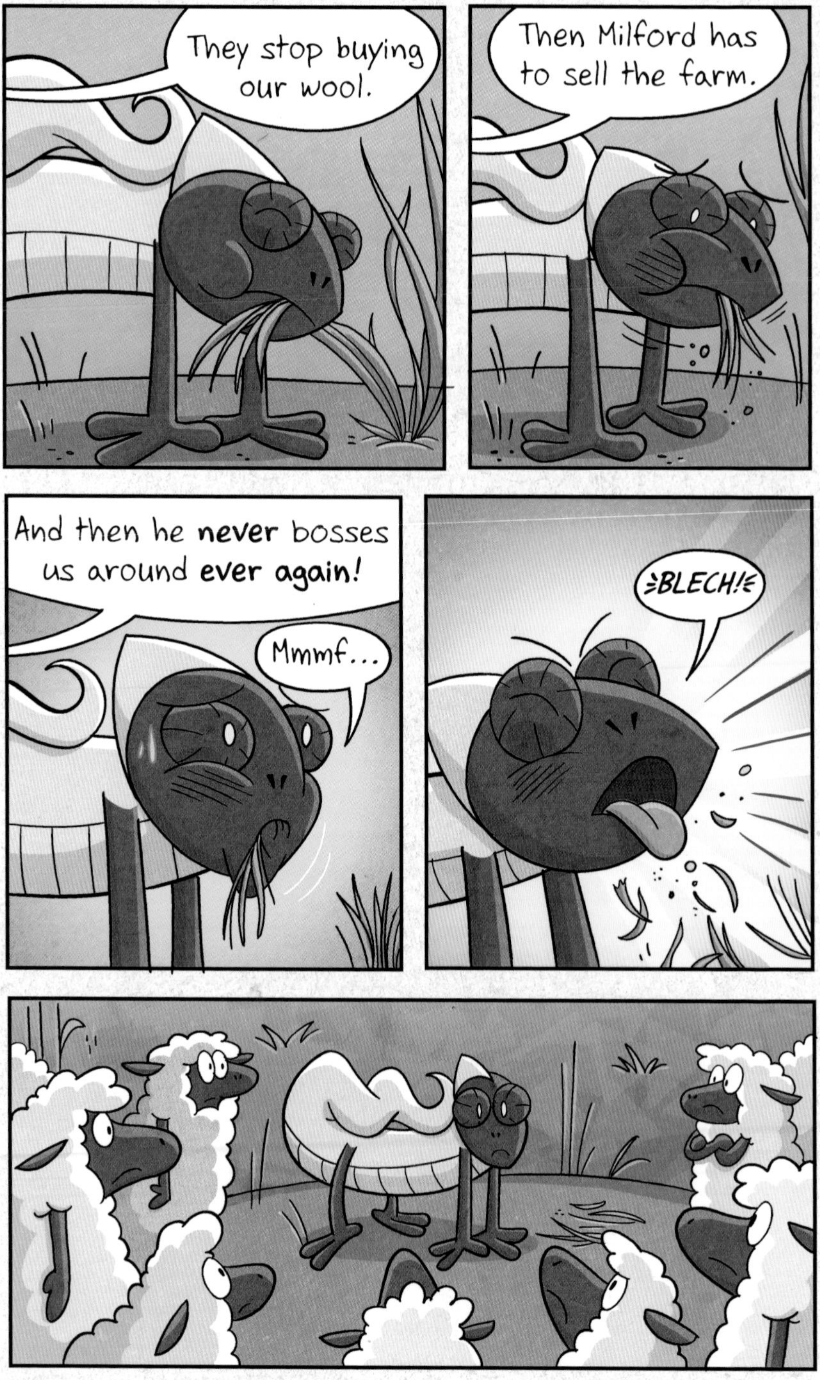
They stop buying our wool.
Then Milford has to sell the farm.
And then he **never** bosses us around **ever again**!
Mmmf...
BLECH!

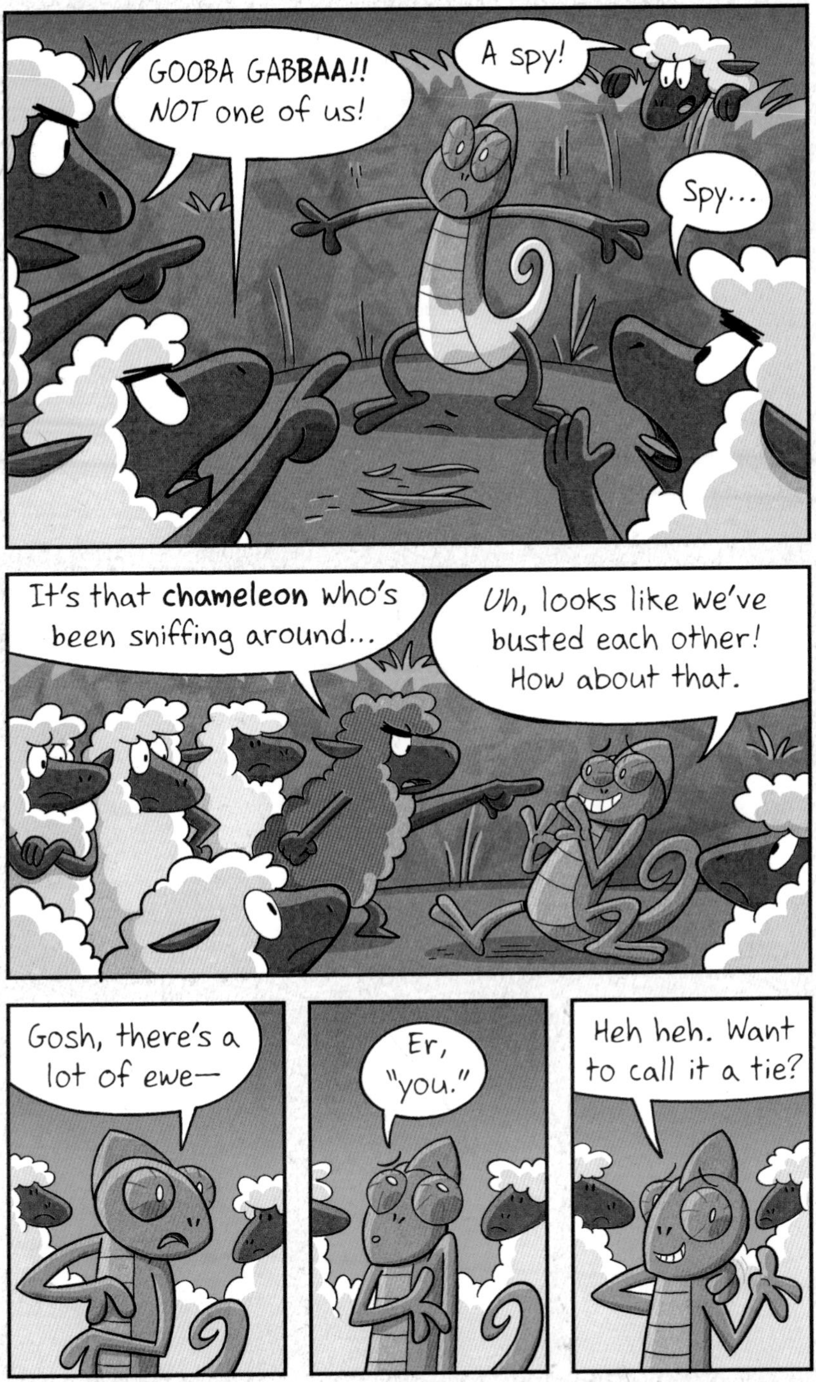
GOOBA GABBAA!! NOT one of us!
A spy!
Spy...
It's that chameleon who's been sniffing around...
Uh, looks like we've busted each other! How about that.
Gosh, there's a lot of ewe—
Er, "you."
Heh heh. Want to call it a tie?

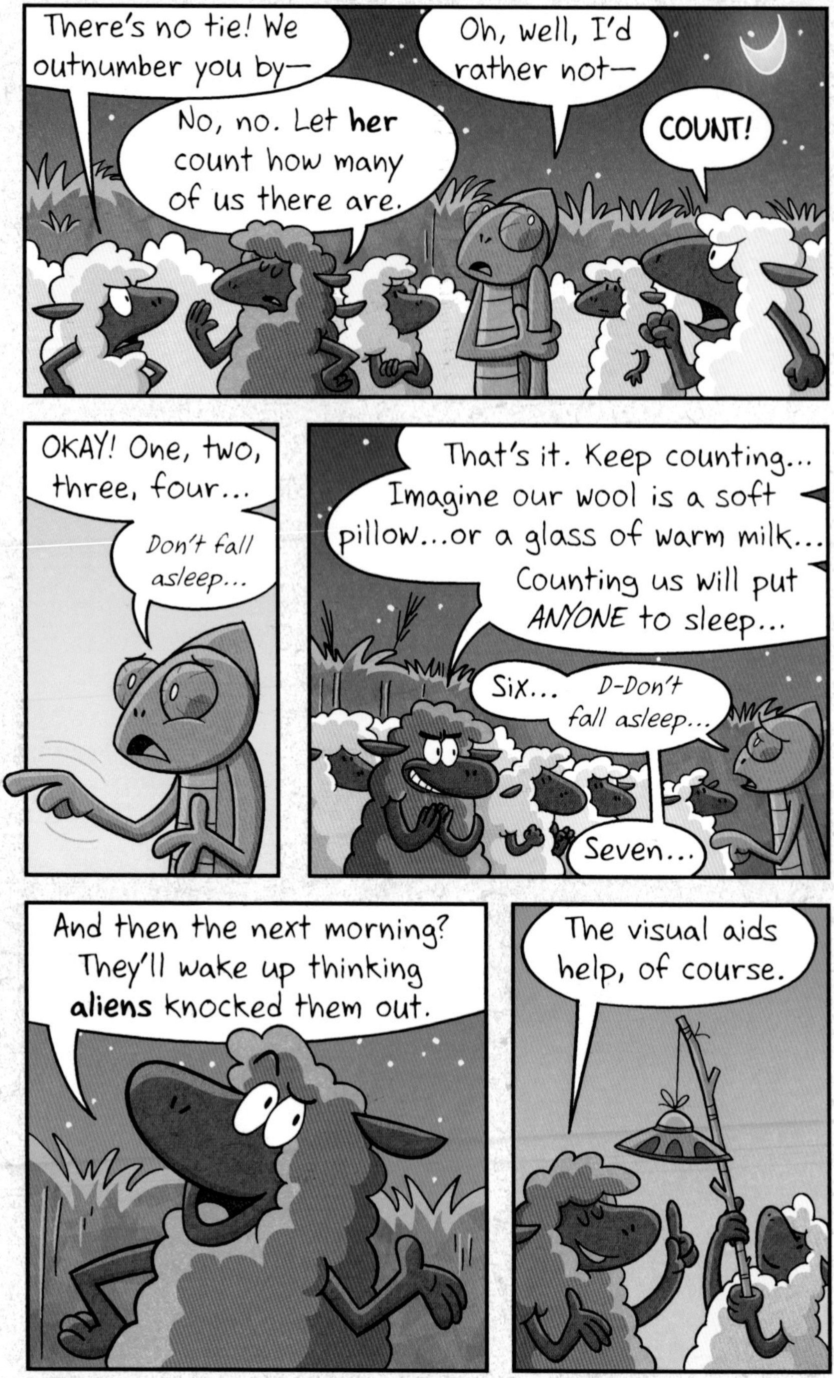

There's no tie! We outnumber you by—
No, no. Let **her** count how many of us there are.
Oh, well, I'd rather not—
COUNT!
OKAY! One, two, three, four...
Don't fall asleep...
That's it. Keep counting... Imagine our wool is a soft pillow...or a glass of warm milk...
Counting us will put *ANYONE* to sleep...
Six...
D-Don't fall asleep...
Seven...
And then the next morning? They'll wake up thinking **aliens** knocked them out.
The visual aids help, of course.

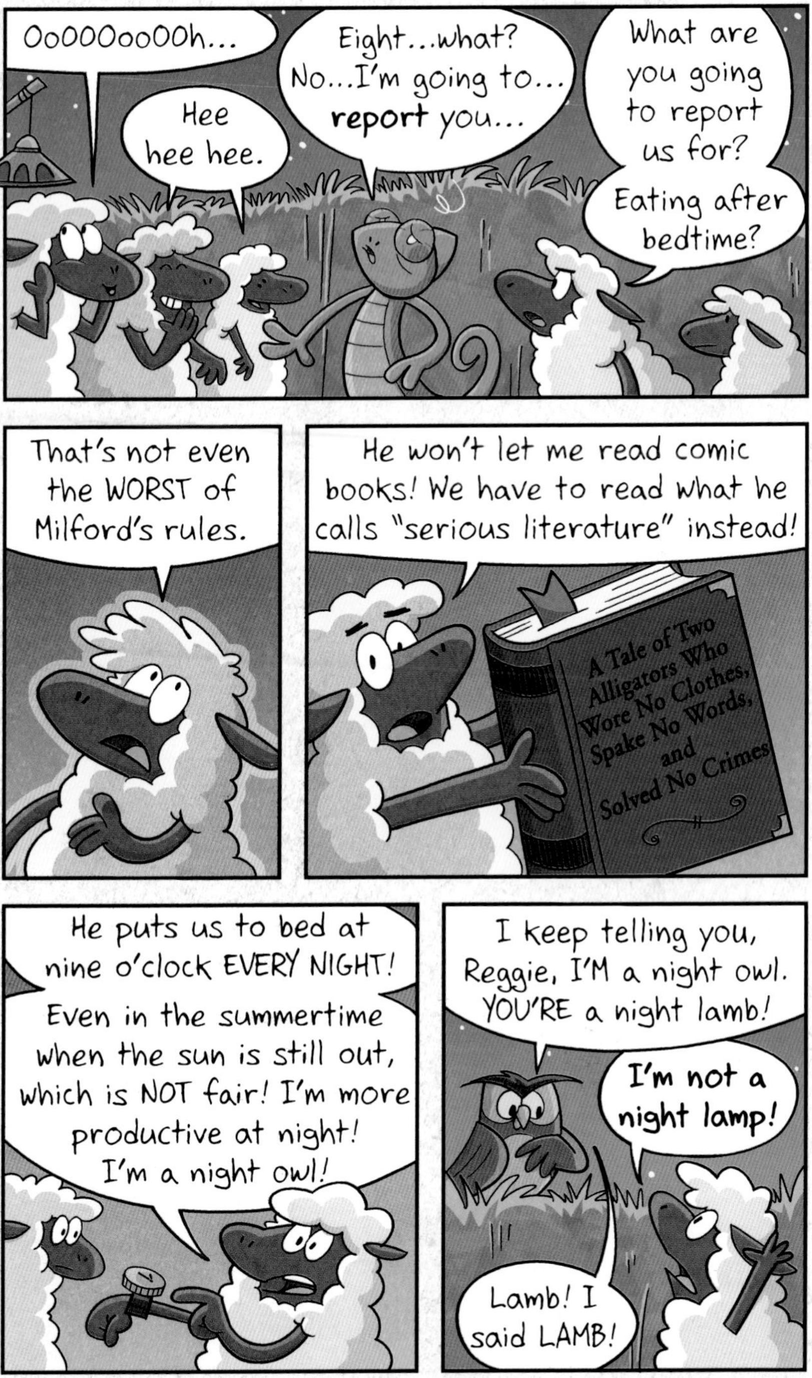
OoOOOooOOh...
Hee hee hee.
Eight...what? No...I'm going to... **report** you...
What are you going to report us for?
Eating after bedtime?
That's not even the WORST of Milford's rules.
He won't let me read comic books! We have to read what he calls "serious literature" instead!
A Tale of Two Alligators Who Wore No Clothes, Spake No Words, and Solved No Crimes
He puts us to bed at nine o'clock EVERY NIGHT!
Even in the summertime when the sun is still out, which is NOT fair! I'm more productive at night! I'm a night owl!
I keep telling you, Reggie, I'M a night owl. YOU'RE a night lamb!
I'm not a night lamp!
Lamb! I said LAMB!

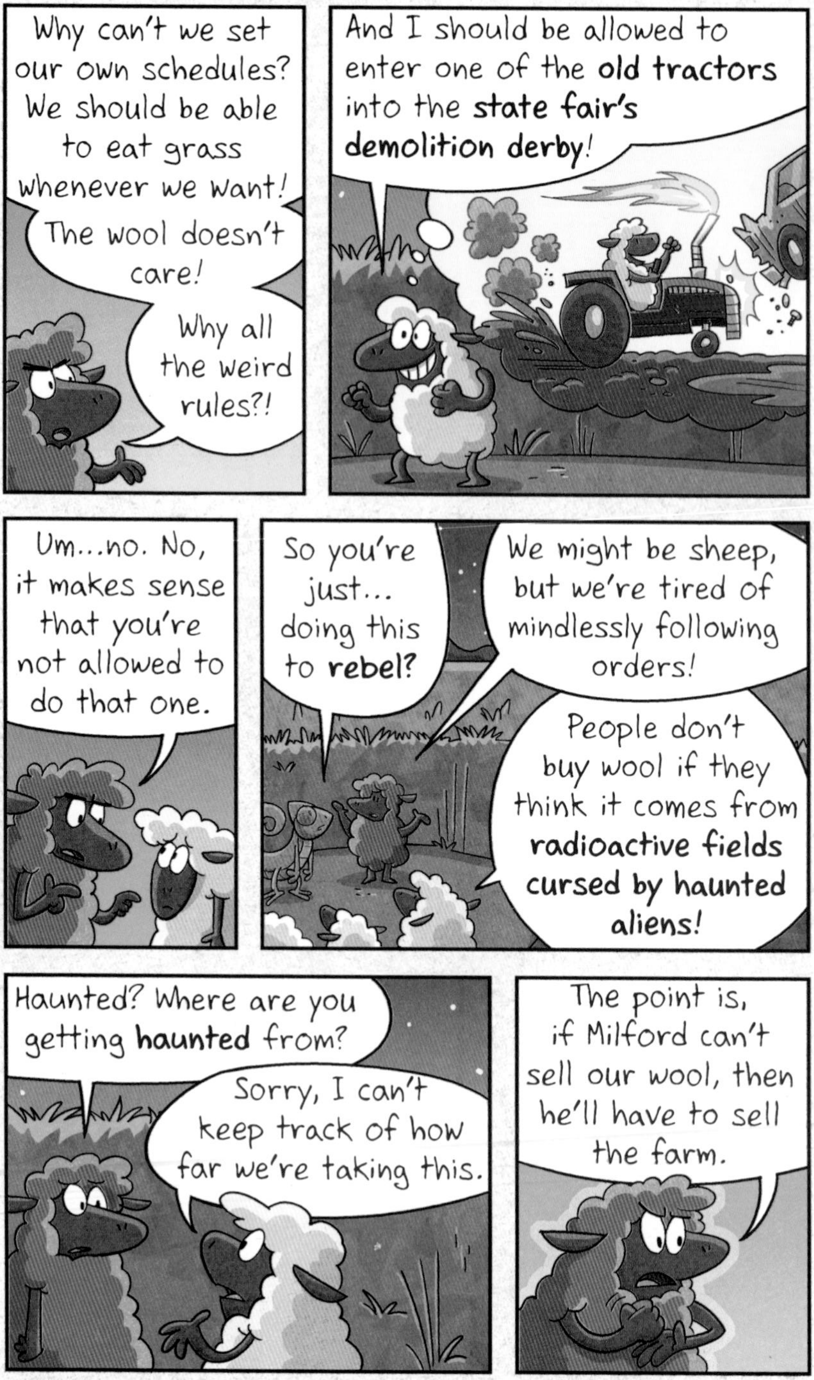

Why can't we set our own schedules? We should be able to eat grass whenever we want!
The wool doesn't care!
Why all the weird rules?!
And I should be allowed to enter one of the **old tractors** into the **state fair's demolition derby**!
Um...no. No, it makes sense that you're not allowed to do that one.
So you're just... doing this to **rebel?**
We might be sheep, but we're tired of mindlessly following orders!
People don't buy wool if they think it comes from **radioactive fields cursed by haunted aliens!**
Haunted? Where are you getting **haunted** from?
Sorry, I can't keep track of how far we're taking this.
The point is, if Milford can't sell our wool, then he'll have to sell the farm.

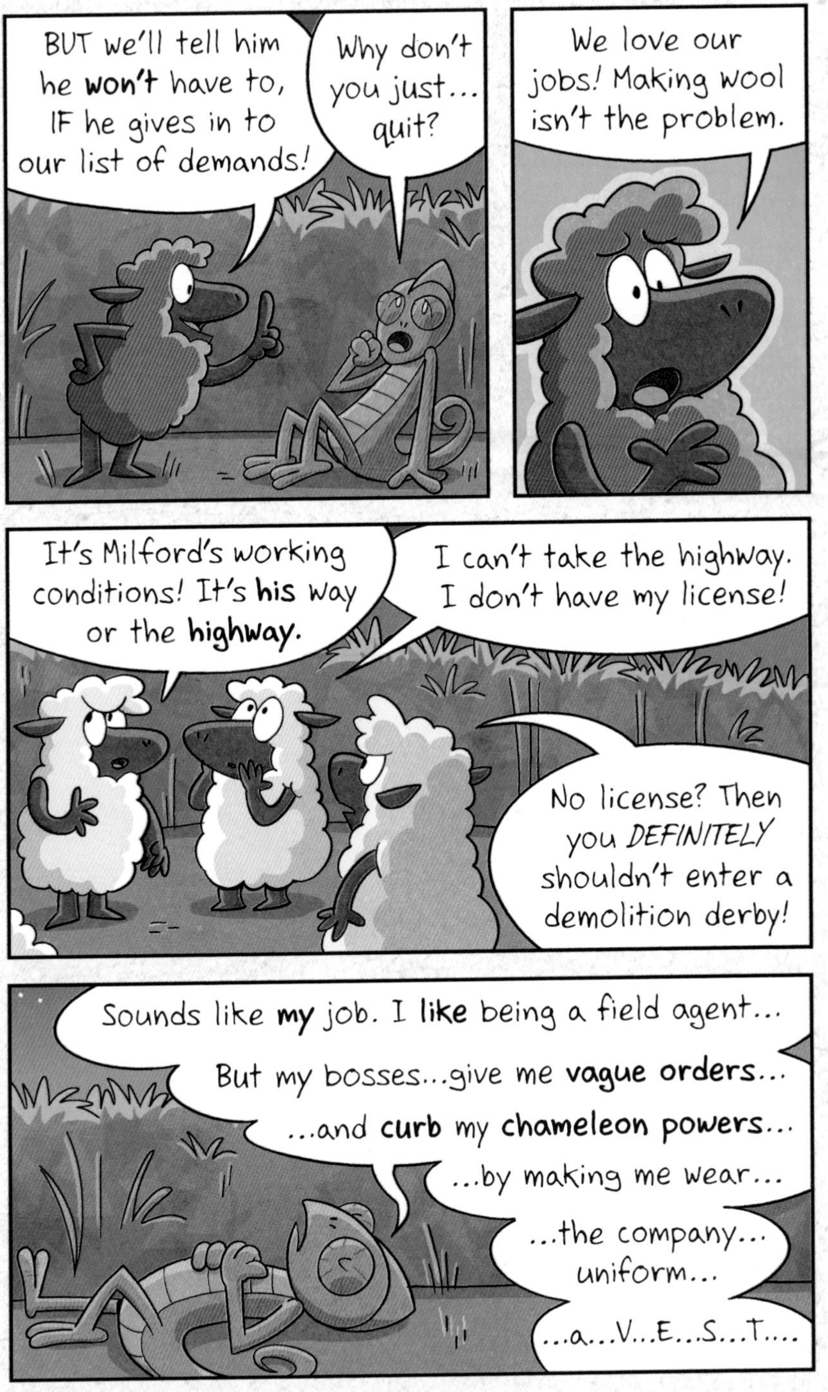
BUT we'll tell him he **won't** have to, IF he gives in to our list of demands!
Why don't you just... quit?
We love our jobs! Making wool isn't the problem.
It's Milford's working conditions! It's **his** way or the **highway**.
I can't take the highway. I don't have my license!
No license? Then you *DEFINITELY* shouldn't enter a demolition derby!
Sounds like **my** job. I **like** being a field agent...
But my bosses...give me **vague orders**...
...and **curb** my **chameleon powers**...
...by making me wear...
...the company... uniform...
...a...V...E...S...T....

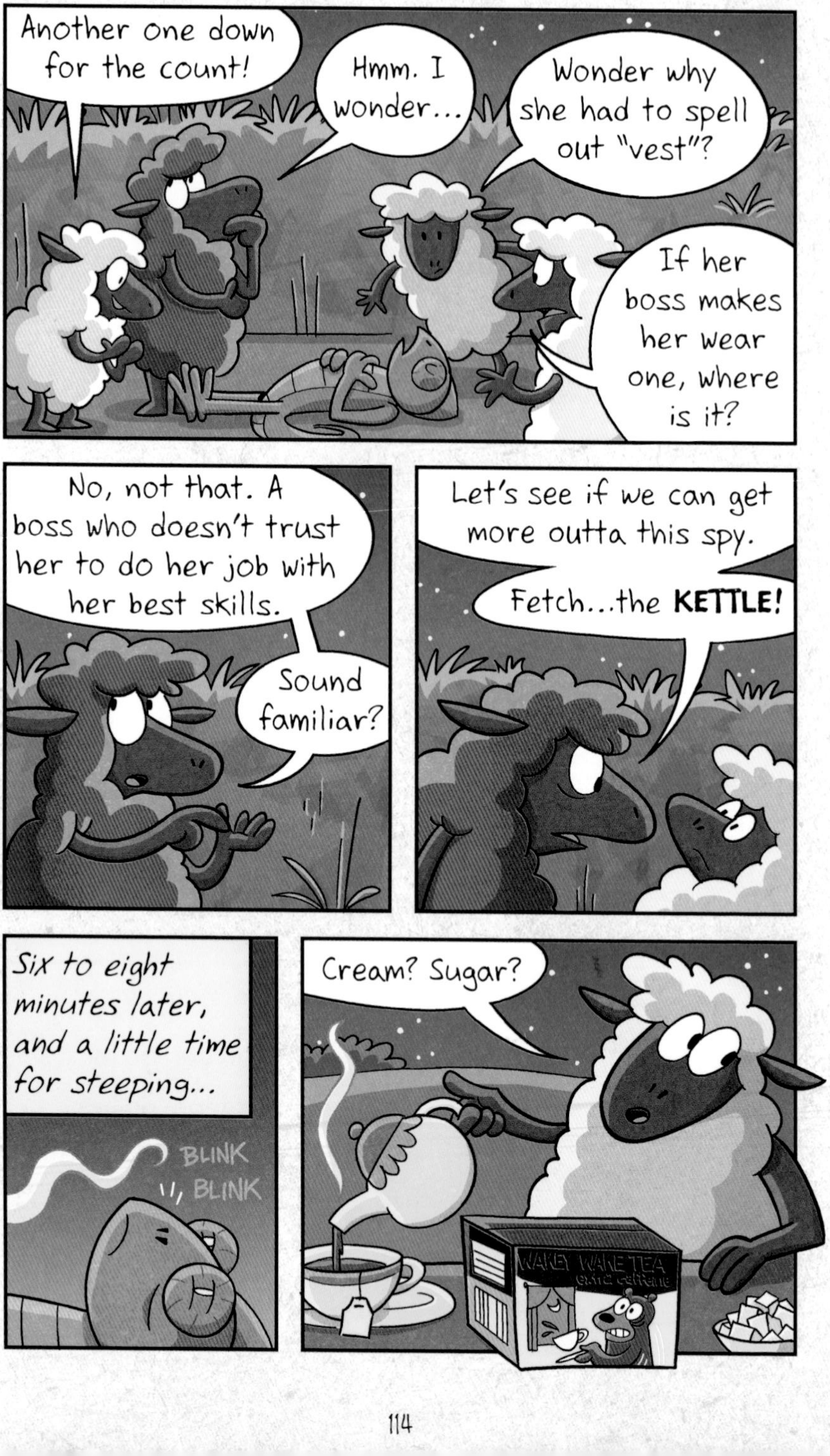
Another one down for the count!
Hmm. I wonder...
Wonder why she had to spell out "vest"?
If her boss makes her wear one, where is it?
No, not that. A boss who doesn't trust her to do her job with her best skills.
Sound familiar?
Let's see if we can get more outta this spy.
Fetch...the **KETTLE!**
Six to eight minutes later, and a little time for steeping...
BLINK
BLINK
Cream? Sugar?
WAKEY WAKE TEA
extra caffeine

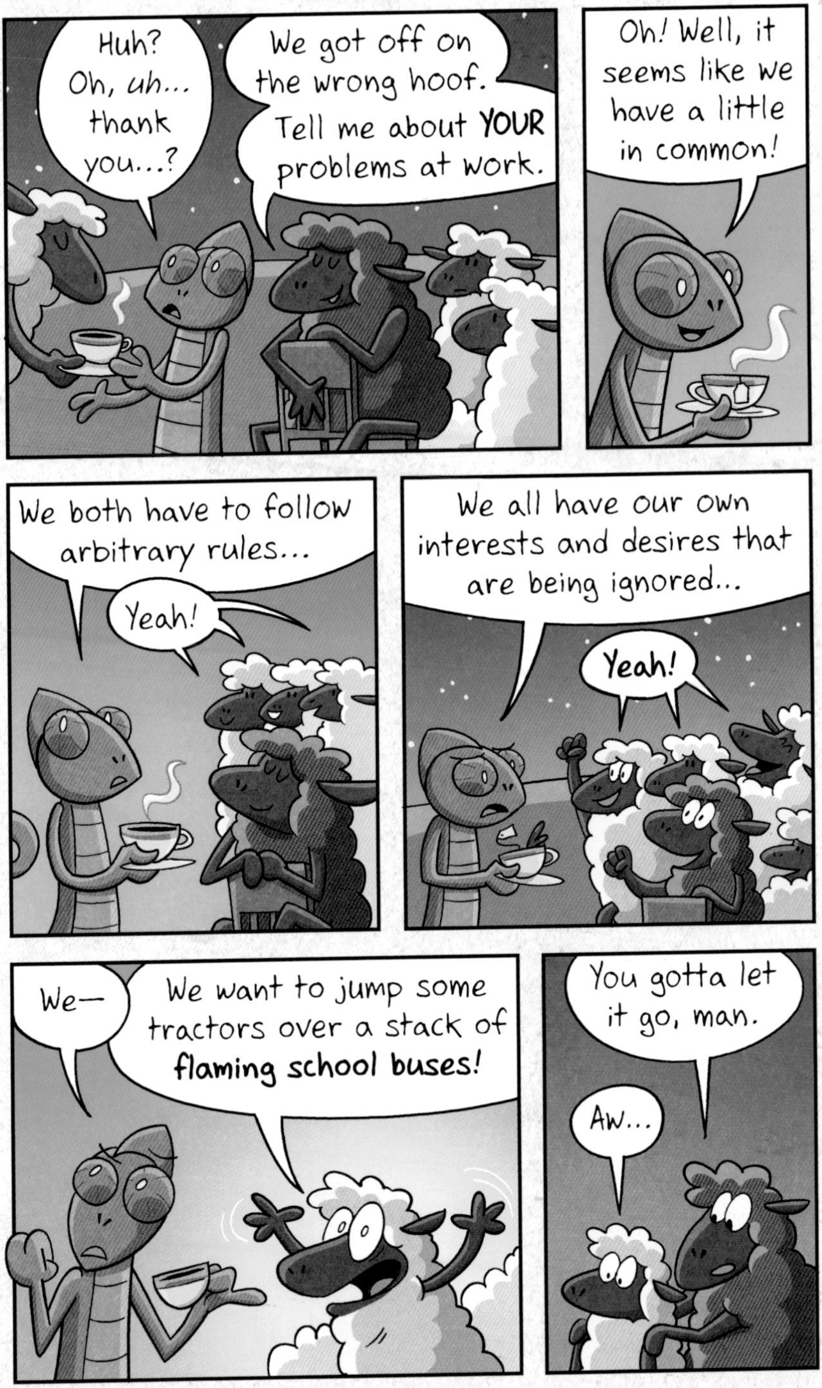
Huh? Oh, uh... thank you...?
We got off on the wrong hoof.
Tell me about **YOUR** problems at work.
Oh! Well, it seems like we have a little in common!
We both have to follow arbitrary rules...
Yeah!
We all have our own interests and desires that are being ignored...
Yeah!
We—
We want to jump some tractors over a stack of **flaming school buses!**
You gotta let it go, man.
Aw...

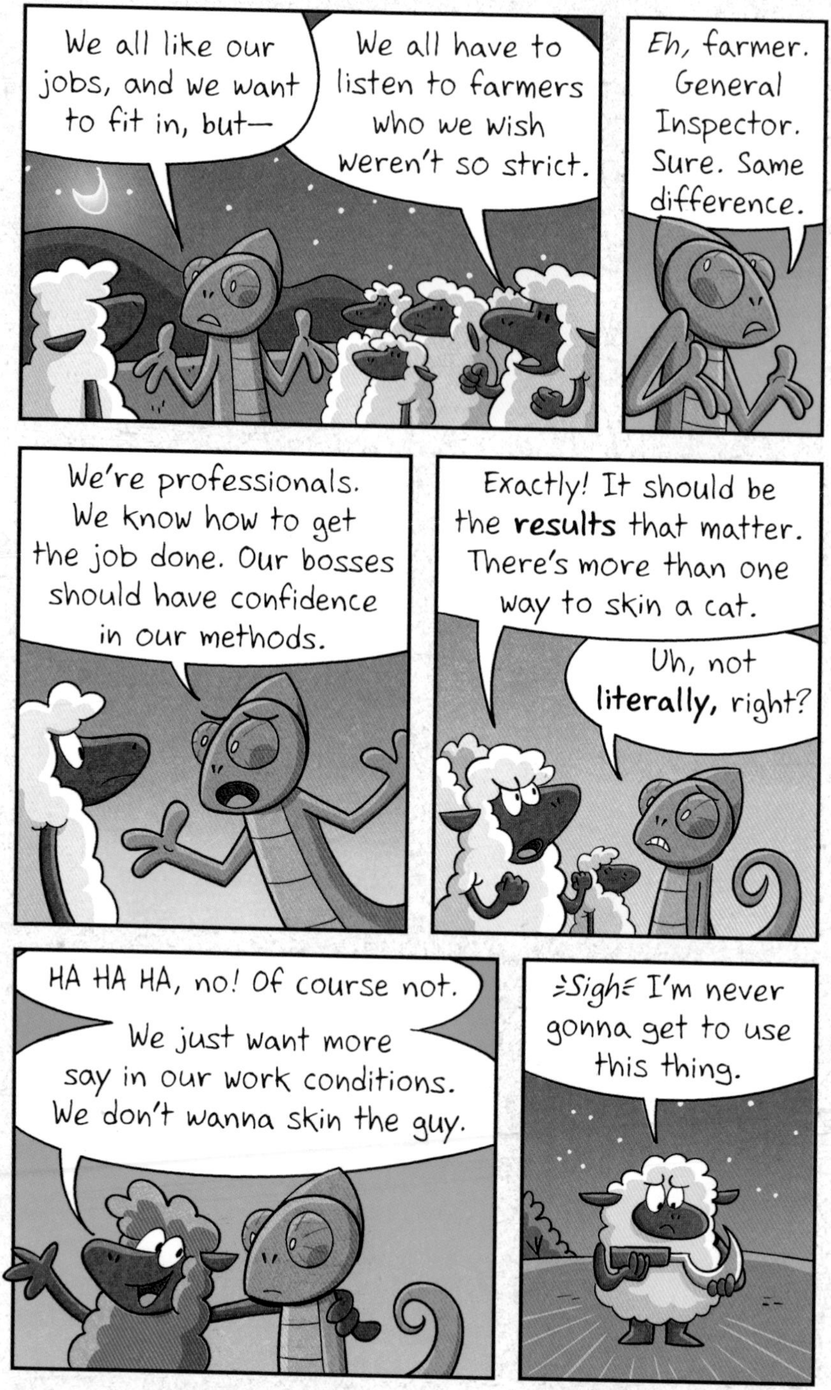
We all like our jobs, and we want to fit in, but—
We all have to listen to farmers who we wish weren't so strict.
Eh, farmer. General Inspector. Sure. Same difference.
We're professionals. We know how to get the job done. Our bosses should have confidence in our methods.
Exactly! It should be the **results** that matter. There's more than one way to skin a cat.
Uh, not **literally,** right?
HA HA HA, no! Of course not.
We just want more say in our work conditions. We don't wanna skin the guy.
Sigh I'm never gonna get to use this thing.

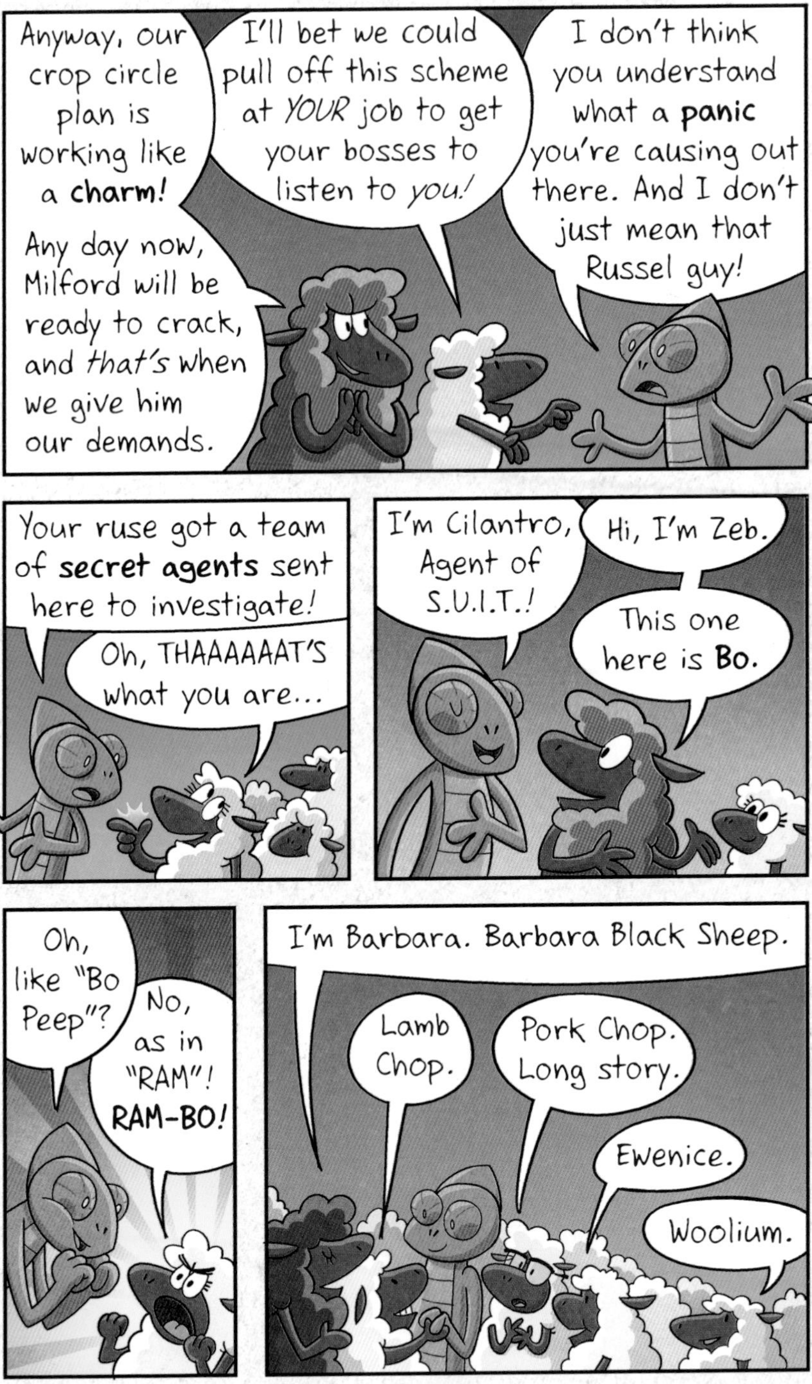

Anyway, our crop circle plan is working like a **charm**!
I'll bet we could pull off this scheme at *YOUR* job to get your bosses to listen to *you*!
I don't think you understand what a **panic** you're causing out there. And I don't just mean that Russel guy!
Any day now, Milford will be ready to crack, and *that's* when we give him our demands.
Your ruse got a team of **secret agents** sent here to investigate!
Oh, THAAAAAAT'S what you are...
I'm Cilantro, Agent of S.U.I.T.!
Hi, I'm Zeb.
This one here is **Bo**.
Oh, like "Bo Peep"?
No, as in "RAM"! **RAM-BO**!
I'm Barbara. Barbara Black Sheep.
Lamb Chop.
Pork Chop. Long story.
Ewenice.
Woolium.

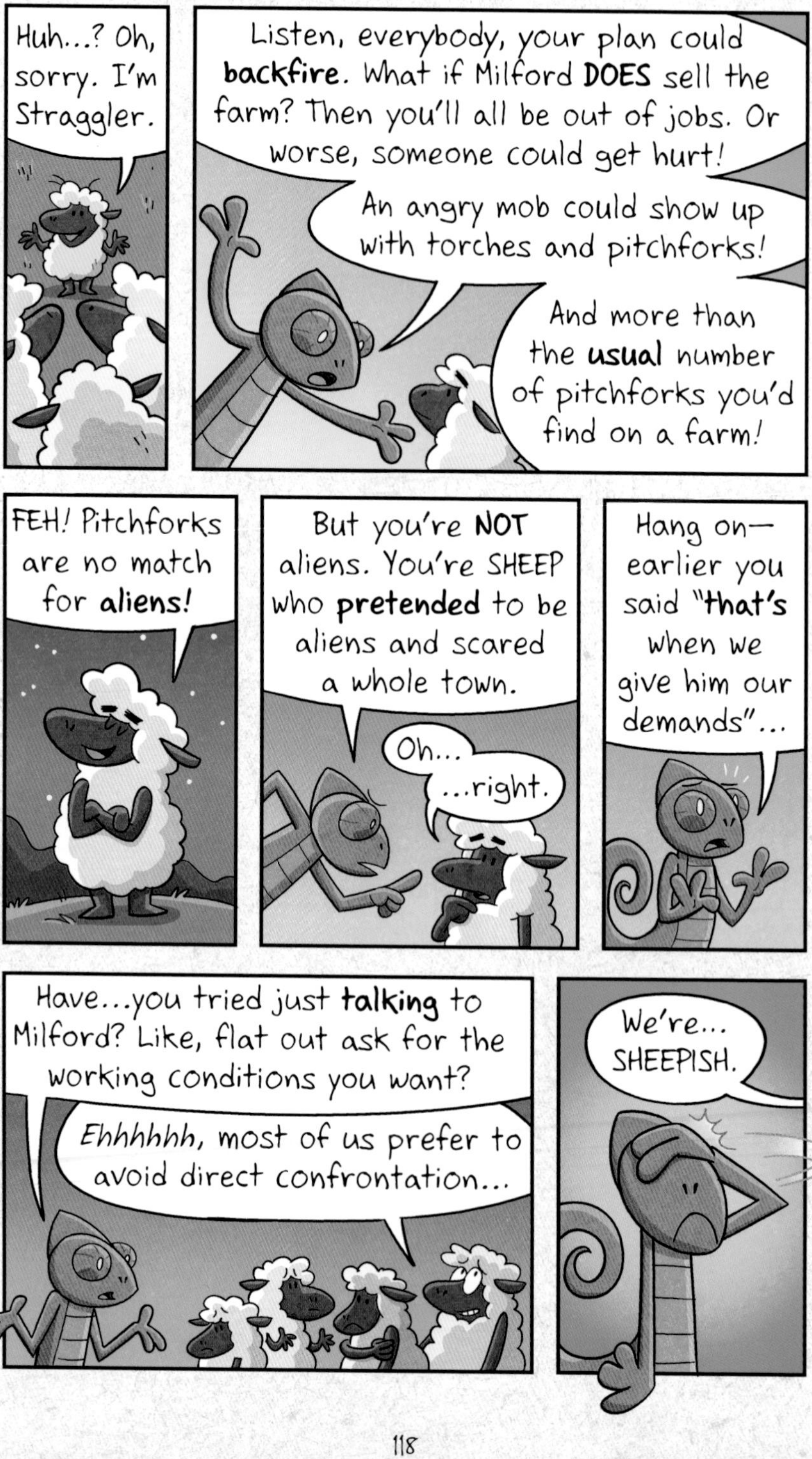
Huh...? Oh, sorry. I'm Straggler.
Listen, everybody, your plan could **backfire**. What if Milford **DOES** sell the farm? Then you'll all be out of jobs. Or worse, someone could get hurt!
An angry mob could show up with torches and pitchforks!
And more than the **usual** number of pitchforks you'd find on a farm!
FEH! Pitchforks are no match for **aliens**!
But you're **NOT** aliens. You're SHEEP who **pretended** to be aliens and scared a whole town.
Oh...
...right.
Hang on— earlier you said "**that's** when we give him our demands"...
Have...you tried just **talking** to Milford? Like, flat out ask for the working conditions you want?
Ehhhhhh, most of us prefer to avoid direct confrontation...
We're... SHEEPISH.

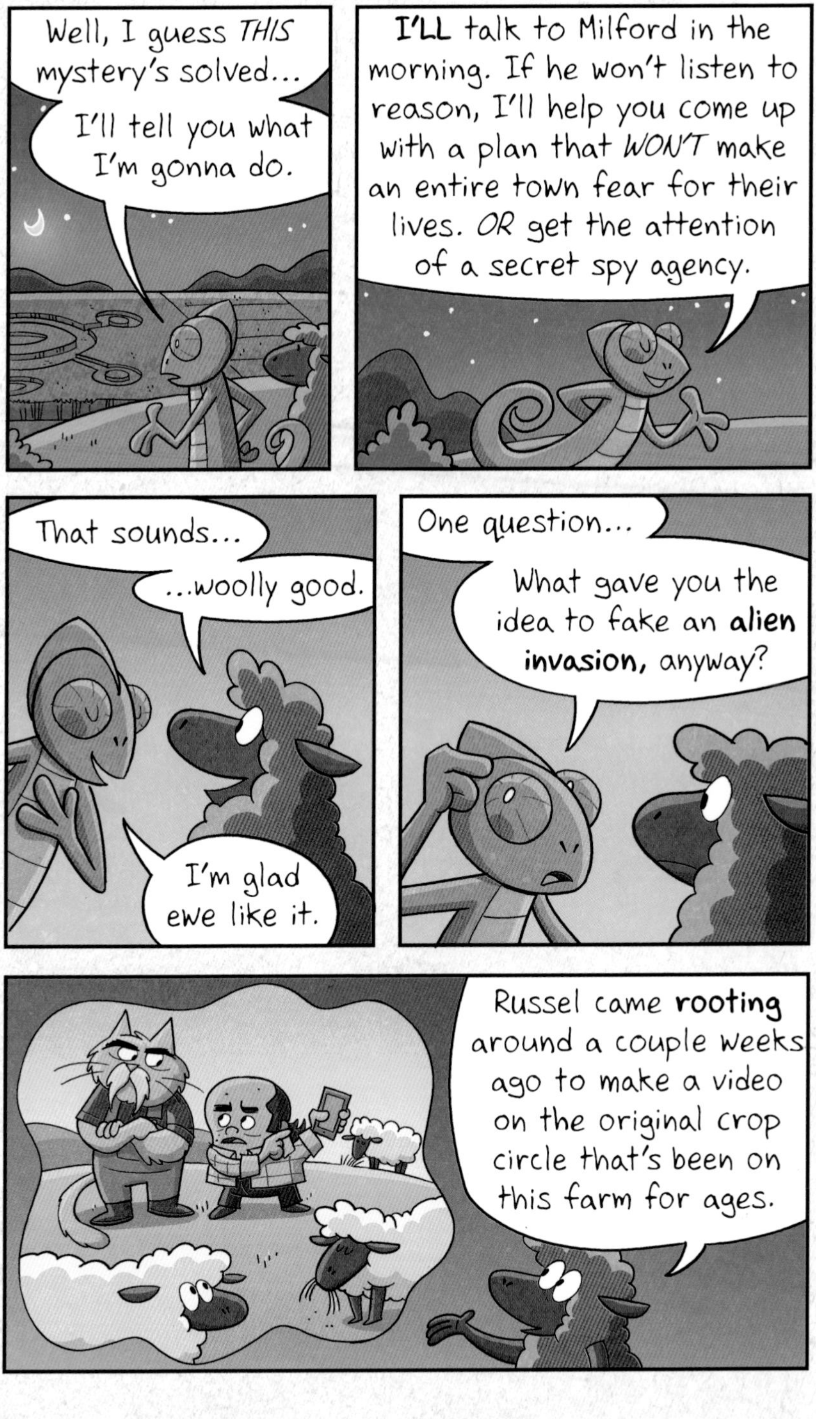
Well, I guess *THIS* mystery's solved...
I'll tell you what I'm gonna do.
I'LL talk to Milford in the morning. If he won't listen to reason, I'll help you come up with a plan that *WON'T* make an entire town fear for their lives. *OR* get the attention of a secret spy agency.
That sounds...
...woolly good.
I'm glad ewe like it.
One question...
What gave you the idea to fake an **alien invasion,** anyway?
Russel came **rooting** around a couple weeks ago to make a video on the original crop circle that's been on this farm for ages.

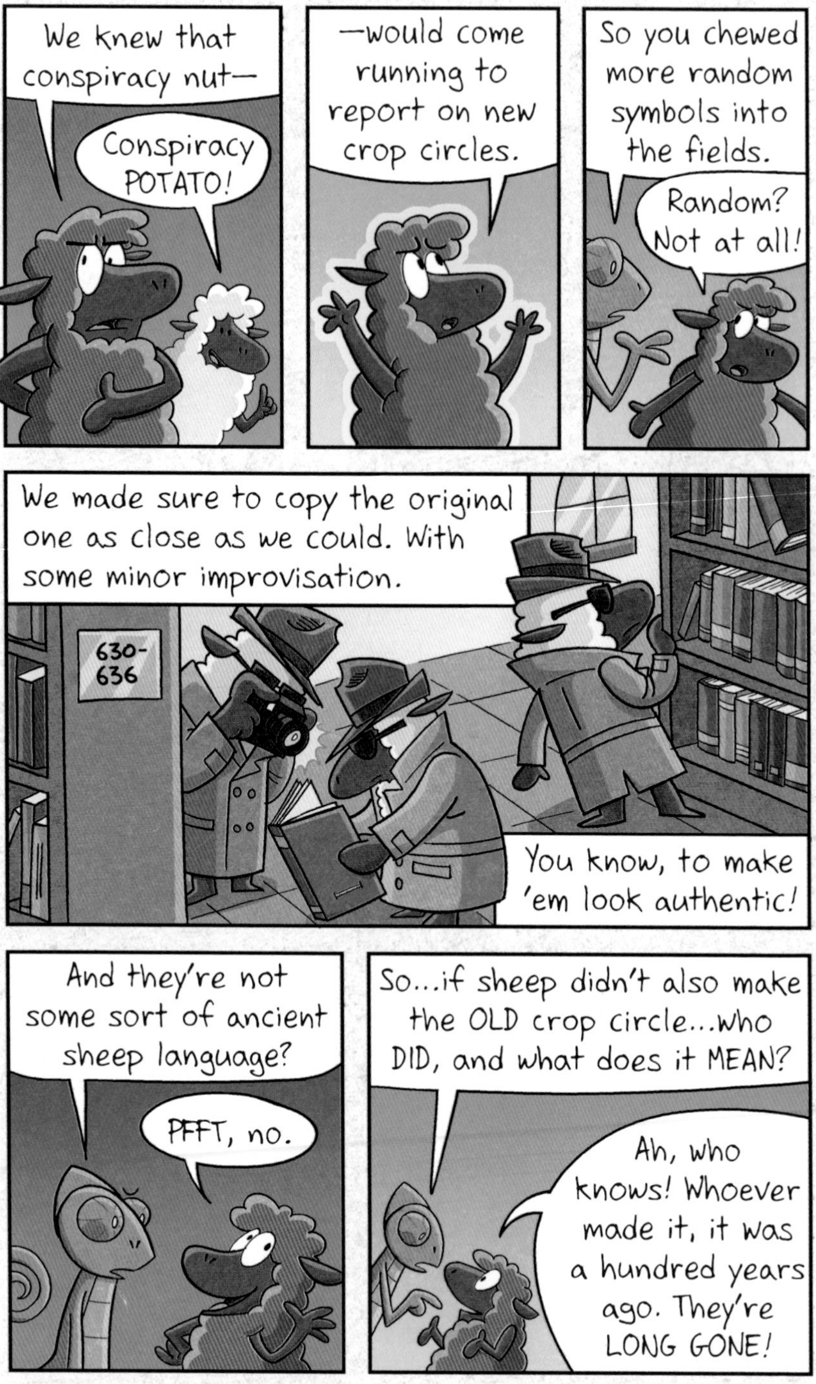
We knew that conspiracy nut—
Conspiracy POTATO!
—would come running to report on new crop circles.
So you chewed more random symbols into the fields.
Random? Not at all!
We made sure to copy the original one as close as we could. With some minor improvisation.
630-636
You know, to make 'em look authentic!
And they're not some sort of ancient sheep language?
PFFT, no.
So...if sheep didn't also make the OLD crop circle...who DID, and what does it MEAN?
Ah, who knows! Whoever made it, it was a hundred years ago. They're LONG GONE!

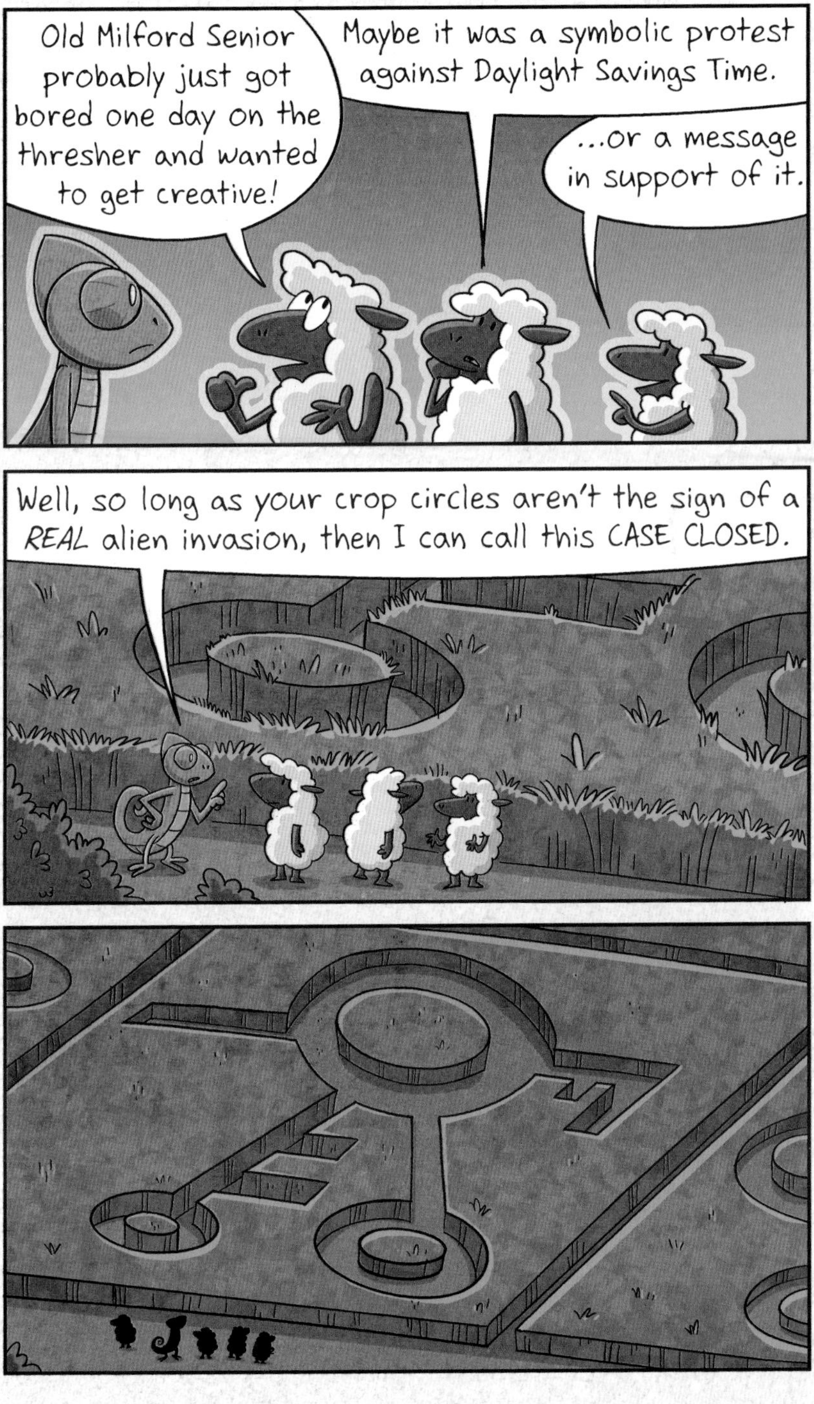
Old Milford Senior probably just got bored one day on the thresher and wanted to get creative!
Maybe it was a symbolic protest against Daylight Savings Time.
...or a message in support of it.
Well, so long as your crop circles aren't the sign of a *REAL* alien invasion, then I can call this CASE CLOSED.

Chapter 9

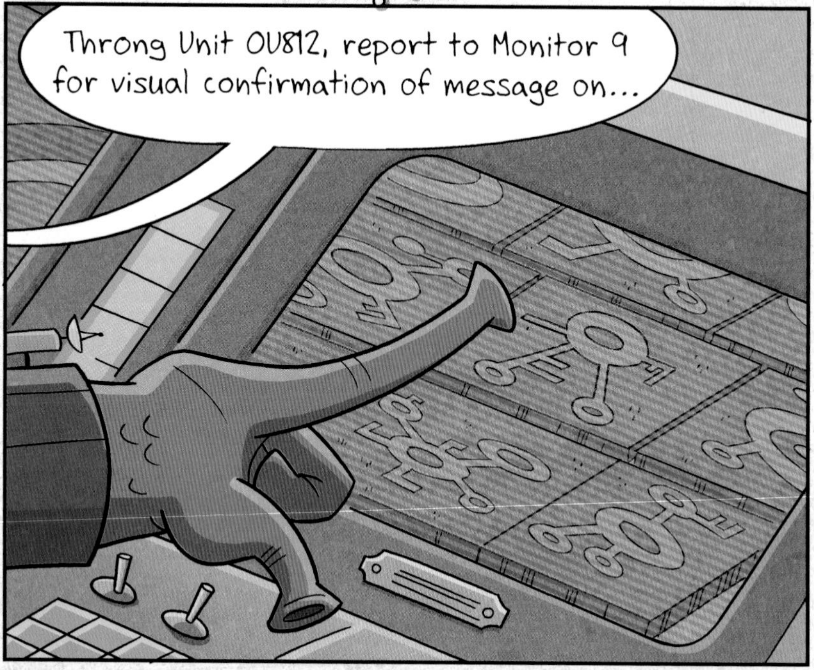
Throng Unit OU812, report to Monitor 9 for visual confirmation of message on...

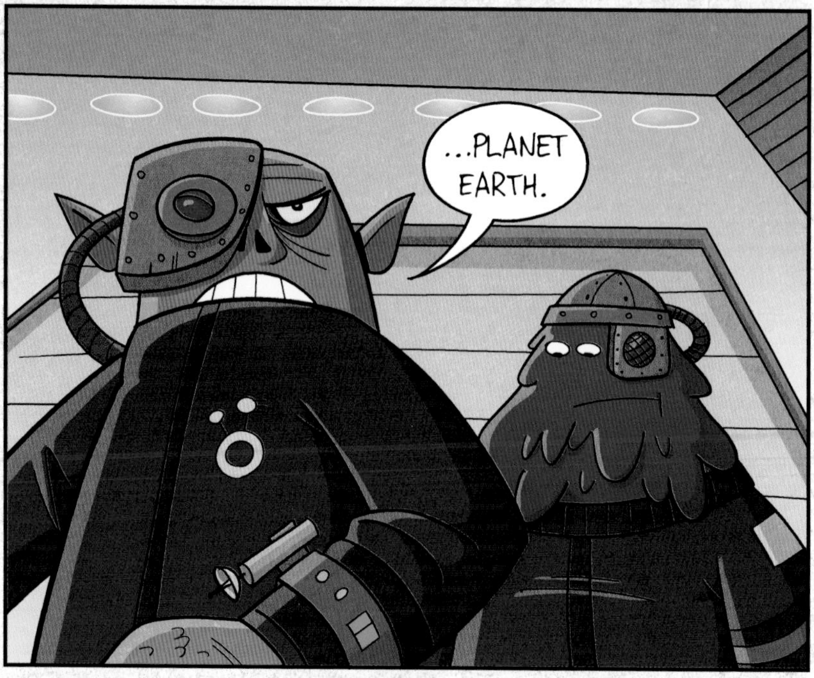
...PLANET EARTH.

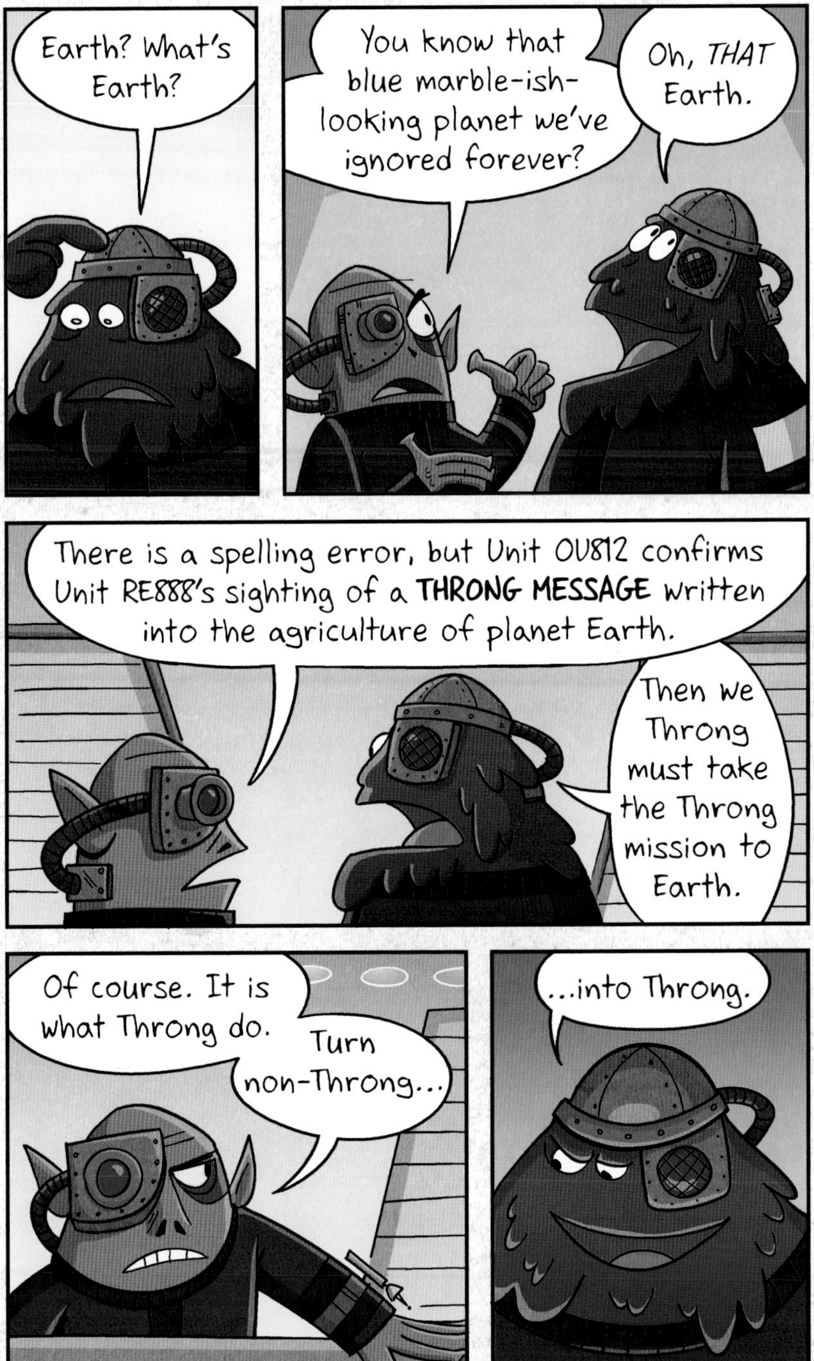
Earth? What's Earth?
You know that blue marble-ish-looking planet we've ignored forever?
Oh, *THAT* Earth.
There is a spelling error, but Unit OU812 confirms Unit RE888's sighting of a **THRONG MESSAGE** written into the agriculture of planet Earth.
Then we Throng must take the Throng mission to Earth.
Of course. It is what Throng do.
Turn non-Throng...
...into Throng.

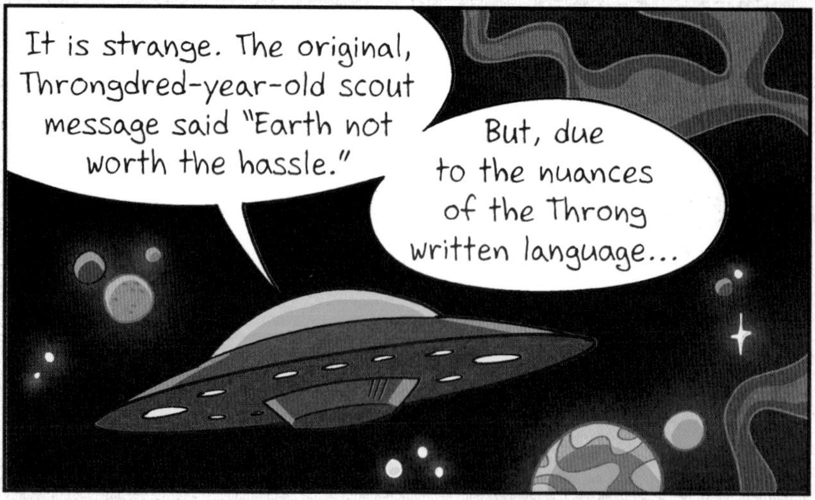
It is strange. The original, Throngdred-year-old scout message said "Earth not worth the hassle."
But, due to the nuances of the Throng written language...

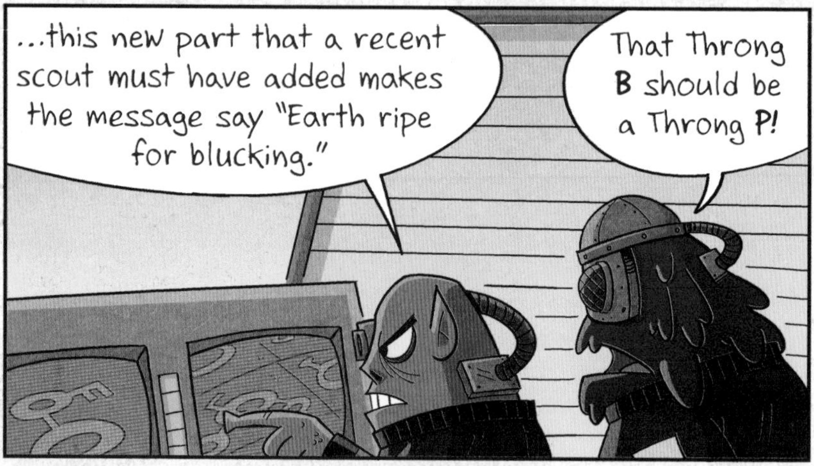
...this new part that a recent scout must have added makes the message say "Earth ripe for blucking."
That Throng **B** should be a Throng **P**!

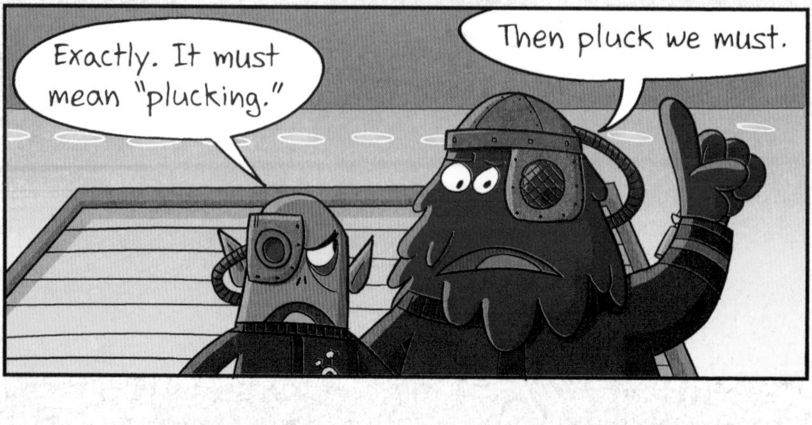
Exactly. It must mean "plucking."
Then pluck we must.

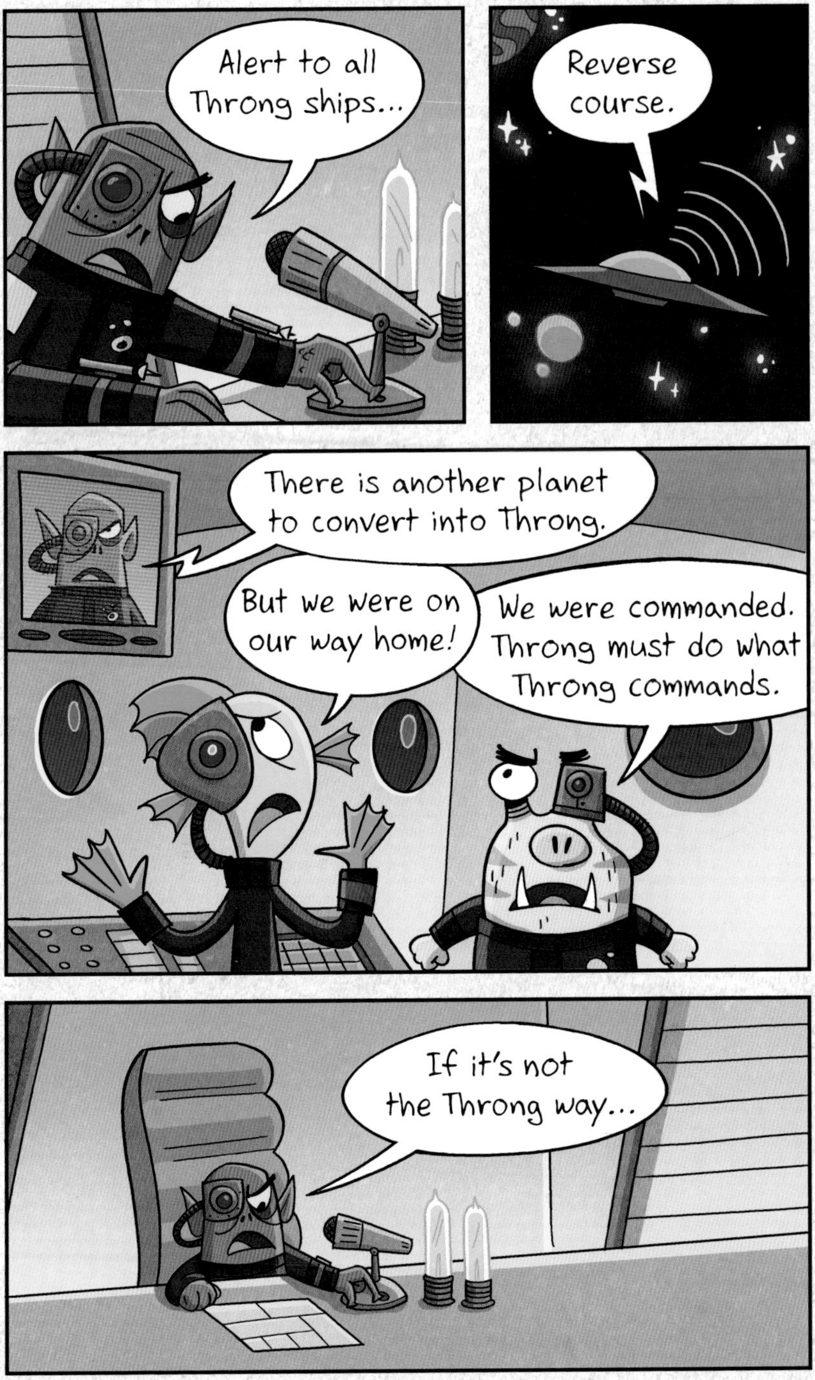
Alert to all Throng ships...
Reverse course.
There is another planet to convert into Throng.
But we were on our way home!
We were commanded. Throng must do what Throng commands.
If it's not the Throng way...

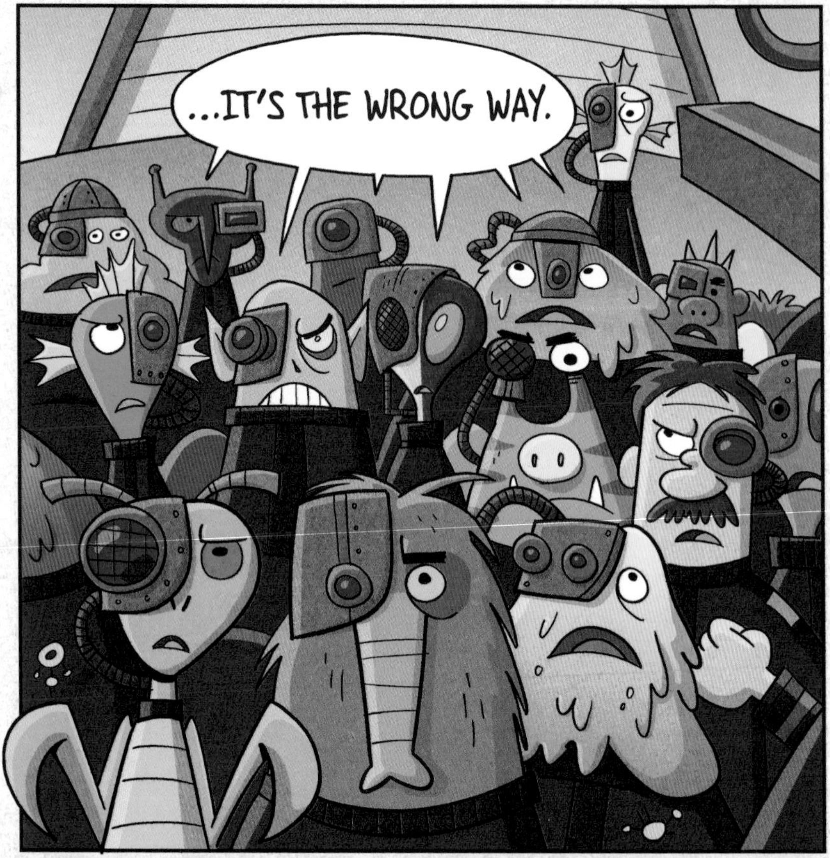
...IT'S THE WRONG WAY.

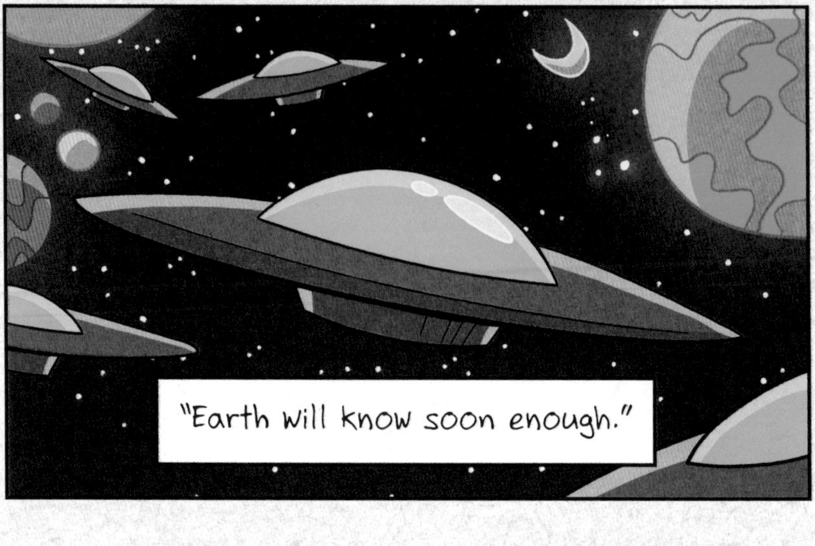
"Earth will know soon enough."

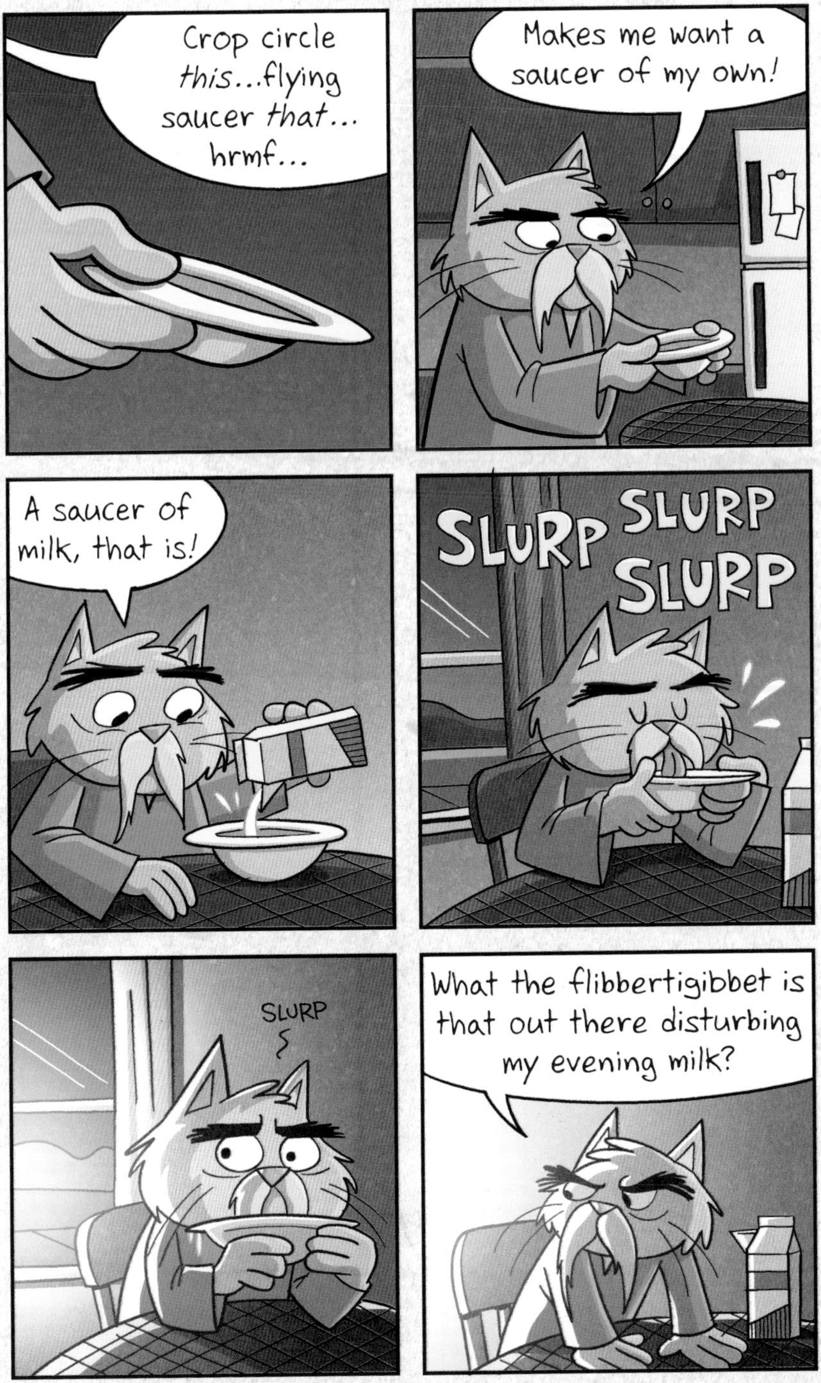
Crop circle *this*...flying saucer *that*... hrmf...
Makes me want a saucer of my own!
A saucer of milk, that is!
SLURP SLURP SLURP
SLURP
SLURP
What the flibbertigibbet is that out there disturbing my evening milk?

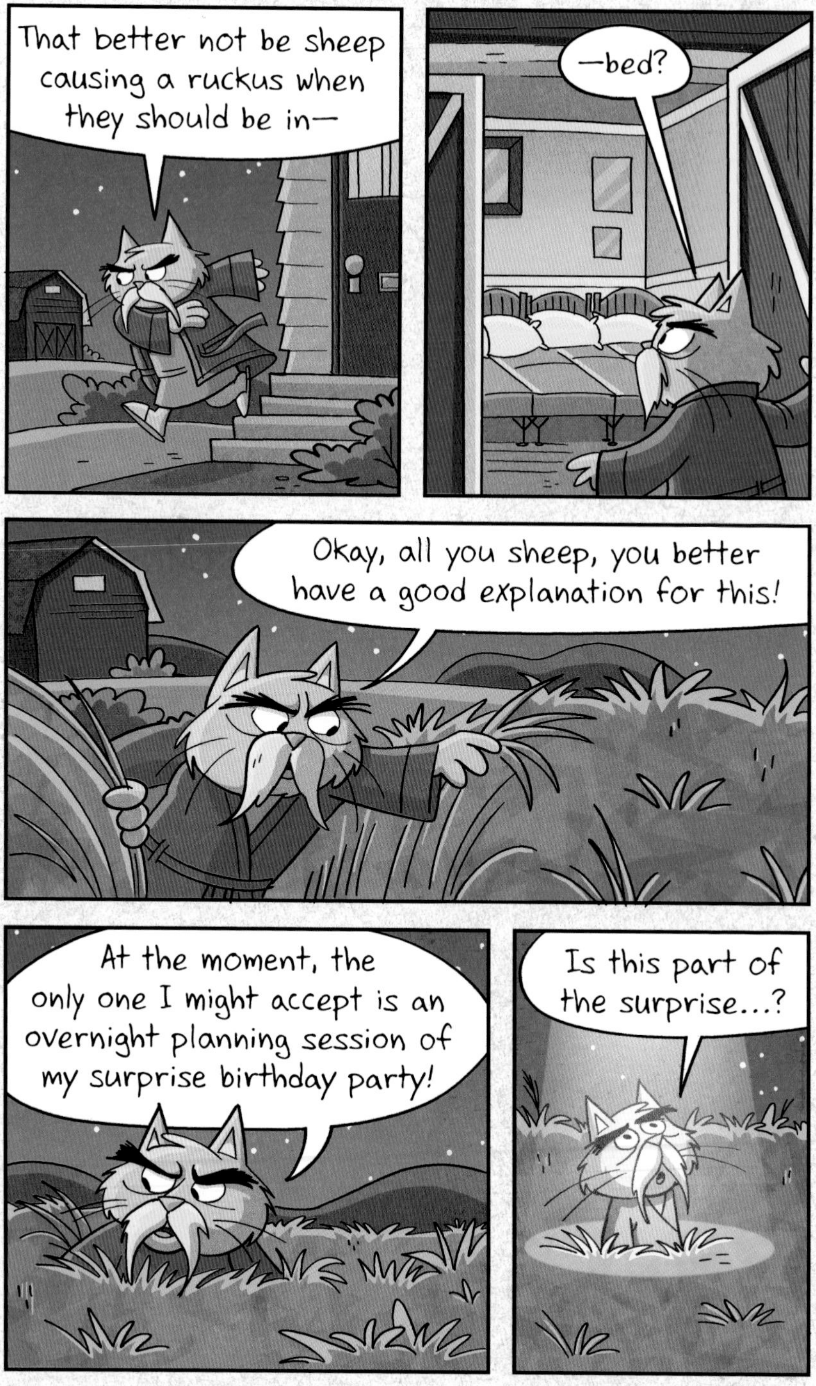
That better not be sheep causing a ruckus when they should be in—
—bed?
Okay, all you sheep, you better have a good explanation for this!
At the moment, the only one I might accept is an overnight planning session of my surprise birthday party!
Is this part of the surprise...?

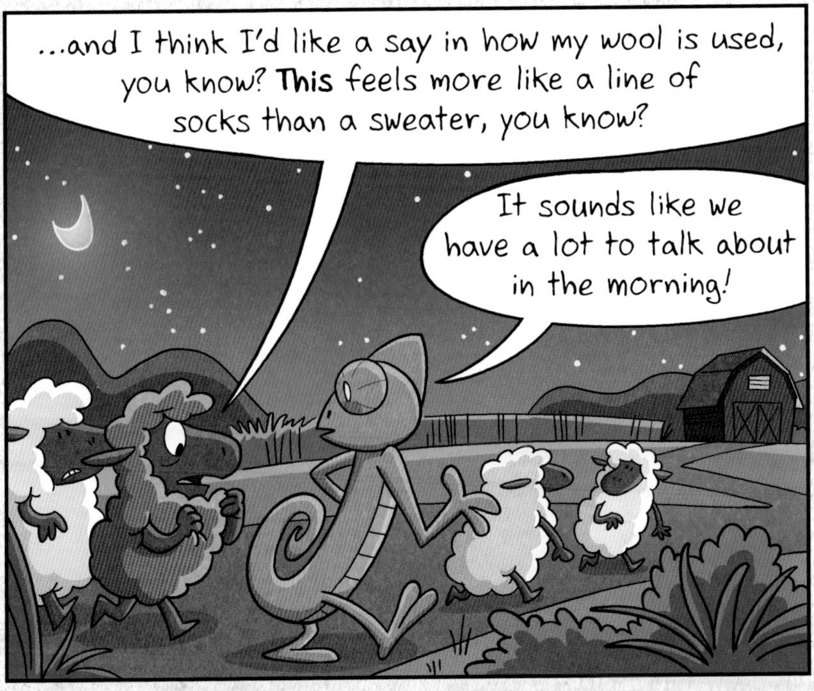
...and I think I'd like a say in how my wool is used, you know? **This** feels more like a line of socks than a sweater, you know?
It sounds like we have a lot to talk about in the morning!

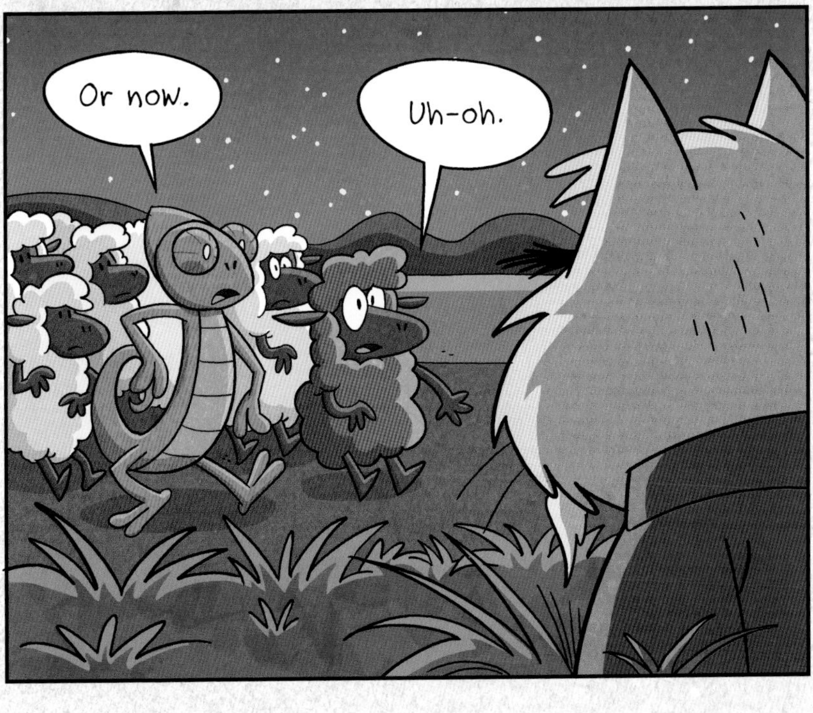
Or now.
Uh-oh.

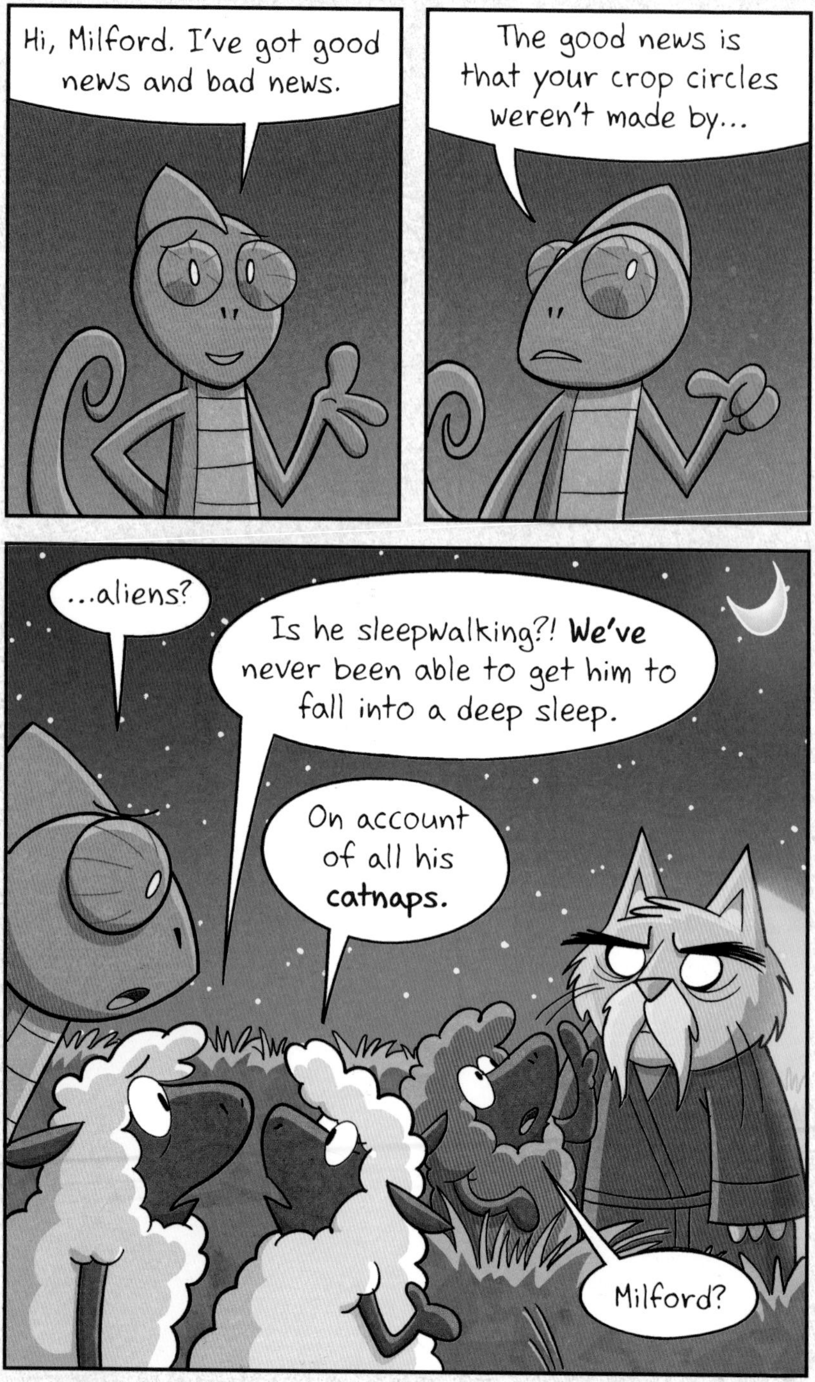
Hi, Milford. I've got good news and bad news.
The good news is that your crop circles weren't made by...
...aliens?
Is he sleepwalking?! **We've** never been able to get him to fall into a deep sleep.
On account of all his **catnaps.**
Milford?

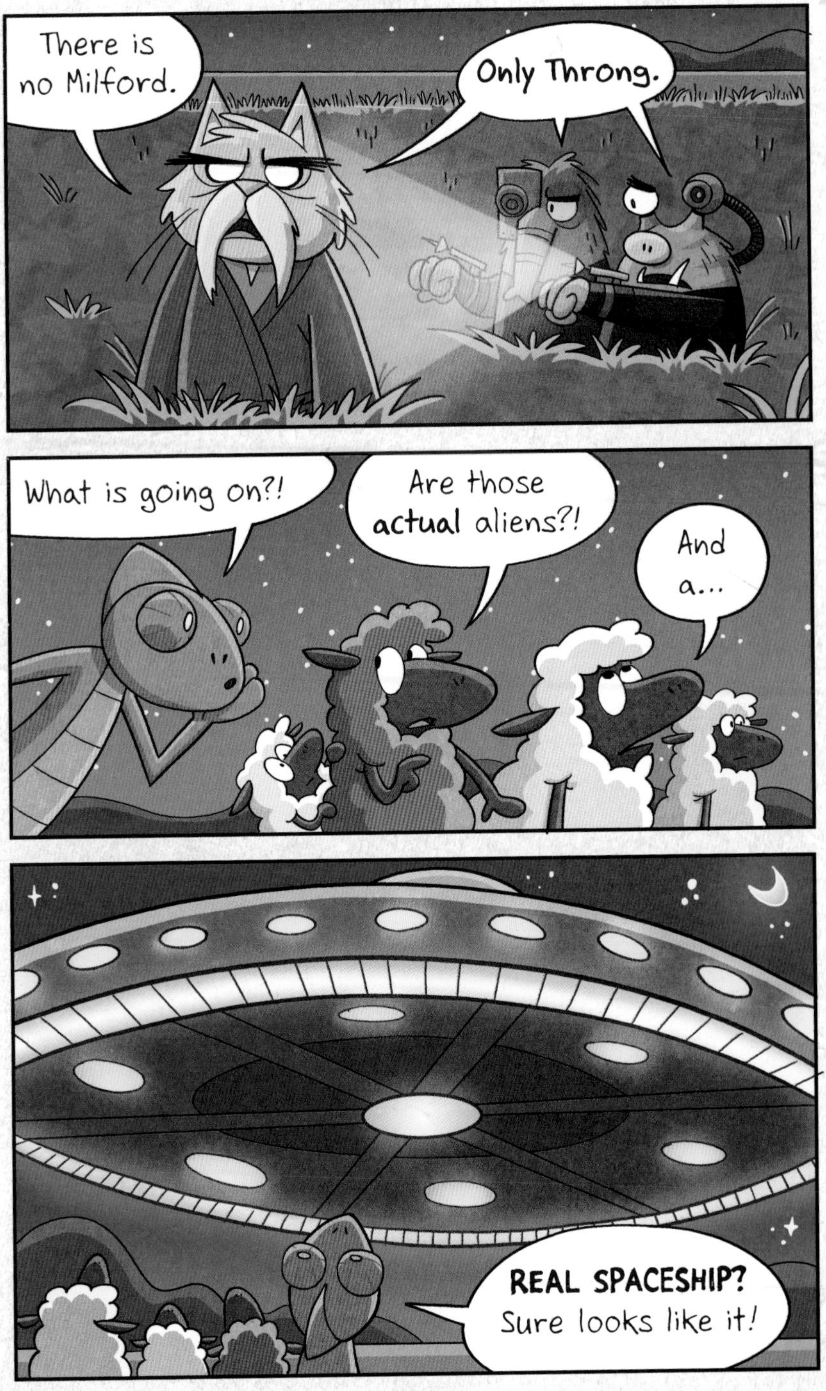
There is no Milford.
Only Throng.
What is going on?!
Are those actual aliens?!
And a...
REAL SPACESHIP?
Sure looks like it!

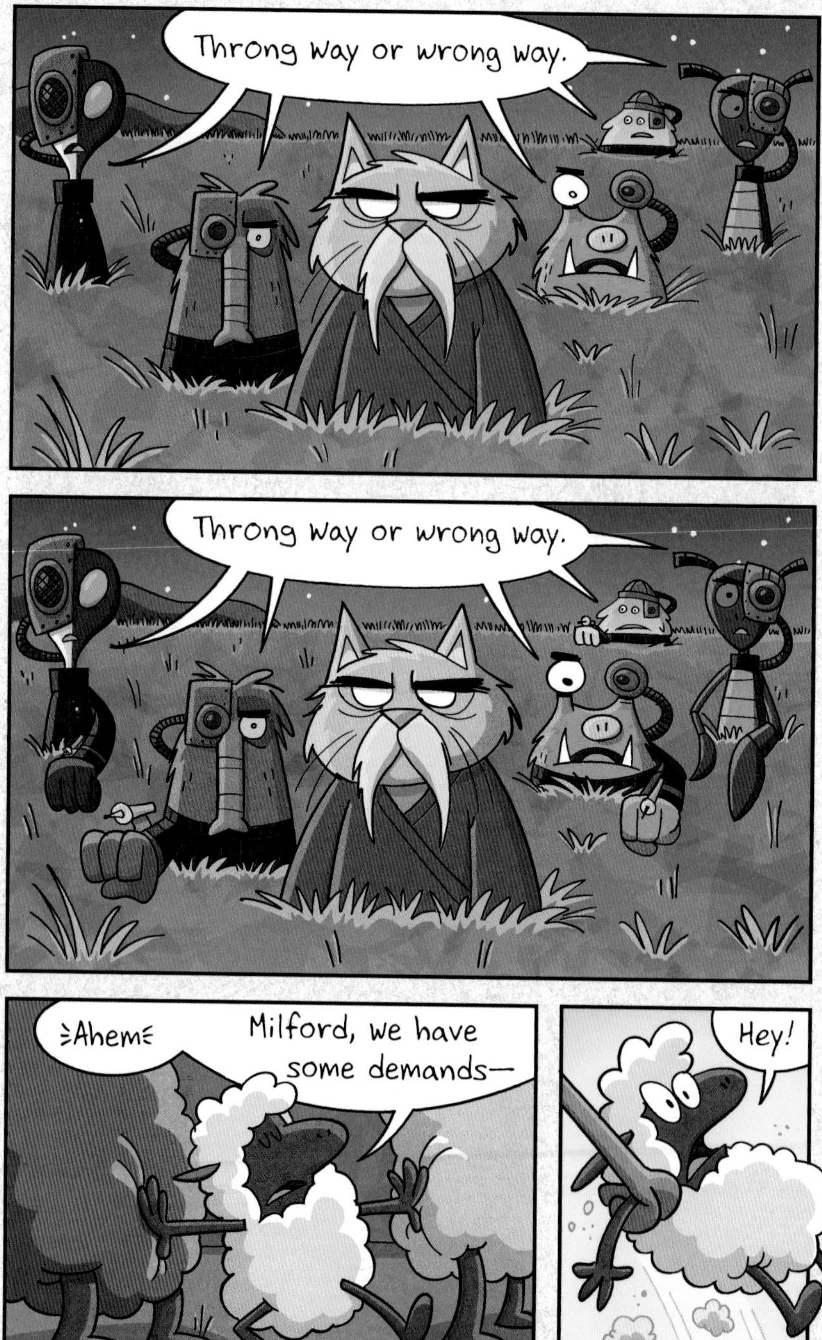
Throng way or wrong way.
Throng way or wrong way.
≷Ahem≶
Milford, we have some demands—
Hey!

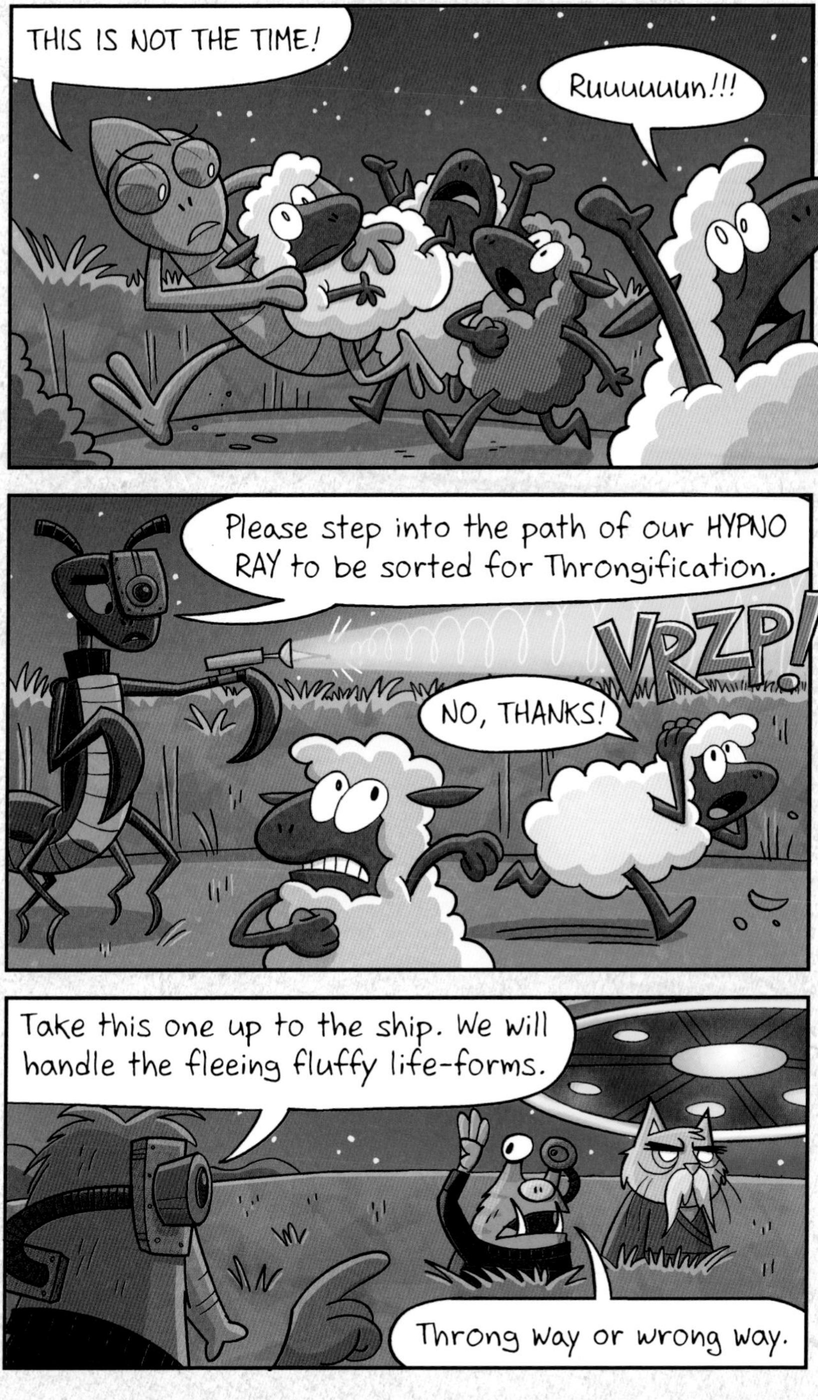
THIS IS NOT THE TIME!
Ruuuuuun!!!
Please step into the path of our HYPNO RAY to be sorted for Throngification.
VRZP!
NO, THANKS!
Take this one up to the ship. We will handle the fleeing fluffy life-forms.
Throng way or wrong way.

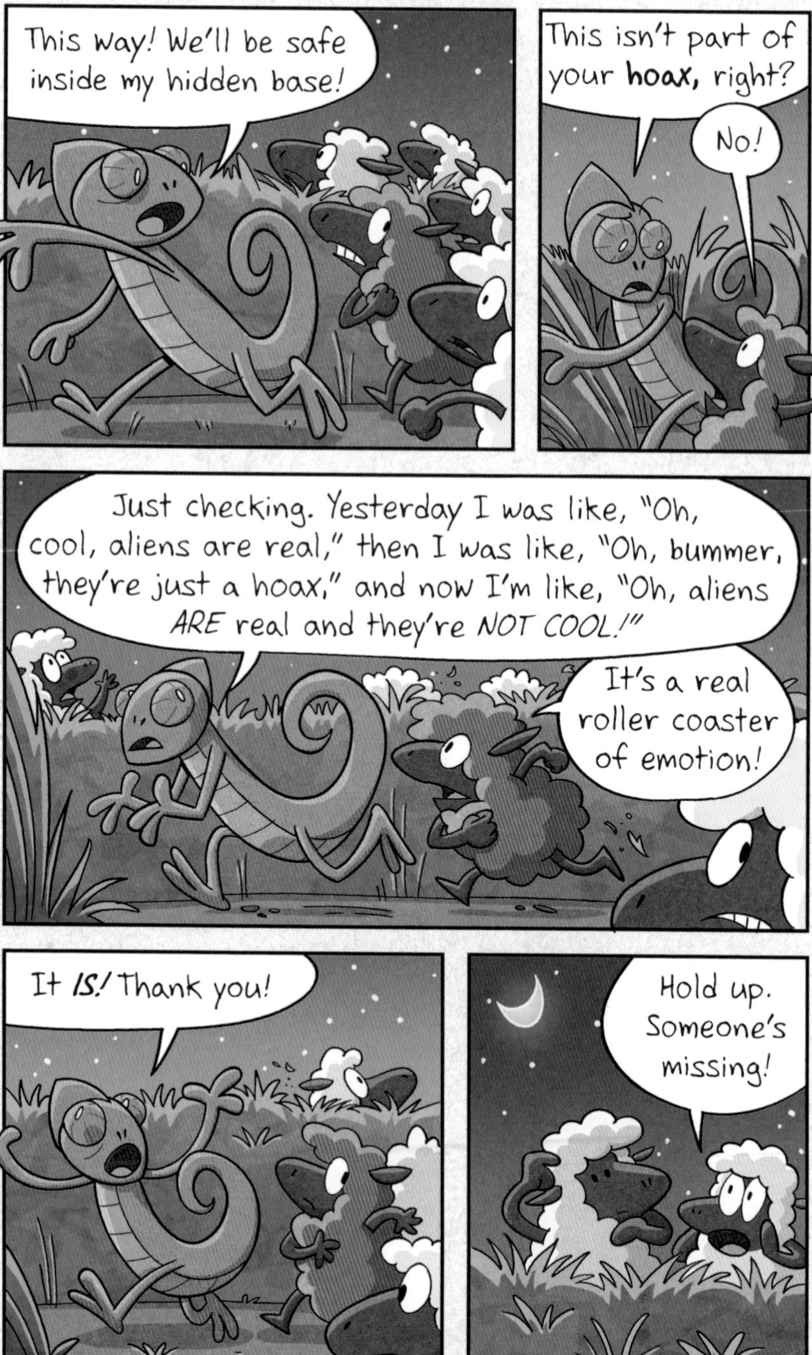
This way! We'll be safe inside my hidden base!
This isn't part of your **hoax,** right?
No!
Just checking. Yesterday I was like, "Oh, cool, aliens are real," then I was like, "Oh, bummer, they're just a hoax," and now I'm like, "Oh, aliens *ARE* real and they're *NOT COOL!*"
It's a real roller coaster of emotion!
It *IS!* Thank you!
Hold up. Someone's missing!

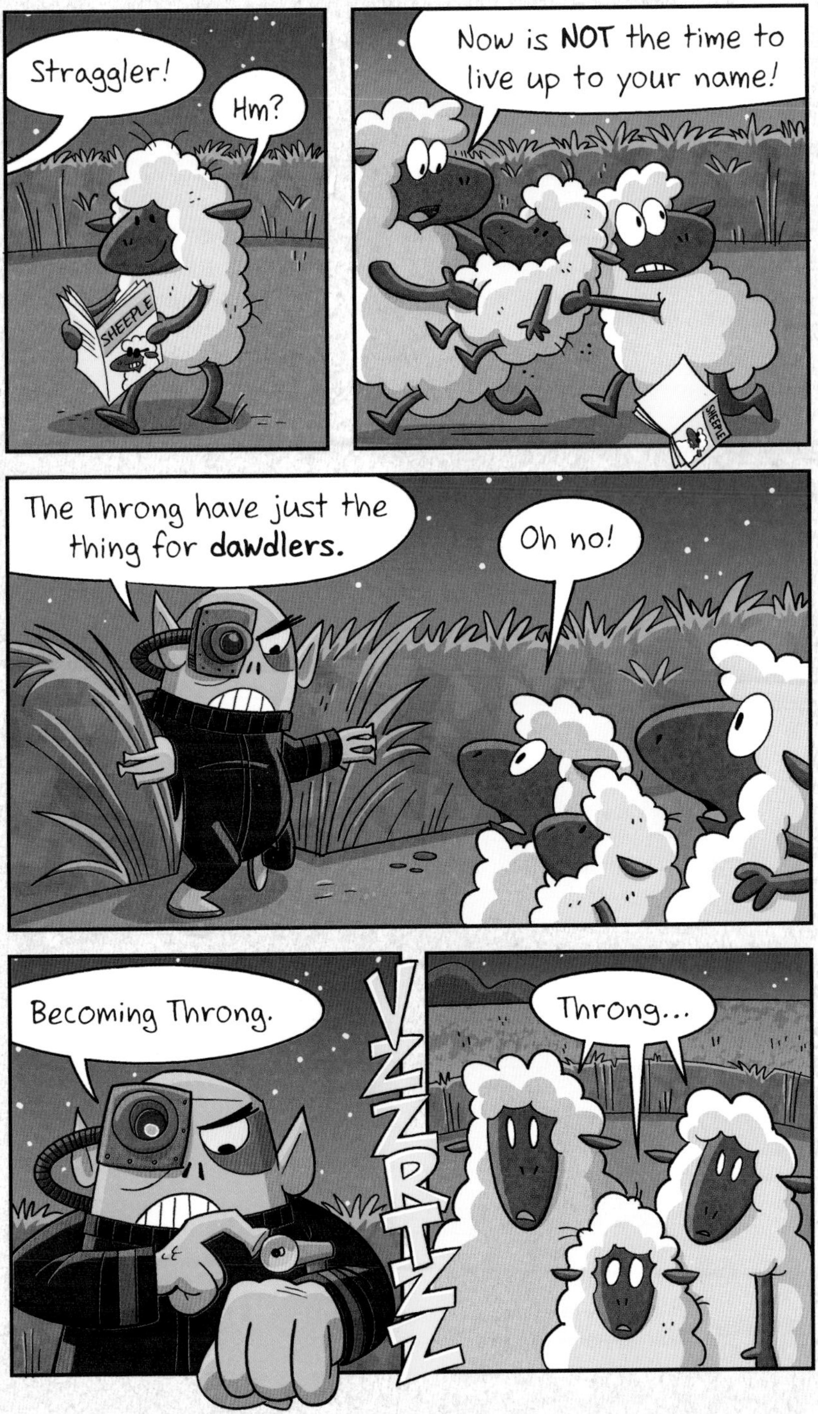
Straggler!
Hm?
SHEEPLE
Now is NOT the time to live up to your name!
SHEEPLE
The Throng have just the thing for dawdlers.
Oh no!
Becoming Throng.
VZZRTZZ
Throng...

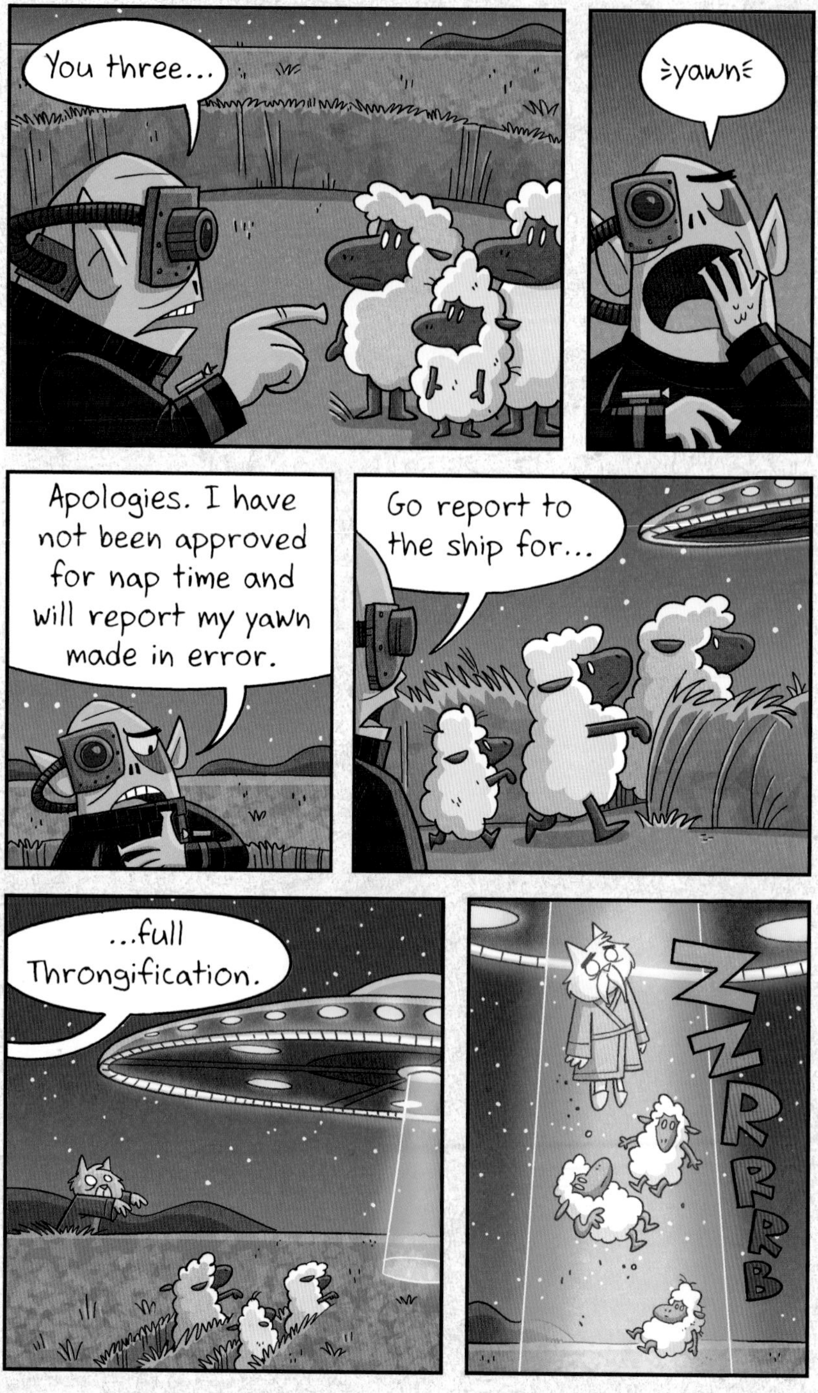
You three...
yawn
Apologies. I have not been approved for nap time and will report my yawn made in error.
Go report to the ship for...
...full Throngification.
ZZRRRB

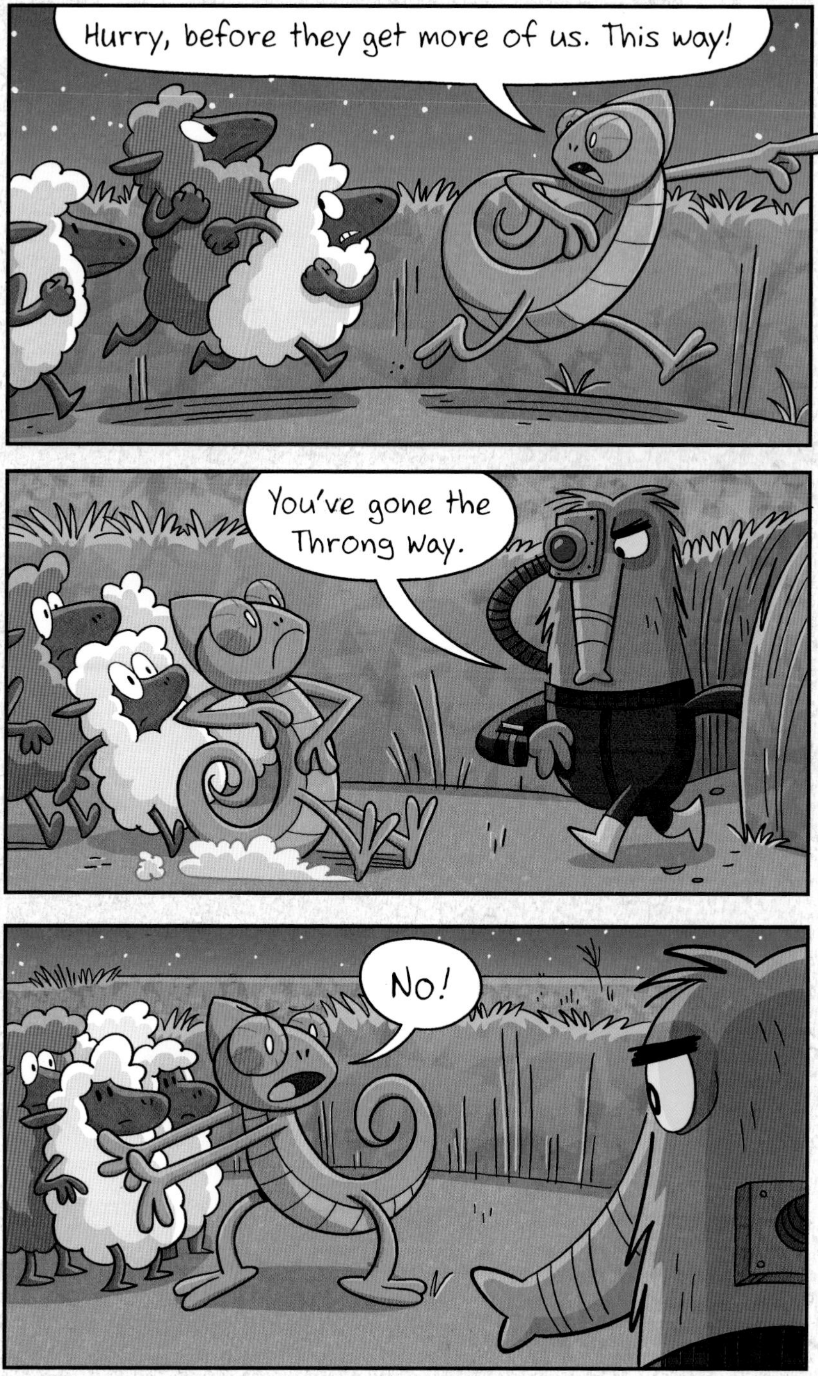
Hurry, before they get more of us. This way!
You've gone the Throng way.
No!

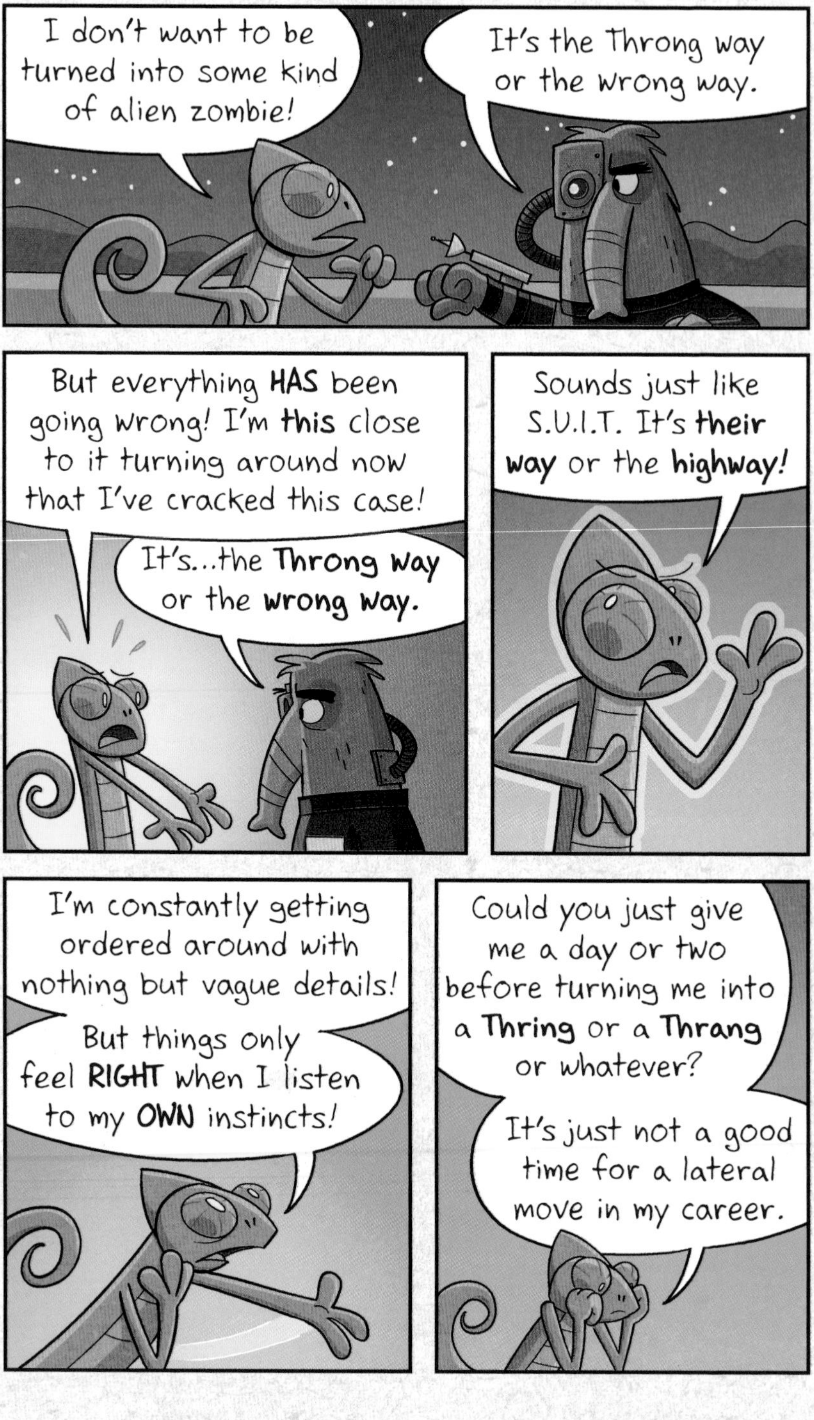
I don't want to be turned into some kind of alien zombie!
It's the Throng way or the wrong way.
But everything **HAS** been going wrong! I'm **this** close to it turning around now that I've cracked this case!
It's...the **Throng way** or the **wrong way.**
Sounds just like S.U.I.T. It's **their way** or the **highway!**
I'm constantly getting ordered around with nothing but vague details!
But things only feel **RIGHT** when I listen to my **OWN** instincts!
Could you just give me a day or two before turning me into a **Thring** or a **Thrang** or whatever?
It's just not a good time for a lateral move in my career.

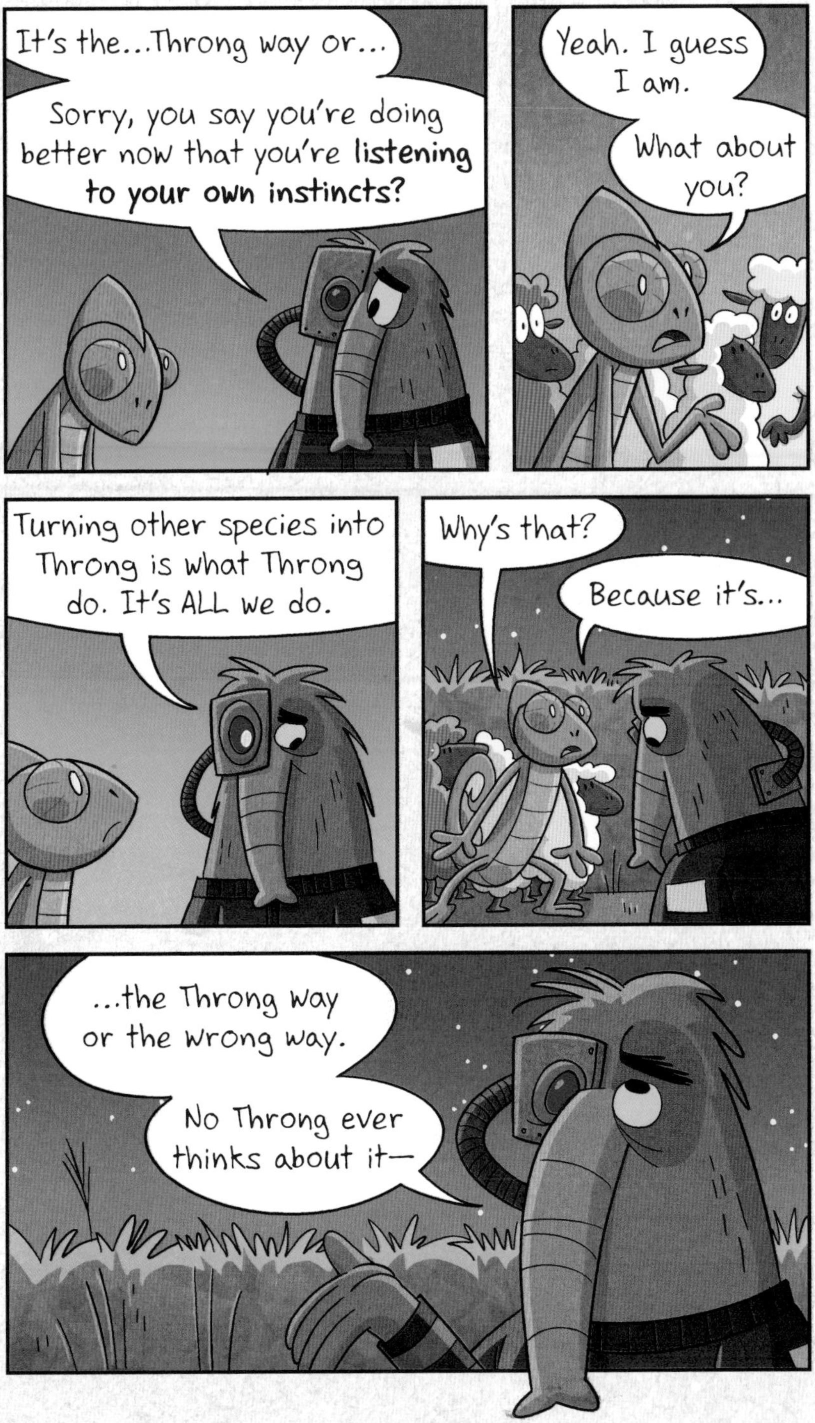
It's the...Throng way or...
Sorry, you say you're doing better now that you're **listening to your own instincts?**
Yeah. I guess I am.
What about you?
Turning other species into Throng is what Throng do. It's ALL we do.
Why's that?
Because it's...
...the Throng way or the wrong way.
No Throng ever thinks about it—

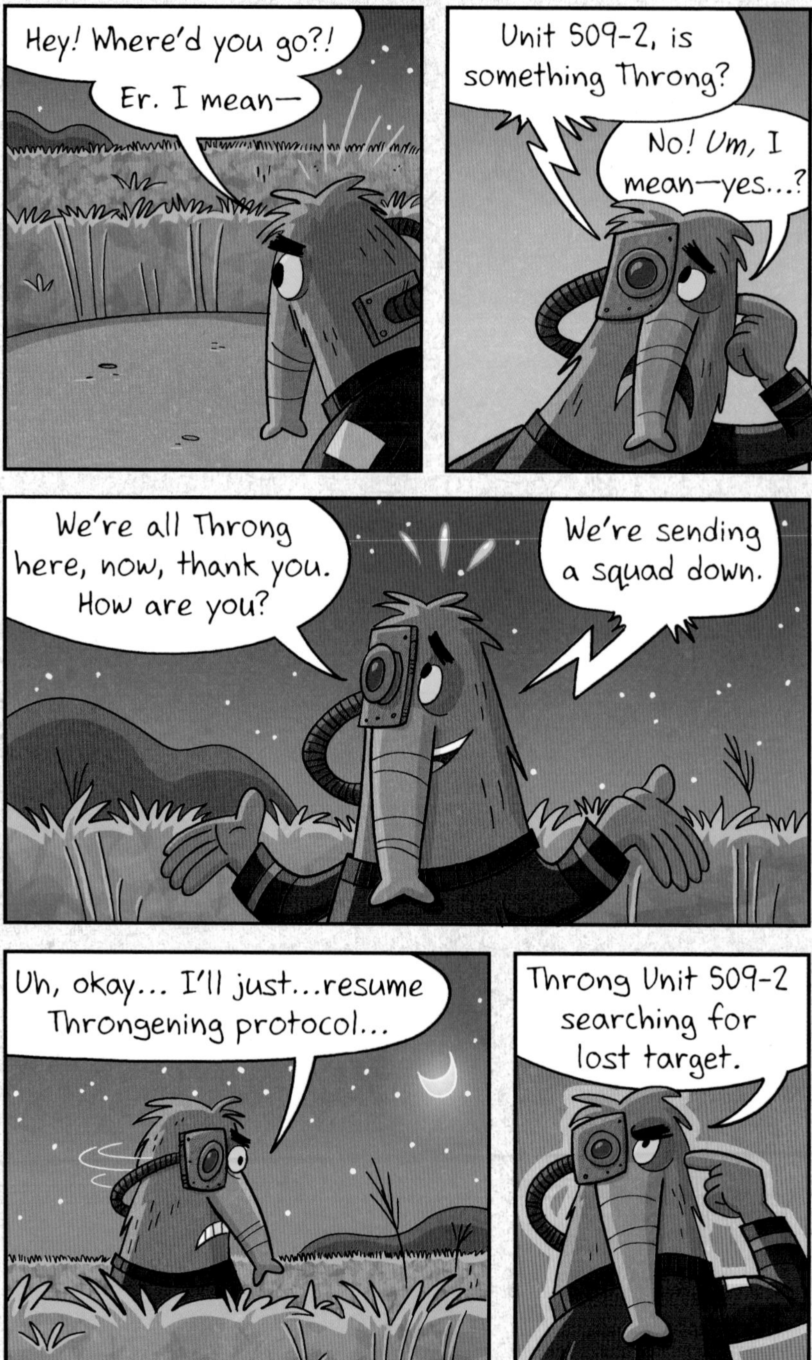
Hey! Where'd you go?!
Er. I mean—
Unit 509-2, is something Throng?
No! Um, I mean—yes...?
We're all Throng here, now, thank you. How are you?
We're sending a squad down.
Uh, okay... I'll just...resume Throngening protocol...
Throng Unit 509-2 searching for lost target.

Chapter 10

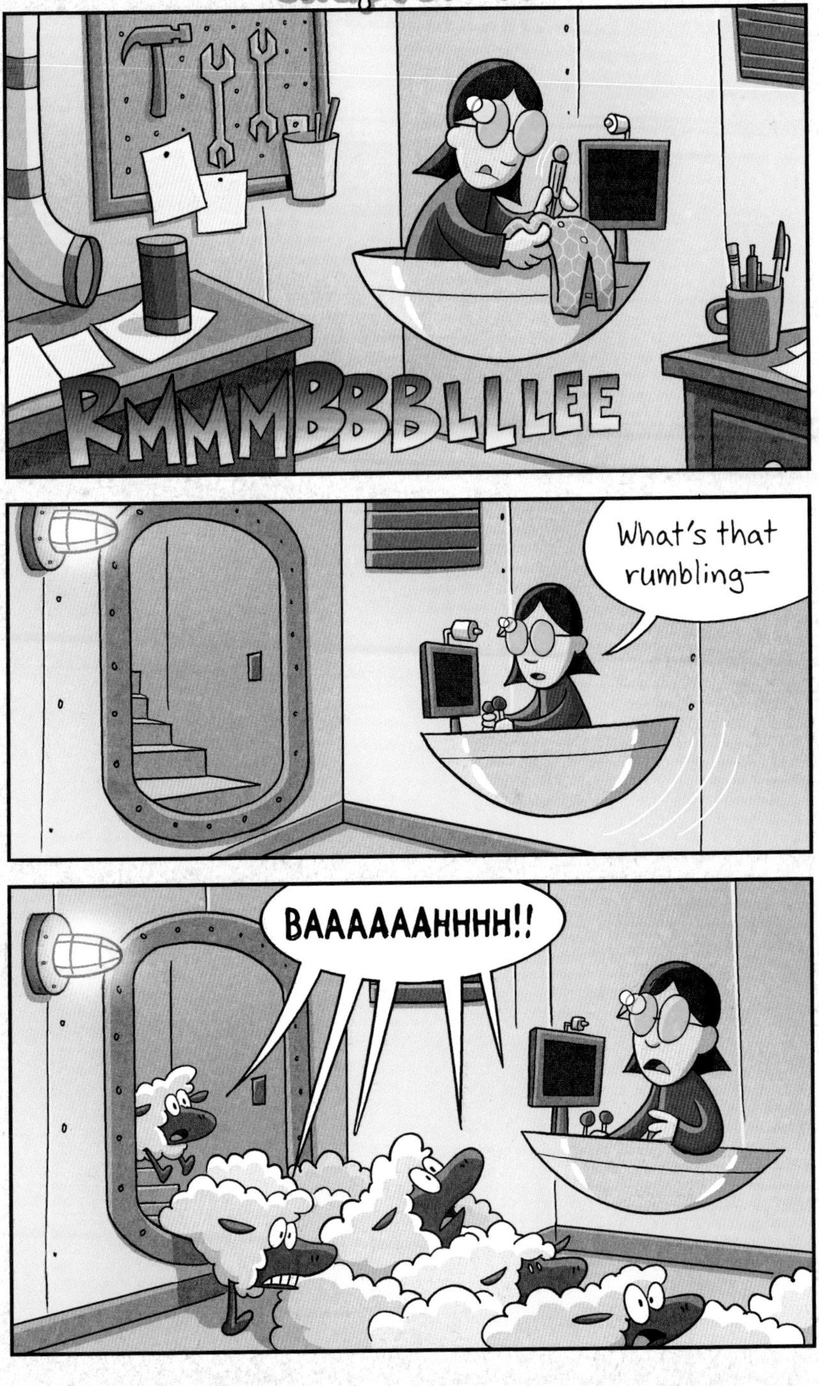
RMMMBBBLLLEE
What's that rumbling—
BAAAAAAHHHH!!

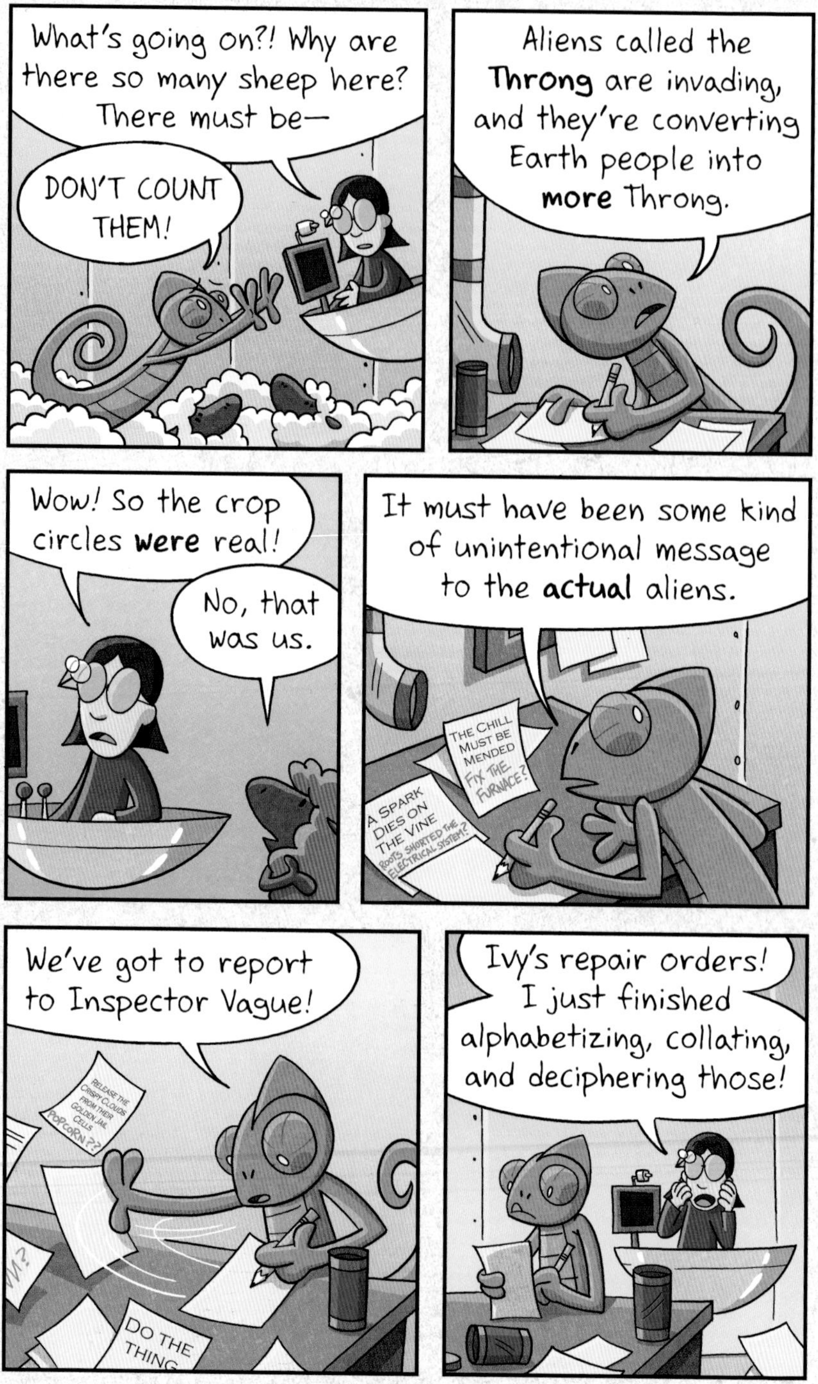
What's going on?! Why are there so many sheep here? There must be—
DON'T COUNT THEM!
Aliens called the **Throng** are invading, and they're converting Earth people into **more** Throng.
Wow! So the crop circles **were** real!
No, that was us.
It must have been some kind of unintentional message to the **actual** aliens.
THE CHILL MUST BE MENDED
FIX THE FURNACE?
A SPARK DIES ON THE VINE
ROOTS SHORTED THE ELECTRICAL SYSTEM?
We've got to report to Inspector Vague!
RELEASE THE CRISPY CLOUDS FROM THEIR GOLDEN JAIL CELLS
POPCORN??
DO THE THING
Ivy's repair orders! I just finished alphabetizing, collating, and deciphering those!

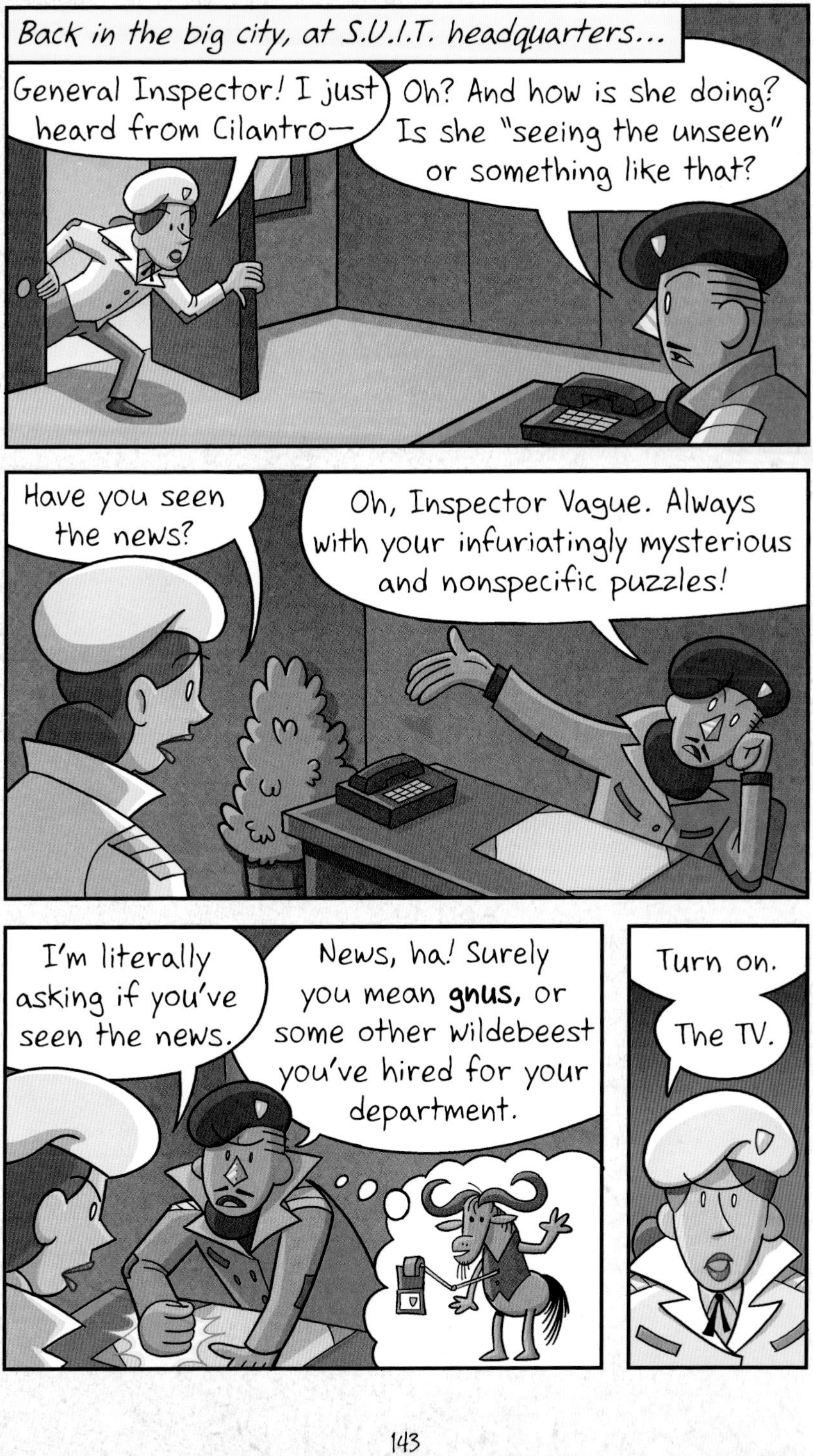
Back in the big city, at S.U.I.T. headquarters...
General Inspector! I just heard from Cilantro—
Oh? And how is she doing? Is she "seeing the unseen" or something like that?
Have you seen the news?
Oh, Inspector Vague. Always with your infuriatingly mysterious and nonspecific puzzles!
I'm literally asking if you've seen the news.
News, ha! Surely you mean **gnus,** or some other wildebeest you've hired for your department.
Turn on.
The TV.

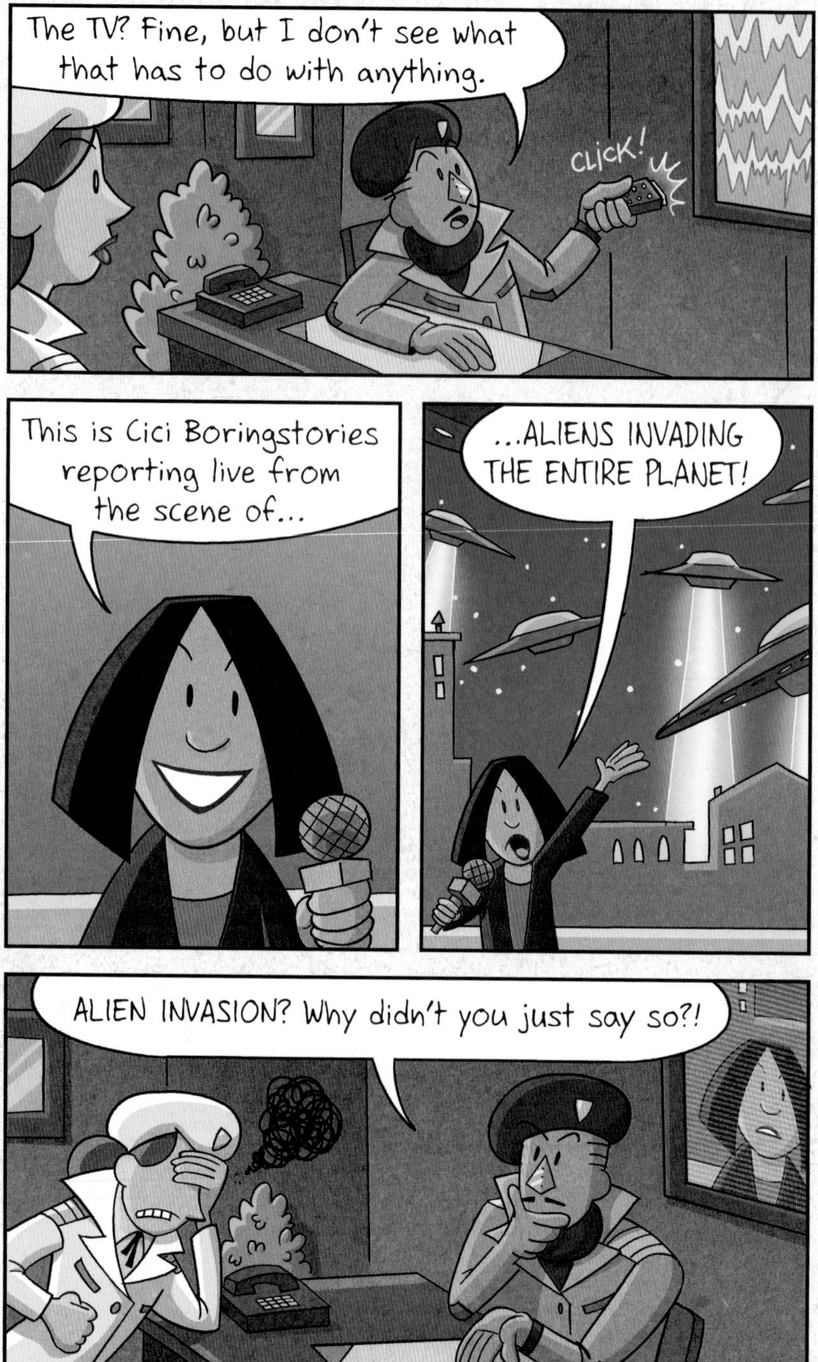
The TV? Fine, but I don't see what that has to do with anything.
CLICK!
This is Cici Boringstories reporting live from the scene of...
...ALIENS INVADING THE ENTIRE PLANET!
ALIEN INVASION? Why didn't you just say so?!

AAAAIEI!

Which of course stands for...

...Activate An All-Agent Important Emergency Immediately!

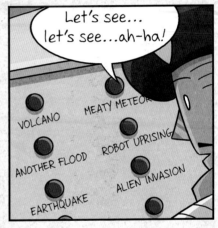

Let's see... let's see...ah-ha!

VOLCANO

MEATY METEOR

ANOTHER FLOOD

ROBOT UPRISING

ALIEN INVASION

EARTHQUAKE

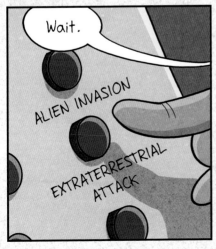

Wait.

ALIEN INVASION

EXTRATERRESTRIAL ATTACK

Oh no. Which one?

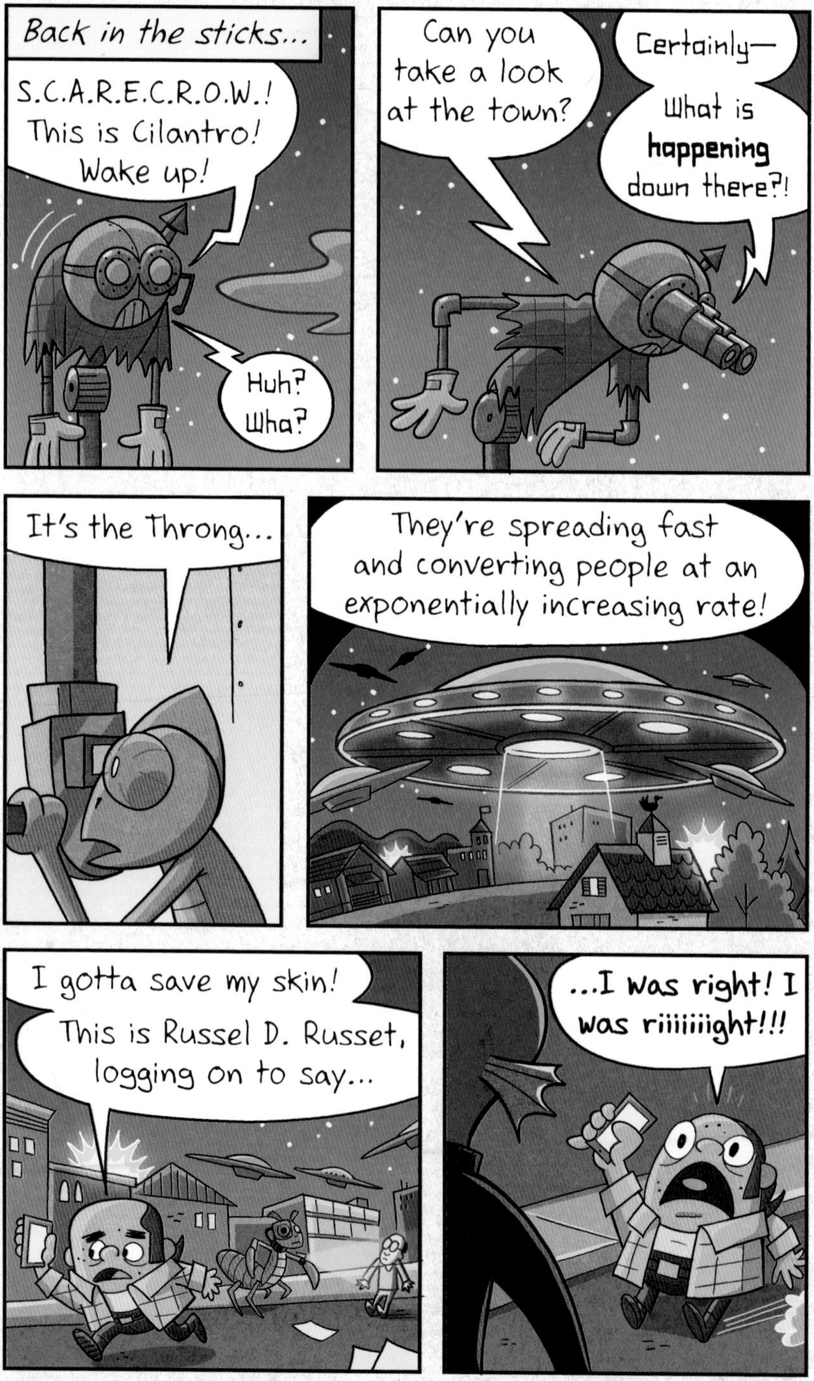
Back in the sticks...
S.C.A.R.E.C.R.O.W..! This is Cilantro! Wake up!
Huh? Wha?
Can you take a look at the town?
Certainly—
What is **happening** down there?!
It's the Throng...
They're spreading fast and converting people at an exponentially increasing rate!
I gotta save my skin!
This is Russel D. Russet, logging on to say...
...I was right! I was riiiiiiight!!!

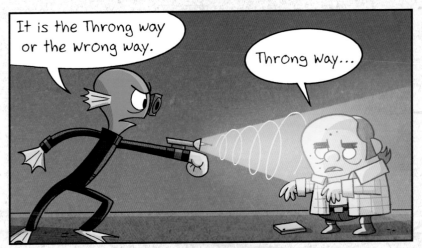

It is the Throng way or the wrong way.

Throng way...

It looks like the Throng's wrist-rays get people to sleepwalk to the ships...

They are tractor beamed up...

...turned into Throng themselves...

...then sent back down to brainwash more people.

Where ya goin' in such a hurry there, fella? That's the wrong way, not the Throng way.

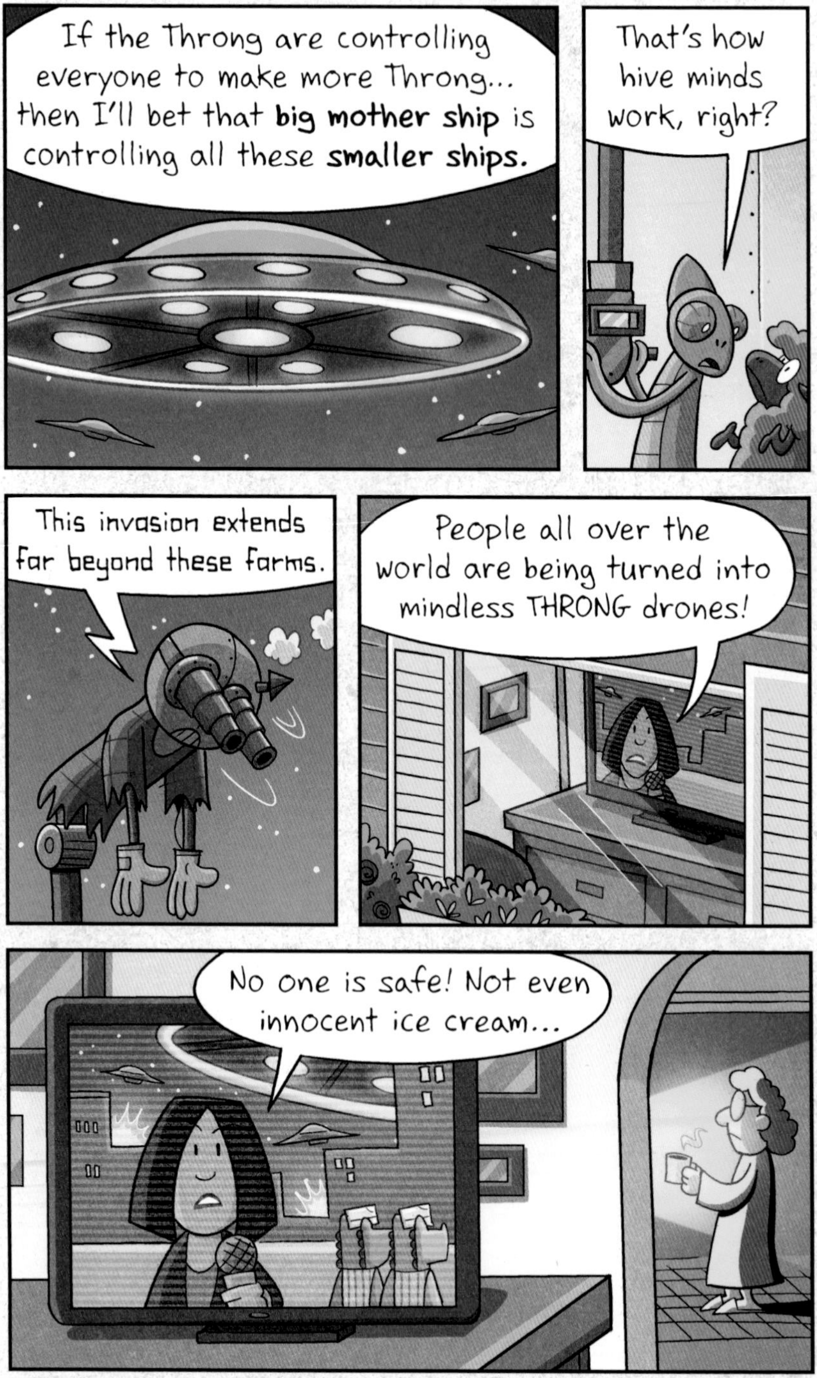
If the Throng are controlling everyone to make more Throng... then I'll bet that **big mother ship** is controlling all these **smaller ships.**
That's how hive minds work, right?
This invasion extends far beyond these farms.
People all over the world are being turned into mindless THRONG drones!
No one is safe! Not even innocent ice cream...

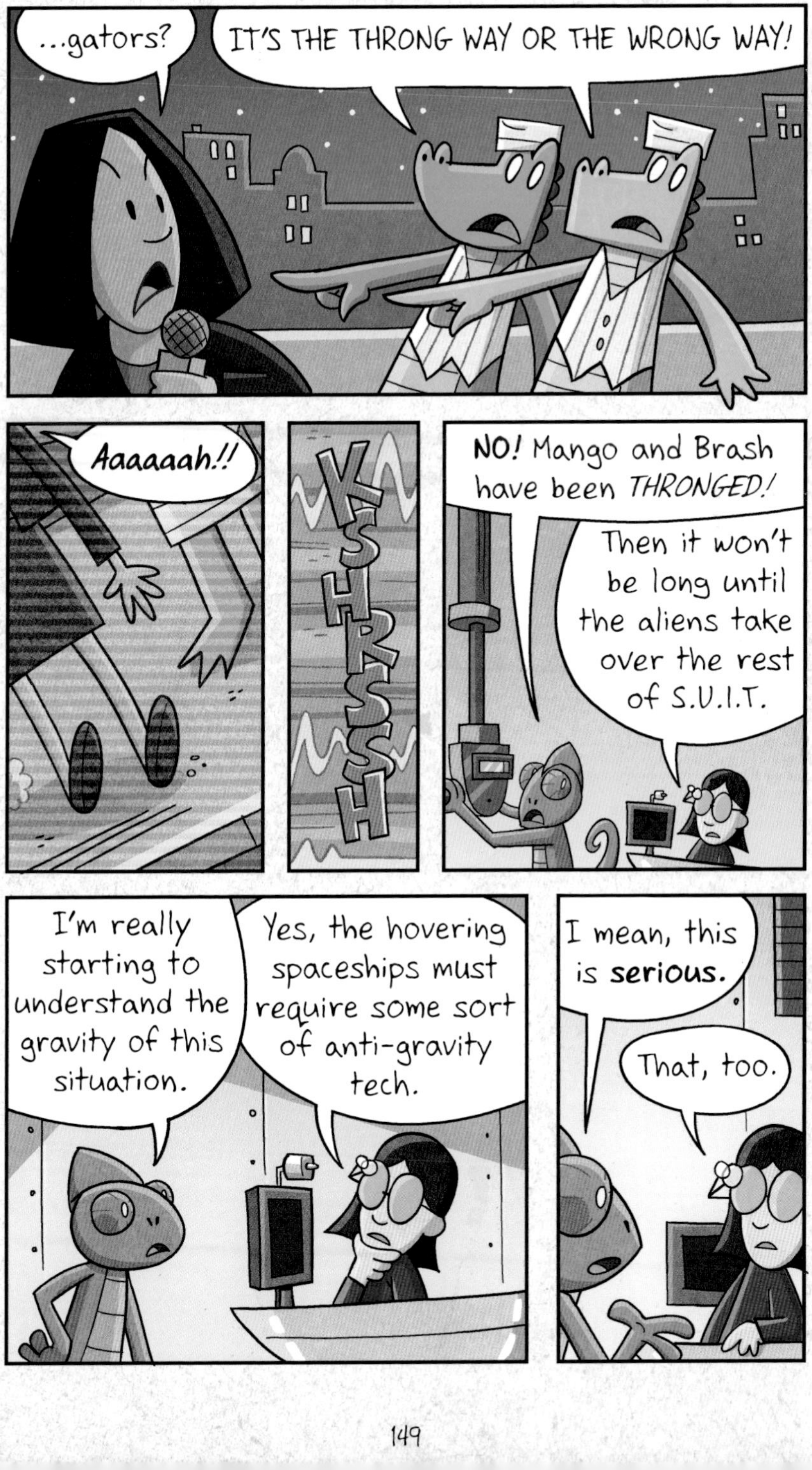
...gators?
IT'S THE THRONG WAY OR THE WRONG WAY!
Aaaaaah!!
KSHRSSSH
NO! Mango and Brash have been THRONGED!
Then it won't be long until the aliens take over the rest of S.U.I.T.
I'm really starting to understand the gravity of this situation.
Yes, the hovering spaceships must require some sort of anti-gravity tech.
I mean, this is serious.
That, too.

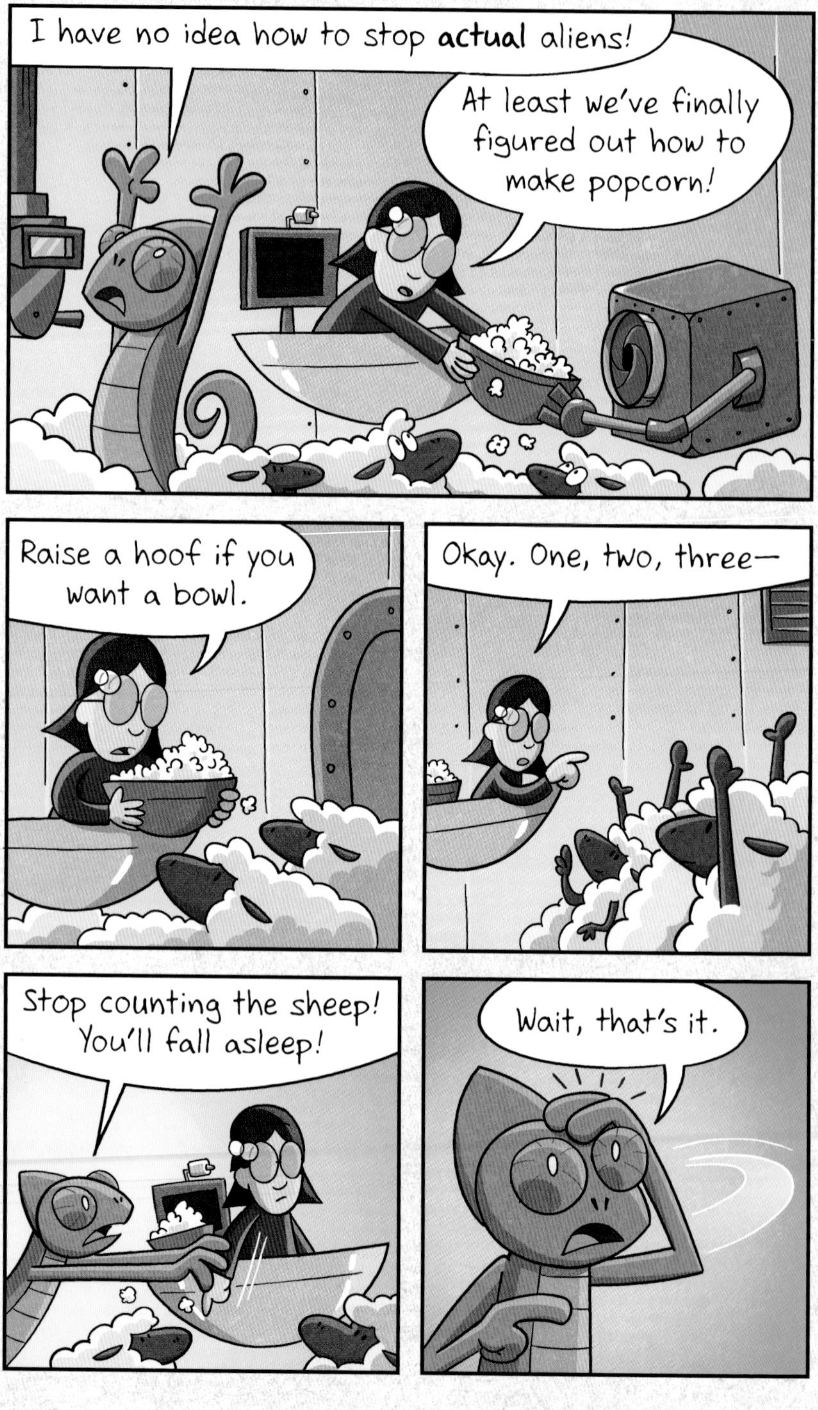
I have no idea how to stop **actual** aliens!
At least we've finally figured out how to make popcorn!
Raise a hoof if you want a bowl.
Okay. One, two, three—
Stop counting the sheep! You'll fall asleep!
Wait, that's it.

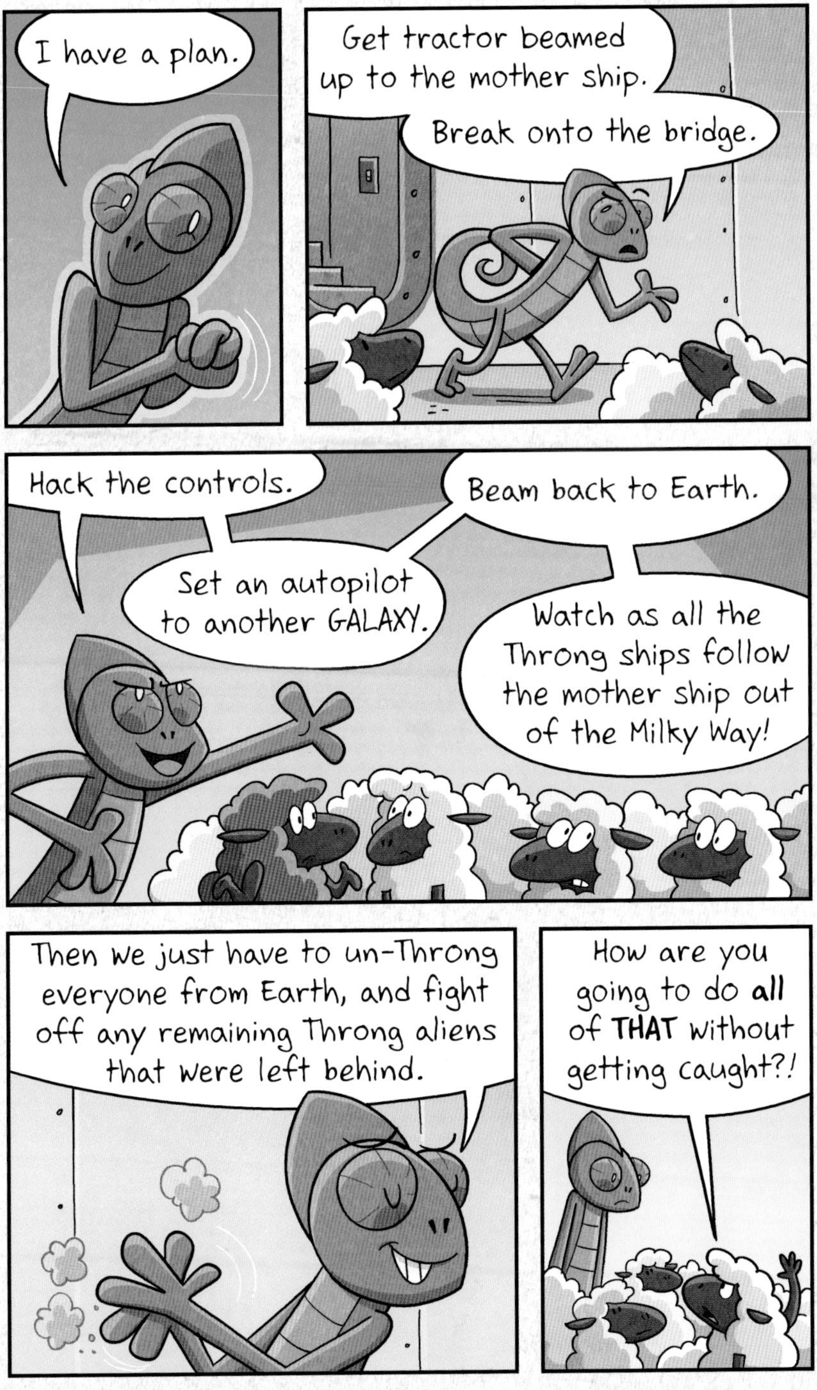
I have a plan.
Get tractor beamed up to the mother ship.
Break onto the bridge.
Hack the controls.
Set an autopilot to another GALAXY.
Beam back to Earth.
Watch as all the Throng ships follow the mother ship out of the Milky Way!
Then we just have to un-Throng everyone from Earth, and fight off any remaining Throng aliens that were left behind.
How are you going to do **all** of **THAT** without getting caught?!

Simple! If we can get enough sheep onto the mother sheep— I mean mother **ship**...

...the Throng will **COUNT** them and fall asheep—I mean **asleep!**

Giving us *plenty* of room to figure out the remaining details of the plan.

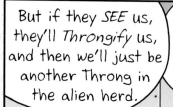

But if they *SEE* us, they'll *Throngify* us, and then we'll just be another Throng in the alien herd.

Can you turn us invisible like you?

No. Actually, the fact that my camouflage only works on my **skin** has been a real source of conflict lately.

About that...

I'd have preferred to test this out in a non-global-alien-invasion scenario, but...

I finally got the parts I needed shipped in from S.U.I.T. HQ and made you...

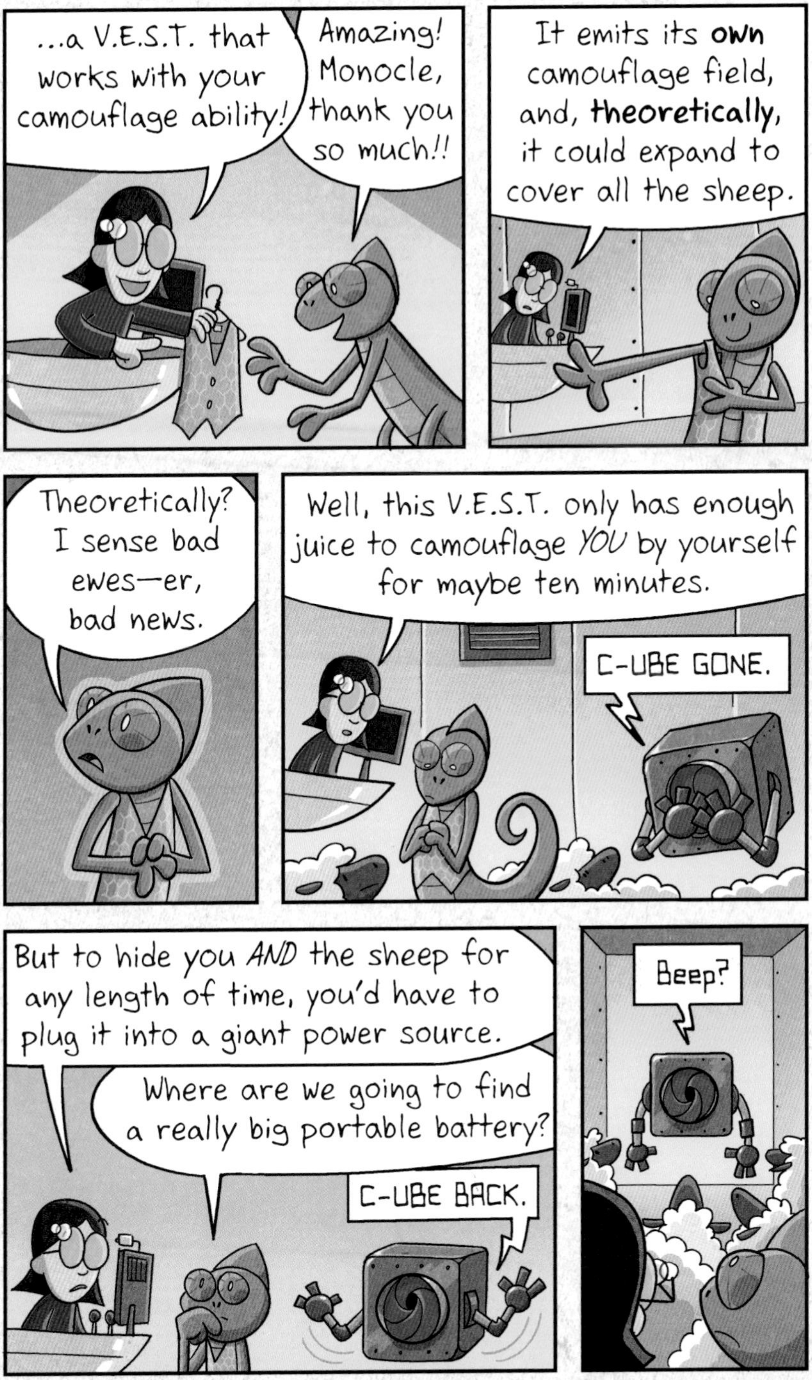
...a V.E.S.T. that works with your camouflage ability!
Amazing! Monocle, thank you so much!!
It emits its **own** camouflage field, and, **theoretically,** it could expand to cover all the sheep.
Theoretically? I sense bad ewes—er, bad news.
Well, this V.E.S.T. only has enough juice to camouflage *YOU* by yourself for maybe ten minutes.
C-UBE GONE.
But to hide you *AND* the sheep for any length of time, you'd have to plug it into a giant power source.
Where are we going to find a really big portable battery?
C-UBE BACK.
Beep?

Chapter 11

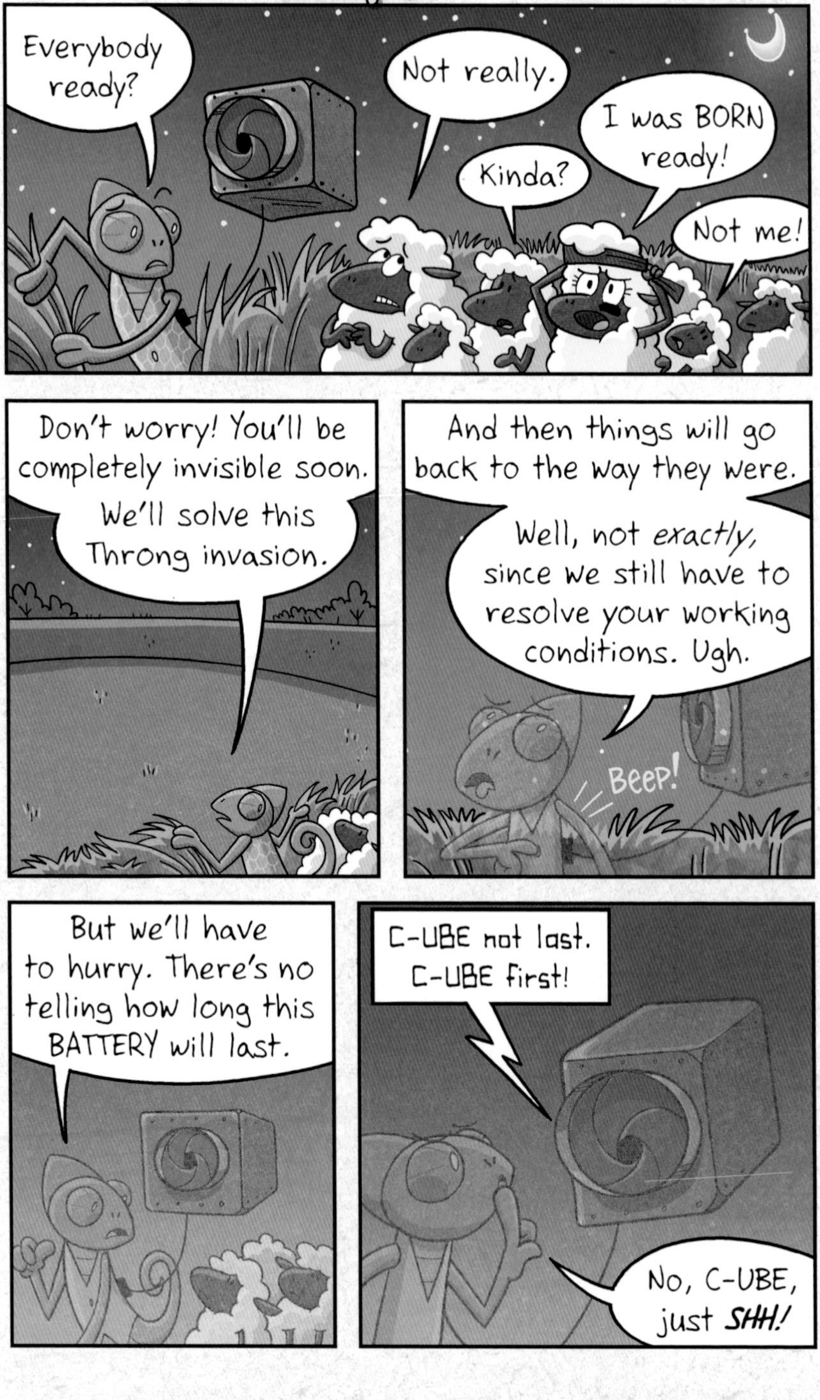

Everybody ready?
Not really.
Kinda?
I was BORN ready!
Not me!
Don't worry! You'll be completely invisible soon.
We'll solve this Throng invasion.
And then things will go back to the way they were.
Well, not *exactly*, since we still have to resolve your working conditions. Ugh.
Beep!
But we'll have to hurry. There's no telling how long this BATTERY will last.
C-UBE not last. C-UBE first!
No, C-UBE, just ***SHH!***

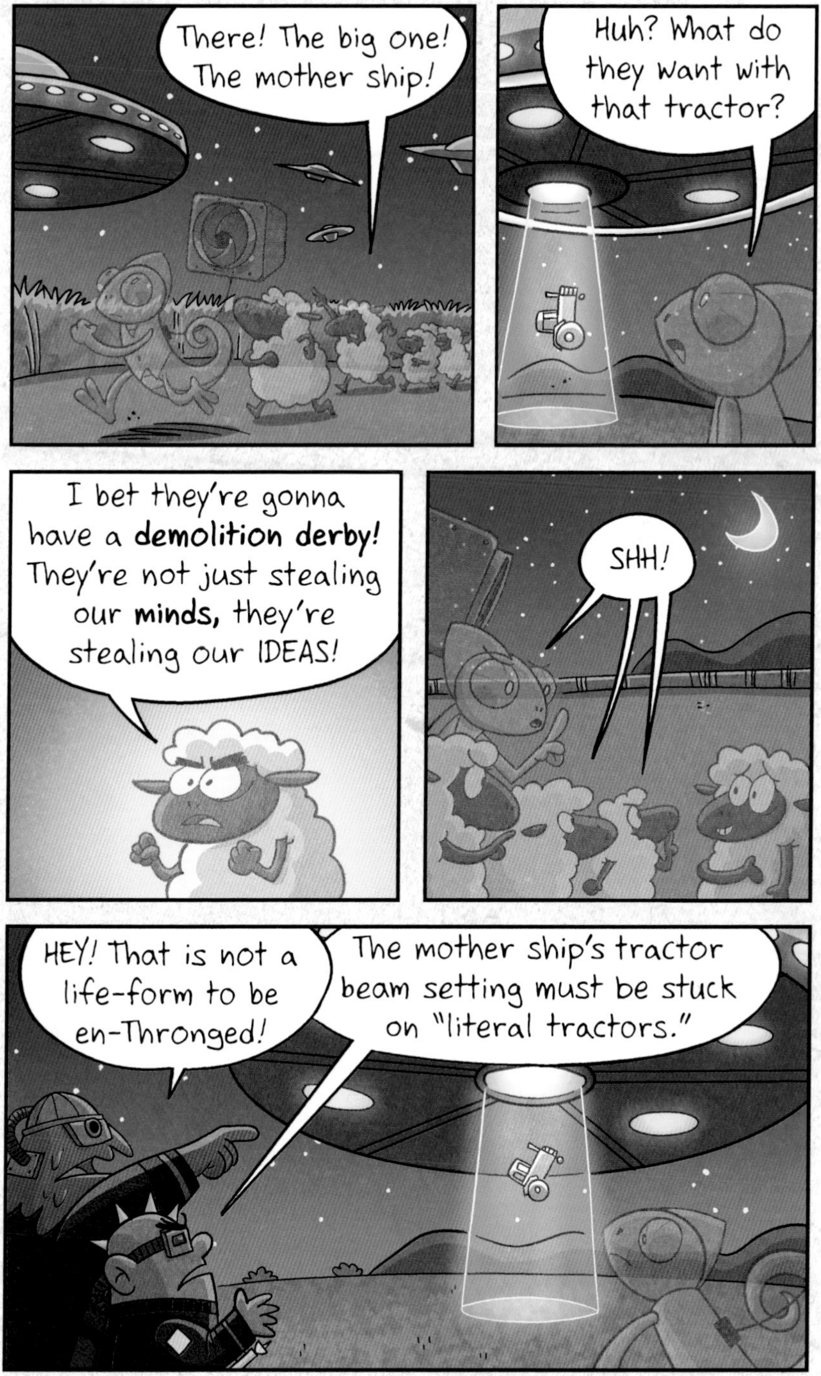
There! The big one! The mother ship!
Huh? What do they want with that tractor?
I bet they're gonna have a **demolition derby!** They're not just stealing our **minds,** they're stealing our IDEAS!
SHH!
HEY! That is not a life-form to be en-Thronged!
The mother ship's tractor beam setting must be stuck on "literal tractors."

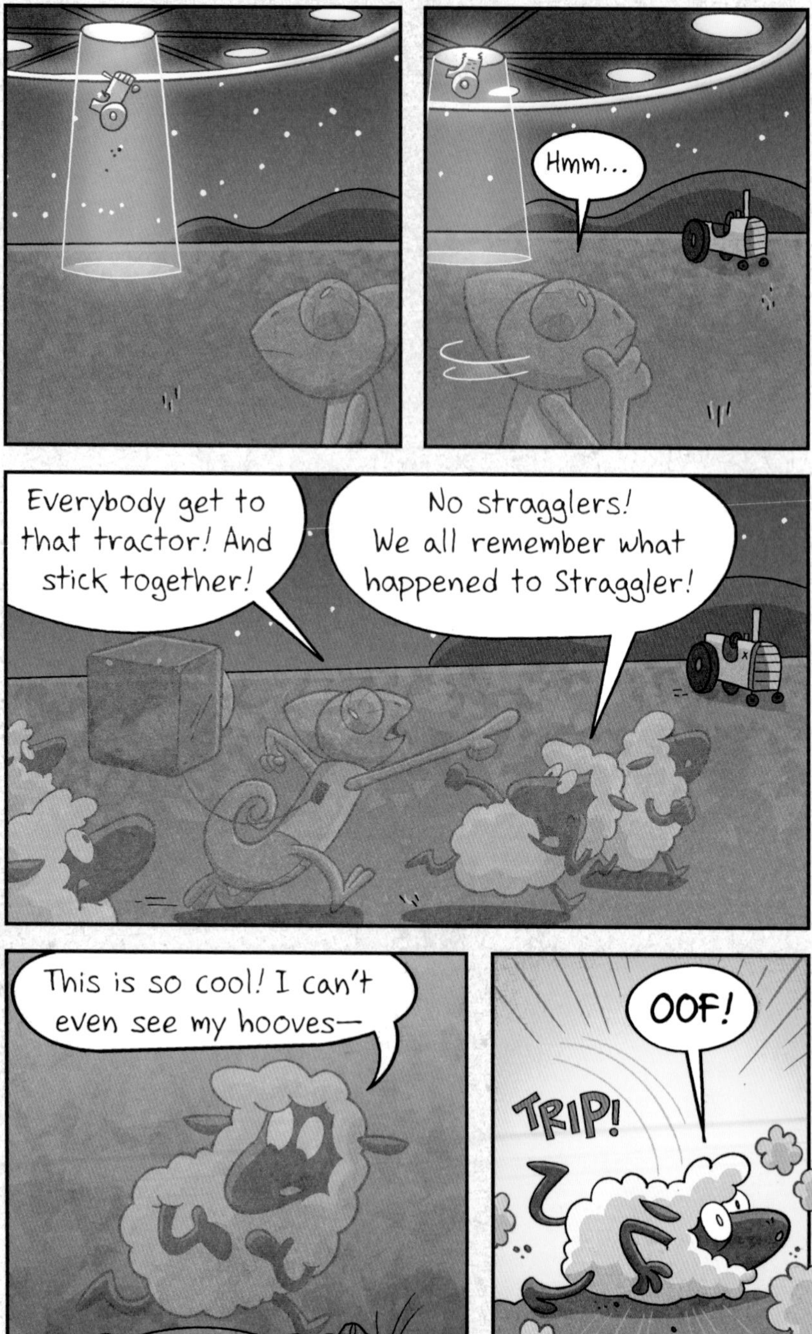
Hmm...
Everybody get to that tractor! And stick together!
No stragglers! We all remember what happened to Straggler!
This is so cool! I can't even see my hooves—
TRIP!
OOF!

Uh...

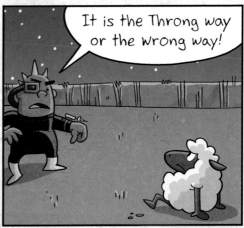

It is the Throng way or the wrong way!

ZAP!

Lost one! No!

Is it hot out here or just me?

It is not just you.

Beeeeeep.

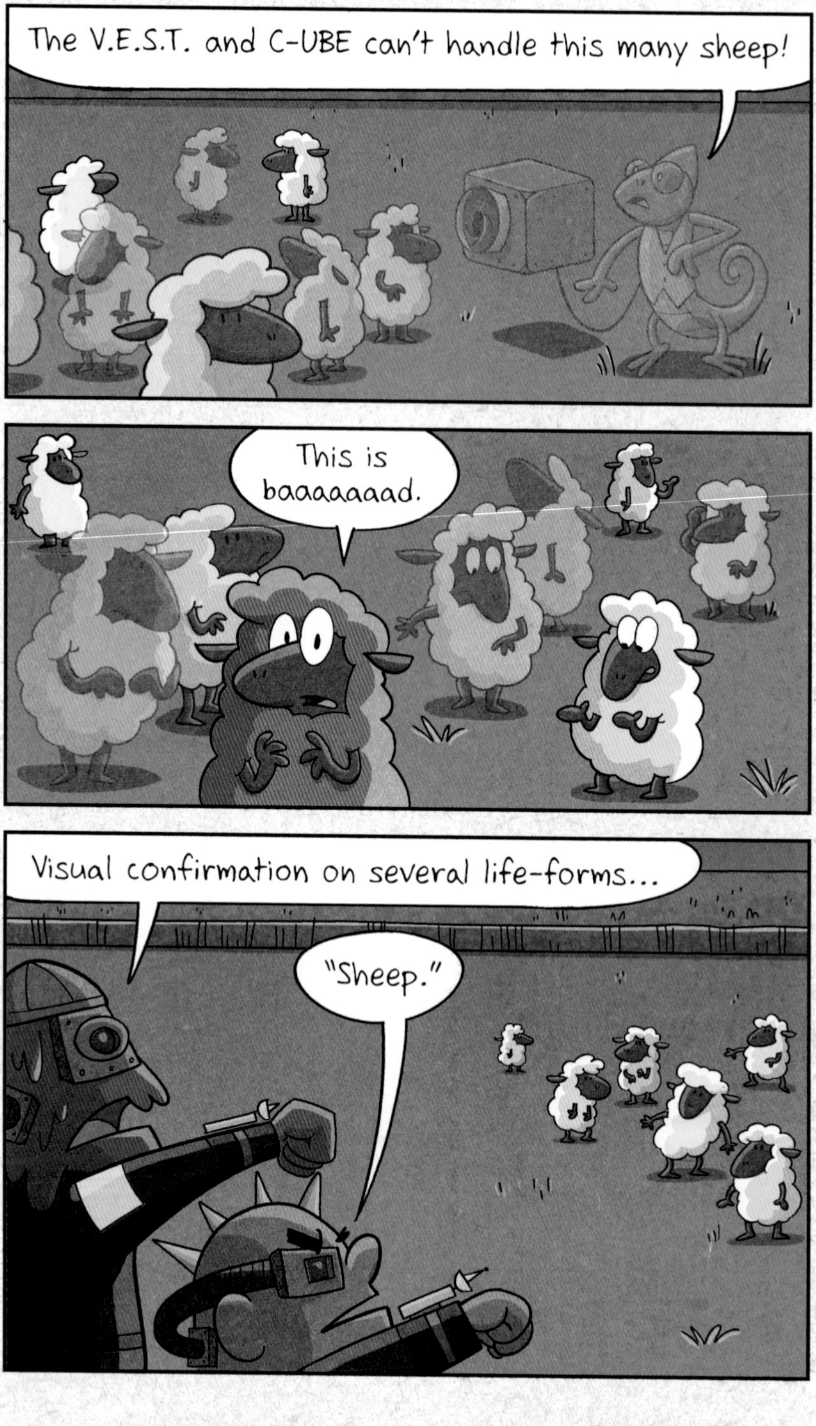
The V.E.S.T. and C-UBE can't handle this many sheep!
This is baaaaaaad.
Visual confirmation on several life-forms...
"Sheep."

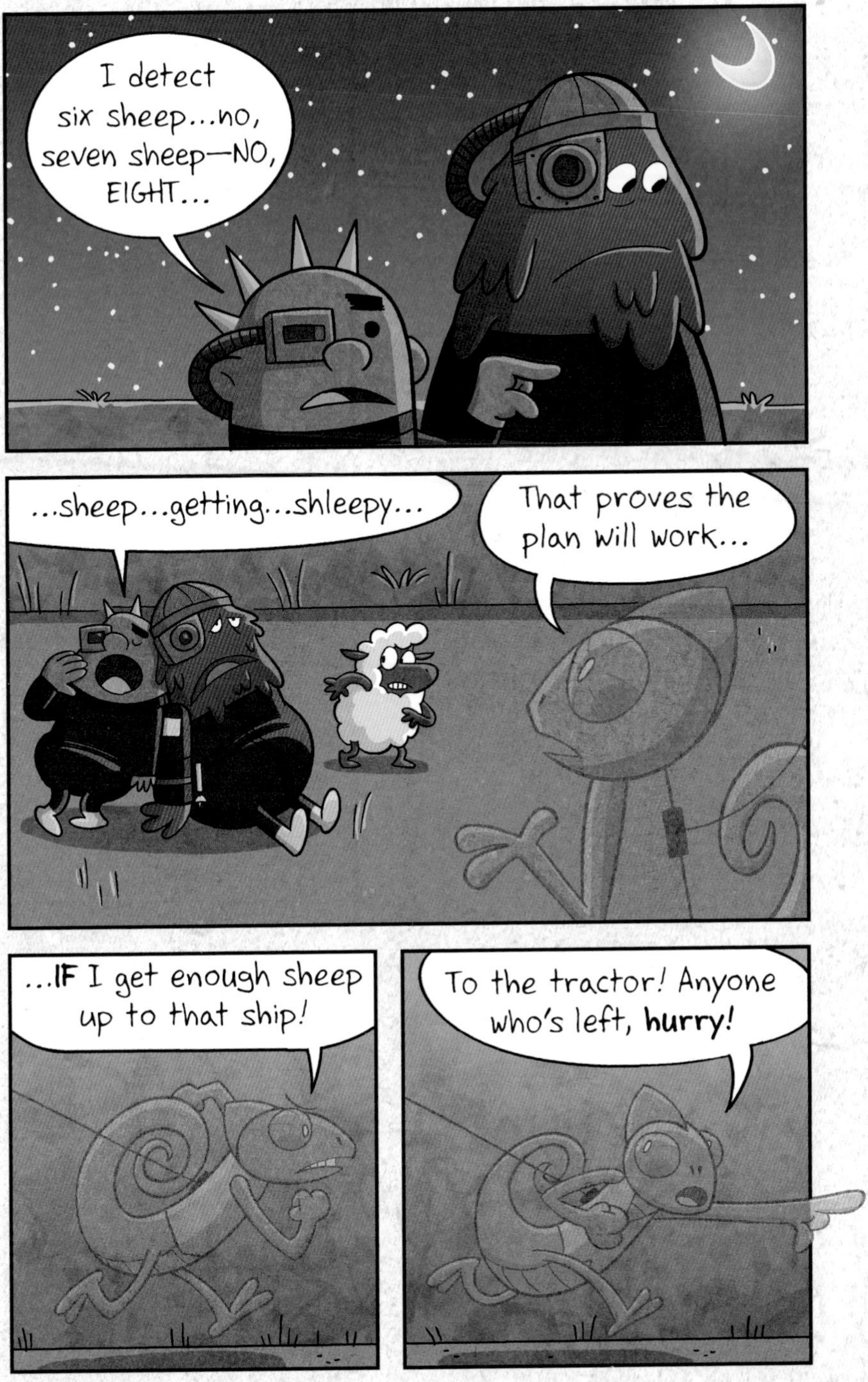
I detect six sheep...no, seven sheep—NO, EIGHT...
...sheep...getting...shleepy...
That proves the plan will work...
...**IF** I get enough sheep up to that ship!
To the tractor! Anyone who's left, **hurry**!

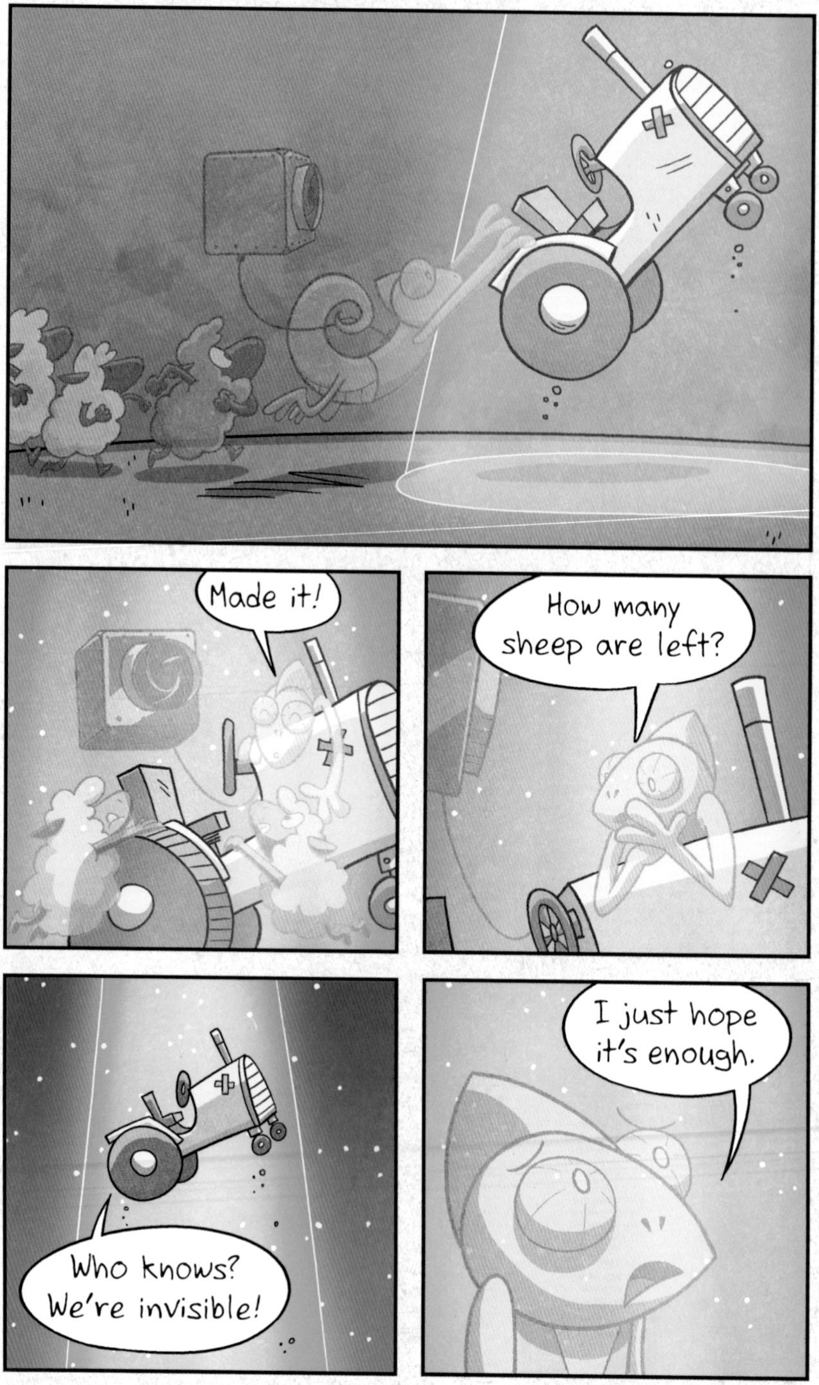
Made it!
How many sheep are left?
Who knows? We're invisible!
I just hope it's enough.

We made it!

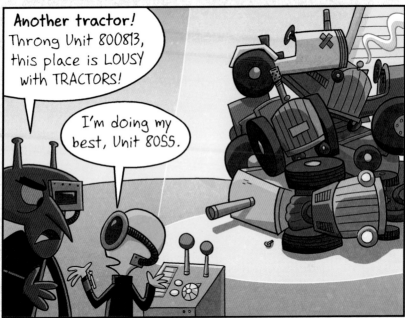

Another tractor! Throng Unit 800813, this place is LOUSY with TRACTORS!

I'm doing my best, Unit 8055.

Psst! This way!

Uh...**which** way?

Look where I'm pointing—OH, RIGHT. Um, just follow my voice!

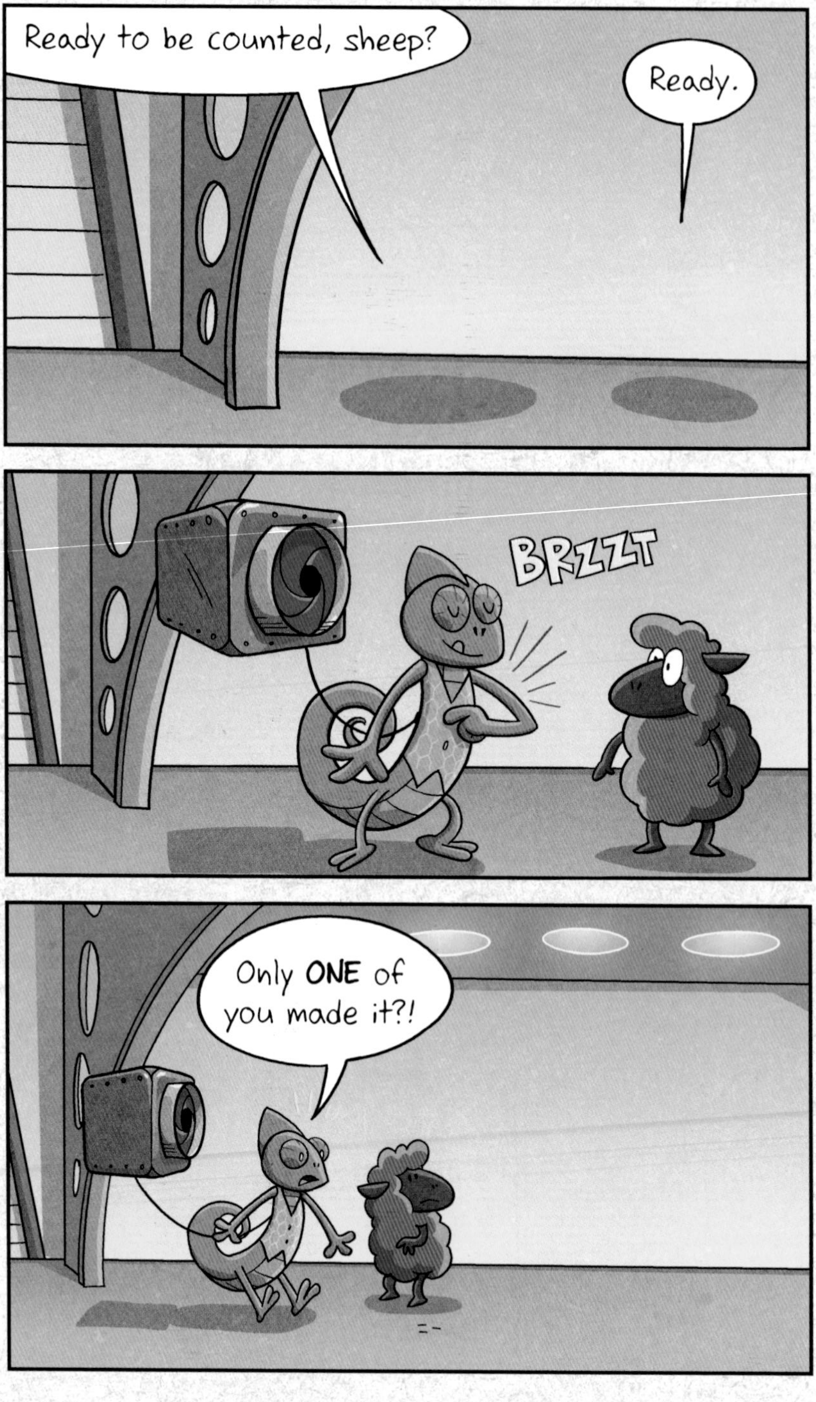
Ready to be counted, sheep?
Ready.
BRZZT
Only **ONE** of you made it?!

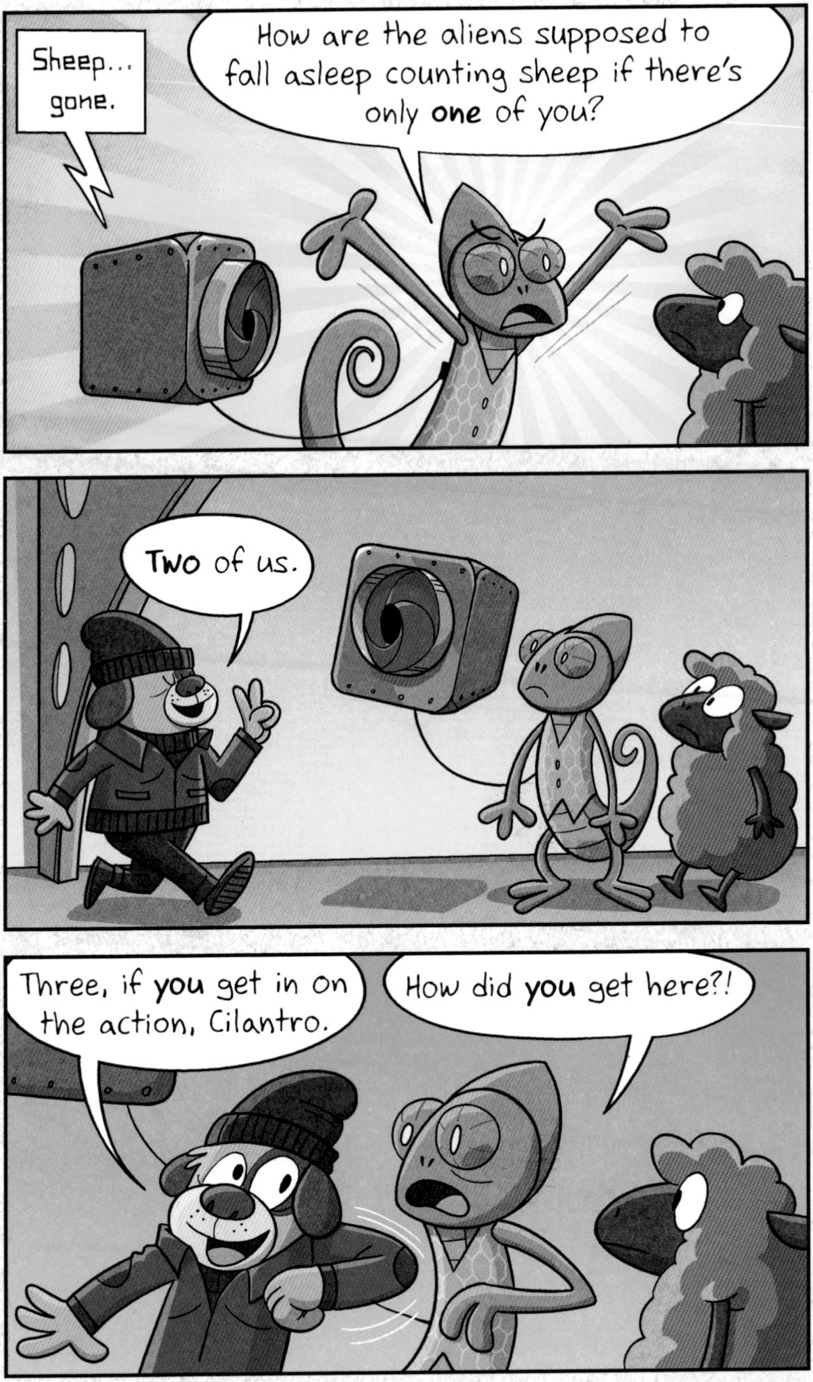
Sheep... gone.
How are the aliens supposed to fall asleep counting sheep if there's only **one** of you?
TWO of us.
Three, if **you** get in on the action, Cilantro.
How did **you** get here?!

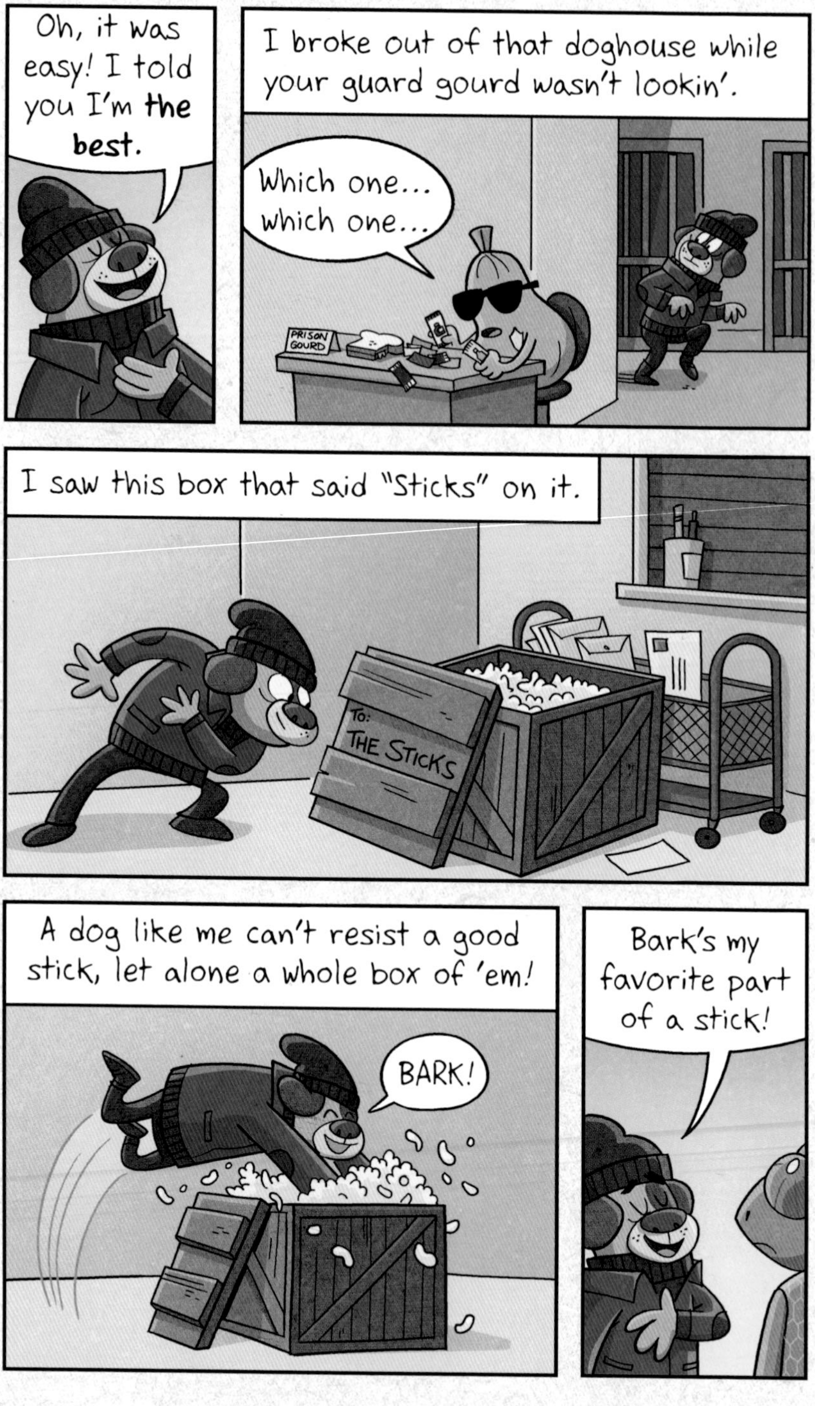

Oh, it was easy! I told you I'm **the best.**
I broke out of that doghouse while your guard gourd wasn't lookin'.
Which one... which one...
PRISON GOURD
I saw this box that said "Sticks" on it.
TO: THE STICKS
A dog like me can't resist a good stick, let alone a whole box of 'em!
BARK!
Bark's my favorite part of a stick!

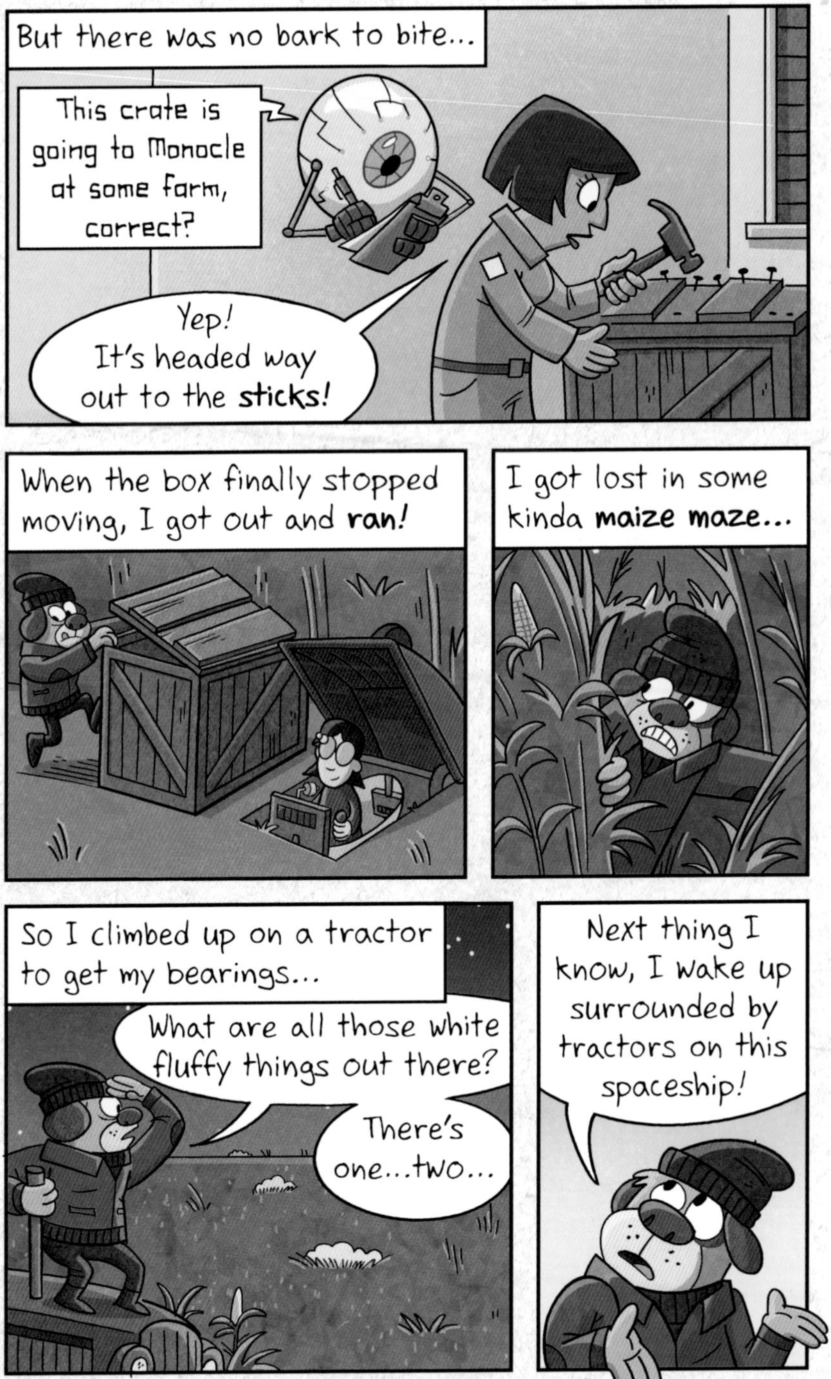
But there was no bark to bite...
This crate is going to Monocle at some farm, correct?
Yep! It's headed way out to the **sticks!**
When the box finally stopped moving, I got out and **ran!**
I got lost in some kinda **maize maze...**
So I climbed up on a tractor to get my bearings...
What are all those white fluffy things out there?
There's one...two...
Next thing I know, I wake up surrounded by tractors on this spaceship!

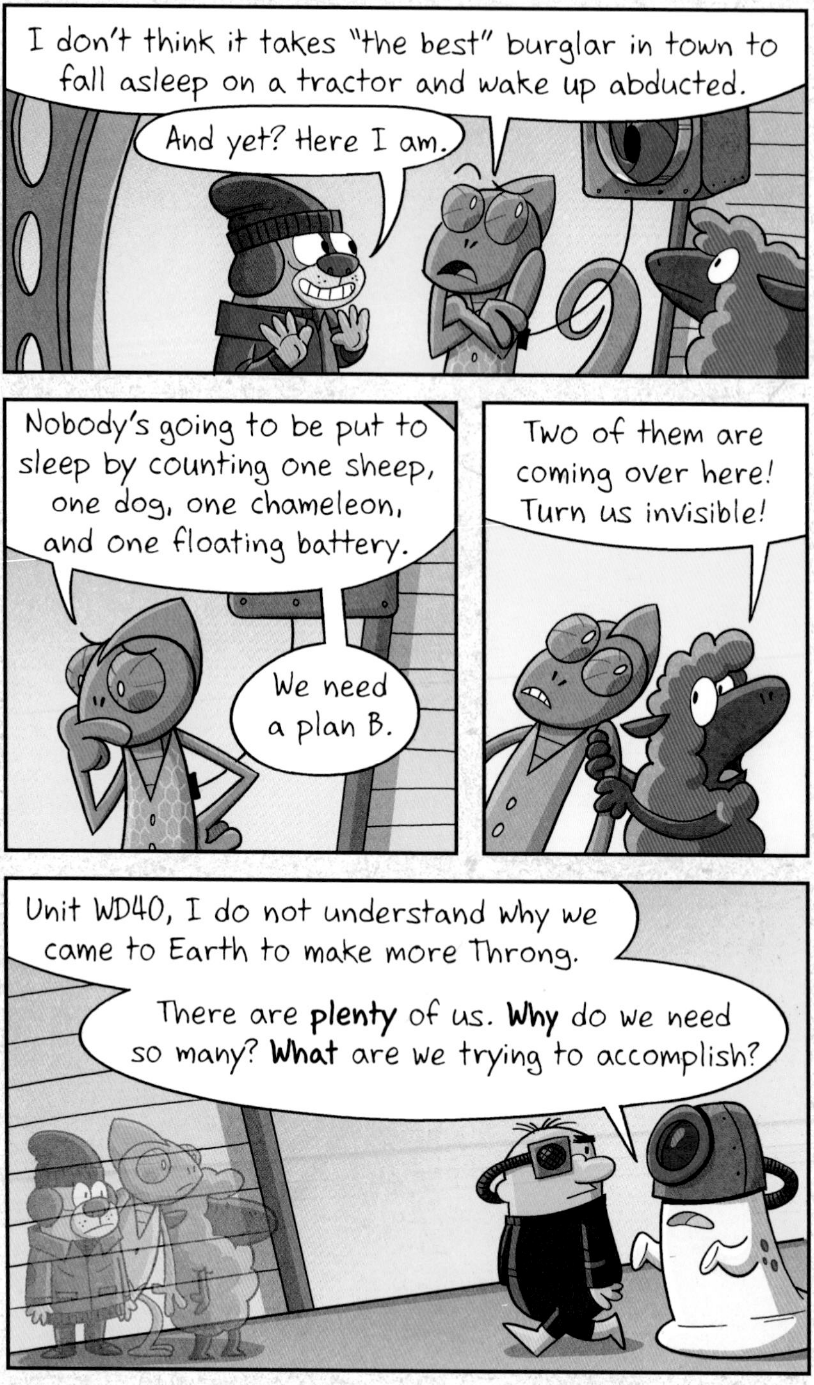
I don't think it takes "the best" burglar in town to fall asleep on a tractor and wake up abducted.
And yet? Here I am.
Nobody's going to be put to sleep by counting one sheep, one dog, one chameleon, and one floating battery.
We need a plan B.
Two of them are coming over here! Turn us invisible!
Unit WD40, I do not understand why we came to Earth to make more Throng.
There are **plenty** of us. **Why** do we need so many? **What** are we trying to accomplish?

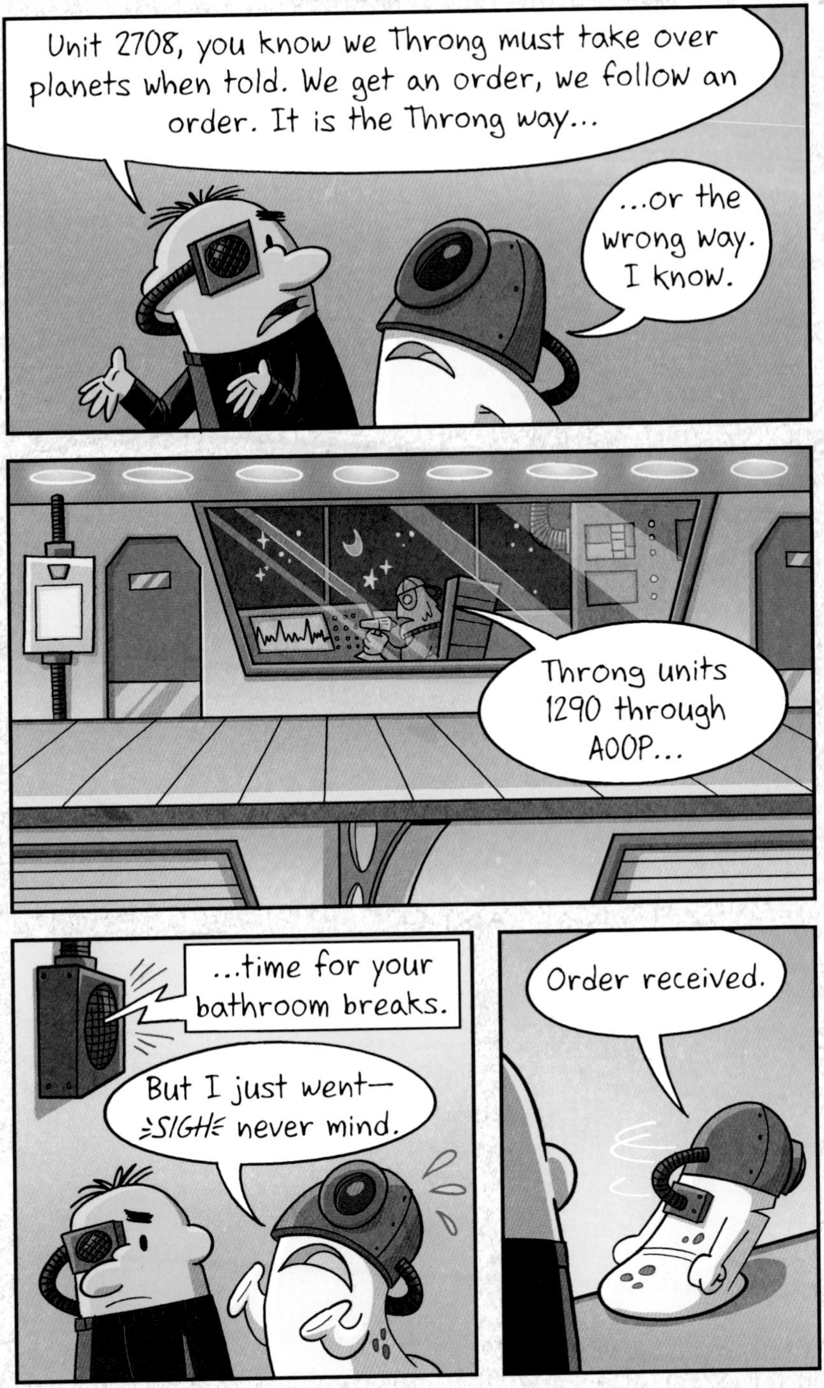
Unit 2708, you know we Throng must take over planets when told. We get an order, we follow an order. It is the Throng way...
...or the wrong way. I know.
Throng units 1290 through AOOP...
...time for your bathroom breaks.
But I just went—
SIGH never mind.
Order received.

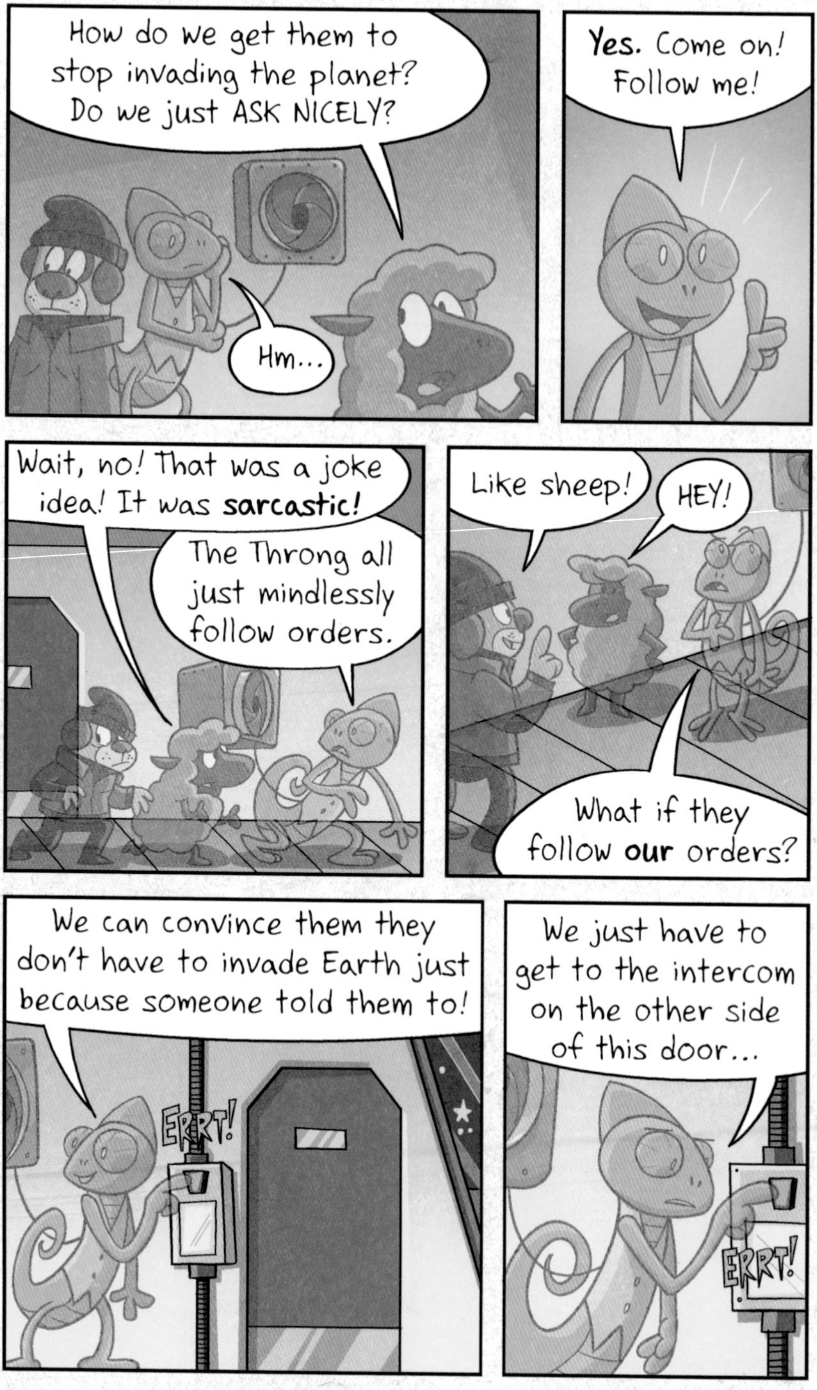
How do we get them to stop invading the planet? Do we just ASK NICELY?
Hm...
Yes. Come on! Follow me!
Wait, no! That was a joke idea! It was **sarcastic!**
The Throng all just mindlessly follow orders.
Like sheep!
HEY!
What if they follow **our** orders?
We can convince them they don't have to invade Earth just because someone told them to!
ERRT!
We just have to get to the intercom on the other side of this door...
ERRT!

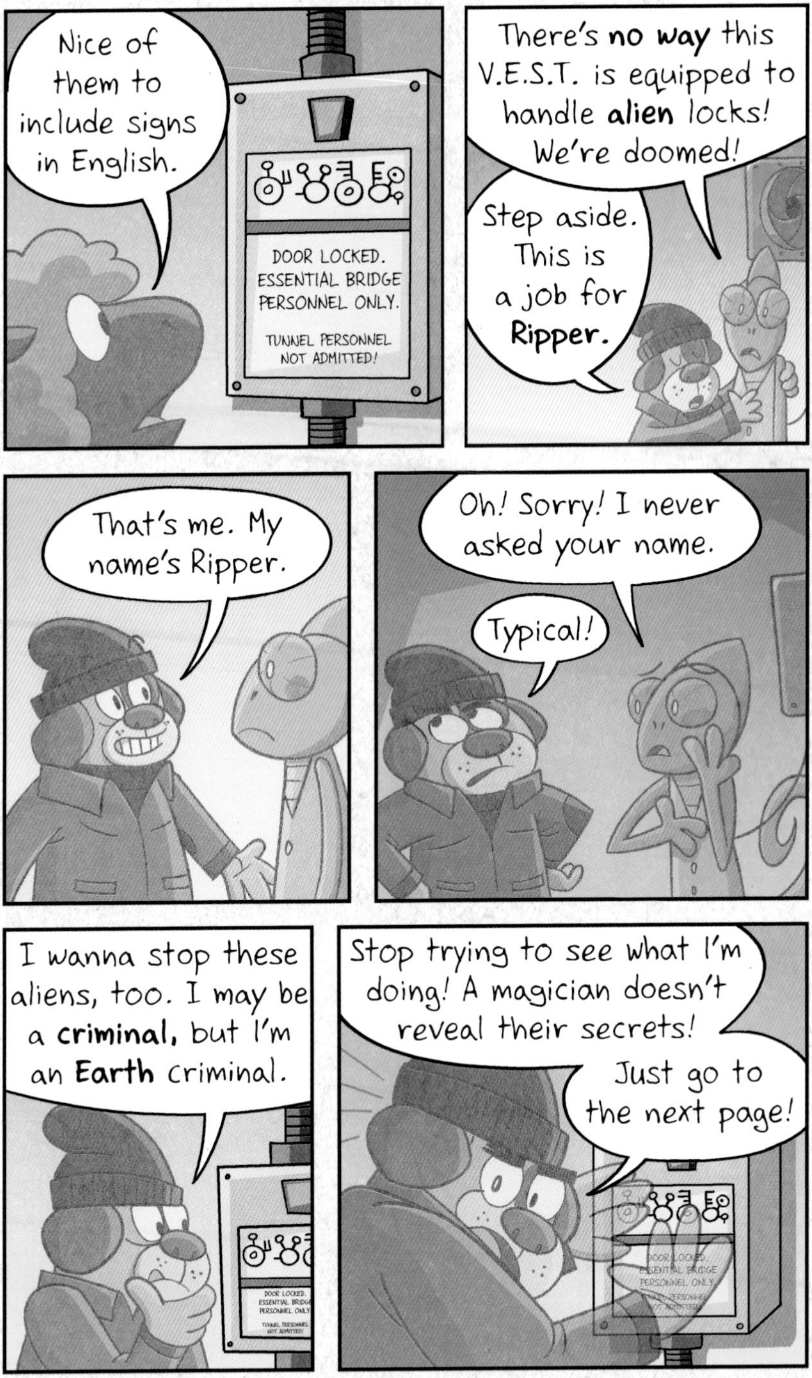
Nice of them to include signs in English.
DOOR LOCKED. ESSENTIAL BRIDGE PERSONNEL ONLY.
TUNNEL PERSONNEL NOT ADMITTED!
There's **no way** this V.E.S.T. is equipped to handle **alien** locks! We're doomed!
Step aside. This is a job for **Ripper.**
That's me. My name's Ripper.
Oh! Sorry! I never asked your name.
Typical!
I wanna stop these aliens, too. I may be a **criminal,** but I'm an **Earth** criminal.
Stop trying to see what I'm doing! A magician doesn't reveal their secrets!
Just go to the next page!

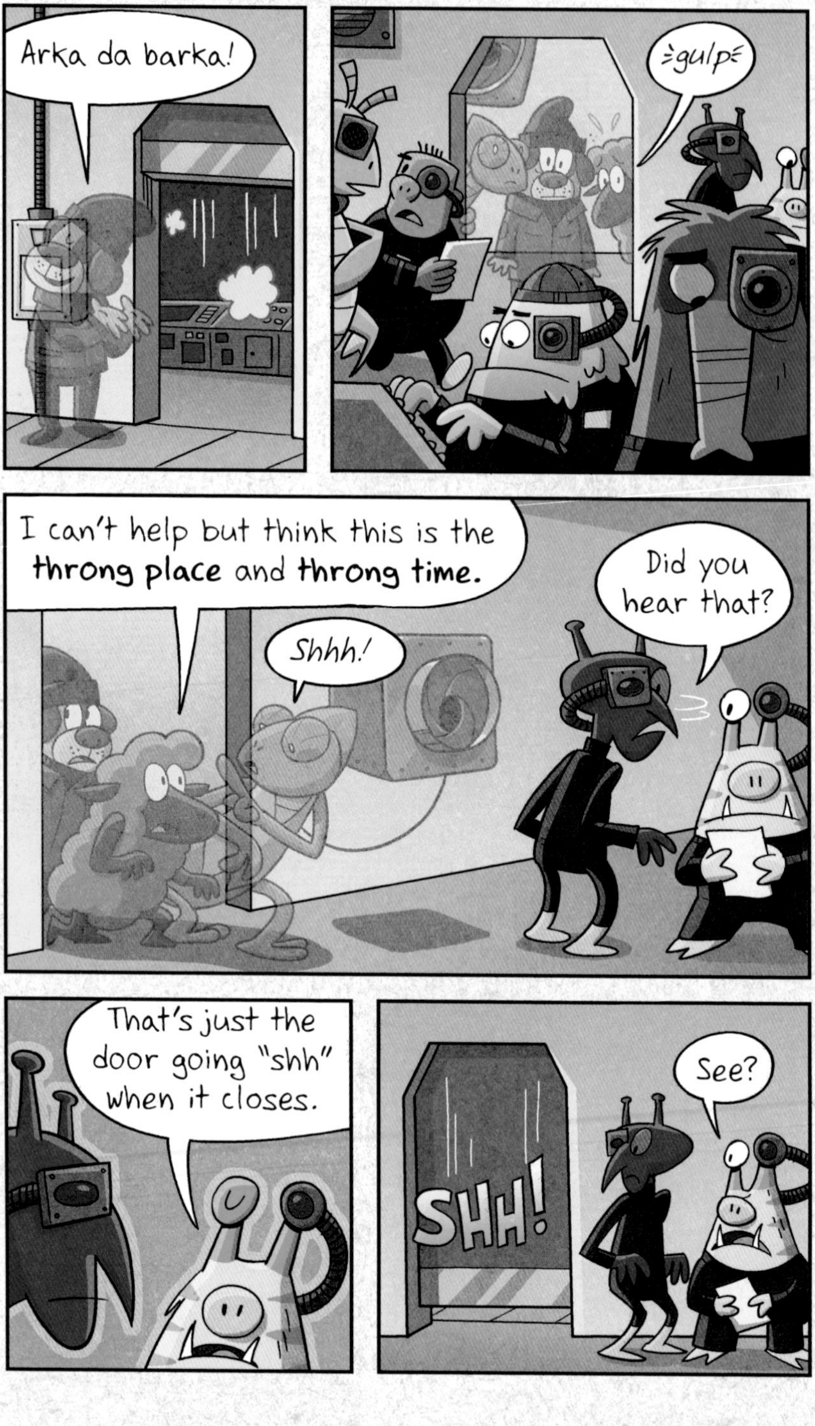
Arka da barka!
gulp
I can't help but think this is the **throng place** and **throng time.**
Shhh!
Did you hear that?
That's just the door going "shh" when it closes.
SHH!
See?

Chapter 12

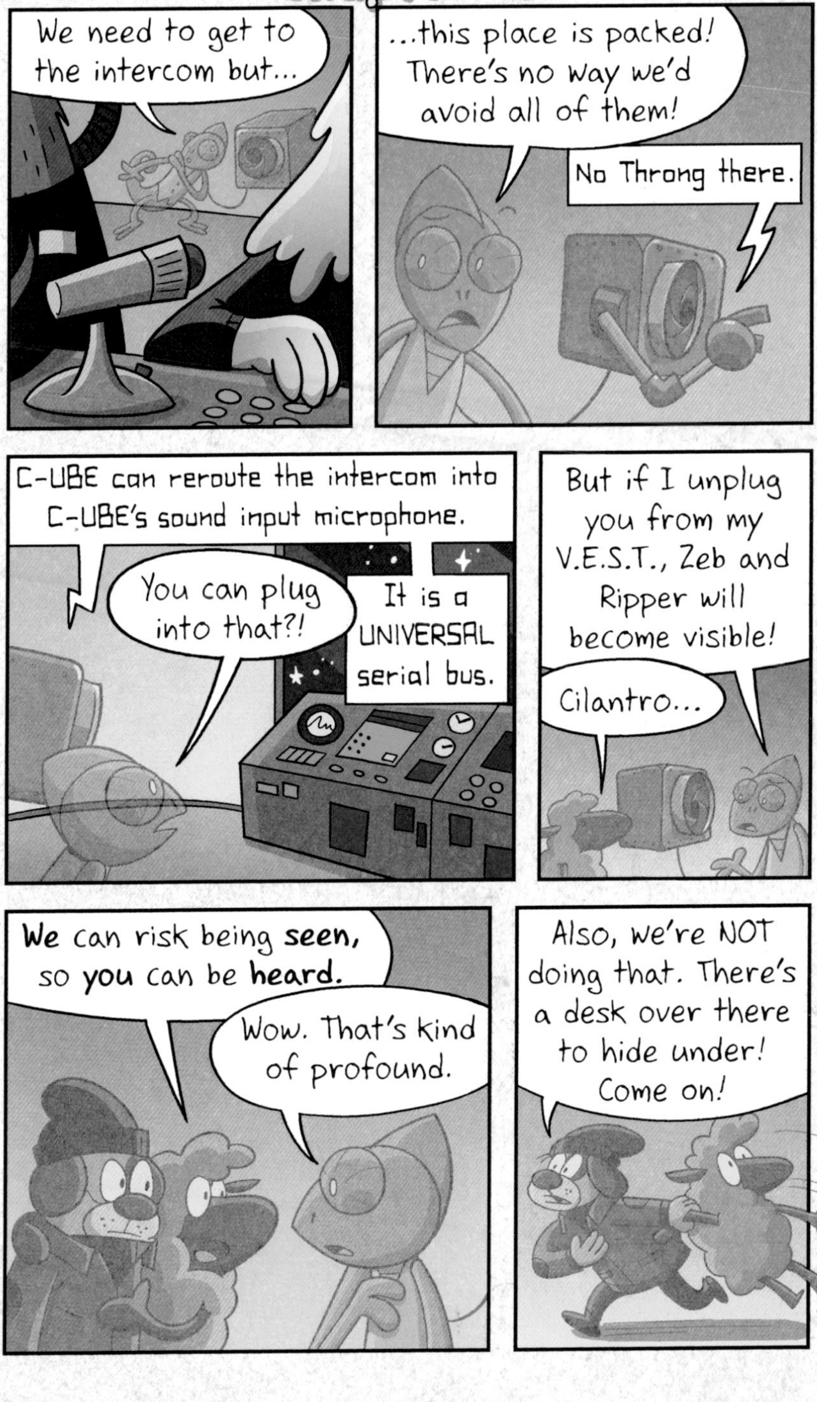
We need to get to the intercom but...
...this place is packed! There's no way we'd avoid all of them!
No Throng there.
C-UBE can reroute the intercom into C-UBE's sound input microphone.
You can plug into that?!
It is a UNIVERSAL serial bus.
But if I unplug you from my V.E.S.T., Zeb and Ripper will become visible!
Cilantro...
We can risk being **seen**, so **you** can be **heard.**
Wow. That's kind of profound.
Also, we're NOT doing that. There's a desk over there to hide under! Come on!

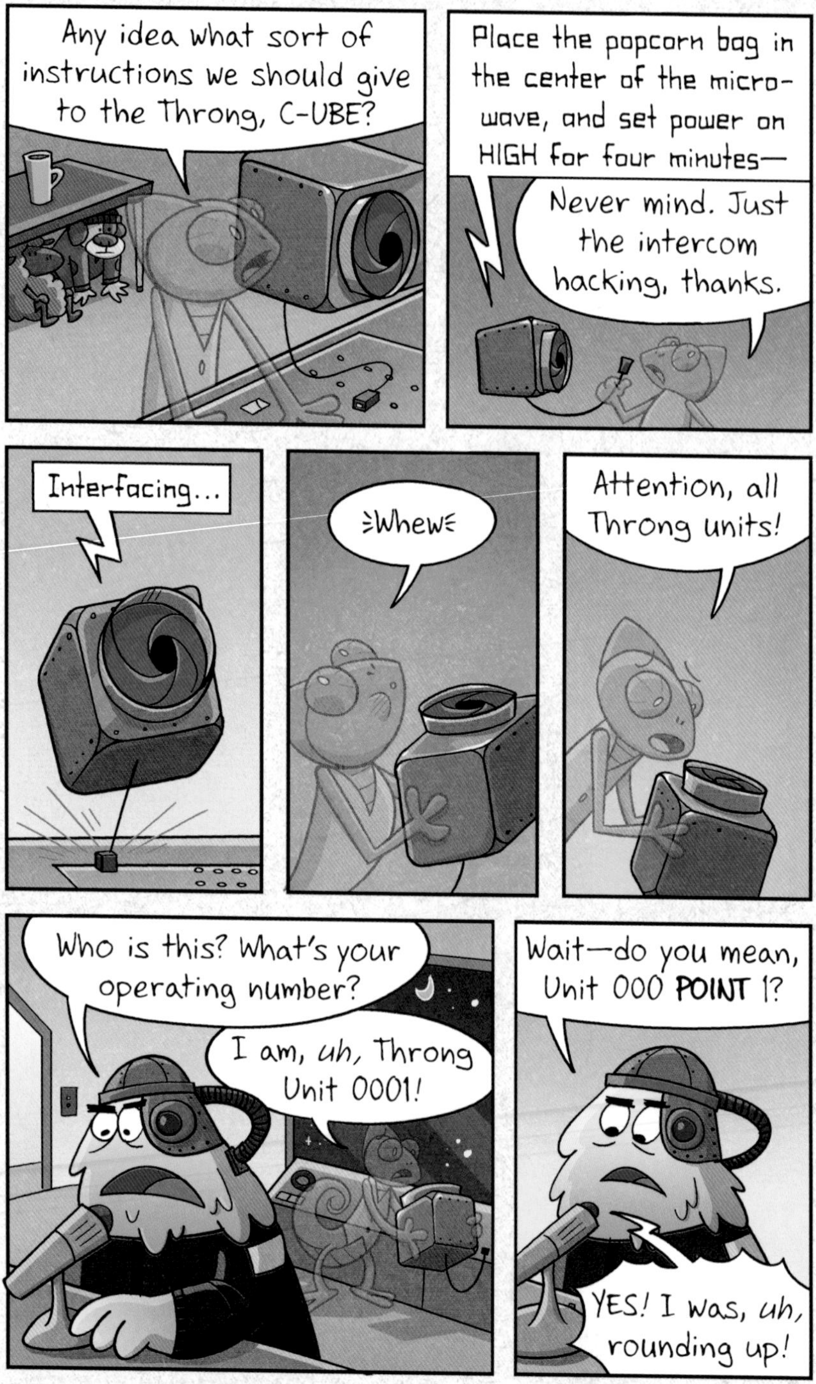

Any idea what sort of instructions we should give to the Throng, C-UBE?
Place the popcorn bag in the center of the micro-wave, and set power on HIGH for four minutes—
Never mind. Just the intercom hacking, thanks.
Interfacing...
Whew
Attention, all Throng units!
Who is this? What's your operating number?
I am, *uh*, Throng Unit 0001!
Wait—do you mean, Unit 000 **POINT** 1?
YES! I was, *uh*, rounding up!

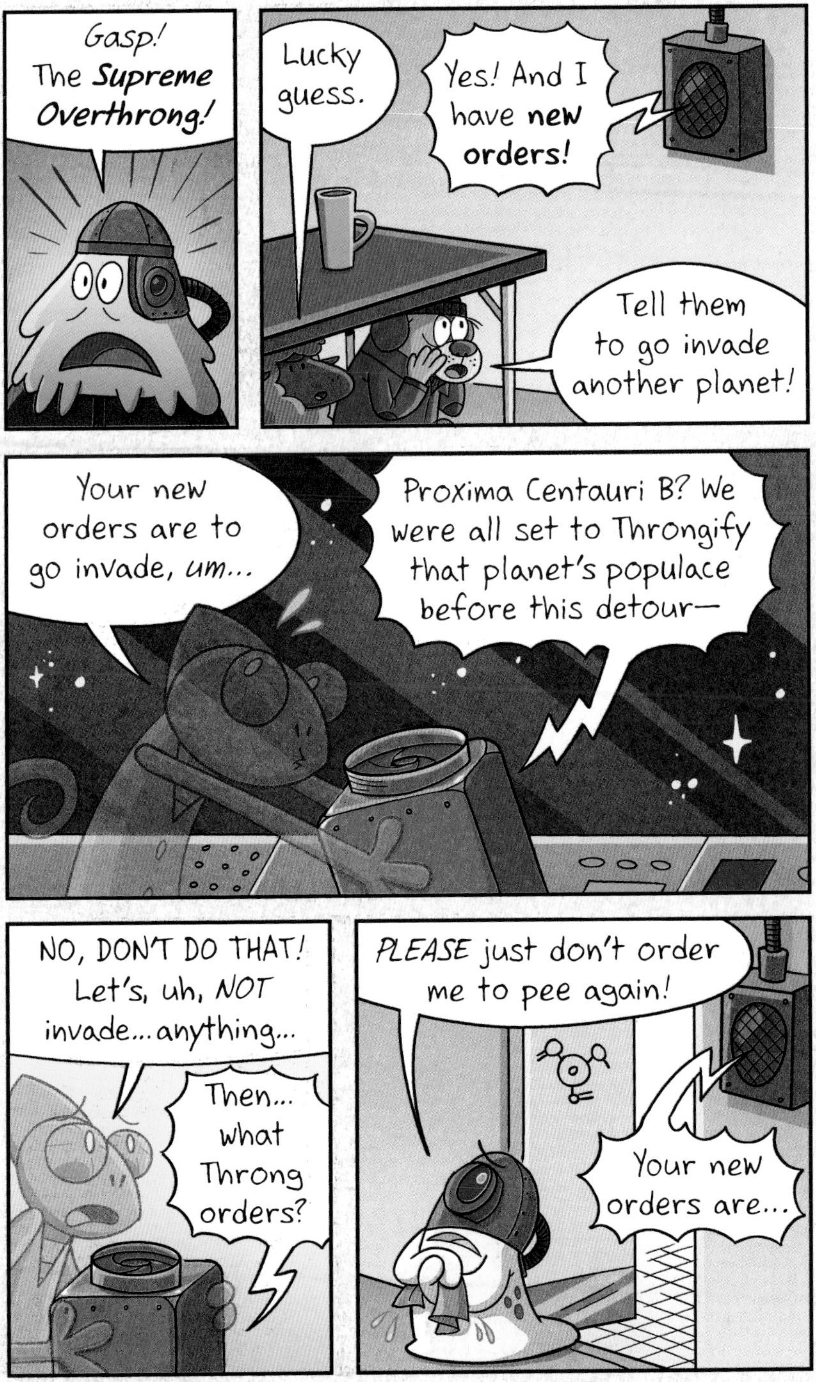
Gasp! The Supreme Overthrong!
Lucky guess.
Yes! And I have new orders!
Tell them to go invade another planet!
Your new orders are to go invade, um...
Proxima Centauri B? We were all set to Throngify that planet's populace before this detour—
NO, DON'T DO THAT! Let's, uh, NOT invade... anything...
Then... what Throng orders?
PLEASE just don't order me to pee again!
Your new orders are...

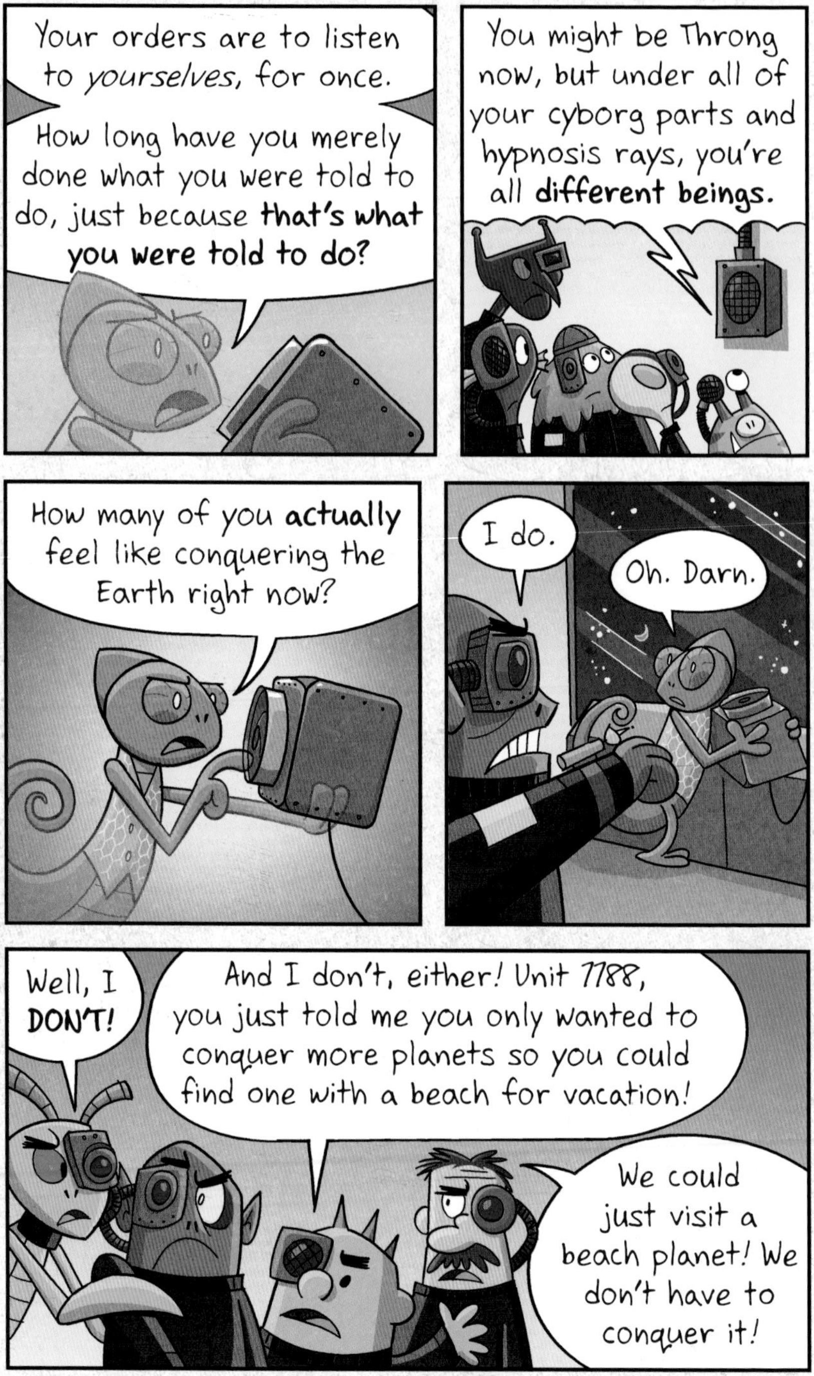
Your orders are to listen to *yourselves,* for once.
How long have you merely done what you were told to do, just because **that's what you were told to do?**
You might be Throng now, but under all of your cyborg parts and hypnosis rays, you're all **different beings.**
How many of you **actually** feel like conquering the Earth right now?
I do.
Oh. Darn.
Well, I **DON'T!**
And I don't, either! Unit 7788, you just told me you only wanted to conquer more planets so you could find one with a beach for vacation!
We could just visit a beach planet! We don't have to conquer it!

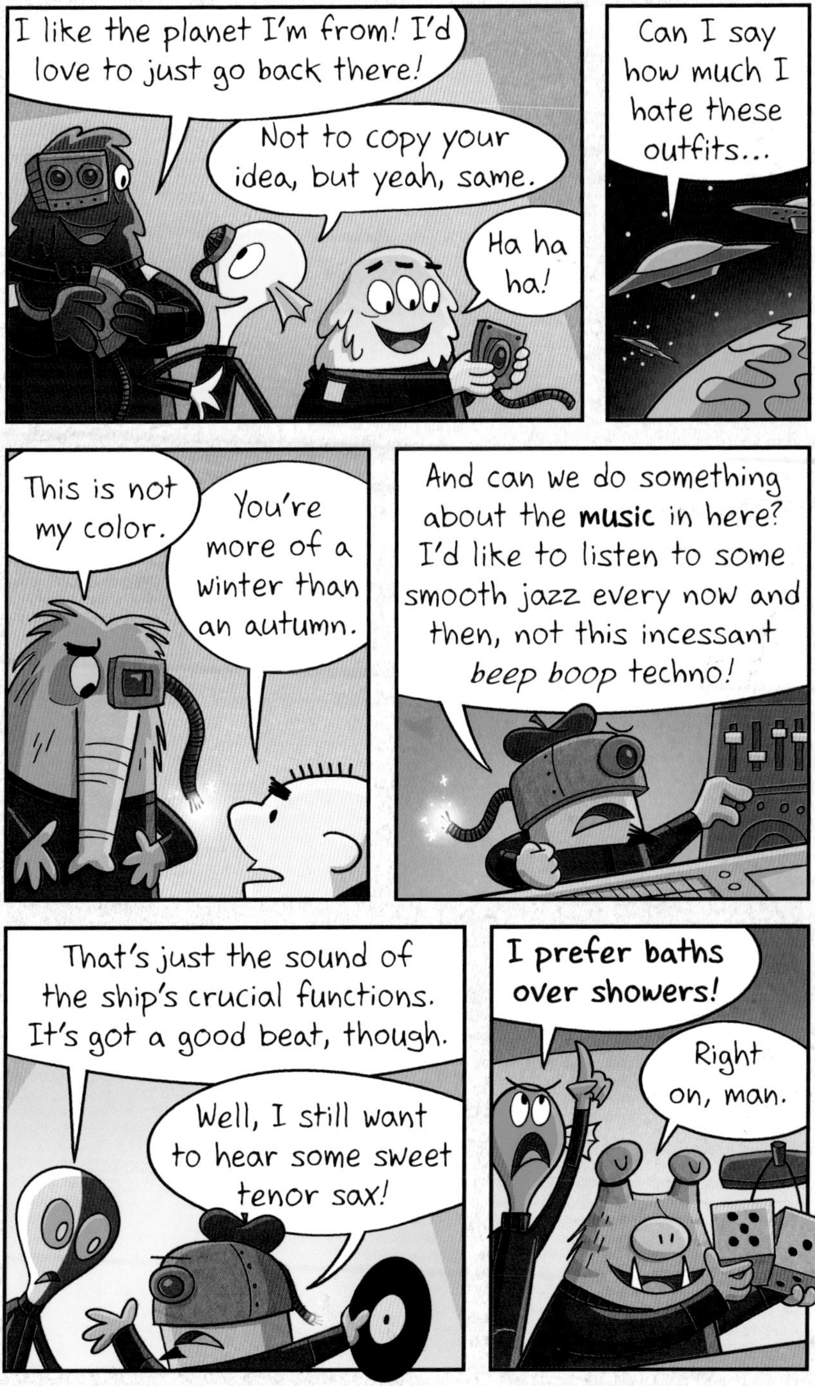
I like the planet I'm from! I'd love to just go back there!
Not to copy your idea, but yeah, same.
Ha ha ha!
Can I say how much I hate these outfits...
This is not my color.
You're more of a winter than an autumn.
And can we do something about the **music** in here? I'd like to listen to some smooth jazz every now and then, not this incessant *beep boop* techno!
That's just the sound of the ship's crucial functions. It's got a good beat, though.
Well, I still want to hear some sweet tenor sax!
I prefer baths over showers!
Right on, man.

The Throng way...

...is?

...the wrong way!

Uh, Brash... What were we just doing?

Hmm... let's deduce, Mango.

We're dressed like **Ice Cream Gators.**

And we're next to an ice cream truck.

We must be on a mission to give everyone FREE ICE CREAM!

Yay!

I'll just take this and be on my way.

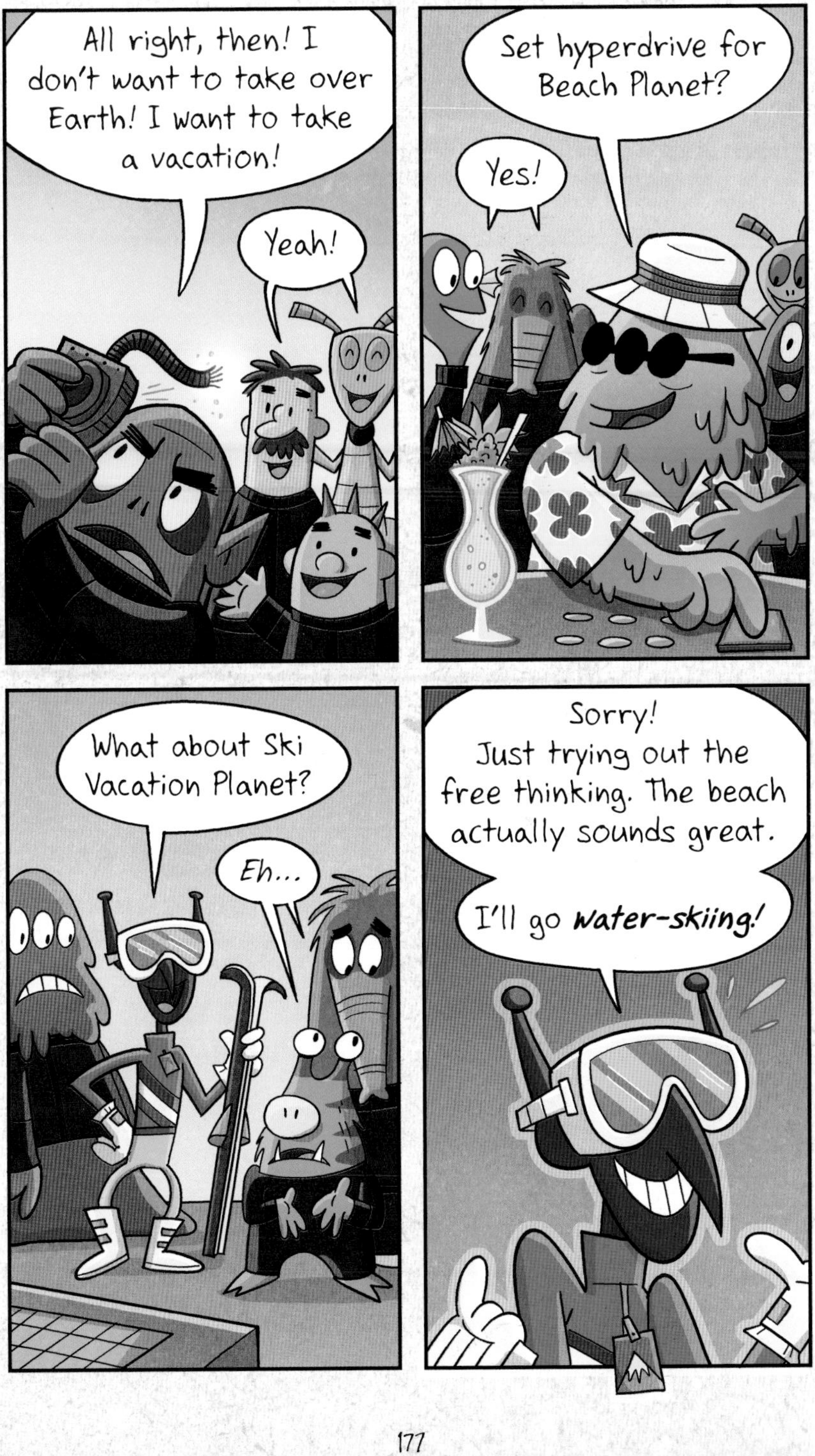
All right, then! I don't want to take over Earth! I want to take a vacation!
Yeah!
Set hyperdrive for Beach Planet?
Yes!
What about Ski Vacation Planet?
Eh...
Sorry! Just trying out the free thinking. The beach actually sounds great.
I'll go **water-skiing!**

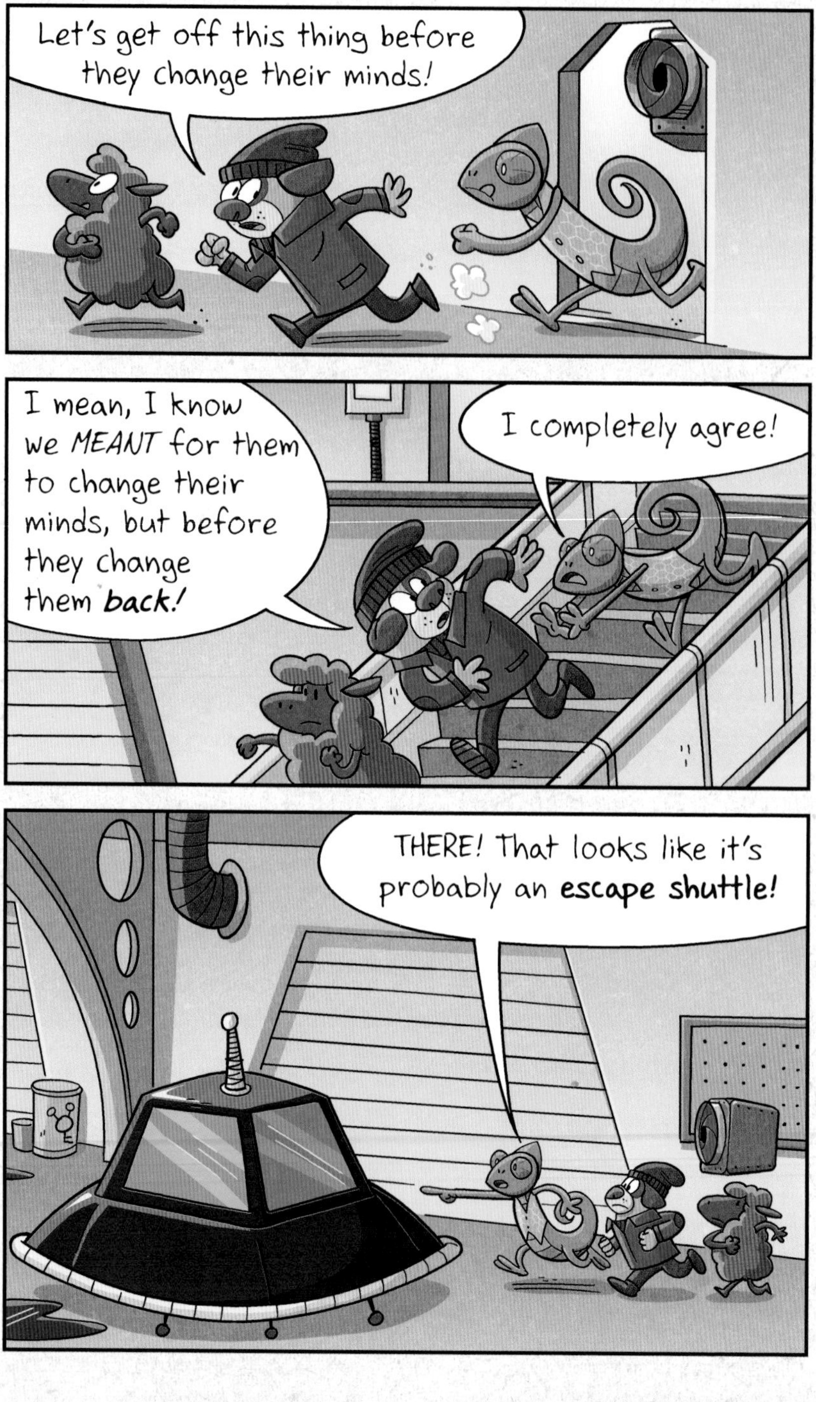
Let's get off this thing before they change their minds!
I mean, I know we *MEANT* for them to change their minds, but before they change them **back**!
I completely agree!
THERE! That looks like it's probably an **escape shuttle**!

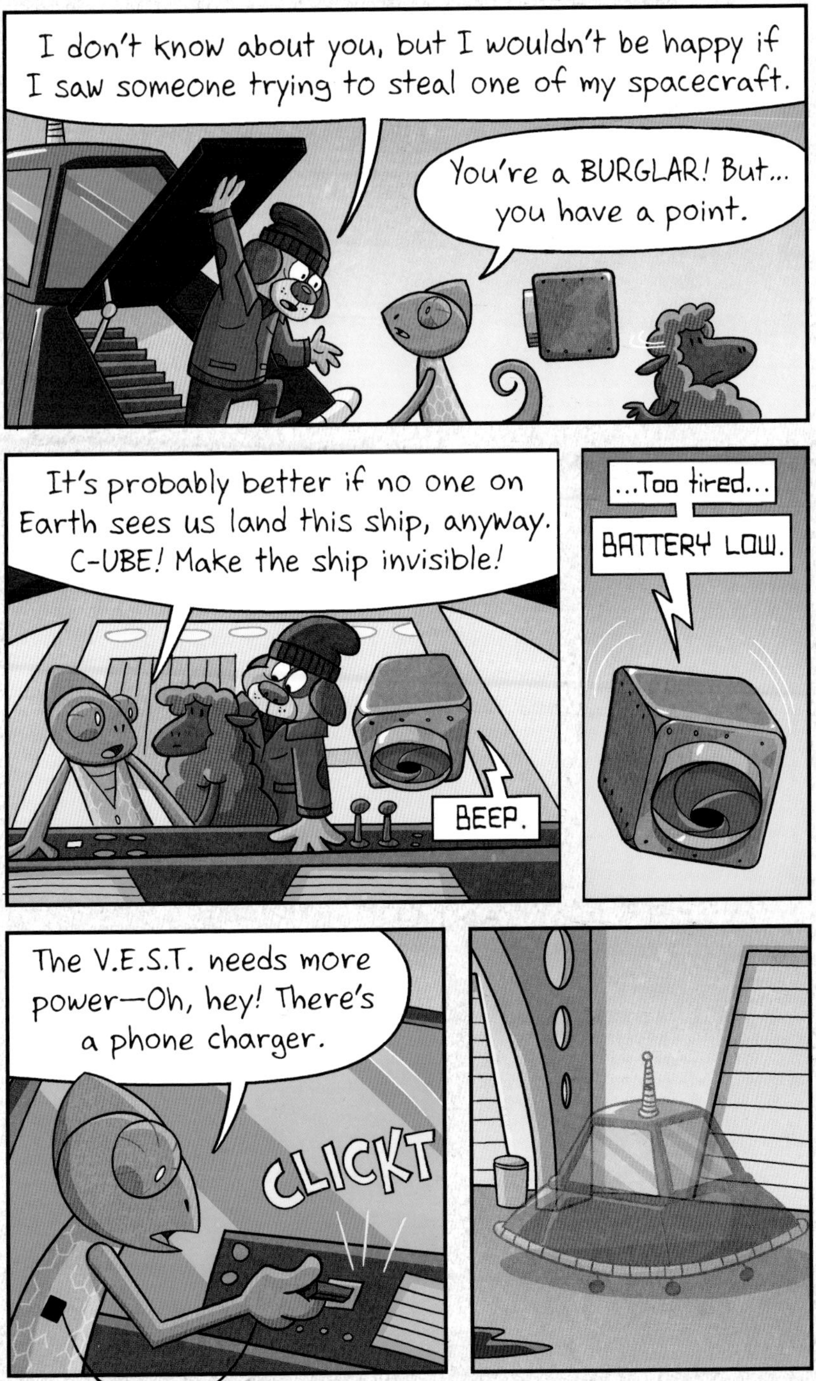

I don't know about you, but I wouldn't be happy if I saw someone trying to steal one of my spacecraft.
You're a BURGLAR! But... you have a point.
It's probably better if no one on Earth sees us land this ship, anyway. C-UBE! Make the ship invisible!
BEEP.
...Too tired...
BATTERY LOW.
The V.E.S.T. needs more power—Oh, hey! There's a phone charger.
CLICKT

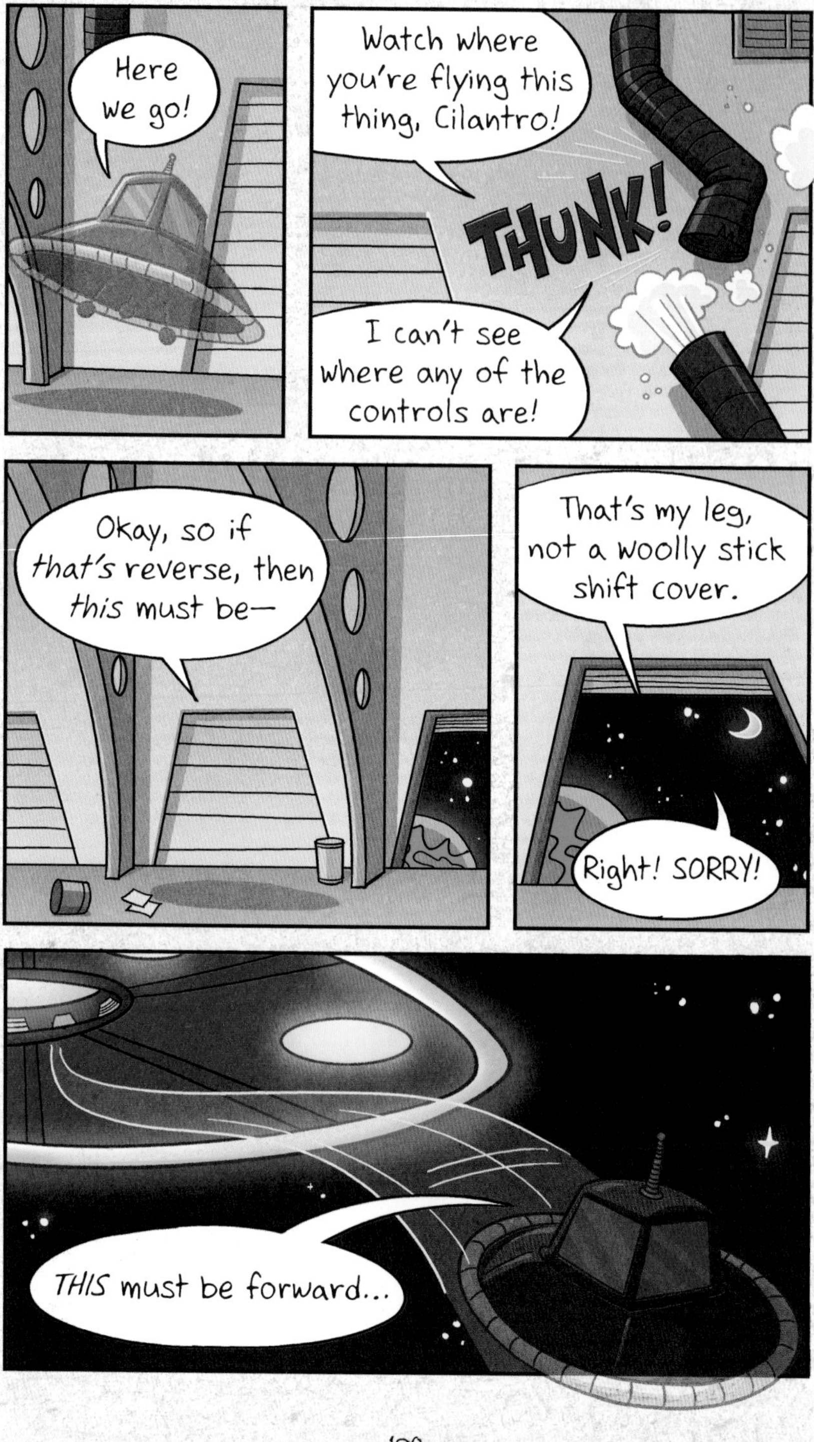
Here we go!
Watch where you're flying this thing, Cilantro!
THUNK!
I can't see where any of the controls are!
Okay, so if *that's* reverse, then *this* must be—
That's my leg, not a woolly stick shift cover.
Right! SORRY!
THIS must be forward...

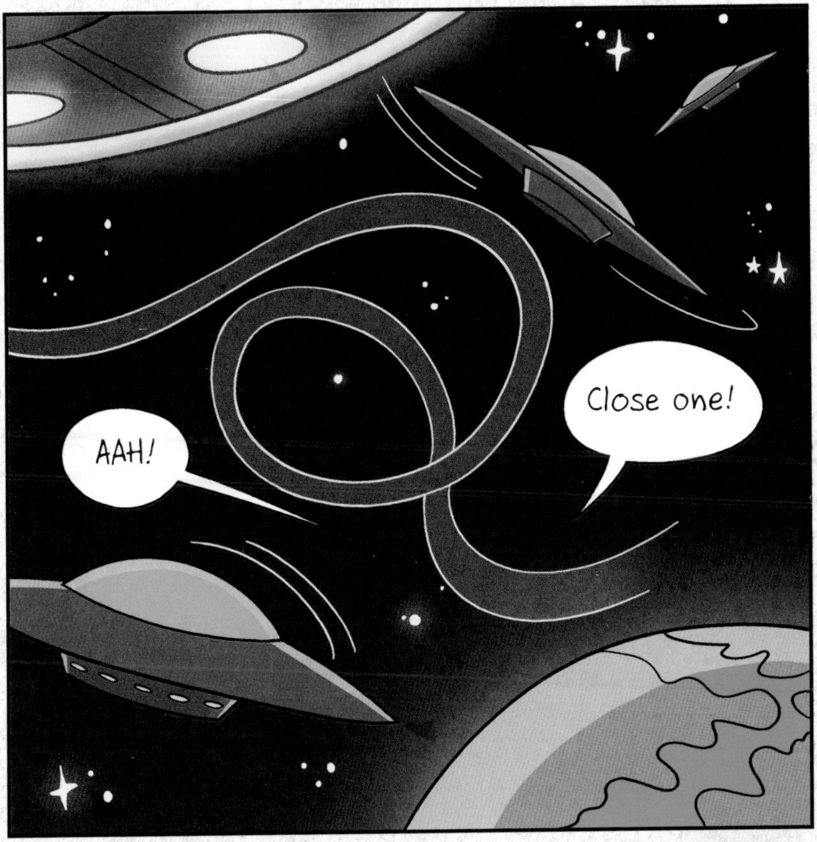
Close one!
AAH!

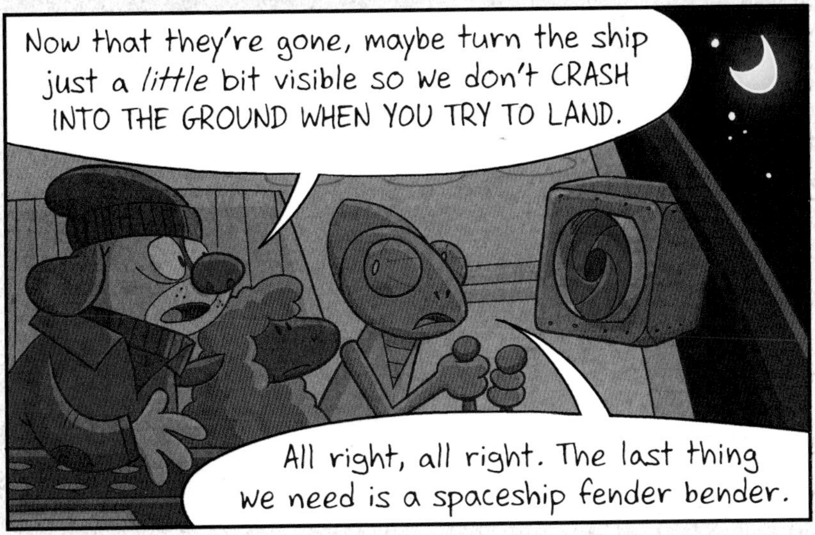
Now that they're gone, maybe turn the ship just a *little* bit visible so we don't CRASH INTO THE GROUND WHEN YOU TRY TO LAND.
All right, all right. The last thing we need is a spaceship fender bender.

Chapter 13

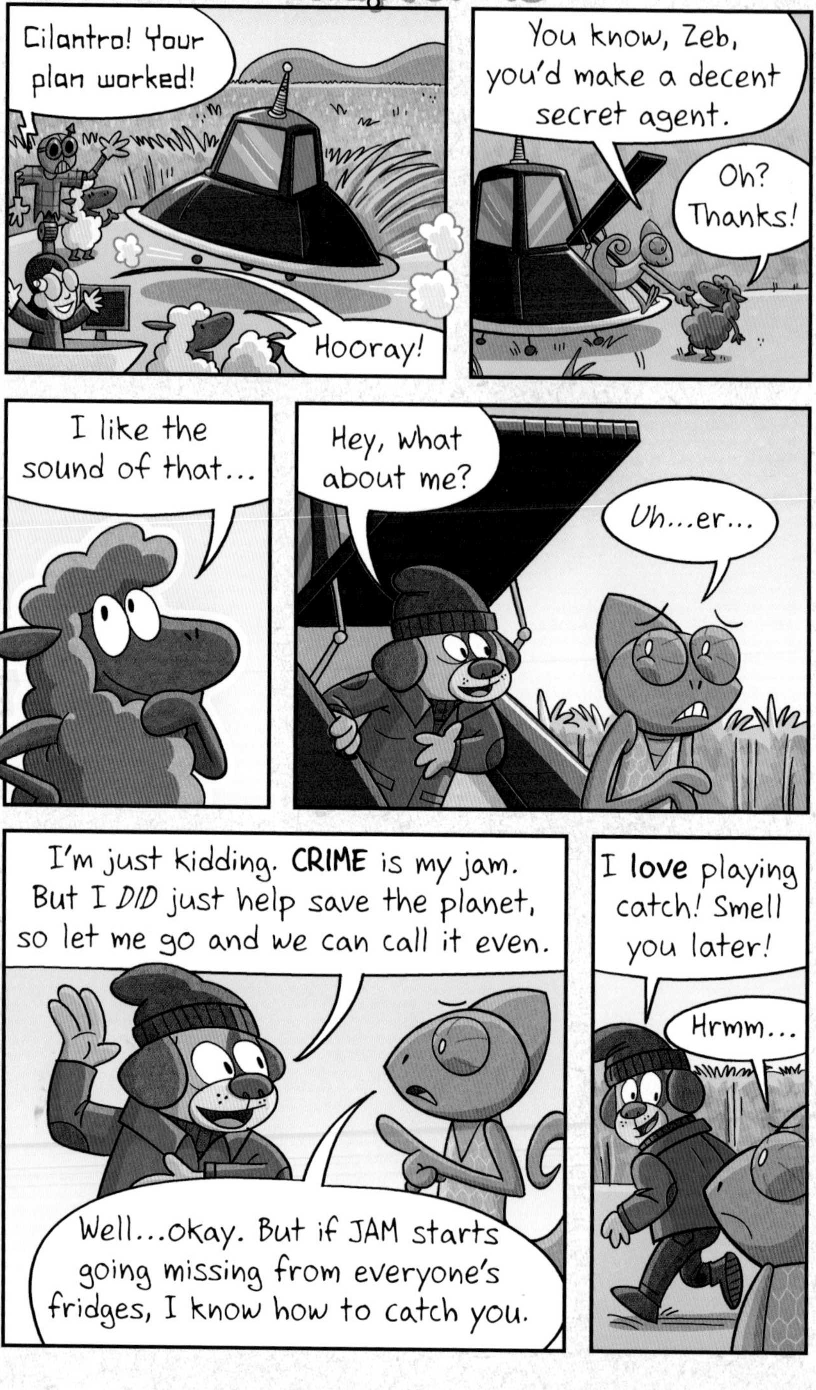
Cilantro! Your plan worked!
Hooray!
You know, Zeb, you'd make a decent secret agent.
Oh? Thanks!
I like the sound of that...
Hey, what about me?
Uh...er...
I'm just kidding. **CRIME** is my jam. But I *DID* just help save the planet, so let me go and we can call it even.
Well...okay. But if JAM starts going missing from everyone's fridges, I know how to catch you.
I **love** playing catch! Smell you later!
Hrmm...

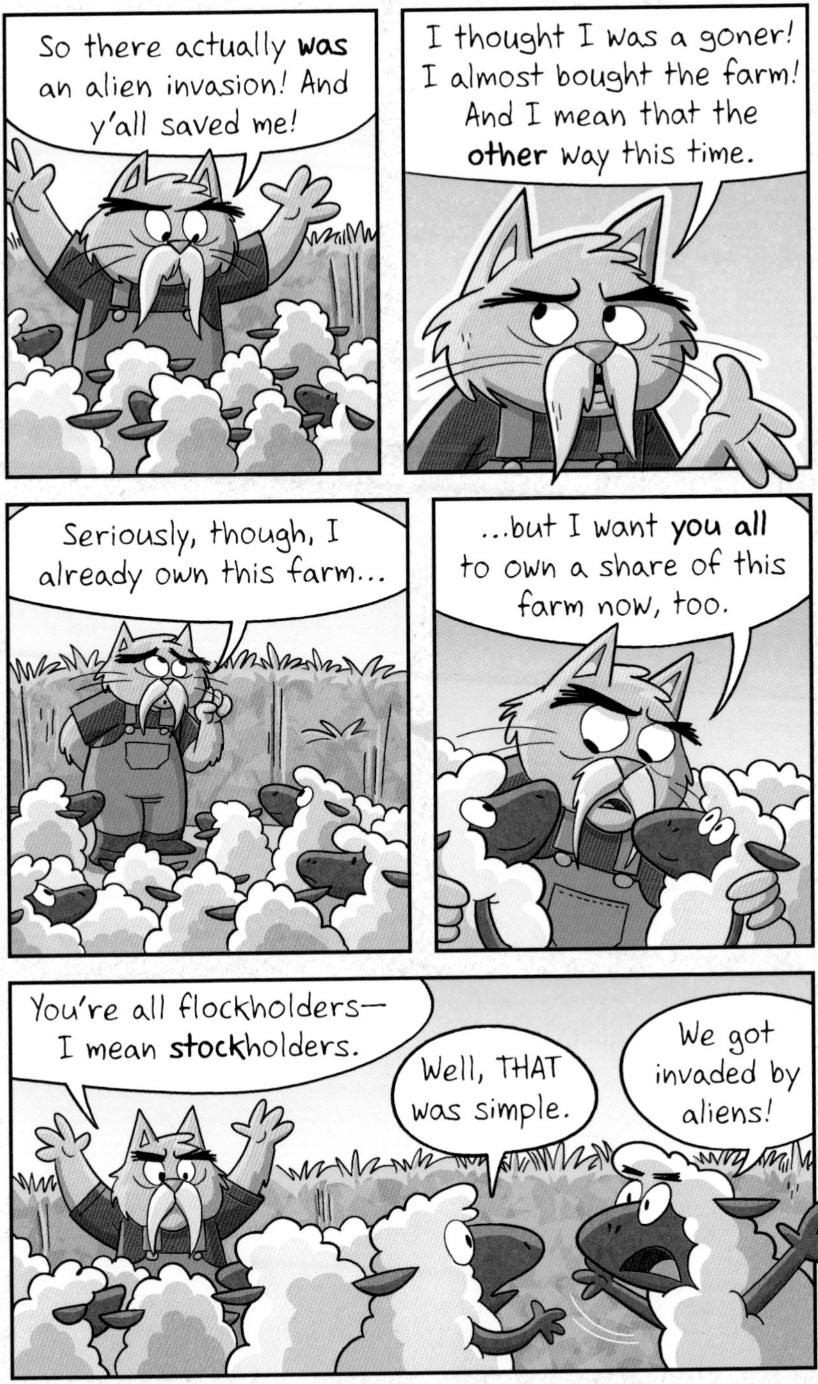
So there actually **was** an alien invasion! And y'all saved me!
I thought I was a goner! I almost bought the farm! And I mean that the **other** way this time.
Seriously, though, I already own this farm...
...but I want **you all** to own a share of this farm now, too.
You're all flockholders— I mean **stock**holders.
Well, THAT was simple.
We got invaded by aliens!

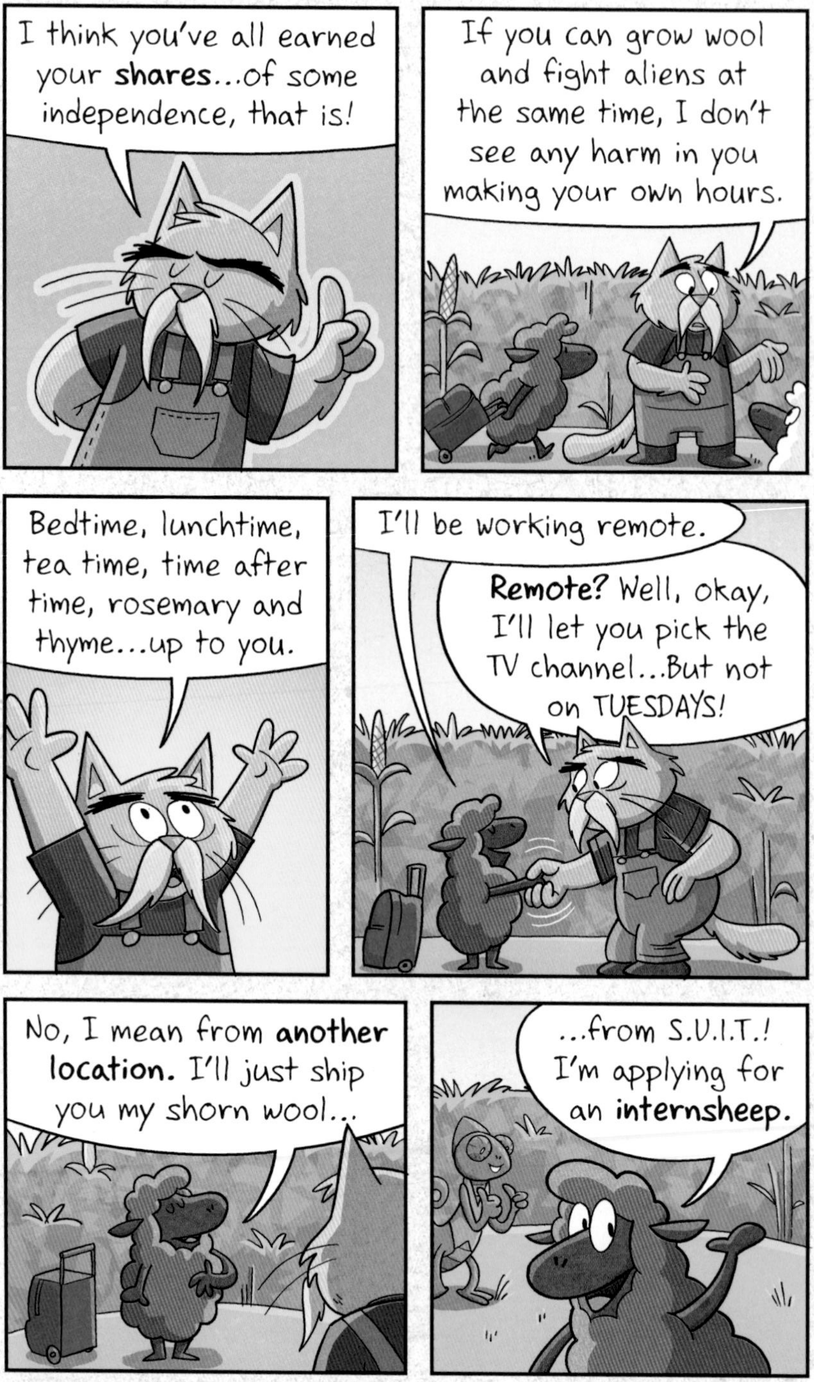
I think you've all earned your **shares**...of some independence, that is!
If you can grow wool and fight aliens at the same time, I don't see any harm in you making your own hours.
Bedtime, lunchtime, tea time, time after time, rosemary and thyme...up to you.
I'll be working remote.
Remote? Well, okay, I'll let you pick the TV channel...But not on TUESDAYS!
No, I mean from **another location.** I'll just ship you my shorn wool...
...from S.U.I.T.! I'm applying for an **internsheep.**

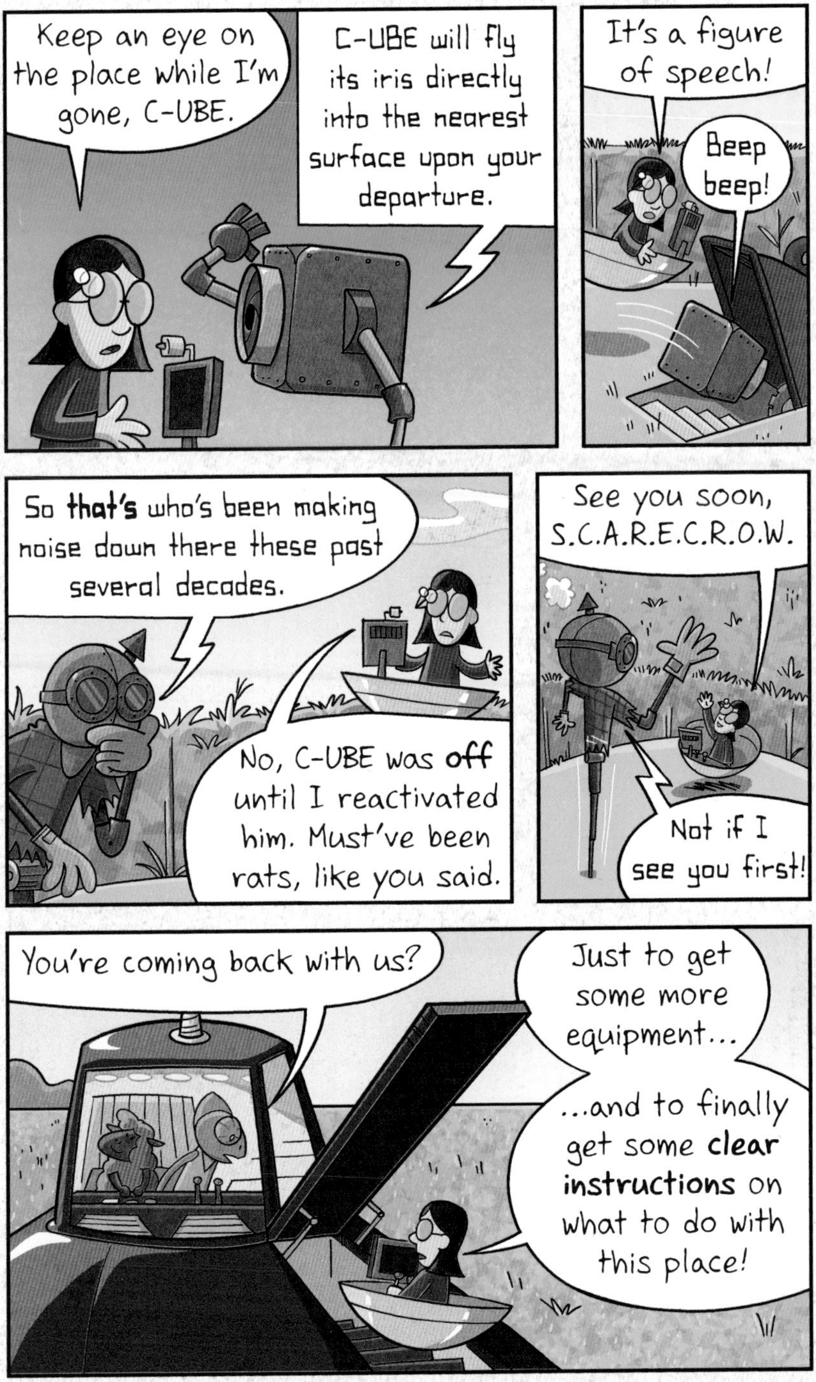
Keep an eye on the place while I'm gone, C-UBE.
C-UBE will fly its iris directly into the nearest surface upon your departure.
It's a figure of speech!
Beep beep!
So **that's** who's been making noise down there these past several decades.
No, C-UBE was **off** until I reactivated him. Must've been rats, like you said.
See you soon, S.C.A.R.E.C.R.O.W.
Not if I see you first!
You're coming back with us?
Just to get some more equipment...
...and to finally get some **clear instructions** on what to do with this place!

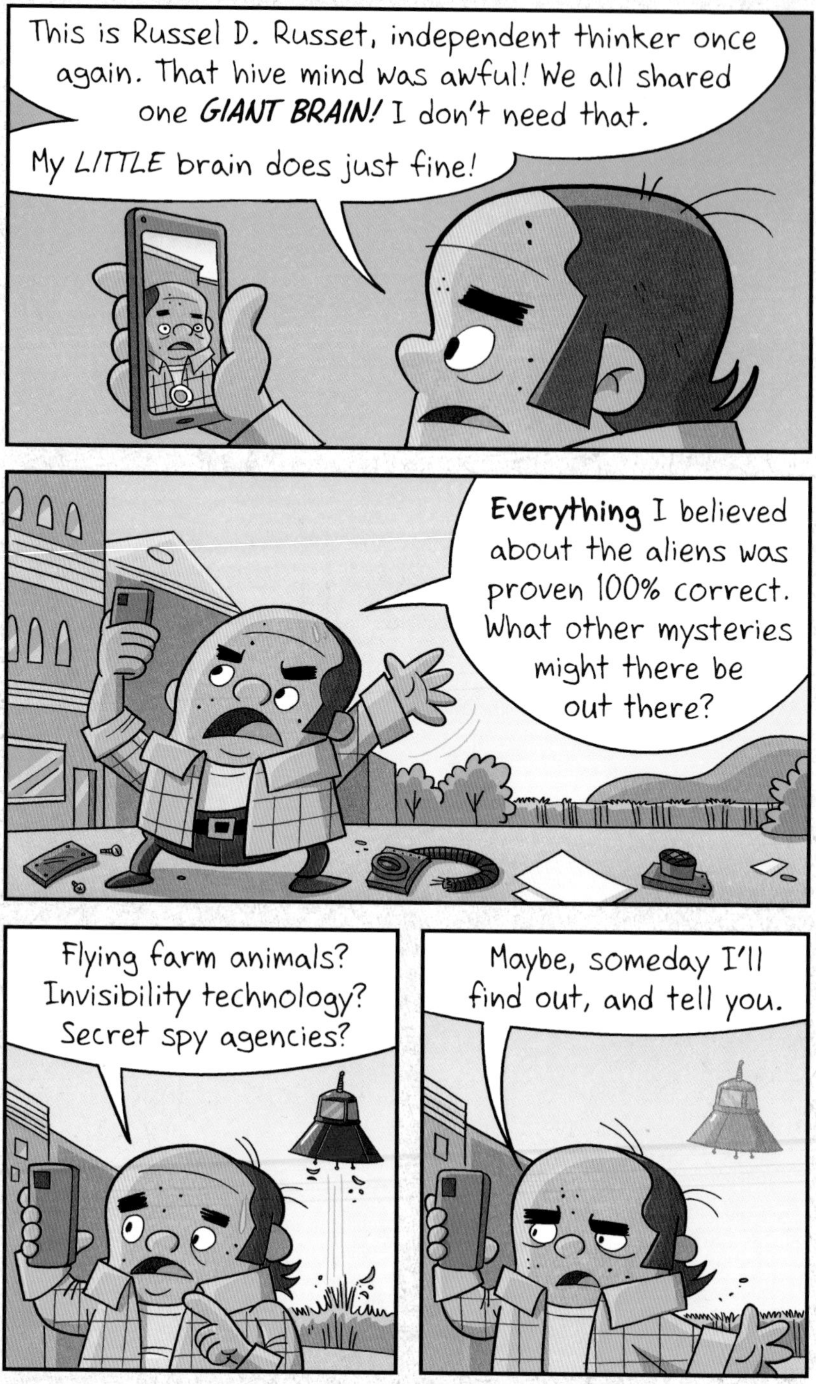
This is Russel D. Russet, independent thinker once again. That hive mind was awful! We all shared one ***GIANT BRAIN!*** I don't need that.
My *LITTLE* brain does just fine!
Everything I believed about the aliens was proven 100% correct. What other mysteries might there be out there?
Flying farm animals? Invisibility technology? Secret spy agencies?
Maybe, someday I'll find out, and tell you.

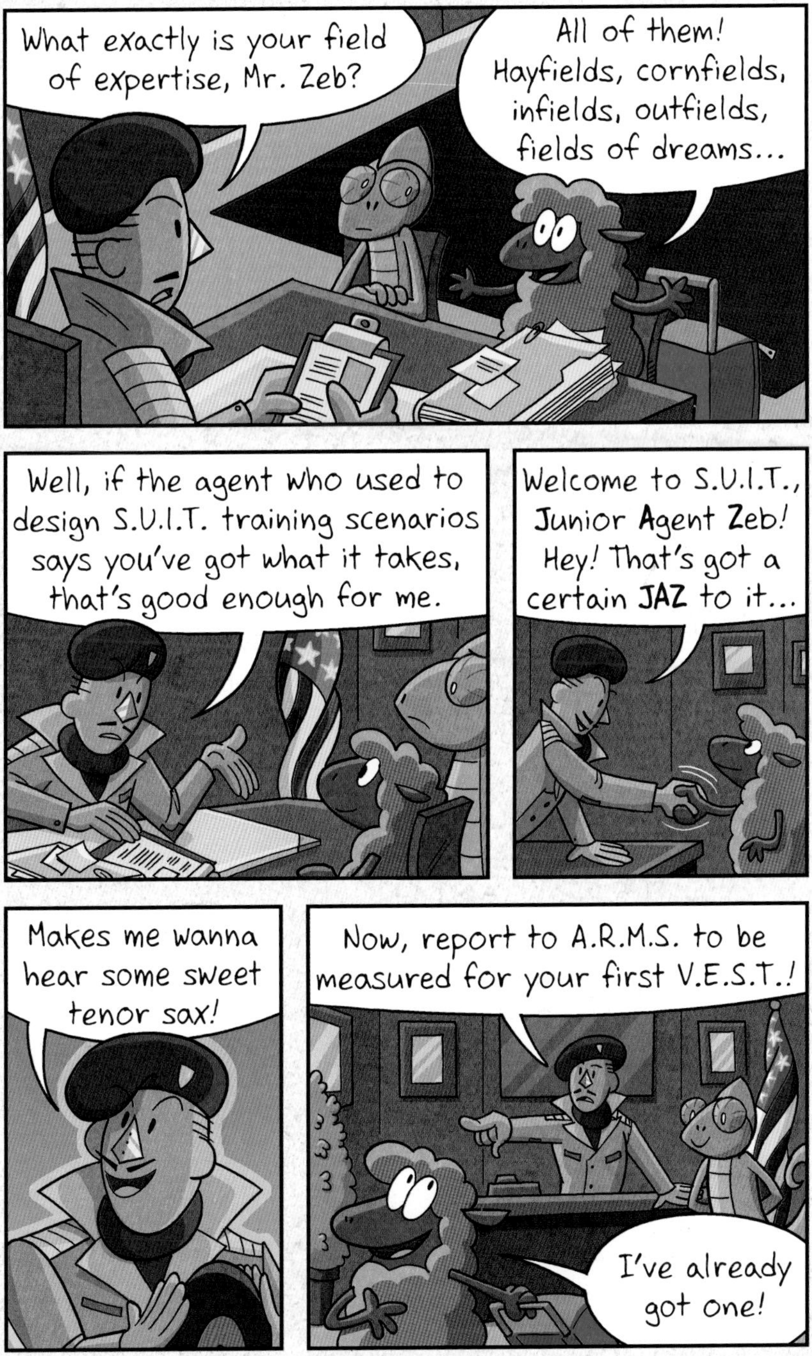
What exactly is your field of expertise, Mr. Zeb?
All of them! Hayfields, cornfields, infields, outfields, fields of dreams...
Well, if the agent who used to design S.U.I.T. training scenarios says you've got what it takes, that's good enough for me.
Welcome to S.U.I.T., Junior Agent Zeb! Hey! That's got a certain JAZ to it...
Makes me wanna hear some sweet tenor sax!
Now, report to A.R.M.S. to be measured for your first V.E.S.T.!
I've already got one!

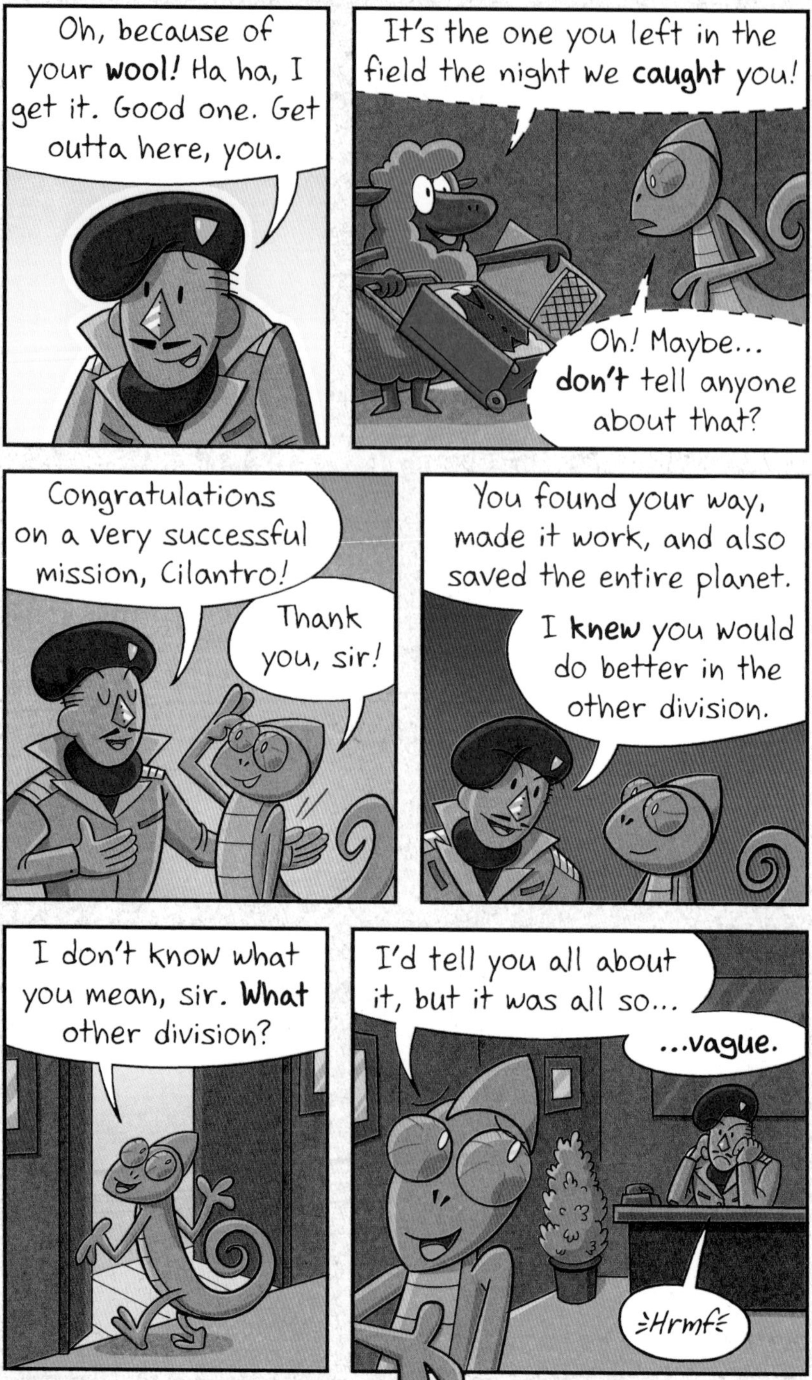
Oh, because of your wool! Ha ha, I get it. Good one. Get outta here, you.
It's the one you left in the field the night we caught you!
Oh! Maybe... don't tell anyone about that?
Congratulations on a very successful mission, Cilantro!
Thank you, sir!
You found your way, made it work, and also saved the entire planet.
I knew you would do better in the other division.
I don't know what you mean, sir. What other division?
I'd tell you all about it, but it was all so...
...vague.
Hrmf

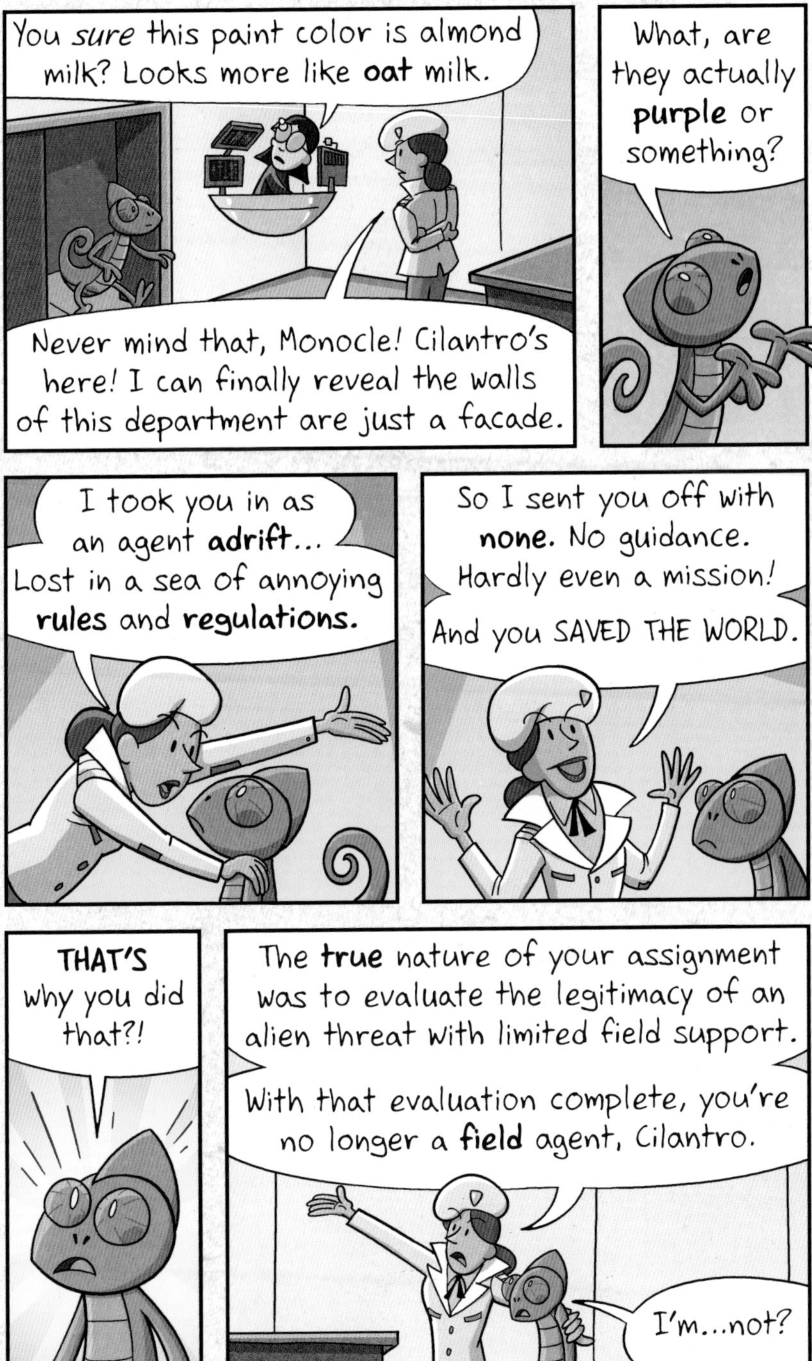
You *sure* this paint color is almond milk? Looks more like **oat** milk.
Never mind that, Monocle! Cilantro's here! I can finally reveal the walls of this department are just a facade.
What, are they actually **purple** or something?
I took you in as an agent **adrift**... Lost in a sea of annoying **rules** and **regulations.**
So I sent you off with **none.** No guidance. Hardly even a mission!
And you SAVED THE WORLD.
THAT'S why you did that?!
The **true** nature of your assignment was to evaluate the legitimacy of an alien threat with limited field support.
With that evaluation complete, you're no longer a **field** agent, Cilantro.
I'm...not?

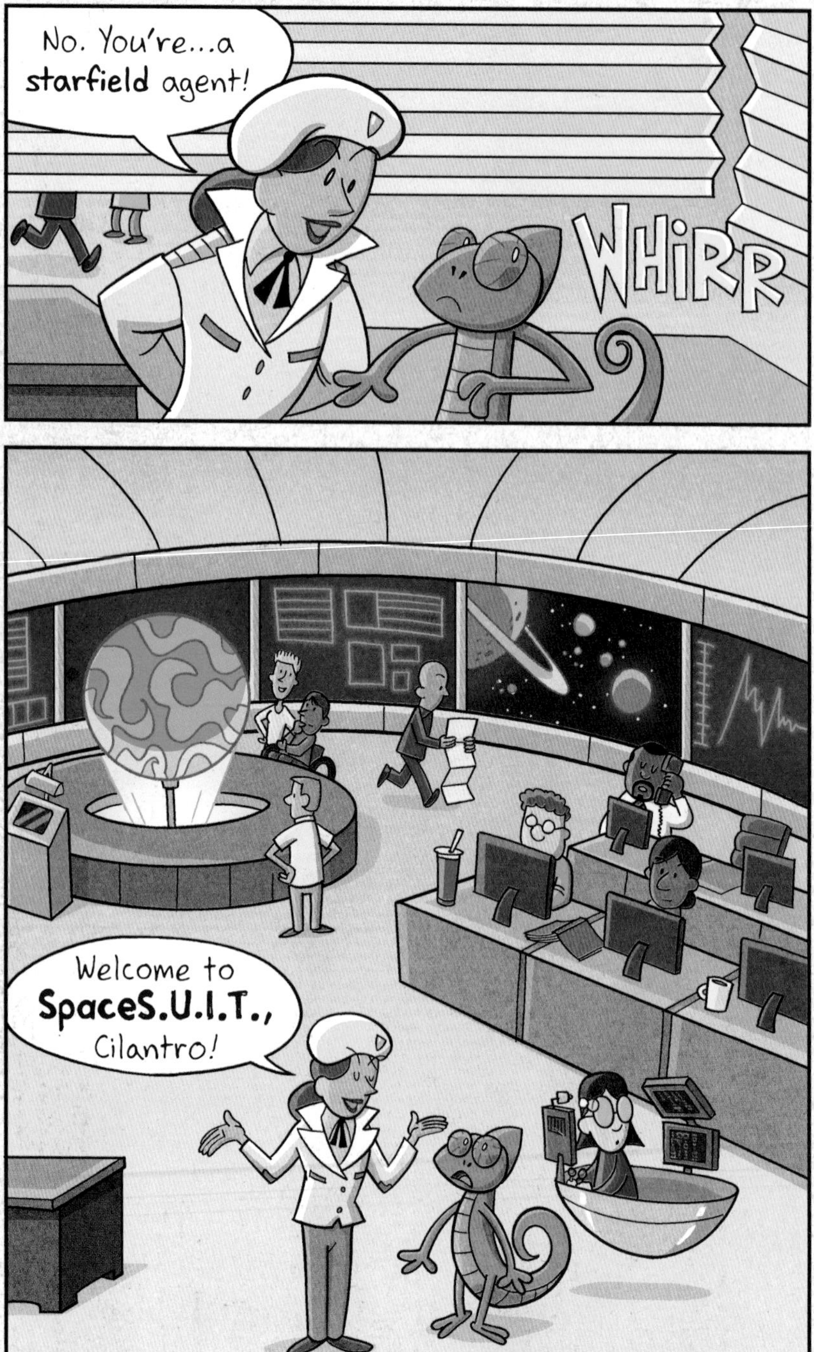
No. You're...a **starfield** agent!
WHIRR
Welcome to **SpaceS.U.I.T.,** Cilantro!

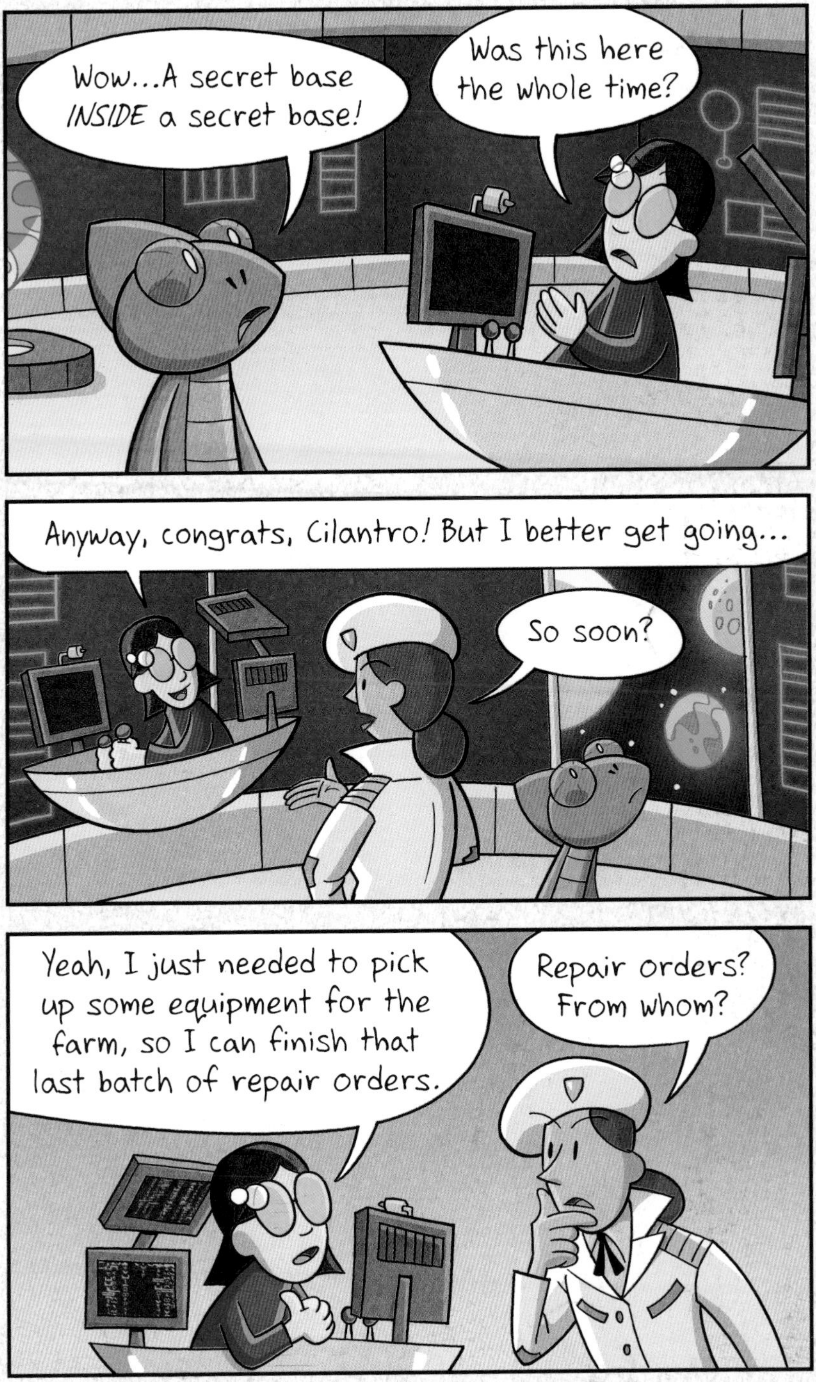
Wow...A secret base *INSIDE* a secret base!
Was this here the whole time?
Anyway, congrats, Cilantro! But I better get going...
So soon?
Yeah, I just needed to pick up some equipment for the farm, so I can finish that last batch of repair orders.
Repair orders? From whom?

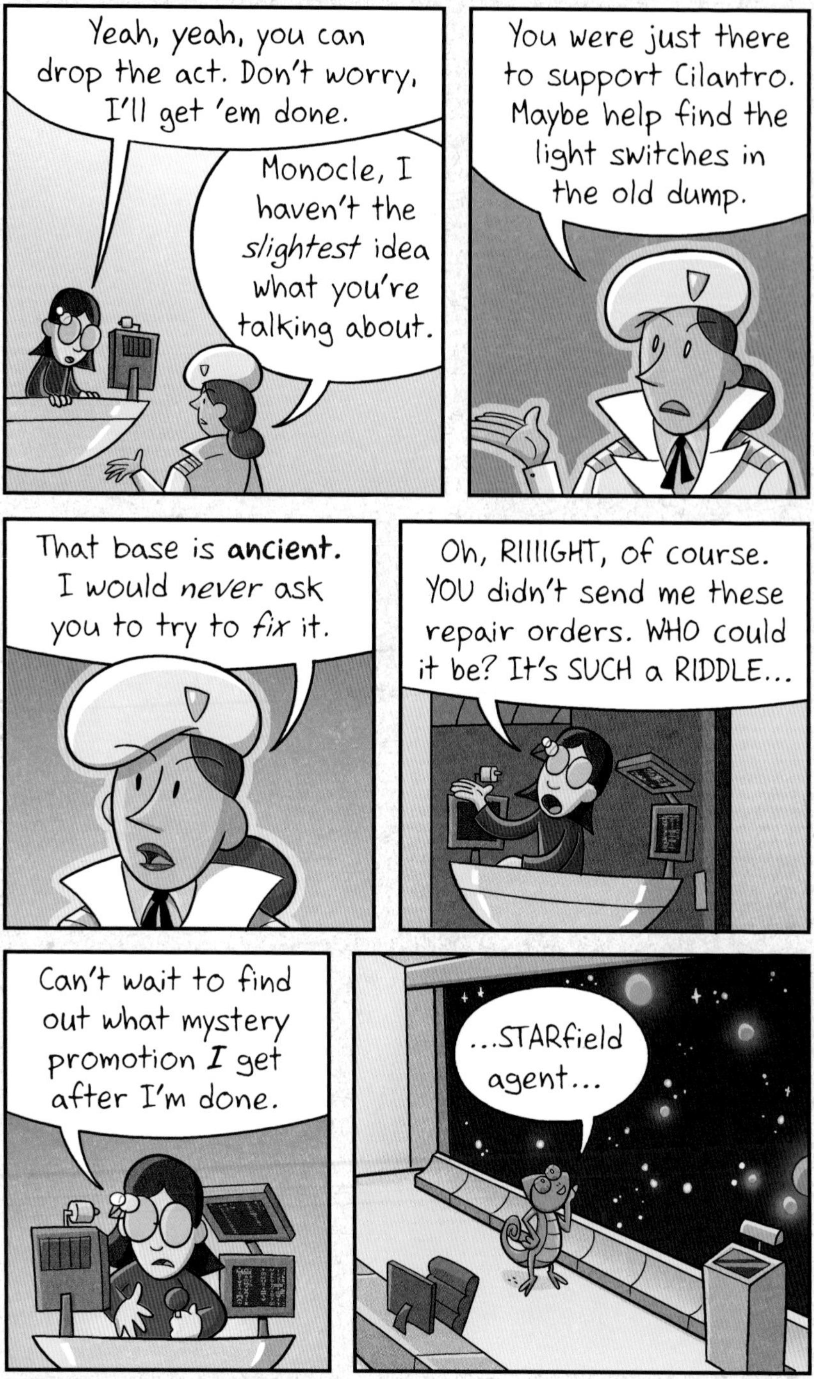
Yeah, yeah, you can drop the act. Don't worry, I'll get 'em done.
Monocle, I haven't the *slightest* idea what you're talking about.
You were just there to support Cilantro. Maybe help find the light switches in the old dump.
That base is **ancient.** I would *never* ask you to try to *fix* it.
Oh, RIIIIGHT, of course. YOU didn't send me these repair orders. WHO could it be? It's SUCH a RIDDLE...
Can't wait to find out what mystery promotion *I* get after I'm done.
...STARfield agent...

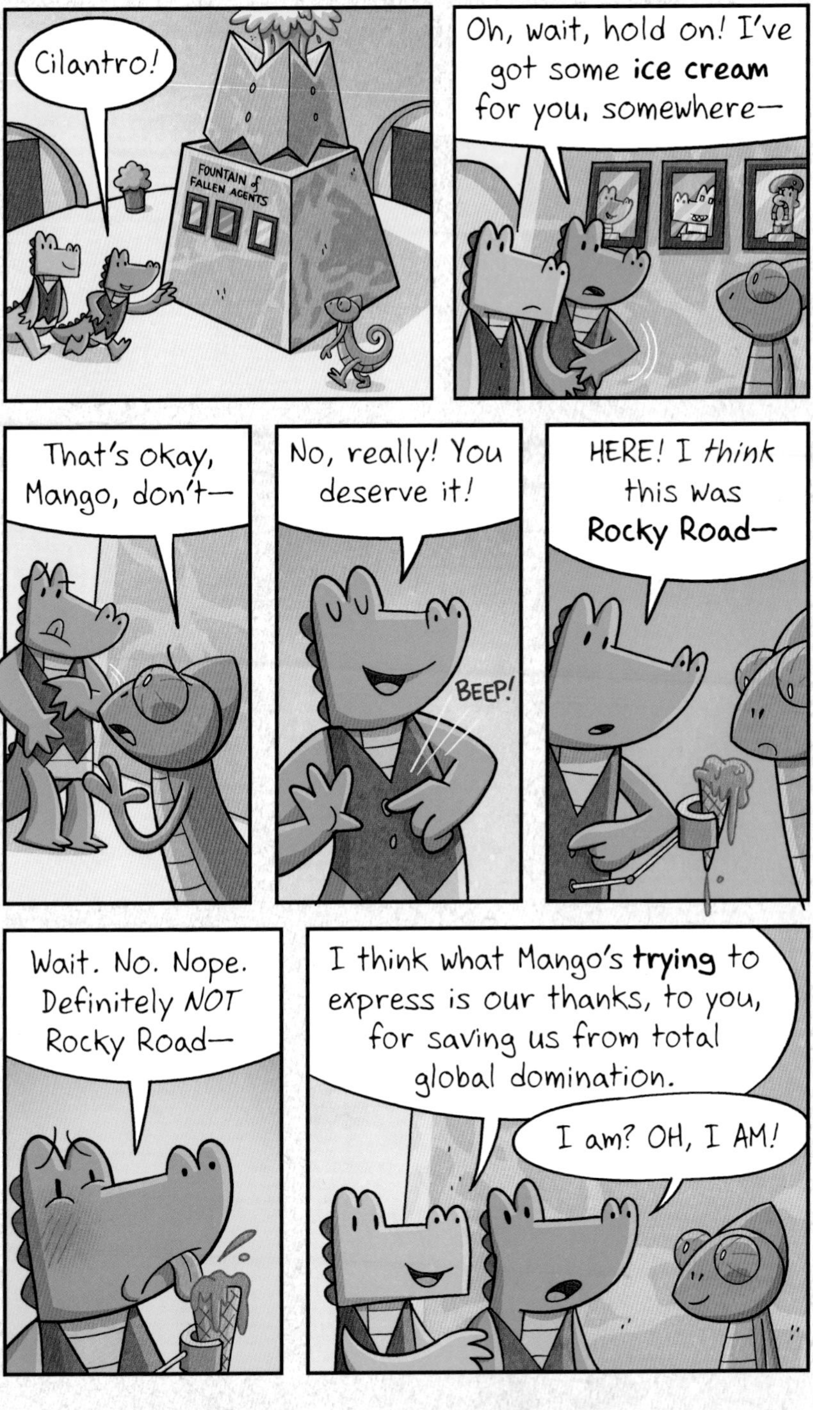
Cilantro!
FOUNTAIN of FALLEN AGENTS
Oh, wait, hold on! I've got some **ice cream** for you, somewhere—
That's okay, Mango, don't—
No, really! You deserve it!
BEEP!
HERE! I *think* this was **Rocky Road**—
Wait. No. Nope. Definitely *NOT* Rocky Road—
I think what Mango's **trying** to express is our thanks, to you, for saving us from total global domination.
I am? OH, I AM!

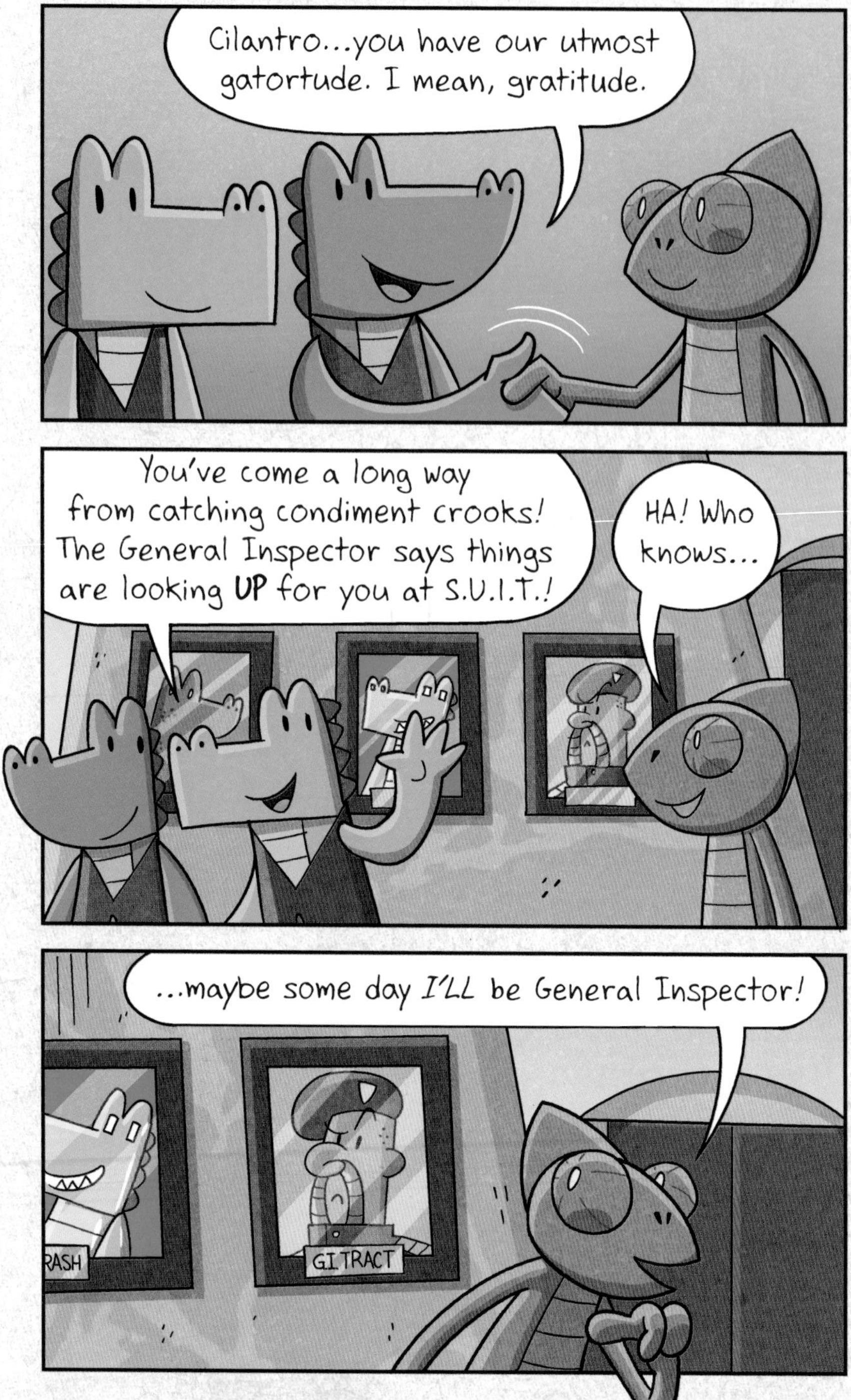
Cilantro...you have our utmost gatortude. I mean, gratitude.
You've come a long way from catching condiment crooks! The General Inspector says things are looking **UP** for you at S.U.I.T.!
HA! Who knows...
...maybe some day *I'LL* be General Inspector!
RASH
GITRACT

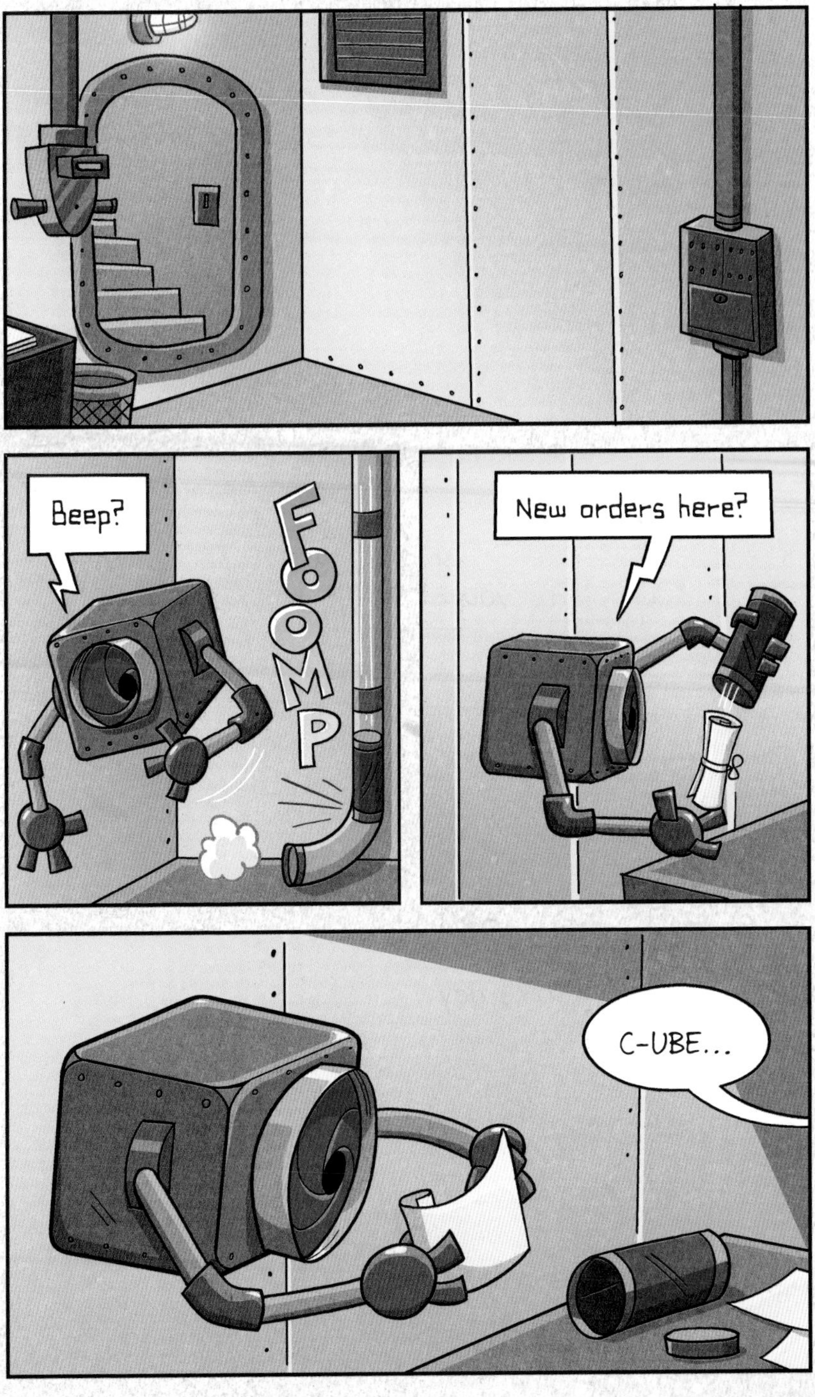
Beep?
FOOMP
New orders here?
C-UBE...

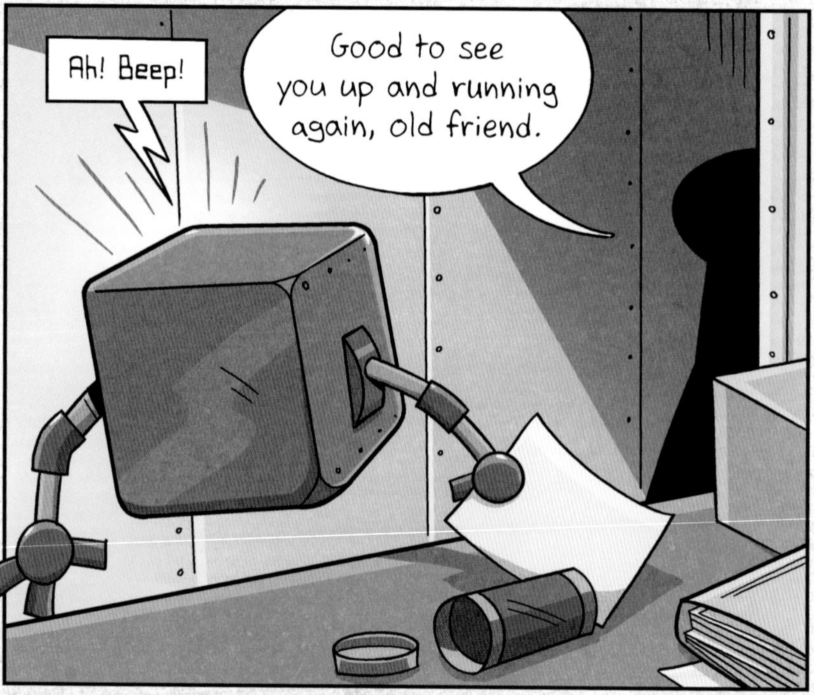
Ah! Beep!
Good to see you up and running again, old friend.

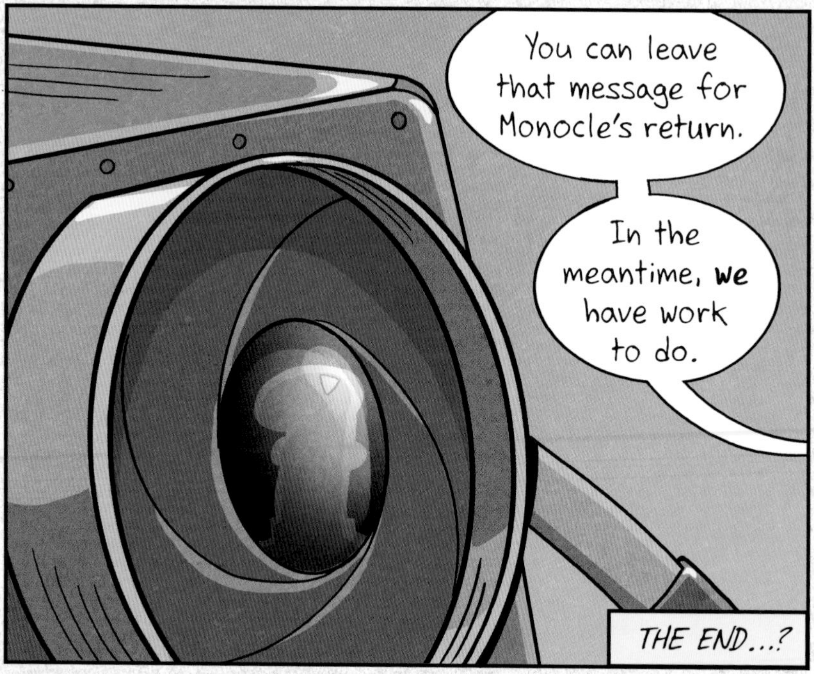
You can leave that message for Monocle's return.
In the meantime, **we** have work to do.
THE END...?

AGENTS OF S.U.I.T.

How to draw **CILANTRO**

1. Start by drawing Cilantro's head. It's shaped kind of like a pointy egg.

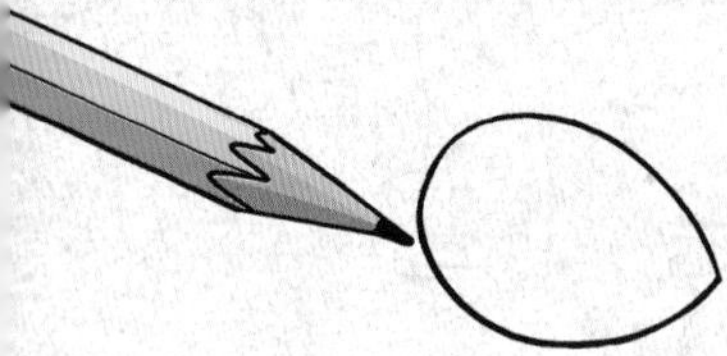

2. Add an upside-down, rounded V for her crest and two circles for eyes. Erase the part of the eye that's hidden by her head.

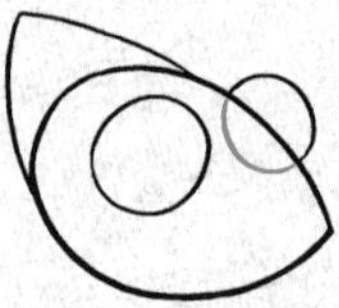

Did you know their weird eyes allow chameleons to see almost 360 degrees around them? I'm just saying.

3. Now draw in the rest of her eye details, plus nostrils and a mouth.

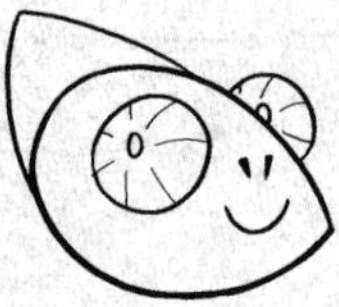

4. To draw Cilantro's body, start with two lines leading down from her head...

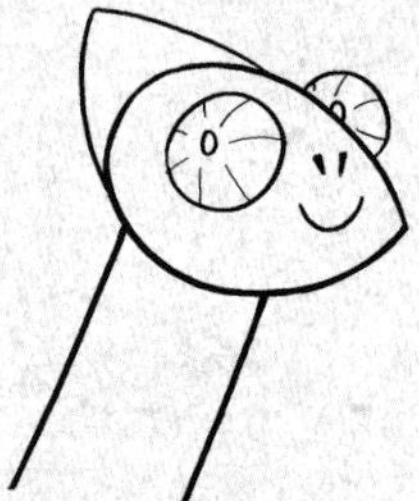

5. ...then add a spiral shape to make the outside of her tail.

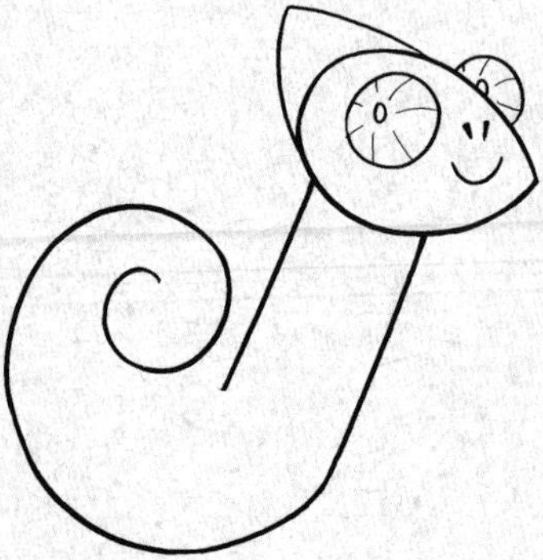

6. A smaller spiral alongside it makes the inside of her tail.

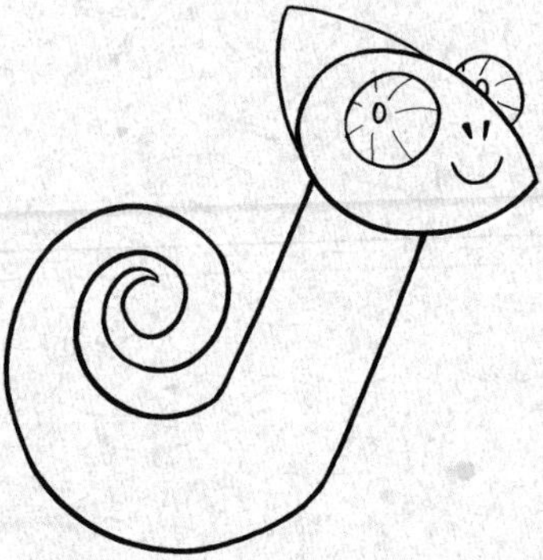

7. Add arms and legs!

8. Now draw in her belly stripes and don't forget her high-tech new V.E.S.T.!

9. Finally, add some color, but be careful...

...It might get hard to find her on the page!

Beep!

Pro-tip: if you really want to capture my likeness, try drawing with *invisible ink!*

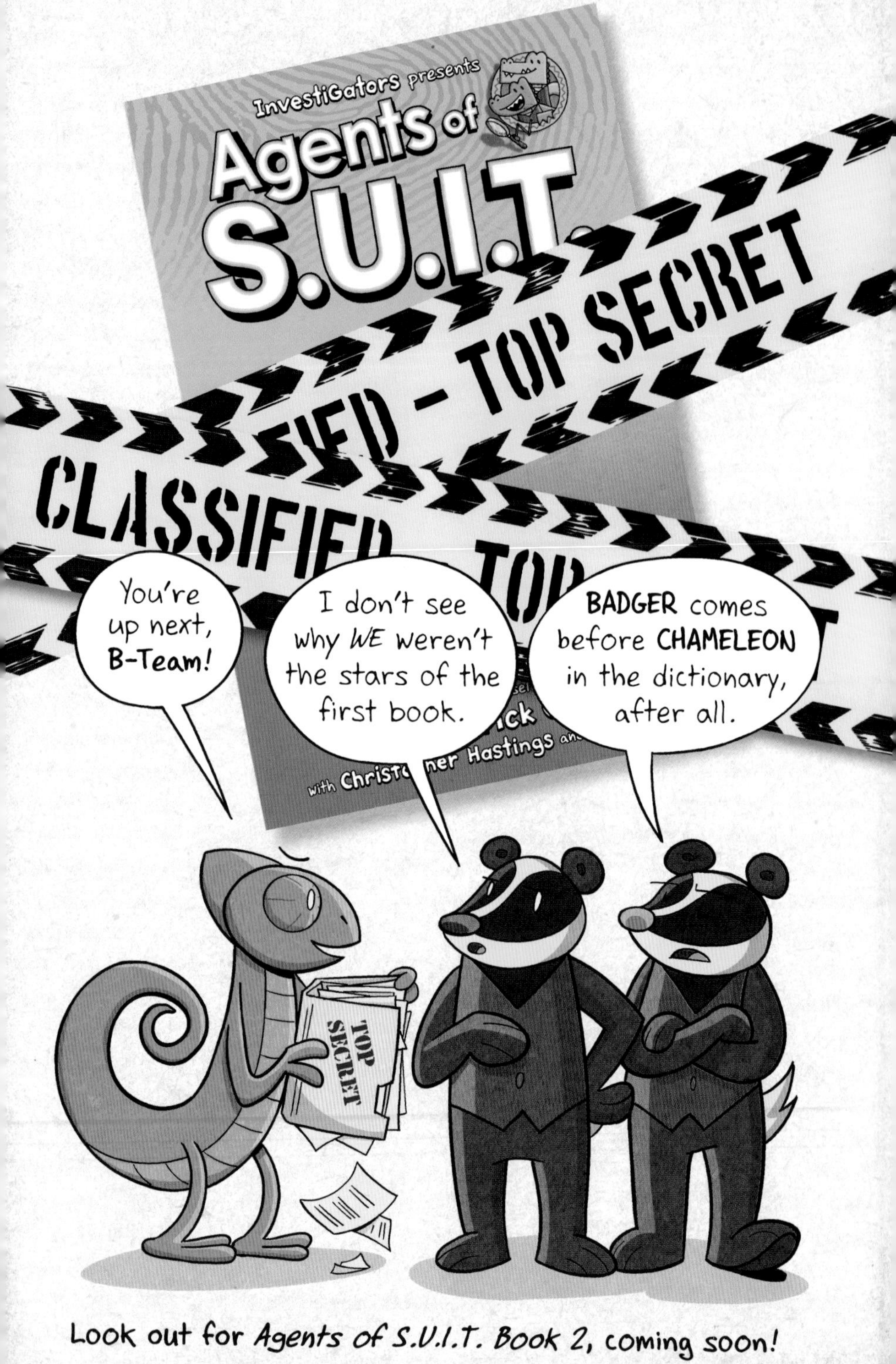
InvestiGators presents
Agents of S.U.I.T.
CLASSIFIED - TOP SECRET
You're up next, B-Team!
I don't see why WE weren't the stars of the first book.
BADGER comes before CHAMELEON in the dictionary, after all.
TOP SECRET

Look out for *Agents of S.U.I.T. Book 2*, coming soon!

Read the John Patrick Green Collection!

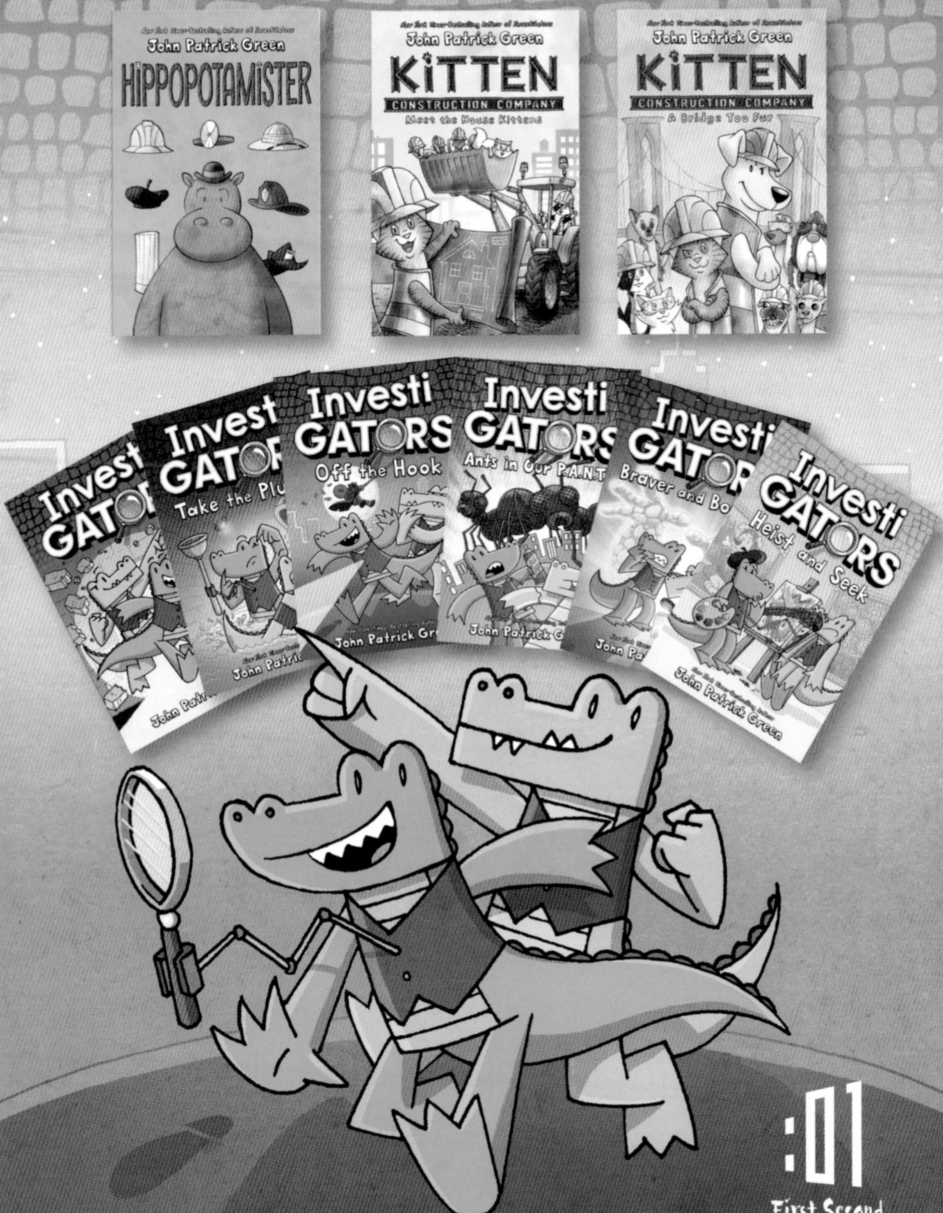
John Patrick Green
HIPPOPOTAMISTER
John Patrick Green
KITTEN CONSTRUCTION COMPANY
Meet the House Kittens
John Patrick Green
KITTEN CONSTRUCTION COMPANY
A Bridge Too Fur
InvestiGATORS
Off the Hook
Ants in Our P.A.N.T.
InvestiGATORS
Heist and Seek
John Patrick Green

John Patrick Green is a *New York Times*–bestselling author who makes books about animals with human jobs, such as *Hippopotamister*, the Kitten Construction Company series, and the InvestiGators series. John is definitely not just a bunch of animals wearing a human suit pretending to have a human job. He is also the artist and co-creator of the Teen Boat! graphic novels with writer Dave Roman. John lives in Brooklyn in an apartment that doesn't allow animals other than the ones living in his head.

Christopher Hastings is a comics writer who lives in the human Earth city of Brooklyn, New York. He is the creator of *The Adventures of Dr. McNinja* and co-creator of Marvel's Unbelievable Gwenpool. He's also scripted many graphic novel adaptations in the Five Nights at Freddy's franchise and has written a slew of other comics, including *Adventure Time*, *Regular Show*, and *I Am Groot*. This bio may be the only thing he wrote in this book that doesn't involve a pun.

Pat Lewis is a freelance cartoonist/illustrator who lives in Pittsburgh, Pennsylvania, with his wife and their two cats. His artwork has appeared in children's magazines such as *Highlights* and *Boys' Life* (now *Scout Life*), as well as books by Workman Publishing, Macmillan, and McGraw Hill. Some of his favorite things in this world are: flea markets, road trips, monster movies, and snack-bar nachos. Oh, and drawing funny pictures for kids and adults.

Wes Dzioba is a Canadian artist based in the city of Winnipeg with his wife and two sons. He was always a fan of comics and animation growing up, and broke into his coloring career by answering an ad in the newspaper for a colorist in 1998. He has worked with publishers like Disney, Dark Horse Comics, Marvel, Nickelodeon, DC Comics, and many more. In his spare time, he likes doing things the THRONG WAY!

Can't get enough of the Investi GATORS?

Don't forget to...

☑ Call the S.U.I.T. hotline
for your next mission:
1-888-SPY-G8RS!

☑ Visit InvestiGatorsBooks.com
for activities, crafts,
and more!

☑ Check out ▸ YouTube
to watch jaw-some videos!

☑ Sink your teeth into
all the books in
the series!